THE QUIDELL BROTHERS BOX SET

A Quidell Brothers
ROMANCE

I'd been a mirror, I think, to protect myself. Maybe also to hide. But I can't now. Touching forces me out from behind my glass wall and I whisper his name. "Tom."

"Sammie." His hand curls into my hair and his stomach suddenly pulls away from me. A kiss takes my mouth, hot and intense. Once again, he pulls the poison from my body....

— THOMAS'S MUSE

Not once since my injury have I shown a woman my scars. Not any of the three whole dates I've been on. None of them made me feel the way Camille makes me feel....

— DANIEL'S FIRE

"You deserve... a real girlfriend." Her hand works into the waistband of my jeans. "Not someone who..." She sucks in her breath before my lips steal more of her air. "... leaves for months."

I pull back enough to see her eyes. She's serious. She doesn't think we can do this long distance.

Maybe she's right. Maybe she's not. But tonight, I'm proving to her how much she means to me....

— ROBERT'S SOUL

THE WORLDS OF
KRIS AUSTEN RADCLIFFE

THE QUIDELL BROTHERS

BOOKS 1-3

A Quidell Brothers
ROMANCE

By
Kris Austen Radcliffe

Six Love Erotic Romance
Minneapolis

www.krisaustenradcliffe.com

Published by
Six Love Erotic Romance

Edited by Annetta Ribken
Copyedited by Juli Lilly
Cover to be designed by Kris Austen Radcliffe
Plus a special thanks to my Proofing Crew.

Third print edition, June 2018
Version: 6.25.2018

ISBN: 978-1-939730-64-0

THE QUIDELL BROTHERS

BOOKS 1 - 3

A Quidell Brothers
ROMANCE

Special thanks to my dear husband Peter for being the inspiration for all the good men.

Also a special thanks to Katie for helping with so many things, the least of which being titles and names.

And finally, an added thanks to Netta and Terry, who polish what I dig out of my psyche. I also want to also thank Kami, Jonel, Kristine, and everyone else who, from the beginning, believed in my stories.

Thank you!

THOMAS'S MUSE

Book 1

CHAPTER 1

Samantha

The first moment I thought *Maybe I need to get my own place* wasn't when I tripped over Rick's bike for the thousandth time. Or when the ripe smell of workout clothes and dirty dishes hit my nose as I opened the apartment door, either. Or when I sneezed. No, none of that.

Rick's an athlete—triathlons, races, modeling to make ends meet because the sponsorship deals haven't quite come through—and he treats it like a career. An investment banker-like, cutthroat, "I work hard so give me my damned Mercedes" career.

The rest of his life sits unwashed and collecting dust.

Making me sneeze.

I knew what I was in for eight months ago when I moved into the spacious wonder of Rick's touched-by-an-architect loft. Into his world of boom and bust. It's exhilarating—I won't lie. When he's up, he's *up*. And he's good at celebrating.

At the time, I thought it a worthwhile trade-off. I received every inch of Rick's scrumptious hardness, a downtown life, and escape from the tired suburban trajectory I'd been born into. But now his bike rattles when I knock it with the door, the place smells like bachelor, and he even closed the curtains before he left.

Shadows force the sunlight onto the rough brick of the loft's walls, making it look like old skin. This place is solid, much like Rick. Sinewy and hard and cut along perfect lines. It's an old refurbished warehouse and it has character.

But it doesn't have soul. And I finally figured out why.

We have no art. Or, more precisely, *he* has no art. No cheap single-man prints. No family snapshots in nice frames. Not one giant narcissistic photo from a modeling gig. The apartment has nothing but a cat who is as bland as the walls.

And deep inside, I wonder what that really means.

৩১৩

Thomas

IT'S TIME FOR ME TO MOVE OUT OF MY BROTHER'S BASEMENT.

My stomach tightens, thinking about it. He did a good job renovating before his ex did her crazy bitch dance and ran off. It's open and sunny, for a lower level. Good light streams in from the big rear windows. I'll miss painting in the warm afternoon glow reflecting off his golden patio out back.

I never wanted to live in his basement, but he needed help with his kid. I needed a place to crash while I finished school. So I cooked mac and cheese for my nephew on the nights Daddy got called into work.

It's the least I could do.

And the kid loves posing. I've covered more canvases than I can count with sweet cherubs and little superheroes.

Right now, a long line of action figures, stuffed toys, books, and video game boxes snakes across the floor of my "studio," running from the steps to the living room upstairs into the box my nephew packs my paints. Bart is quite reverent of my supplies, for a four-year-old.

He holds up a tube of vermillion, his shoulders square, and speaks to his army. "Apples," he says, and nods once before placing it in the box.

I watch, wondering. He asked wide-eyed if he could pack my paints, like it was the most important thing in the world. No way could I say no.

He picks up a tube of indigo, stares at it for a moment, and mouths the label, sounding out the word. "Almost night!" He looks proud.

I squat next to him and squeeze his shoulder. His ever-present superhero costume crinkles under my fingers and he looks up at me, a bit glassy-eyed.

"What are you doing, little man?" He makes rivers of toys all the time, so that's not new, but color naming is.

"I remember the colors, Uncle Tommy. When you used them." He holds up a tube of yellow and points to a summer portrait I painted of him a couple of weeks ago. It hangs on the wall, next to the stairs, in a spot bright in the morning sun.

I don't know what to say, though I remember doing the same thing when I was his age. Lining up my toys. Making patterns on the floor. I drew and drew and taped my stuff to the walls so I could watch the light play over my crayon colors.

I'd seen Bart stare at his markers, his nose crinkled like they weren't *right*. As if they didn't have the scent he expected a color to have.

I give him a hug. "I'm going to miss you." I'll miss my brother too, but I need room. Dating is impossible when you live in your brother's basement. Sex while my nephew lives upstairs seems wrong on so many levels that the elevator between each floor of wrongness is itself wrong.

So I've been unofficially celibate for my last two years of undergraduate studies. It's been... tough.

Bart's eyes widen again. "When will you be home?"

He's got a special scent, one I can only assume is what little boys smell like. He's the only one I know, so I can't say for sure. But he sort of smells like my brothers. And me, I suppose. It's not attractive, just family. "I'll come visit, okay?"

My new place is closer to downtown, not far from my new job. I'm just thankful to have work. I know a lot of people my age who moved home after graduation.

"Uncle Robby says you're selling monster food." Bart blinks, his eyes wide again. It's amazing what kids hear, when adults speak.

My younger brother, Rob, scoffed when I told him about the job in the art department of one of the big multi-national food corporations. Called me a sell-out.

The beers flowed that afternoon on the deck, now that Rob is legal. He chewed his burger and said the last thing he expected was for me to be drawing happy pictures of frankenfood and GMO yogurt. Bart must have heard him.

But it's a job and jobs paid the rent.

"Tell you what," I say. "I'll draw you some 'monster food.'" I curl my fingers and growl, tickling his belly.

Bart screeches, his plastic costume wrinkling. "Uncle Tommy!" He lets loose a little four-year-old-boy fart and screeches some more.

I roll around on the floor with him, laughing. He'll be okay. Little Bart, he's just like my brother, except for the farting. Dan's the biggest and the best of the three of us.

And like my brother, I hope to do the best I can, with what I've got.

CHAPTER 2

Samantha

Andy leans against my cubicle's overhead bin and looks down at me with his baby blues. The metal groans when he crosses his arms. His well-sculpted biceps strain his perfectly-pressed button-down and I swear the fabric groans too. I tell him to call Rick's agent but he just smirks and says he likes his job here in our wide-open land of cubicles, usually with a flourish and a wink.

Andy, my usual lunch mate and the best work-husband a girl could want.

"Let's see them." He wiggles his fingers in front of my face.

Andy's had a crush on Rick since we started dating. Not a *real* crush—more like a supportive best friend showing approval—but he does enjoy the photographic evidence that I am, in fact, living with a hot hunk of man model.

Who took a cab to the airport this morning for another photo shoot, after I left for work. He hadn't really talked to me, not even to ask me to take care of the cat.

"I didn't bring any," I say to Andy. Rick didn't *share* share—he sent me a link with the equivalent of *lucky you* in the subject line. I didn't print them, either. This time, I didn't even load the shots onto my phone. I know he was being snarky, but *lucky me*, indeed.

Shaking my head, I point at my monitor. "Work. Deadline." Honestly, I don't want to think about Rick right now.

Andy rolls his eyes and the walls of my cubie groan again when he stands up straight. Sometimes I forget how tall he is. "You write press releases in your sleep."

"It's not a press release. Product testing." Every year, our company prototypes new cereals, yogurts—anything in garish packaging they can slap with a "good for you" logo and call "healthy." It's a complicated process involving several departments, including ours.

"Ah." Andy's nose wrinkles when he nods at my monitor. There are aspects of our work he likes, and aspects he doesn't. Just like me. That's why he's a wonderful work-husband.

He keeps his arms crossed as he turns to go. "Oh!" He lifts his hand off his elbow and twirls his finger in the air like a magician. "I have noon meetings all week so you'll need to find some other sucker to lunch with you." He winks.

Guess I'll eat my frozen boxes of well-tested midday meal product alone this week. I nod toward my computer. "Probably be at my desk, anyway."

My entire cubie rattles when he wraps his fingers around the top edge of the wall. "Don't do that. It's supposed to be nice. At least take your tablet and go outside." He frowns like a big brother, or an uncle, or a father.

"Yes, Dad." I frown back.

Andy laughs and shakes his head full of perfectly cut, chocolate brown hair. He really should call Rick's agent.

"Back to work, you slacker." He walks off, toward his own cubie. "Next time, pictures!" he calls over his shoulder.

My chair squeaks when I lean back, thinking about pictures, and I realize my cubicle is as ugly as Rick's loft. The gray-blue nylon fabric walls feel like they were textured to mimic office furniture, or burlap, or maybe someone's unfortunate Christmas sweater. They do their job —cutting neighbor noise and fading into the background while I work —but they're flat. And completely lack personality.

I've pinned up a few items: Pictures from a Museum of Modern Art calendar I bought a few years ago. A couple photos of Mr. Pickles —Mickles, I call him—Rick's sweet cat. A page or two out of one of the clothing catalogs featuring Rick and his picture-perfect ah-shucks smile. That's it. Nothing special. Nothing unexpected. Not even a plant.

My cubicle's door opens toward the windows, so at least I see daylight. The tint on the glass turns the morning a weird green, but it's natural light. I can tell when it's time to eat and when it's time to leave, all by the pitch of the sun.

Maybe I should get a plant. Something living.

A message pops up on my screen: The boss wants me to go down-stairs and pick up mock-ups from the Art Department. I stretch, leaning back to see past my cubicle door to the wall of industrial windows not far away.

It looks like a nice day. Bright, and not cave-like. Maybe I should go outside. But first, I need to pick up fresh new designs for America's freshest and newest breakfast foods.

The stairwell door hisses shut behind me as its hydraulic closer keeps it from slamming. The company recently painted the stairwell and my floor's door is purpleberry purple, a cereal box color so vividly bright it looks like a monitor screen and not paint. The tangy, chemical stink of "low odor" paint also lingers. I rush down, trying not to breathe too deeply.

The standard big building metal and concrete stairs clunk as I jog, and my skirt rubs against my legs. Tight black pencil skirts and heels don't make the best running gear, but I try to take the "dress for success" bullshit to heart. The shoes, though, stay in my desk drawer when I leave for home each evening. Bus rides call for sneakers.

The door to the Art Department has a graffiti look, as if someone spray painted versions of all the company's product logos onto it. It's graphic design all the way, with very little "art." But it gets the point across. I pull open the door.

The windows are different down here. The day doesn't shine through weirdly green, like upstairs. It bursts into the wide open space, white and clear and warm. The entire floor is flooded with natural light

9

—and no cubicle farm messes it up, though cubies do line the inner wall next to me, on either side of the door. The Art Department prefers big tables and open spaces.

I walk in, breathing in deeply, and memories of my undergraduate days flood back. I took a lot of art courses, Art History mostly, and I spent my time in studios. They have a particular smell to them, an art-in-progress scent of dyes and metal and clay. Real tools, real media, and the hands of real people.

I loved it. I might marvel at what the Art Department here whips up with software, but nothing beats the sound of brushes on a canvas and the smell of paints.

There'd been this guy, too, my senior year. A tall, skinny kid with sandy brown hair and bright, pale eyes. I saw him once or twice, walking near the art building, a pad under his arm and a pack on his back. He moved around in a sort of awe, like a lot of freshmen, so I stayed away. At the time, I had a month before graduation and an eighteen-year-old boyfriend didn't seem like a good idea.

Sometimes I don't remember his face well, but I remember the look of his hands. And I imagine how they would have felt. How he would have smelled masculine but naïve, with a hint of charcoal from his work, if I had been smart enough to throw my reservations to the wind and come close. How he would have watched me in the morning light with his artist's eye, planning the next expression of his art.

I brush my fingers over the gray-blue nylon of the cubicle wall next to me. Time to retrieve mock-ups, not to pull up old fantasies, no matter how richly wonderful they are.

A body swings out of the cubicle—a big body with a wide chest and broad shoulders—and pulls up short, right in front of me.

"Oh!" pops from my mouth and I look up at the most wonderful blue-green eyes I have ever seen. Eyes more moving than Rick's. Beautiful eyes framed by thick, masculine lashes—not too long, but perfect for the shape of his face.

The man in front of me stands at least six inches taller, even with my heels. I get a good look at his strong jaw and expressive lips. Stubble covers his chin and I doubt he shaved this morning. His hair's messy too, as if he also forgot his comb. But his clothes are neat and clean, and he smells nice.

Quite nice, like real art, not the moused-over kind. Like texture and color and enough care to do it right. My forehead wrinkles. "Caring" didn't have a smell, but with this guy, it did. And it smelled brilliant, as if his potential reflected off his skin with the warm sunlight pouring through the window.

"Sorry," he says, grinning. One of his big hands grips the wall of his cubicle and it grumbles, much like mine does. His other reaches out to steady me, a reflex, I'm sure.

His hand cups my elbow. Strong, warm fingers grasp my flesh, not hard but with just enough pressure to steady me as I stagger back on my three inch heels.

"You okay? I didn't knock you, did I?" He watches me carefully, his gaze first searching my face before it drops for a quick glance at my chest. A tiny arch of approval moves from one eyebrow to the other before his eyes return to where they are supposed to look.

"No, no," I stammer. God, he's built like a man. Not Rick's obvious inverted triangle and twenty-six inch waist. No, this guy looks like he could pick me up and carry me out of a burning building while wearing full firefighter gear. He works, not trains.

His fingers release my elbow. "I didn't mean to startle you."

God, he has wonderful hands. Hands like the ones my remembered freshman would have now, four years out from my graduation. I look down at my arm, feeling, suddenly, as if I'd just been offered the best touch in the world and now he takes it away because he never should have offered it in the first place.

Then I remember the reason: Rick. I stand up straight, determined to regain my composure. I'm in a relationship and I need to act like it.

The new guy—because I'm damned sure I would remember him if I'd seen him before—smirks and looks away. As he shifts his weight, his hips move side to side in the centered way only men with strong abs and assured personalities move.

In this moment, as I stand no more than two feet from him, I know I'm blushing. I feel the heat move down my neck to my breasts and my nipples are so damned hard I'm *sure* they're showing though my bra. I'm starting to feel slick and I want to press my thighs together, but I don't. Because the blush is embarrassing enough.

He blinks a few times and I wonder if he can smell how much I want him, even though—God knows—I shouldn't. I wonder if he's going to turn me around right here and now, throw open the stairwell door, and back me against the ugly graphics on the door just so his fingers can find out for themselves in relative privacy what his sense of smell already knows.

Sometimes being horny all the time has its drawbacks. It's a plus, with Rick. When he's in town. And not too tired from training. Or too busy making sure his tan is just right or his chest is smoothly shaved. I stifle a frown, hoping the new guy won't think I'm frowning at him.

He's a gentleman. One obviously raised well, because he's fighting to keep his eyes on my face. I imagine he's holding in a growl, too. A deep baritone growl, one full of resonance from his huge chest.

He sticks out his hand. "My name's Thomas. Tom Quidell."

I wrap my palm around his, doing my best to be a gentlewoman. "Samantha Singleton. Sammie for short."

He winks and nods toward the door. "Do say, m'lady, from whence level of our dungeon of foodstuffs and factory numbers did you escape?"

I chuckle, smiling, thankful he's found a way to break the awkwardness, but his charm just makes me want him more. Which I *shouldn't*. The broken spell lets in a sudden and unwanted burst of guilt. I look away.

"Campaign Relations. I came down for—"

"Oh!" He snaps his fingers and backs into his cubie. "The mock-ups."

My body doesn't like that he's moved away. I feel a pull, as if I'm supposed to walk forward into the gap between his cubicle walls, so when he turns around again I'm right there, waiting for him to run into me, in full body contact.

A cardboard tube pokes out of the cubie, held in the air by his luscious hand. "My first." He winks again, his chest out, but he shoves his fingers into his pockets when I take the tube.

"When did you start?" I roll the tube between my hands, flipping it around like a wand. Why do *his* hands seem so familiar? Maybe it's because they're so masculine. And wonderful.

"Last week." He watches me, captivated. "I graduated Spring semester."

How could this huge, gorgeous man be a baby? Except he graduated, and was most certainly legal to drink. And no more than five years younger than me.

He turns back to his desk to grab something and I take in the square perfection of his backside. The man in front of me was definitely not a baby.

He holds out a card, a big smile lighting up his handsome face. "Just delivered this morning. You're the first."

I take the card, glancing at his name, title, office phone, and e-mail, knowing full well I will have it all memorized before I return to my floor. "A business card virgin, huh?" I tuck it into my pencil skirt's one pocket.

His face takes on a raw edge as he watches my hand smooth across my hip. I don't know if it's because I said "virgin" or because he likes what he sees. Or a combination of the two. But he catches his look quickly, like a true gentleman, and offers his hand once more. "Nice to meet you, Samantha Singleton, Sammie for short."

We shake again. I back toward the stairway door, watching him and not where I'm walking. A chuckle rolls from his cubie, but his phone rings, and he turns away.

So much for him following me into the stairway.

As I open the door I frown at myself, as indignant as I am embarrassed. I just met a good guy, a smart, sexy guy, and a gentleman. I live with someone. I sleep in the same bed with another man. And I'm flirting like some horny high schooler?

It's not the first time my libido has gotten me in trouble.

But part of me screams I need to pay attention. Would this temptation have occurred if the best part of my home life wasn't Mickles rubbing my ankles and demanding a good petting?

I stand in the stairwell for a long moment, wondering what to do.

Thomas

I JUST HANDED MY FIRST BUSINESS CARD TO THE HOTTEST WOMAN I have ever met in my entire life. Auburn hair so shiny it gleams. Hazel-green eyes sparkling with life. Full, round lips and the most beautiful smile I have ever seen.

Holy shit, I think, barely keeping my mind on the chatter coming at me over the phone. I write down a few things, say a few *ah-hahs* and ask for an e-mail confirming the conversation before I hang up. My brother Dan told me before I started to "always get an e-mail. Believe me, you *always* want an e-mail." Times like this, when all I can think about is getting into that tight little skirt to find what other tight little treats await me, I know my brother is a genius.

Sammie Singleton. I do a quick search in the company directory. An assistant to an assistant. Been with the company four years. Started here my sophomore year at the University.

So she's a little older than me. And has the lushest *real* breasts I ever wanted to rub my face between. Big, little, I don't care, but I like real. Fake looks fake. Fake feels fake. Some men don't care but I swear I can taste the silicone.

And her hips screamed *fuck me*. Pull up my black skirt and fuck me long and hard.

I close my eyes and force myself to count as I inhale. I can't get this worked up over a woman, especially one I just met. She could be married, for all I know. Or living with someone. If there's one thing I learned from Dan's divorce, it's to make sure you know who you are sleeping with.

CHAPTER 3

Samantha

I spend the rest of my day refusing to think about one Mr. Thomas, Tom Quidell. About his white shirt or the leather cord tied discretely around his neck. Or how soft his hair would feel between my fingers. Because every time I do, I see Rick standing in front of our bathroom mirror, a towel around his waist, as he checks out his chest stubble.

Watching Rick used to be the sexiest thing I could imagine. He'd come out of the shower and stare at me until I couldn't take it anymore and went down on him. I'd suck him off and he'd throw me onto the bed and fuck me missionary style.

At the time, it seemed so exotic. But now I wonder if it was just erotic.

And maybe not all that erotic, either. Maybe simply expected.

The bus bumps along the city streets and I look around at my fellow passengers. I've been riding this line, at this time, every day for eight months. In summer, it's bright outside and the morning dew covers the sidewalk. I wait at the stop, my bag in my hand and my sneakers on my feet, with the same three people. In the evenings, I ride home with a different set, a guy and two older women with their bags and their sneakers.

We take up our places but we don't talk to each other. Sort of like how I take up my place on my knees in front of Rick and don't know what it means to him.

Or what it means to me.

Inside, I wonder if there's any beauty to the movements of my life.

As I walk up the stairs to the loft, I remember, once again, Rick is gone on a shoot. This time, he's in L.A. He won't be back for four days.

I stop outside the door, my key in hand, and stare at the heavy wood slab. It's hung on massive iron hinges setting off its rough, original look. I think it must have been part of a worktable at some point, or maybe a floor. This door, it has history. And now it's trying something new.

I drop my bag on the floor and hit the light switch, even though there's enough evening light I should be able to see. But the curtains are closed. Rick must have shut them before he left this afternoon.

Flinging them open, I flood the loft with low sunlight. The main window faces west, and we're high enough in the building we see the sunset. Tonight, the sky spreads out red and gold, and lights up the world.

There's a piece of paper on the table, but I know what it says. Itinerary notes, flight numbers, and the unspoken reminder to feed Mickles. It's the same every time.

The cat prances around my legs, starved more for affection than for food. I pick him up and he rubs his soft fur against my cheek, purring and licking and meowing.

He might be a boring kitty, but he's a good boy. And he prefers the curtains open, just like me.

I set out his food and drop onto the couch. It crinkles as I lean back, its not-so-buttery leather muttering about my invasion of its domain. I pull a pillow under my head and look up at the solid beams crossing the ceiling. In the evening light, I see a few cobwebs, and wonder how to get the vacuum up there. Then I wonder if it's worthwhile.

My hand wanders to my thighs, as my mind wonders about other unknowns. I have a steady life with Rick, a good-ish life, but my brain's screaming *excitement! Possibilities! New new new!*

The handsome and huge Mr. Quidell.

I can't think about him anymore. I can't think about either man. So I dip back into my old fantasy, the one of the art student with his huge pad of paper under his arm.

He sits on the mound of lawn in front of the library, his pad propped against his pack. He's a puppy, tall and not quite filled out yet, with big hands and big feet. Bright, pale eyes watch me as I walk along between the buildings and the bike path. His gaze is intense, piercing, as if he likes what he sees. Wants what he sees.

On the couch, my hand pulls up my skirt and my thighs part. I end up here more often than I want to admit. Training makes Rick tired. Perfection comes at a cost, and usually it's our sex life.

I've gotten quite good at dealing with it on my own.

In the fantasy, I bite my lip, watching the gorgeous art student watch me. When I duck through the sliding doors into the library, his eyes narrow, and he's up off the grass, pad in one hand and pack in the other.

I duck through the second set of doors, into the library's cavernous lobby, glancing first to the left, then to the right. I need someplace private—a quiet corner to study. But I know he's right behind me, his tall stride long and purposeful. He'll follow. But how deep into the stacks will he go?

On the couch, my fingers find their private place, their quiet corner. I rub my clit lightly at first, feeling my fantasy self stride between shelf after shelf of books. In the fantasy, I want to rub myself, but I roll my hips instead, pushing my thighs together.

I know he's there. I know he's watching.

This part of the library has wide, tall windows, but it's a corner rarely visited. I stroke the spine of an old book, one untouched for ages, and I know I don't want to end up like it. Not in my fantasy, and not on my couch, where I wiggle.

He's there, at the other end of the long row of books, standing square to me, his pale eyes intense. The pack hangs from one of his hands, the pad from the other. His grip is strong, firm, and I wonder how those fingers will feel on my skin.

I back against an old metal desk, one that's been pushed into the forbidden corner of this forbidden section of the library. Sun streams in from the lone window behind it, but scattered by a rolling shelf full of books. I lean back into the dappled light, knowing my legs are parting and my nipples are pressing through my thin t-shirt.

On the couch, by myself, I sigh.

In the fantasy, he's right there in front of me, looking down at my face, his head slightly tilted. He drops the pack onto the desk on one side of me, but holds the pad.

He wants me to see.

The pages flip and then there's me. And me again. Walking. Smiling. My hand on my pack's straps. Another of me watching as the world passes by.

He's been drawing me for days. Weeks, maybe.

The pages turn again. Me, now in places I've never been. In a studio. On a bed I don't know. They are his fantasies. His desires.

Me, naked, reaching out to him.

His eyes intense, he closes the pad and drops it on the other side of me, trapping me between his possessions. The pad crinkles and a rustling breaks the silence.

He wants me. This beautiful boy wants me and he's been shy—too shy to say hello, but not shy enough to keep from drawing me on my back, nipples erect, his hope that I want him as much as he wants me blistering from the page.

In the fantasy I rub my hand over the bulge in his jeans. A groan rolls from his throat and he looks up at the ceiling. I see his smile.

Leaning forward, he reaches around my side to smooth the paper, his gaze locked to mine. I'm breathing hard, this close to him. He's gorgeous up close—thick sandy brown hair and beautiful blue-green eyes. I trace the leather cord tied around his neck.

When he leans toward me his shoulder brushes my breast and I gasp. He doesn't pull away, just stares at my chest, a hungry look making his young features seem older than he is.

"My muse," he says, his voice low and resonant. He may not have filled out yet, but his voice has. "You are *perfect*."

His mouth descends onto mine, searching and a little naïve. But he's strong and his stomach feels wonderful and rock hard under his shirt. I yank on the fabric, pulling it up to get a look at what my fingers feel.

"Take off the shirt." I say, rubbing my hands all over his skin.

He glances back into the library, but does as I say. His shoulders and arms do not disappoint. I rub cheeks and lips against his chest.

I'm so hot that when he tongues my mouth again, stealing my breath, I almost come. He chuckles, his hand moving under my skirt to my itty bitty panties, and a finger finds its way underneath.

"I want to see," he growls. "Let me see." His other hand yanks on my shirt as he backs away enough to see both my breasts and my pussy. He doesn't let go. I'd scream if he let go.

My fantasy man watches his finger dip in and out like he's never seen a woman's parts before. His other hand is working hard on my nipples, yanking and twisting, and I'm dying, it feels so good. He moves two fingers inside me and I'm bucking now, moaning, and his face is pure carnal joy. He likes how I react to him, and it just makes me want to fuck him more.

Just how he's looking at me makes me so horny I want to scream. The bulge in his jeans is too much and I unbuckle his belt, balancing carefully on the edge of the desk. He's cupping my pussy now, rubbing against my clit with the palm of his hand, and also keeping me from falling. His arms take all the work of holding me still, one hand working my fantasy clit the way my real finger works my real clit, the fingers of the other curled into the front of my bra. His biceps may be developing, but they are beautiful. A groan rolls from his throat, a deep groan, one urging me on. I work at it, but it takes effort to release his glorious cock from his boxer briefs. He's big—long and thick—and I can't believe my luck. Those hips are going to pound me hard and I'm going to come again and again.

I stroke him with a firm grip. He's hard—unbelievably hard—but his cock feels velvety and smooth. Wonderful. I roll my thumb over the tip, spreading his pre-cum, before licking the pad of my thumb.

God, my fantasy man tastes as good as he looks. Clean and wonderful and like a man who knows how to work.

His eyes narrow, his lids dropping, as he watches me suck at the pre-cum on the tip of my thumb. "Suck me," he demands, holding me where I am.

Oh, I think about it—how the crown of his cock will feel against my tongue. How taut his muscles will be as he tries to thrust into my mouth. How my throat will take all of him.

But this is my fantasy, not his. "You first." I widen my legs, leaning back. I want him to lick me. To taste and want to fuck me so bad he's gripping my hips enough it hurts.

His hand pulls off my pussy and cold air washes in behind it. Both hands pinch my nipples. Both flicking and squeezing and I let out a whimper. My pussy convulses, a pre-orgasm rippling up my belly. When he gets his tongue on me I'm going to come all over his face.

"Oh, God," I moan.

In my fantasy, his cock pushes into me. Hard.

On the couch, where I lay in the real world with my pencil skirt hitched up, I moan. Shudders flood from my contracting pussy all the way to my toes and my fluttering eyelids. I drop down, my fingers still rubbing. I'd forgotten the brilliance of this fantasy.

How much better it is than Rick's hard abs and his demanding stare.

I open my eyes. Mickles sits on the back of the couch, licking his paw like he doesn't care one bit what the human is doing.

I sit up even though all I want to do is take a nap, and think back to that last semester on campus. I spent a lot of time in and near the arts buildings as I finished off my last few classes and I remember my fantasy hottie and his pack and his artist's pad. Lots of students set up to draw passersby. He was one of many.

It dawns on me that the details of my fantasy could just be my new crush entering my desires. Maybe I added them this time. But no. Those details have always been there: pale eyes—blue-green in the bright sun—broad shoulders, even if they hadn't yet completely filled out, and the leather cord around his neck.

And the luscious hands.

I grab a pillow, suddenly so embarrassed I don't want anyone to see my face, not even Mickles.

And I realize why Tom seemed familiar.

All these years I've been using a memory to get myself off that, more often than not, worked better than thoughts of Rick. A memory of a hot guy I didn't know.

Until today.

CHAPTER 4

Thomas

I bounce my pen on my desktop—*snap, snap, snap*. My foot is going at the same rate—*tap, tap, tap*. And I've been semi-hard for three days, thinking about Ms. Sammie Singleton.

We crossed paths twice since she appeared on my cubicle threshold all sweet smelling and lickable. Both times she smiled and looked away and I wished I was better at reading people. Coy or embarrassed, I couldn't tell.

I think she's avoiding me, so the second time I stood my ground. "Do you want to have lunch today? It's nice out." I waved my hand at the weirdly green windows of her floor. They hazed Campaign Relations and everything within reach. Except her. They did nothing to cut her beauty.

She just blinked at me, not answering.

"Did I do something?" I didn't know what else to ask but I can't stand her not talking to me. It's driving me nuts.

She nodded and stood up straight, as if she'd decided to not be embarrassed anymore. Or coy. "No, no, of course not."

"Did *you* do something?" I grinned the most disarming grin I could, attempting to charm her out of whatever issue she's got going on.

For a long moment, she watched me with her hazel eyes, but she didn't answer my question. "Twelve fifteen? I'll meet you at the stairs by your cubicle?"

I got through. We made a lunch date.

That was at ten. The last two hours have been excruciating.

She's not wearing a ring, wedding or otherwise, so there's hope. And she's wearing another tight skirt today, a bright indigo number that screams *look at my hips*. And *look at my ass*. And her legs. And her waist.

Lunch better go well or I'll be punching holes in men's room walls.

I close down my illustrating program and push back my chair. The wheels do their squeaky pinging and it flows into my backside. Not a pleasant sensation against my balls.

Part of me wants to find a fuck buddy and work out all my pent-up issues over a few hours of itch scratching. Hook-ups serve a purpose, even if I've never liked the practice. There's something about not waking up with the person you went to bed with. I want to see a woman in the morning light, even if she doesn't always want to be seen.

Maybe I'm old fashioned.

It's twelve thirteen. I'll wait for her in the stairwell. Nothing beats watching a beautiful woman descend a staircase.

I push open the ugly door, absently wondering why someone thought the "graffiti" was a good idea. No sense of form, no flow, it looks like six or seven of the company's mascots threw up. I step into the landing, looking more at the lack of design in front of me than where I'm going.

"Tom!"

I look up. Sammie stands two steps up, her hand gripping the railing tight. Her gorgeous breasts are right there. Right at my eye level. So close all I need to do is walk one pace forward and bury my face in her chest.

She doesn't say anything. I blink, a sudden fear that I've been staring at her chest for minutes—*hours*—and next thing she's going to do is take a good strong swing and punch me right in the mouth.

But she doesn't. And when I look up at her face, she's wearing an expression I don't understand. Is she angry? Embarrassed? Disappointed?

Oh, shit, I think. How can I be this clueless with women?

"Ready for lunch?" She's tilted her head a little and looks away again. I wish I had better light than the buzzing fluorescent donut hanging in the center of the stairwell shaft.

I may paint this anyway. Sammie, the one bright spot of beauty against an ugly concrete backdrop.

She steps down to the landing. "When I was in school, the artists I hung around with all made that face." Her delicate finger swirls in front of my nose. "I called it the 'composition snarl.'"

I laugh, happy she's not going to smack me upside the head, like I deserve. Happy, too, she seems to like artists. "What did you major in?" We turn to walk down the remaining stairs to the first floor and the cafeteria, and I touch her back without realizing what I'm doing.

A tingle runs up my arm as I feel her muscles sway under my fingers. Shit, I could hold onto those hips all night, with her riding me.

I pull my hand back before she can get mad.

"Communications." She glances at my hand as I move next to her on the stairs.

I shove it into my pocket.

"Minored in Art History."

I smile. She becomes more and more perfect with each passing moment. We chat as we walk into the main lobby. I keep my hands in my pockets, trying to be a gentleman. It's difficult. All I want is more touches. More fingers along her back. To feel her skin. To see more smiles.

Her heels click on the granite floor and draw my eyes to her calves. Smooth, rounded, her legs look strong, like she works out.

In the cafeteria line she gets chicken salad and an orange, plus tea. Me, I get the same, but bigger, with a breadstick and two oranges.

At our table she snickers and wags her finger between the two pieces of fruit, an eyebrow up, another blush rising up her neck. "What's with the matching orange globes?"

I'm barely able to draw my gaze from the warm glow of her face. God damn I want to kiss her. Right now, right here in the company cafeteria in front of the entire staff. I feel myself harden and I glance away, down at my tray, trying to think about something stupid, like baseball stats or the bad graffiti on the Art Department door.

My bread stick is tipped slightly but propped up between the two fruits. Like my cock. "Oh, geez." Quickly, I move the stick to the other side of the plate. I peel one of the oranges, doing my best to ignore the heat creeping up *my* neck.

Sammie laughs and sits back in her chair. "I'm sorry. Can't help but give the new kid a hard time."

She still looks uncomfortable but not as much as before, and I relax some. But the "kid" reference annoys me. I yank the rind off the orange and drop it on my tray. "I'm not that young."

Chewing, she sets down her fork and her fingers cover her mouth. "That's not what I meant." But embarrassment returns, like I pulled up some memory she doesn't like.

What am I up against, here? The phantoms in women's heads are more terrifying than any real bad guy. They lunge at you out of nowhere and rip to shreds the world you've built. Like what Dan's ex-wife did to his life.

I must be frowning because now she looks worried. "Believe me, no one looks at you and thinks 'kid.' You're..." She waves her hand at me.

"A moose?" Dan started calling me "moose" when I put on twenty-five pounds during my sophomore year. Wasn't even lifting that much, other than helping at his work.

Sammie laughs and shakes her head. "You *are* big."

I shift in my chair, trying to keep my semi-hard state as comfortable as possible, and our knees bump.

She jumps, startled, and glances under the table. "And long legged."

The front of her shirt opens enough for me to see the edges of her little lacey bra. It's indigo, like her skirt. Her bra matches her *touch me* skirt.

I almost blurt out a dinner invitation. Hell, I almost knock aside the table and take her right here on the floor of the cafeteria.

But Sammie's phone chirps. She pulls it out of her bag and, holding it out, she narrows her eyes as she reads the text. "Damn."

She's not happy. Or she is happy. I can't tell.

"Rick got a second shoot. He's staying in L.A. for an extra few days." Her shoulders tighten, as do her fingers around the phone. She's sitting uncomfortably, the way I would paint her if I wanted to convey anxiety.

My stomach drops and all of a sudden I don't want to eat anymore. This Rick is the reason she's been standoffish.

He causes her discomfort and it leaves a bad taste in my mouth.

He shouldn't treat her that way, I think. Except I don't know what *that way* is. Maybe he never does the dishes. Maybe he leaves his underwear on the floor. Or maybe he doesn't touch her the way she likes.

She looks up from her phone. "You're awfully quiet."

She's right—I haven't said anything for a couple of minutes. Thing is, I don't know what to say. Everything swimming around in my head sounds idiotic. I want to pick her up and set her on my lap and stroke her back instead.

I don't like seeing her upset.

I blink. We've had one lunch and a fair amount of staring and this guy is raising my hackles? Did I learn nothing from Dan's divorce?

Sammie leans forward, her face unreadable, poised to put down her phone. But it chirps again and she stops, looking at the screen with the same narrow eyes as before. Until they widen.

Her entire body stiffens.

"What?" I ask. Probably not what she wants to hear.

Sammie turns the phone around, holding it out. I gently touch her fingers as I take it, knowing I shouldn't be thinking about her skin right now. Whatever is on the phone has her upset.

I look down at the screen. *What time pick you up?* the text reads. *Have exactly what you need. Don't worry baby.*

It's from her asshole boyfriend. I know immediately it wasn't meant for her. So does she. And I know immediately what it means.

"It's vague, right? Maybe he's talking about a script or something." She looks more shocked than anything else.

The phone is still in my hand. "Don't answer it." My head is spinning with options: Wait and see if he realizes who he texted. Wait for his excuse. But what I want to do is type out *Sammie's new boyfriend here. Fuck off.*

I hand back the phone before my thumb gets me in trouble.

She drops it into her bag without looking at it again.

"You alright?" I want to reach across the table and take her hand.

"Why did you say to not answer?" Her face looks blank. She's dropped her hands to her lap like some school girl.

"Let him explain without prompting." I sit back. *Let him dig his own hole.*

Her eyebrows bunch together and she frowns. "Why?"

I look away. *Damn it*, I think, *my chances with her just imploded.* Showing up in the middle of messes like this only leads to problems. "My brother went through a bad divorce a couple years ago. Best thing is to let stuff like that spin itself out without interference." *You get better evidence of infidelity.*

"Oh." Sammie sits for a moment, staring at her half-eaten lunch.

Now my phone beeps. "Shit." I hold it out so Sammie sees my calendar reminder. "I have a meeting in ten."

She nods and drops her napkin on her picked-at lunch. I don't like that she's not eating. It means she's more upset than she's letting on.

"If you need to talk, text me. Okay?" I pile my dishes on the center of my tray. I don't stand and I won't either, until I know she's okay. If I'm late for the meeting, so be it.

Sammie watches me and her face is impassive again. But she nods finally and stands up.

"I'm glad I met you," she says. "Thank you."

If we were alone, or in a restaurant, or outside, or—damn it, I don't know. Anyplace but here. Anyplace other than the cafeteria where we both work, I would have kissed her. Straight up and over the table, a full kiss right on those beautiful lips.

But I breathe because she doesn't need a scene right now. "You're welcome." I lift my tray as I stand, partly to hide my hopefully not that obvious desire to be near her. "Text me." *Or call.*

We walk up to our respective floors and I wait by the Art Department door as she ascends to her level. The indigo skirt hugs lovely hips as she steps one leg up, then the other.

I know one thing for sure: That asshole boyfriend doesn't deserve what he's got.

CHAPTER 5

Samantha

I made it through my embarrassment and ate lunch with Tom. Yes, I can act like an adult. But then he had to go and be perfect. Eight months and Rick has never cared if I'm *okay*. He brought me tea when I had the flu but mostly he stayed back, saying he didn't want to catch my bugs. He never makes sure I'm *okay* okay. He's never even asked me to text when he's gone.

And I doubt his last text was meant for me.

This time, when I open the door to the loft, I don't hit his bike. I hit nothing.

Mickles rubs against my leg, meowing for his dinner. I pick him up, cradling him in my arm, and he headbutts my shoulder as I drop my bag on the floor.

He's soft and smooth under my fingers, a sweet vibrating ball of fluff and love. I breathe, listening to his purr, and try to clear my mind. All I need to do is open the windows. And let in the light.

Part of me thinks I should be ecstatic. My wanting to move out is Rick's fault. All the rolled eyes and the ignoring weren't just his crabby moods. It's always been Rick's fault and I've been picking up subtle cues. But if that's so, then why do I feel so *empty*?

Something needs fixing and I don't know what.

Mickles's food smells terrible but he likes it. I dig in the freezer, the cold numbing my fingers and the rattling drone of the fridge filling the empty loft—and my head—with a constant buzz. I pull out a random microwave dinner and drop it on the counter. Mickles scarfed his entire bowl and now sits in the center of the kitchen floor, cleaning his face.

The cat knows what he wants.

My dinner tastes like paste. I push it away, wishing I'd eaten more of my lunch. An orange right now would taste good.

Some orange on the walls would brighten the entire loft. A little paint, maybe some laughter.

An orange held by one Mr. Tom, Thomas Quidell, peeled slowly and with great care, the way his fingers would peel away my blouse.

Or how I fantasize he'd treat me—gentle pressure along the tight muscles of my neck, strong hands cupping my breasts, his warm, masculine breath teasing my neck.

What am I doing? I think. I pick up my phone. Rick's freaky text is still there, still vague and still weird. I stare at it, thinking it's as strangely lifeless as his loft and I wonder what attracted me to him in the first place.

But I know: I like sex. I like men with hard muscles and strong jaws who like sex, too.

And once again, I wonder why I feel empty.

I absently flick through my contacts. Maybe right now I need a friend more than I need a hot guy. Or maybe a hot guy friend who understands where I'm coming from.

Except my finger brushes past Andy's number. It brushes by all my girlfriends, too. And stops on a place I wasn't expecting: Tom.

Damn it, I think. *Why does he have to be so perfect?* And then I stop thinking. My impulses take over.

I tap away: *Thank you again for lunch.*

A second passes and I drop onto the squeaky couch, staring at what I just did. He said *text me* and I did like some horny kid.

A response pops up: *You are welcome.*

Now what do I do? Ask him if he'd like to get some dinner? Tell him I want a booty call? Lie back on the pillow and add the new and improved Tom to my favorite fantasy?

I'm so fucked up.

Another message pops up: *You okay?*

He didn't type *I'm coming over.* That's what Rick did, the first night we met. I left the party and an hour later I had my ass in the air and a male model pounding away groaning how much he likes chicks who can take what he gives them.

Just a little disoriented, I message back.

Lunch tomorrow.

I stare at my phone. Part of me is screaming *Yes!* while another is screaming *No!* The worst of it is that I don't know why.

Sure. Lunch tomorrow. I set down the phone. Mickles watches me from the back of the couch again, purring like he always does. He drops onto my lap and curls up into a ball of happiness. A cat knows when a moment is good and a cat doesn't care if what's done is bad. Or if what's coming is worse. Cats just know what they like in the moment.

Maybe I should pack my stuff. Or maybe I should wait until Rick is back and we have a moment to talk.

But Rick's not a talker. I don't even know where to start with him. Never have. Never will.

I stroke Mickles's back, thinking about that space between me and Rick. That big, empty place we often filled with sex because sex is something we can both do. And do well. But when the sun comes up, the curtains are always closed. Nothing gets in.

I lie back on the couch, thinking about how correct I was before: I'm so fucked up.

Thomas

BART'S RUNNING CIRCLES AROUND MY LEGS. "UNCLE TOMMY! UNCLE

Tommy!"

I'm not paying him the attention I should because Sammie texted me back: *Lunch tomorrow.*

My brain's yelling *Score!* but I know I shouldn't be smiling like some stupid kid. I need to be careful. Don't need to do dumb shit and end up like Dan.

"Uncle Tommy!" Bart's in his superhero pajamas and he's bouncing on his toes, his arms out, ready to be hoisted into the air.

"Sorry about that, little man." I tuck away the phone and swing him up to my shoulders. "Shouldn't you be in bed?"

He wraps his little hands around my forehead as we bounce along. "Daddy said Uncle Tommy was coming over and that I could stay up so you could tuck me in and then I'll go to sleep because I have school tomorrow and I'm tired." He makes a show of yawning so he can touch the ceiling.

"Well then, we need to do just that."

Dan's leaning against the wall next to the door, grinning. He's set the last of my boxes out for me. With tonight's load, I'm officially out of his basement.

I carry Bart over to his dad and bow so he bops a little on my shoulders. A massive giggle curls from his little boy throat.

"School, huh?" I ask. Bart's four and a year out from kindergarten.

Dan ruffles his son's hair. "Mister Smartypants here got accepted into the Early Childhood Arts program at the center, didn't you?"

Bart bounces on my shoulders. "I did! I did! I told them I want to be a painter like my Uncle Tommy and Ms. Frasier is my teacher and she's really pretty."

"Really pretty, huh?" I look to Dan and he nods *Oh yeah*. I laugh. We're three peas from the same pod, us Quidell men. "Is she a really good teacher?"

"She's got Bart here painting pictures every day, doesn't she?" Dan lifts his son off my shoulders and sets him down.

"Yes!" Bart's pantomiming painting and he squints, holding out his thumb.

Dan laughs and scoots Bart toward the stairs. "Off to brush your teeth. Uncle Tommy will tuck you in when you're done."

Bart stands straight. "I brushed my teeth!"

Dan kneels down, his face exaggerated into an unbelieving smirk. "And when did you do this?"

"Yesterday."

I laugh again, remembering saying the exact same thing to our dad when I was little.

Dan shakes his head and sends Bart off. "Go on." He watches his son climb the stairs and we both listen to the soles of Bart's footie bottoms whiff on the carpet.

"You texting with a woman?" Dan doesn't look at me. He's watching Bart turn on the bathroom light.

"Yes." No use lying about it or acting upset about the question. He's my big brother. "Her name is Sammie. Met her at work."

Dan nods but doesn't say anything more. I know what he's thinking, though: Please be careful. Don't do what I did.

I glance up the stairs. Dan went through hell with his divorce. But at least he got Bart. "Thanks for packing up the last of my stuff."

Dan rolls his eyes. "Why do you keep all those old drawings? There's stuff from high school in there."

High school, college—some people keep a journal. I keep my drawings. "I'm a hoarder. You'll need to commit me in a few months. Start planning now."

Dan chuckles. "You got some hand drawn porn in there." He smirks and kicks at one of the boxes. "That's why you keep it. Admit it."

"If only." But I used to draw every pretty woman I saw. Out on the mall in front of the art building, while sitting on the grass in front of the library—

A memory slaps me hard: My first month on campus, an upperclassman walking by, her lovely auburn hair in a ponytail, her head turning as she watched me watch her.

"Man, you alright?" Dan slaps my shoulder. "You look like you just saw a ghost."

Maybe I did. A ghost I share with Sammie.

And maybe *my* phantom is big enough, strong enough, to wrestle into submission whatever is swirling around in her head.

BACK HOME, I KNEEL IN MY "LIVING ROOM" NEXT TO MY apartment's big sliding glass door. The balcony is three feet deep, just enough for a chair and a pot of tomatoes. It's the reason I took this place. The door lets in brilliant afternoon light.

The room has one chair. My monitors sit on my desk, in the dining area off the little kitchenette. I usually eat on the balcony or at my work table, which sits where a normal person would have a couch.

The place screams bachelor—working bachelor—but it gets the job done. I did spring for a big comfy mattress, the only furniture in the apartment's one bedroom.

Inside the box of old drawings, I find some comic book-inspired work from middle school, a couple still lifes from high school, and my target: one of my small drawing pads from my freshman year of college.

The memories rush back in: The play of light on the grass I favored. The laughter and the sounds of bikes rushing by. The smell of coffee and fast food.

Some of the pages are smudged. Some not. I flip through the book, searching.

And there she is, walking by, her lush hair in a ponytail and her backpack riding high on her back. She'd glanced over her shoulder, watching me more than where she was walking, and I had to draw her. I had to capture that face.

Sammie, four years ago, just as she was graduating. We'd had a moment. Too brief and never followed up, but it happened. And I had proof.

I stare at the drawing for a long second. I'd used pencil for this one. It had faded some around her shoulders, but her face lifts off of the paper, beautiful and perfect. Somehow, I'd managed to get it right.

I'll give it to her tomorrow. Even if nothing comes of it, she needs to know not all men see her the way her boyfriend does. Some men see what's truly there.

That asshole is going to lose her, if it's the last thing I do.

CHAPTER 6

Samantha

We're outside today, sitting at the picnic table under the sad maple tree in the tiny municipal park next to our building. There's an ugly piece of seventies public art at the intersection of the two sidewalks bisecting the lawn, and the tree shades it as much as the picnic table.

But we take what we can get. This is one of the few open grassy areas in the entire downtown that hasn't been turned into a parking lot and there are always employees out here, taking in a bit of sun.

Tom is telling me about his family and I'm chewing my sandwich. We're eating the same thing for lunch again today, but I'm pretty sure he chose the same I did on purpose this time because he keeps making a face when he bites into his Reuben. I didn't think anything could make him more handsome, but the frowny-face does.

His eyes light up when he talks about his nephew and his gestures become more animated when he tells me how Bart likes to draw just like his Uncle Tommy. When he shows me Bart's picture I can't help but smile. I'm watching Tom, listening, thinking he's not only unbelievably hot, but also a good person. And interesting.

"You have two brothers?" Two other Quidell men walk the world, probably both just as flawless as Tom.

He nods. "Dan used to be a firefighter, until his injury. Now he has his own company." A new frown works across his face as he takes a bite of his lunch, chews, and swallows it down. "Rob starts grad school next year. Cultural Anthropology."

Smart, too. But I could have guessed that.

We're quiet for a moment, both finishing our sandwiches. After we'd ordered he'd tucked his hand around my back and ushered me through the crowd using his big shoulders to clear a path.

I don't know why, but it made me feel special.

"Rick's coming home tomorrow night." I blurt it out. I never blurt. I think I need some insight, some support on this, and for some reason, my instincts tell me to talk to Tom about it, and not Andy. Maybe because Andy's always had a crush on Rick.

Tom sits back. He watches me with his intense blue-green eyes, and his jaw hardens. He truly is a big guy; he's wide enough to block all the glare bouncing off the public art behind him.

"What are you going to do?" He wants to cross his arms but he doesn't—I can see his shoulders twitch like he's fighting it.

Move out and spend the rest of my life subduing my sex drive by masturbating to my old fantasy of your former self? I think.

A blush creeps up my neck and I look away. I've been doing pretty well on keeping control of the color creeping up my neck. I don't want to lose a friend because I can't keep my hormones in check. "I'm thinking I should move out." I can't read his response. He's holding his body perfectly still and with the bright light out here it's difficult to read the subtle twitches of his face.

"Do you have a place to stay?" He says it slow and I can tell he's watching me carefully.

"I don't know. I haven't asked anyone." Sitting straight, I look around. I could ask Andy, but I haven't seen him all week. This isn't something to text someone about. "My family is in Grand Forks. Finding a new apartment first would probably be the best idea."

His phone beeps. "Shit. Listen, I have another meeting." Stuffing it back in his pocket, he stands up. "I think I need to work on scheduling, huh?"

He's smiling and I feel better. The wonderful person in front of me is willing to go through the hell of rescheduling meetings in our meeting-heavy workplace just so he can spend longer lunches with me.

I don't think I've ever had lunch with Rick. When he comes downtown, he's always too busy.

"Drinks after work?" Tom touches my elbow but pulls his hand back like he's afraid he did something bad.

I don't think Rick ever touches my arms, either, except to hold me down.

"Okay," I say. Drinks with a friend is, I think, what I need right now.

"We'll get this worked out. You don't have to live somewhere you don't want to." Tom takes both trays and waits as I stand and loop my bag over my arm. The shadow he throws is almost as big as the one cast by the art, and for a second I wonder if I should be intimidated. I'm not. But his presence offers a comfort I'm not used to.

As I stand in this little park surrounded by coworkers chatting on their phones and the constant downtown traffic noise, I wonder why I've been fighting moving out. Because I have.

Why do I keep going back to the loft? For a split second, I wonder if it's as simple—and as pathetic—as not wanting to be alone.

But I don't think so.

I smile. "After work it is. I'll come down and meet you. Okay?"

Tom smiles too, a big grin like I'd expect to see on this little nephew's face when the kid wants to share a secret but can't because he *promised*.

"Okay, what's up?" I throw him an exaggerated look of suspicion just to see what he'll do. He doesn't disappoint.

The grin turns into a big, full-body wiggle of happiness. When a man does the quick body dance of excitement—not a kid, but a gorgeous guy—it's like every glacier on the planet has melted and everything's blooming. He's not just a big dude capable of scary things, but a full person with joy in his heart.

"I have something for you." He's still grinning, and still just as gorgeous.

"Oh my God you didn't buy me a car, did you?" I'm sure I'm smiling just as much because there's no way I couldn't be, even though I'm joking.

A wonderful, hearty laugh rolls out of Tom. "Been on the job three weeks, my lovely, beautiful Sammie. A new car won't be coming for at least six months." Tom ushers me back toward the door, winking.

He said *lovely, beautiful Sammie.* He stacks the trays and lays his hand on my back, at waist level the same way he did when we came outside.

But this time I feel the strength of his fingers. This time, I want more than just his forearm rubbing my skin through my blouse. I want to be against his side, feeling those arms wrap around all of me. I want to be close enough to smell his subtle-but-rich scent. To breathe in masculinity and consideration and art.

He's juggling the trays and lifts his hand off my back, his attention completely on the tip weight of what he's holding and not at all on what's playing over my face. And I'm glad, because if he did see, I'd be embarrassed beyond anything I felt when I realized *he* was my fantasy freshman.

Much more embarrassed.

Which I shouldn't be. Or maybe I should. I walk alongside Mr. Tom Quidell, chatting small talk. He won't tell me what he has for me. And I don't say anything about wanting right now, more than anything else in the world, to kiss him.

And the embarrassment just grows.

When we walk the stairs to our floors, he smiles again and watches my face like he can't quite figure out what he's seeing. "Drinks in four hours. No backing out." He gives me a mock stern look.

I must be hiding my embarrassment well, so I grin and wag my finger at him. "You said you have something for me. I want it."

Tom laughs as he opens the graffiti door. "Off to your dungeon my queen, before the knaves find us missing from our tortures." He bows and vanishes from the stairwell, hurrying off to his meeting.

Ahead, I have four hours of stewing in the emotions rolling around inside my body. Four hours of a clenched gut that can't decide if it wants to force me to run and hide or jump for joy.

I stare at the door thinking, once again, the one thought that's been blinking in my mind for the past few days like a giant neon light: I'm so fucked up.

But this time it's dancing with another thought: I know how much Rick likes the "fucked up" me. I think, for him, it's useful. It's that bit of distance that allows him to do whatever the hell he wants.

I never hid it from Rick. We never talked about it, either. I suppose it's not fair to hide it from Tom. So the question is, how much "fucked up" will Tom tolerate?

CHAPTER 7

Thomas

The bar across the street from our building serves a good selection of beers, but Sammie sits across from me in the dim booth with a glass of malbec in front of her. She leans forward, playing with her napkin, and for a second I get a good look at her cleavage.

I want to crawl over the dark table top to the deep red leather of her side of the booth and pull her into the corner. I want to kiss that frown right off her face while I rub my palm across her exceptional breasts.

And maybe get her to look at me.

She's been avoiding eye contact since we came in. We chatted about work and weekend plans, because it's Friday. All it did was remind her that her asshole boyfriend would be home tomorrow evening.

Now she's on her second glass of wine. She hasn't eaten anything, either. So I'm wondering. "You going to be okay on your bus trip home?" She's not that big, though she is taller than most women. To me, she's the perfect size.

She looks up this time, meeting my gaze, and sighs. "What do you have for me?"

I shake my head. "It's in my truck. And don't change the subject."

She sits up. "In your truck, huh?"

I can't tell what she's thinking but her body looks tentative. "When we leave, I'll get it."

Quiet, she watches me. After another sip, she sits back. "You're too perfect, do you know that?"

I almost spit my beer across the table. It's not that good anyway—it's bitter—and I set it down instead. "I'm too perfect?" *God damn*, I think. Is she flirting with me? It's dark in here and a shadow fell across her face when she sat back. Could I be lucky enough to have her *flirt* with me?

"You're right. I don't need to live someplace I don't want to." Her delicate hand lifts her glass off the table and it disappears into the shadow as she sips. "I think I should have had something to eat."

"We can get something. Or go down the street to the new Thai place." *Or I can drive you home*, I think. Drive her to her door, go in with her, and pack up all her possessions and take her back to my place.

"At least I have my work shit together." She shrugs and sips again. "And you, to make sure I'm not a hazard to my fellow bus passengers."

Her gaze flits to my face as if she's waiting for me to run away. But I know what she's doing. She's laying out her insecurities because every woman knows nothing chases off a man faster than showing "senseless vulnerability." Or at least that's what Dan says.

I'd rather see her demons now, though, and not three years into a marriage, thank you very much.

I blink, watching her, and my chest tightens. Thinking about Sammie and *three years into a marriage* at the same time is, in all honesty, much scarier than any of her self-doubts.

"You know why Rick likes me?" She sniffs and swirls what's left of her wine. Then she thrusts out her breasts.

I almost spit out my beer again. "That can't be the *only* reason."

She opens her mouth like she's about to spill every detail of their sex life but snaps it shut. Her jaw clenches.

It *is* the only reason he likes her. What kind of asshole is this guy?

She waves her hand in the air. "It's my fault. It's the only reason I like him."

I don't know what to say. Living with someone just for the sex would be fun, I suppose. For a while.

"Why do you do that to yourself?" It's the only question my brain musters.

Across from me, Sammie steels herself. She's going to give me an honest answer and I know from the way she's looking at me that this is a test. I know it the way I know she's unbelievably beautiful. I may not be able to read women's faces, but this body language screams louder than Bart when he wants a new video game.

"I like sex," she says. She's owning it, not flinching or backing down and goddamn, it makes her hotter. I want to rub my face between her breasts. And my cock.

"That doesn't explain why you're living with him." I own it too—if she's testing me by showing what she considers her warts, then I'll give her honest answers. I won't be chased off by my own discomfort.

"No, it doesn't." She takes another sip.

My napkin bunches up under my fingers. "It seems like you're ashamed."

She doesn't look at me. "Why would I be ashamed?"

That's just it. I don't know why she would be ashamed. She's lovely and fun and if she needs to own anything in her life, it's that. "You can like sex. You don't need to separate it from the rest of your life. Well, maybe work." I grin, trying to ease some of her tension. Though backing her against the wall under the stairs would be a nice distraction between meetings.

Sammie grins back at me and taps her temple. "I grew up in the suburbs of a small city. Maybe I have stuff in my head I don't know about."

"Don't we all?" Blaming her ghosts wouldn't change anything, though.

"I'm frustrated when I can't have the sex I want." She takes another sip. "Rick's been tired lately. Says he's been training too hard and he'd rather sleep."

Whoa, I think. I suspect my eyes got big. "No *fucking* way." He's denying Sammie? Who the hell would deny Sammie? My hand slaps the table top. "I'd rather be close to my woman than train, or play video games, or drink, or anything else. A weight bench is no one's muse."

Her face changes. Her cheeks soften and her eyes grow big. Just for a second.

I wonder if I just passed the test.

"You have a much healthier view of sex than I do."

I laugh. "If you think abstinence is healthy." I roll my eyes.

"What?" Now she looks equal parts shocked and confused.

I laugh again. "Been living in my brother's basement, remember? Makes a man bad dating material."

"Oh my God. I can't believe I'm talking to you about this. You must think I'm a crazy person." She downs her wine, a new embarrassment creeping up her neck, and glances at her watch. "Who is about to miss her bus."

My hand wraps around her wrist before she can stand up. "I'll drive you home. Besides, I have something for you, remember?"

"Oh..." She's staring at me and her eyes are huge. Really huge.

"Sammie, you're not crazy."

"But I am fucked up," she whispers.

Ah, the ever-present ghost haunting a lot of women. I wrap my fingers around her hand, holding gently. She looks down at our clasped fingers, our touching palms, and sighs again.

"My brother's ex was fucked up. You are not fucked up. You just need to figure out a few things."

She nods, still looking at our hands. "Will you drive me home?"

"Of course." I'll do more than drive her home. I'll do everything I can for her.

CHAPTER 8

Samantha

Tom digs around behind the seat of his clean-but-older truck. It's flame red and looks like it's had work done to it and I wonder if it's an old firefighter's vehicle.

I stare at his ass. It's magnificently framed by his black slacks and I can't help myself. I'd be staring at it even if I hadn't drunk two glasses of wine on an empty stomach and had a frank talk with him about sex.

Sometimes my mouth just blabs.

"Ah!" Tom pulls his head out and stands up tall, a cardboard tube in his hand. "Here it is." He hands me the tube.

It looks just like the one he handed me at the beginning of the week, when we first met, and for a second I wonder if it's more mock-ups.

He must have read my mind because he chuckles. "No logos. I promise."

I pop off the top. Inside, there's a single rolled up sheet of paper and I finger it carefully, making sure I don't damage it.

It unrolls as I pull it out.

I'm looking at myself. Me, with a backpack over my shoulders and my hair longer, and in a ponytail. Like I used to wear it, when I was still at the University.

That day, the day of my fantasy, when I was looking at him, he was looking at me. And he drew a picture. Of me.

"I found it last night." He's grinning like a kid again, and his happiness reasserts itself when he points at the drawing. "I did this my first semester. It's you. I'm positive."

It's stunning. The emotions he captured sing off the paper: I'm tentative and unsure. There's desire in my eyes, but it's not to be. And there's a sadness to the lines, as if he, too, wanted a connection, but also decided it wasn't to be.

"I don't know what to say." In my hands right now is a real, physical manifestation of what, for me all these past four years, had been nothing but a dream. A desire I could never make real. "This is beyond beautiful."

For a moment, long ago, I had been Tom's muse.

"I'd like to draw a new one."

I look up at his handsome face and his tousled hair. He still wants me to be his muse? Even after I did my damnedest to scare him off?

My answer popped out of my mouth before all the embarrassment —all the fucked-up-edness—can cut it off. "When?" Not *Why?* or *Really?* I ask *when*.

Somewhere in my brain, I understand what I want. Damn it, I need to own it.

Something about his stance changes. He feels closer all of a sudden, as if we're touching. Like I just passed a test for him.

Because I want this. I want to be his muse. I want to give to him across all his senses.

Hunger overtakes his face and his eyes darken for a moment. When he speaks, his voice is low and deep. "Now."

"Now?"

Tom nods. He's got a look of determination about him and I realize this is as much about him not letting me run off to my loft-cave as it is about wanting to draw my picture.

Maybe more.

"But it's night."

"Candles, then."

"Right now?" Why am I waffling? I want this. But maybe I don't deserve it.

Tom takes my hand, his grip firm but polite, and my body responds before I can think. Again. I'm tingling. Up my arm from where he holds my fingers. Down my belly to between my legs. Into my neck and up across the back of my mouth.

I suck in my breath and my breasts thrust out. My lip curls in and I bite down.

He pulls me around his truck and opens the passenger side. "Up you go. We'll get take-out and you will eat low mein out of a box while you sit for me in the candlelight."

My heel slips on the running board but Tom has me. He keeps me from falling, his hand on my ass.

He's cupping my backside, his fingers splayed, like he knows how to give me the right kind of spanking. I must have shivered because he let go.

"Buckle in, my lovely Sammie," he purrs, the wonder of his baritone flowing over me. When I settle in, he's walking around the front of the truck, but his eyes are on me.

I feel like I'm on that desk in the library, the one in my fantasy. But this time, it's twenty-three-year-old Tom bending over me with his breath tickling my nipples and his palm rubbing me just so.

When he gets into the truck, he slams the door and I jolt back into the here and now. *Shit*, I think. *I'm going to fuck him tonight.* It's going to happen.

I want to crawl onto his lap as much as I want to run away.

"You will be my first guest." He starts the truck but he's looking at me with his gorgeous eyes and I can't read his face.

How is this going to help me feel less fucked up? A sane woman would say next weekend, let me move out first.

But I'd waffle about that, too. Why, I don't know. It's not Rick I want anymore.

CHAPTER 9

Thomas

Sammie stands in the center of my living room, her back to me and her smooth little ass tight and her heels together like she's trying to keep her pussy clenched. Fucking her right now, on the floor between my easel and balcony door, would be as easy as taking those five strides across the room. But I walk into the kitchen instead, though the walking is uncomfortable, and drop dinner on the counter.

I can wait. I *will* wait. She's not going to leave here thinking I'm no different from her dumbass soon-to-be ex-boyfriend.

"Your curtains are open." She says it in a dreamy voice, as if seeing the outside world makes her happy.

I dig around for forks. I have to do something to distract myself. Damn, she's beautiful. "I like the sun." Glancing over, I see the last of the sunset play along the lines of her body. She's silhouetted in golds and reds, her black and gray patterned skirt curving around her hips and her hand, holding a bottle of water, at her side.

Her lovely hair is up in a loose ponytail. Little wisps frame the line of her perfect jaw when she looks over her shoulder. "I like it, too."

No more of that boyfriend. She makes a decision tonight. Then I clean out her stuff from that apartment. If I need to take her to her friend Andy's, so be it. But she deserves better than what she's letting herself have.

"Is the floor okay?" I point at my work table and shrug. Six or seven drawings lay scattered over the top and I don't want to move them. "I have a system."

Sammie laughs, pulled, it seems, from her dreaminess. "Men with systems are always better."

I didn't think I'd want her to stay more than I do right now, but I can't let her go. Not without a good reason. I hand her a box of takeout.

She stares at it for a second. Winking, she pulls off her heels and drops to the floor, both her legs off to one side so she can sit like a lady. Patting the floor, she reaches for me.

Me. Not the food. My hand.

I almost drop the food and roll on top of her. Almost rip open her blouse and lay kisses over her chest while growling some vague words declaring my possession. Because for a flittering moment, those primal needs surface above my civilized caution and the lower parts of my brain—and the lower part of my body—all scream *my woman*.

Jealousy flicks into my vision and for a split second I see some manscaped douchebag model-boy pawing at her chest and forcing her down on him.

I blink. I'm still standing, still holding the low mein. She's looking me up and down—at my face and my chest and my crotch. My boxer-briefs can only keep my cock under so much control.

I grin sheepishly and drop down next to her, handing over her meal. She takes it, looking away again, over her shoulder and out the window. "You don't seem like a candles kind of guy."

Her skirt hikes an inch or two up her legs when she sets down her food. The top of one thigh-high stocking peeks out.

She says something. "What?" I ask.

Her gaze moves from the moon to the easel. "You said candlelight. Will you be able to see well enough to draw?"

The sun's gone and the full glory of the evening moon scatters across her hand. She dances her fingers across the carpet. Rustling drifts in from outside—the wind has picked up. A cloud rolls through the sky and for a second my living room drops into shadow.

I don't say anything. I stand instead and she watches me as I rise, her lovely face turning up. She looks hungry, but not for the food next to her. She looks like she wants to escape.

I need to capture her state on paper. I need for her to understand that I see it when I look at her, and that I'm here for her. She has a choice.

"Don't move," I say. She blinks, but follows my command, staying perfectly still as I walk to the linen closet in the hallway. Dan sent a box of pillar candles, old ones his ex left. I think he wanted them out of his house.

A couple are sweet smelling. A few, spicy. One smells like vanilla and I pull it out when I set the candles down next to my work table.

Sammie watches me, her hand still splayed in the moonbeam, her face in shadow. Bending down and kissing her would be the easiest thing in the world. Tasting those perfect lips. Flicking my tongue against hers. But I back away toward the kitchen for a lighter and plates for the candles.

The apartment drops into twilight when I turn off the kitchen light. Only the silver glow of the moon frames Sammie where she sits on the floor, her long legs to the side. I set a candle next to the easel. The lighter bursts on, a little sun in our night, and the candle sputters alive. A new glow brightens Sammie from the front, a warm wash of light and vanilla.

"It smells nice." She sits up a little, obviously uncomfortable leaning to the side because of her skirt.

I pull two pillows and a throw off my chair. Leaning toward her, I catch the tiny hint of wine still left on her breath. But mostly I hear the small hitch in her breath and the whiffing of her blouse's fabric against her bra.

The first pillow I tuck under her arm. The second, behind her back. The throw, I bunch up under her hip.

"Thank you," she whispers, and lays down, rolling against the pillow behind her and stretching out along the throw on the floor. Her breasts thrust up. She sighs softly, her eyes closing for a second, then reopening to look up at the moon now dappling her face.

Her fingers wiggle. Her hips sway. And I swear she's having a tiny orgasm right now, right in front of me.

I want to rub against her. I want to pull those legs apart and nip her skin along the top of those stockings. I want to pump into her fast and hard and make her come more times in one night than that dick ex of hers has the entire time they've been together.

But it's not my choice when he becomes her ex. It's hers. And she might tease—consciously or not, I'm not sure—but she's going to say it to me. She's going to tell me explicitly what she wants.

And she's going to want me.

"Take out the ponytail." I'm growling. I swear to God I sound like some animal. When I get between those thighs I will be an animal.

She lifts her head and a small wicked smile curls up her lips, but she doesn't say a word. Her fingers smooth up her side and pull free her hair. It cascades over her shoulders, over the throw, and into the moonbeam. When she lays her head down again, her fingers stay next to her lips.

"You are killing me." It comes out even deeper than before. I can barely talk. But I somehow manage to pull my pad down from the easel and my pastels from my case.

The moon casts silver from behind and the candle golden orange from the front. She's bathed in contradiction and I need to capture it as much as I need to capture her. The candlelight flickers over her skin, over her flimsy blouse, and I see the outline of her bra underneath as it curves around her full breasts. Her nipples must be hard little nubs under it, but I can't see.

If I ran my hand over each breast, first the left, then the right, squeezing, I'd find those rock hard nipples. Flick them each with my tongue. Make her scream my name.

I drop onto the floor and prop the pad against the easel's leg. Sammie watches me, calm and almost dozing. We don't speak.

I draw.

CHAPTER 10

Samantha

Tom settles into brilliant intensity and I'm hypnotized. He sits three feet away behind his paper but I feel his gaze on me, assessing, reading, wanting. He moves his hands to draw an arc and I feel his fingertips on my skin. My need for him lifts away with his artist's touch, but it doesn't leave. It floats above my hip like a ghost waiting to be given permission.

He tilts his head and my frozen soul lifts up as well. I feel the ice that's been locking me into one place hover now just outside my mind. Like it's a separate thing that's been too close for me to see. But Tom draws a line, makes a sweep of color, and pulls it to his paper, giving the phantom a visible shape.

I've been, I think, a mirror to Rick, reflecting back his physical attraction to himself. He banks it, lives it, sells it, but it's flat and thin.

But when Tom watches me, I can tell he sees the dimensions he wants to lay down on his page—and, from the brilliant hard-on outlined in his pants, to touch. He's not flat. Or thin. And I want, more than anything right now, to get rid of my phantoms. To let in this living man.

Slowly, carefully, I unbutton my blouse. If Tom is willing to look beyond my surface to find what's below the mirror, I'll show him. I'll open up.

I hear his pastels scrape across the paper. The candle flickers and the scent of vanilla fills the air, and Tom's gaze wraps his strong will around my body. Tom yanks away the sheen I've been using since college to reflect back to the men I want to bed what they want to see.

Somehow, it became my cover. I could have as much sex as my body wanted but I never showed my partners *me*. Mostly, they didn't want to see me, anyway. They just wanted their cocks sucked.

But Tom wants me. He wants to see. I don't think he wants a relationship with someone who hides from him, and with each fill of gold or blue on his paper he's demanding I tell him the truth.

His hand stops for a moment as he watches me undo my blouse, but he doesn't set down his work.

I know why. He's not seeing me yet. That mirror is still there, and I'm still behind it. I feel it, drifting over my skin. It's cold, frosty. And I need to shed it.

Slowly, I arch my back and slip off the blouse. A groan rolls from his throat, a deeply male vibration. His fingers set down the pastel and without looking at his paper he flips it over to a fresh page.

He's taking in the curve of my back and the line of my legs. His gaze stops at my hip and he tilts his head again, his eyes piercing, but he doesn't ask me to take off my skirt. He only watches.

I unhook the button and undo the zipper, easing the fabric down my legs. It rubs against my stockings, sounding much like his charcoal against the page.

I want him against me. I want to see the hard muscles of his thighs. To feel the v of his abs. I want to know if he keeps his chest smooth or if I'll rub my face against hair. Will he whisper when we make love? Will he make the small sounds that drive me crazy?

He's beautiful, my Tom. He sits, one leg propped up, leaning toward his paper, a charcoal in his hand. A smudge marks his cheek where he rubbed his face. I want to lick it, to feel with my tongue what this wonderful man does with his hands.

I smell the hot scent of the candle and its flickering heat, but it's

Tom's focus that reddens my skin. He holds me without touching even as I release the skirt from around my hips. The tops of my stockings grip my thighs and I'm suddenly very aware of their tight hold.

It should be Tom holding my thighs. Tom widening my legs. Tom staring down with all the intensity I see in his eyes right now.

I could crawl across the floor. Pinch the zipper of his trousers between my thumb and finger and release what's waiting for me. How smooth is he? Is he velvet, like in my fantasy? Is he thick and hard enough to make me scream? Will I swirl my tongue around the head of his cock and hear his groans?

Can I make him crazy enough to thrust into my mouth even though he's a gentleman?

"Sammie."

I blink, pulled from my revelry, and I realize my hand is between my thighs. I'm stroking myself, thinking about the gorgeous man in front of me. About his beautiful eyes and his wonderful hair I want to tangle my fingers into. About his chest and arms, so large they cover me completely. About his dexterous fingers and the joy they promise.

My mind knows what's possible and my fingers are determined to give me a touch, a taste.

"Sammie, look at me."

The candle's light flickers over his arm, his shoulders. His white dress shirt—his work shirt—glows. The leather cord around his neck stands out as a deep line. I want to lick it, to take it away. Nothing should mar this man's skin.

He sets the pad against the easel without turning it. I can't see what he's drawn and I think he wants it that way. For now.

"Talk to me." Tom wipes his smudged fingers on a cloth from the easel.

No words have passed between us for so long I feel mute. The moon's silver slices across my bare shoulder, into the glow of the candle, and I shiver. I'm stuck between two places—between the cold out there and the warm hardness in here.

"Tell me what you're thinking. Please." He's still rock hard. All this time he's been drawing me and I've been stripping for him, he's been straining the seams of his trousers. He hasn't touched. Hasn't slipped his fingers into the cup of my bra and plied my breasts, his hot breath on my neck.

"You haven't touched me." I'm spread before him with only the deep red lace of my bra and panties between me and his strong hands. Between me and his cock.

"You haven't touched *me*, Sammie." He's next to me now, so close I feel the heat rising off his skin, but he keeps his hands away. "God, you are beautiful."

I want to know this man, to be tasted by him, to feel his tongue and his lips against my mouth, my nipples, my clit. The fantasy won't work anymore. I need the real Tom.

I reach to unbutton his shirt but he stops me, his hand wrapping my wrist and holding me firm.

"You have no idea how much I want you." Tom's voice fills the room, a booming, low call that plays up my spine.

His words resonate inside my head and chest, flooding between my legs. He has no idea how much I want *him*. The need flickering in my belly is like an animal. It wants out. It wants Tom *in*, his cock gliding in and out on my slickness.

"Then let me touch," I whisper. "Let me suck you." Let me feel.

His eyes narrow for a split second. He releases my wrist but leans away toward his easel. Chest out, body elongated, for a moment Tom is on his back and the full wonder of the bulge in his pants is plain to see.

I groan, staring, wanting nothing more than to touch. I need to know. My fingers work his belt.

But he sits up again before I undo the clasp. "Wait."

He has the cloth in his hands. The one with the smudges he used to clean his fingers. He folds it over and over until it's a clean, white, long rectangle and all evidence of his work is on the inside.

I watch the cloth. Other men have tried to tie me up. I don't like it. Why, I don't know, but it's not my thing.

His face crunches up in frustration. "I want you to feel the difference between what you had and what you could have now." His hand tightens around the fabric. "I'm not him."

"No, you are not." *You are much, much better*, I think. His art, his work, his soul, his body all curl around me. Tom is focused, but he's not Rick. He's not *flat*.

Maybe I can distract him from his cloth. I fumble with his zipper again but he pulls away my hand.

"Sammie, wait."

"I don't want to wait. I can't wait. Not any—"

His mouth covers mine. I lose all my breath to this man—he draws it out of me as if he's sucking out poison. I'm left a blank slate.

No more words circle in my head. That place I go when I hit the fantasy is here, alive. It's his world, his context. It's this room he's filled to the brim with creation, with paints and charcoal and paper. With his weighty easel and the stacks of canvas against the wall. With the lone candle on the floor and the pool of heat it throws. The room lacks the expected bits of life he's supposed to have. Chairs. A couch. But what Tom has is so much better. So much more alive.

He tastes the same as his scent—male and warm. His lips work hungrily over mine and I respond with a greedy need I didn't know I had. This isn't just about wanting to feel his muscles tighten and flex as he fucks me or about knowing he wants it as much as I do. Nor is it about moving on.

His hand finds my breast and he palms my nipple through the cup of my bra, groaning into my mouth, and my back arches in response. Maybe he whispers my name. Maybe he's like me, unable to talk. We both shudder.

His tongue flits into my mouth and tangles with mine. I lose my remaining breath.

Why is he still dressed? I paw at his shirt, pulling and tugging. I need access to his chest. To his skin. I feel his hard muscles under my palms but I can't see. I need to see.

He wraps the cloth from his easel around my eyes.

I stiffen.

"I want you to feel, Sammie," he rumbles, his lips taking my earlobe much the same way they took my mouth. Nibbles flicked my skin, both cold and hot at the same time. My scalp tingles and I sigh, letting him tie the blindfold. "That's all. Just feel."

The world drops into darkness, but Tom is against me, pressing his still covered erection into my belly, and I somehow know where everything is. The candle's heat gives the room directionality. The pillows and throw feel soft against my bare back, the carpet rough. And Tom's clothes rub against the lace of my panties, demanding entrance.

"Tom..." I whisper. He's on top of me, heavy and strong, and his mouth works along my jaw.

His fingers stroke mine, weave into mine, and he pulls my arms up over my head. "Touch me, Sammie." But he lifts away.

Cold air rushes over my breasts and I gasp, wanting him back. How did I live before, without his body on mine? Why, four years ago, did I pass this up?

I reach for him, my hands grasping, though I can't see. But I know where he is. I know he's kneeling between my legs, my magnificent Tom, waiting.

I won't disappoint him.

CHAPTER 11

Samantha

Sitting up, my fingers find his hips. I glide them along his belt, feeling a hitch with each loop. His zipper feels hot, the metal teeth vicious, and I need to release him from his torture. He's rubbing against my hand like he can't help himself and a rush of power rolls through my body. He blindfolded me, but not to dominate, and I understand what he meant by *I want you to feel.*

First, my hands pull his shirt out of his waistband. The fabric crinkles in my grip, crisp as a white dress shirt should be. I find the bottom button and carefully, slowly, undo it.

A low groan rolls from Tom. I imagine him looking down, his face intense. His eyes are full of carnal joy because he's watching me— blindfolded me in only my bra and panties—and I trace my fingers over his abdomen as I undo the next button.

But I don't *know* what he's experiencing. "What do you see right now?" I have to know. I undo another button.

The shirt twists and his hand touches my shoulder, my cheek. "What I want."

I'd been a mirror, I think, to protect myself. Maybe also to hide.

But I can't now. Touching forces me out from behind my glass wall and I whisper his name. "Tom."

"Sammie." His hand curls into my hair and his stomach suddenly pulls away from me. A kiss takes my mouth, hot and intense. Once again, he pulls the poison from my body.

I pull away and he groans, his hands finding my breasts. He's pinching, rubbing and the fabric constrains. I wiggle, reaching for the hooks, but his fingers find them first. My bra lets go.

A vibration moves through his torso as if he's let out a subsonic growl, and his mouth descends to my chest. No man has responded to seeing and sucking at my breasts with so much masculine joy. I almost burst apart, broken into little bits of sensation caused by Tom's roving mouth and possessive hands.

I force his shirt down his arms and he lifts off me. Cold rushes between us and for a split second I don't know where he is, but fabric crinkles—I hear him pull it off—and I orient again. My body knows where Tom is. As does my focus.

Undoing a belt while blindfolded is more difficult than I expected. A giggle pops out and Tom laughs too, until he cups my breasts.

"I want to rub my cock right here." His palm slides between them, over my heart. "I want you to feel it everywhere."

Oh, God, I think. I'm through his belt, through the zipper, to the cotton weave of his boxer-briefs. I have no idea what color they are, but my mind screams *black*. His briefs lie flat over the hard muscles of his hips and I run my hands between his trousers and fabric, feeling the square perfection of his ass. I don't touch his cock. Not yet.

When I pull his hips toward me, I get the full wonder of his hardness against my face. A breathy moan pushes between my lips. My mouth waters—I want to taste him. I *have* to taste him. He releases himself from the boxer-briefs and his cock springs against my lips.

His shaft feels velvety under my fingers, and rock hard. He's long and thick—perfectly shaped. And all I want is to run my tongue over his sensitive head.

I smooth his pre-cum over my lips, tasting him. He's intense, exotic, and I take him into my mouth, working slowly. He wants me to feel, and I want it too. I want this with him, to be aware of his entire body's responses, and not just the force of his cock as it hits the back of my throat.

"Jesus, Sammie." His hips tense under my hands.

I'm taking him deep, swirling my tongue and sucking so hard my cheeks pull in. One hand helping my mouth while the other brushes through his trimmed pubic hair.

I want to see. I feel the v of his hips and the ripple of his abs, and I want to *see*. I lift away my hand to fiddle with the cloth over my eyes.

"Leave it on," he croaks out as he stops my fingers from lifting away the blindfold.

I stop vacuuming his cock, but I keep its perfect head in my mouth, waiting. What else is he going to do? My body screams—I can't take much more. Every inch of my skin ripples as if my nerves are jumping up and down like screaming fanatics. Tom makes every single one of my cells swoon.

His hands grip my breasts again and he pulls them up, making me arch my back. My head falls back and I exhale hard. My entire body moves and the next thing I feel—the next thing I know—is his cock rubbing against first my left nipple, then my right. I want to scream. It feels *good*. So, so good. How can this be? I have to have him in my mouth again.

But he's between my breasts, pumping hard. My saliva on his cock offers some lubrication but it dries fast and only his hot skin rubs against my breastbone. But before it starts to hurt, he groans and pulls away, vanishing from my perception. For a second, I'm disoriented again, lost without his body to give me direction.

Then his hand pushes me back onto the pillows and I flop, bouncing off the softness. He grips my hips; my panties vanish down my legs, pulled off faster than I could do it alone. And he's spreading my legs.

Is he going to fuck me? Will he pump into me the way he pumped between my breasts. "Please," I whimper. "Now. Please."

Fingers rub along the top of my stockings. A palm descends to my mound, grinding into my pussy. I whimper again, my back arching.

He's on top of me, covering me completely. His cock burns against my lower belly and I whimper, but his mouth covers mine. This kiss is deep, lingering, hungry. It rolls through my entire body, a wave of brilliance I've never experienced before. It's Tom. Only *Tom*.

Each of his touches is more possessive than the ones before. More demanding, as if he's losing patience. As if he truly, honestly wants me.

It makes me hotter.

"Fuck me, please. Tom! Now. I'm on the pill. Come in me. Please. I want you to come in me." I wrap my legs around him and push my feet into his hamstrings, making his hips grind against mine. I want him inside. I *need* him inside.

The noises he makes lack words but carry meaning: *Quiet*. The muscles of his shoulders tense under my hands. Tom breaks the force of my hold and his body pulls off mine.

"Tom!" Why is he doing this? "What's—"

His mouth descends onto my pussy and his tongue immediately finds my clit. I buck against him, my entire body suddenly, completely electric. I know he wants me to come. Now. Right now, as his fingers probe and his tongue dances. Before he's inside me.

The orgasm quakes me down to my bones. My throat constricts. My hands jitter. And Tom doesn't stop.

He licks and finger-fucks me, drawing my orgasm out into one shudder after another. How long it lasts, I don't know. I'm lost.

Until he takes a hold of a handful of breast again.

His cock is against my belly. He's flicking my nipple, and his mouth is working along my jaw, toward my earlobe. "You are beautiful. How can you be so beautiful?"

His words filter through me, washing over me like rain water. He's the beautiful one, my hard Tom. He dominates this moment. He dominates my world.

He's curled against me, rubbing, his muscles so tense I almost hear them hum.

I squirm, trying to move so when he pumps, he's pumping into me and not against my bellybutton. But he's holding me tight, his grip on my arms intense. He's not letting me move. And his thrusts become stronger, more powerful.

"Tom, in me. Please. Fuck me."

"*Ah!*" His head lifts away from my neck as his orgasm spurts onto my belly.

What just happened? Why didn't he come inside me? Confusion strangles my thoughts and I can't think. What did I do?

"Sammie," he whispers. He's still with me, holding on. His arms tighten.

I touch his head, feeling his soft hair. He's fiddling with the blindfold, untying it. When I see again, he's using the cloth to wipe his cum off my belly.

"Why?" I should be angry, but only confusion fills my head. He felt so good. Extraordinary. But I feel like something's missing, and it's not just him pumping into me.

I don't know what to say. I just don't want him to let go.

He makes a face like he doesn't want to talk.

This is complicated, I think. I've never dealt with complicated before. It's always been clear-cut fuck-and-go. Or fuck-and-sleep, like with Rick. But with Tom, it's more. He's kissing my forehead, his arms tight around my body.

I could run away. Go back to the loft. But Tom pulls me into his arms, even if he doesn't want to talk, and I don't want to be anywhere else.

I need to admit it. To myself. To him.

I curl around him. He feels warm, strong. Perfect. His skin, his body, his muscles, all fill my perception, my world, even without the blindfold.

I see, finally.

And I see Tom.

CHAPTER 12

Samantha

Full and glorious sun streams into the bedroom through the wide open curtains. I lay on his bed, naked, next to the beautiful and still sleeping Mr. Thomas Quidell. The bright morning dances over the strong, sculpted muscles of his back.

In the sunlight, I see what I couldn't last night. The sheet rides low on his hips, revealing a toned and perfect body. He's no longer the kid I fantasize about; he's someone I know in detail. But not full detail, the way I want it.

All I want to do is start in the center of his wonderful lower back, laying a kiss on his skin one inch at a time, up between his broad shoulders to the nape of his neck.

But I don't. He's snoring softly in that steady male way guys do when they lie on their stomachs. I should let him rest.

Carefully, I swing my feet over the side of the bed. A pile of clean and folded clothes sits on the top of his hand-me-down dresser, and I root through it, looking for a t-shirt. I don't want to put on my work clothes. It's Saturday morning and...

I look back at the bed. We didn't talk last night. We had sex—not penetration sex, but sex—and we didn't talk about it. He carried me into the bedroom instead, pulling me tight to him and kissing my forehead until we both fell asleep.

I didn't speak, either. We were together, in his bed, and for once I felt calm and safe. And I knew I could let my subconscious figure it all out.

I pull a t-shirt over my head. It's worn, old, with a fading logo of a nineties band on the front. It drops over my ass but I should find my panties. When he wakes up I'll ask to borrow some sweats.

He shifts a little and the bed groans. It's a comfortable mattress. I grin to myself, remembering those days right out of college when I, too, had no furniture.

I still don't. Everything in the loft belongs to Rick.

Frowning, I look down at my hands as my gut suddenly clenches up. I didn't end it with Rick before I left the bar with Tom. I didn't call. Hell, I didn't even send a text.

But I know why: revenge. And now I wonder if I'm just as shallow and flat as the man I'm about to leave behind.

Tom mumbles something, his deep baritone washing through the room as if carried on the sunlight, and I wonder how such a wonderful man—such a good person—could ever want to be with me.

Softly, I tiptoe out of the room. Sun streams into the living room as well, and his entire apartment is bright and shadow-free. It's cleaner than many bachelor's apartments, but that could be because he hasn't lived here long enough for the place to turn into a man cave.

But I don't see that happening. Tom is sensitive to his environment, and to what his environment brings to him.

Yet he still brought me home last night. Samantha Singleton, the fucked-up work fuck-buddy.

His sketchbook leans against the easel leg still. I pad over, the soles of my feet rubbing on the apartment's carpet, and pick it up.

There I am, half naked and stretched out on the pillows—and I'm beautiful. He's drawn me, arms out to him, my face full of contradictions. There's unvarnished, intense desire in my eyes. The tip of my head suggests uncertainty, but it's not in my body. He's what I need.

But he's hazed it, too, as if he can't quite see me. Like I'm hiding something from him.

I grip the sketchbook. He wouldn't have kept me in his bed all night if I was just some fuck buddy. And it's not what I want. I see it in this mirror he's made for me and I feel it all the way to my bones.

Standing here in the full glory of the light he throws on his life, I realize I need the light thrown on me, too. Because before, I couldn't see what I'd been groping for.

But will he tolerate me while I figure things out? I know, deep inside, hell, from *outside* too—from my skin and my elbows and my earlobes where he nibbled last night—I want him to. Sharing with him, being open no matter how scary it is, will be worth the pain.

The sounds of shuffling turn me around. Tom stands in the hallway, a pair of plaid sleep pants low on his gorgeous hips, and his hand rubbing across the top of his head. "Do you like it?" He points at the sketch.

I'd half expected him to ask why I'm still here, but I know that's not him. That's my own fears talking.

"Have you done gallery shows?" I hold out the book and the wondrous drawing. "You need to do gallery shows. This is beautiful. I've never seen anything like it."

He blinks, but a small grin works across his lips. "Do you want breakfast? I could make us eggs."

"I..." It's time to be open and honest, not just with him, but with everyone. And with myself. I look around for my phone. "I need to text Rick." It's not the most wholesome way to break—

Tom's face changes. Sadness rolls off his entire body. Anger creeps in, and his nostrils flare. He whispers, "*He* doesn't love you, Sammie."

I stop, frozen. Tom turns his back to me and takes a deep breath. Then he's gone, vanishing around the corner into the kitchen.

Did he...? I can't finish my own thought. I follow him into the kitchen.

He slaps a spatula onto the counter when I round the corner. "I didn't *fuck* you last night because I don't want it to be *fucking*. That's what it will be if you go back to him. Straight-up side-action fucking." He steps away from the counter, then back again. "Damn it, that's what it was, wasn't it? I wanted to be with you so badly I let last night happen even though I know you haven't made up your mind. I wanted to wake up next to you."

My mouth opens and closes. "You wanted to wake up next to me?"

He's watching me from his spot next to the counter, his jaw tight and his hand clenching the spatula. "Yes."

I realize this moment isn't just a test, it's *the* test. Am I going to be that woman he's afraid I am? The one who does side-action fucking? The one who lives with a guy because I like the sex and won't move out because...

And it's there, finally, in the front on my mind, a label on my little issues: because I think my main worth is the fucking.

I gasp, holding in a sob. Oh my God, how can that be? I'm doing well in my career. I'm happy with my friends and my life except when I'm not.

But I'm lonely. And I finally understand why.

"Sammie." Tom drops the spatula onto the counter and scoops me up into his big arms before I take another breath.

I can barely speak. How can I think such things? It's stupid. Tom doesn't see me that way. Though I am pretty sure Rick does.

And there's my answer to what's been feeding that stupid little thought.

"You're..." I curl against Tom's chest, my cheek pressed against his breastbone, over his heart. It beats strong and steady, like him. Strong, steady, and...

And accepting.

"What, Sammie?" His arms tighten around my waist, drawing me closer.

I don't finish my thought. I can't. I know what I'd say: *You're perfect. You're wonderful. You're better than I deserve.*

And *I think I'm falling in love with you.*

I'm terrified by this new thought. Will I ever deserve this man?

"I know what you're thinking." He speaks softly, into my hair. "You're thinking that you're fucked up again, aren't you?"

I nod against his chest, sniffling. My tears streak his skin but I don't want to let go. I don't want to move out of his embrace ever again.

"Then we take this one step at a time, okay?"

I nod again.

But I feel a small quake move through his body and his jaw tenses against my forehead. "What were you going to text to Rick?"

That I never want to see him again, I think. I so very much want to leave him—and the part of my life he represents—behind. "That I'm moving out. That I won't be there when he gets home tonight."

A quick, controlled sigh brushes against my hair. Tom's arms tighten again and for a moment, it's hard to breathe.

He's not letting me go. Even with all my fucked-upped-ness, he's holding on.

I kiss his jaw, holding on for dear life. He threw me a life preserver and I'm not going to lose it. I'm not going to ruin this. "Can I store my stuff here until I find a place to live? I don't have a lot."

A snort pops against the skin over my ear. "You can stay here as long as you want. Not just your stuff. You." He backs away enough to look me in the eye. "If you need space, I'll sleep on the couch."

I giggle as much from the release of tension as from his chivalrousness. "You don't have a couch."

"Then I will blow up the air mattress and sleep on the floor. I'm not letting you go. And I'm not letting you run away, either. I'm a Quidell. We fight for what we want." He pulls me back into his arms.

I bury my face in his chest, even though my head's spinning.

"Sammie." A gentle kiss touches my temple. Another falls on my cheek. When I lift my chin, yet another brushes my lips. "We'll take this slow, okay? So we're both sure."

I nod, not speaking. He's right. Figuring this out will take some time.

Another warm, sweet kiss finds my mouth. "Let's get your things."

Tom takes my hand to help me into my future.

CHAPTER 13

Thomas

"How did you live in this dungeon?" I ask Sammie. How someplace as architecturally interesting as her building could be rendered so deeply dark and soulless, I do not understand. Yet here I stand in the huge, open center space wondering if I'm about to hear bats flitting around the ceiling.

Sammie kisses my cheek as she sets another box next to the door. She's filled storage containers, laundry baskets, even plastic grocery bags and I've been hauling them down to the truck. All that's left is an antique table lamp from her grandmother and a wide assortment of frozen dinners.

"No you don't." I scowl at the bag holding the contents of the freezer. "You don't need this crap. I'm going to feed you well." Looking her up and down, I give her my best charming grin. "How can you be so blazing hot when you eat this stuff?"

She laughs, grinning back at me. "And how am I supposed to 'take it slow' when you're always flirting with me?"

How am I supposed to *not* flirt with her? Running up and down in the elevator has kept my mind occupied, but my balls ache. The "taking it slow" is excruciating.

She laughs again when I don't answer. My face must have given me away. But a hint of nervousness filters through with her chuckle. She must still feel uneasy about all this.

I jam my hands into my pockets. "I'm sorry. I don't mean to—"

A kiss silences my apology. It's quick—she's out of reach before I can wrap my arms around her—but it's still a kiss. I grin again, watching her put the frozen dinners back in the freezer.

"I'll leave the bad food, how's that sound?" She slams the door and looks around the kitchen one last time.

Leave the bad food here. And all the bad memories, I think. She needs to leave it all behind, especially Rick the dick.

The cat—Mickles, she calls him—rubs against my shin. He's a sweet fluffy animal and every time I come in, he meows a greeting.

"Is Mr. Pickles coming too?" I pick him up, stroking his back. "He likes me. See?" The cat headbutts my chin and I scratch his ears, doing my best to make her some new, good memories.

Sammie watches for a long second. Her face softens and she smiles a sweet, wonderful smile. "He was wandering outside shortly after I moved in. Rick brought him in, so I've always thought of him as Rick's cat. But I'm the one who takes care of him."

"She calls you Mickles, did you know that?" I rub under the kitty's chin. "You let her get away with that? Have you no dignity, man?"

Mickles meows his answer and headbutts me again.

Sammie laughs. "And here I thought he was aloof and standoffish. He's never like that with Rick."

"Well then, I shall liberate the woman *and* the cat." Bowing, I look around. "Got a carrier for him?"

I get a thrill from stealing the douchebag's cat. Juvenile, I know. But I'm not leaving the kitty here to have him end up on the street again.

"It's in the hall closet." She points down the dark corridor.

This place really is a cave.

Sammie opens the cabinet door next to her head. "I'll get his food and dishes. There's a bag of litter in the closet. Grab it too, please."

Nodding, I set down Mickles and walk away, toward the kitty's carrier. We'll be out of here in a minute or so, and then she's mine. She can take as long as she wants to ease into it, but it's going to happen. Her key to this place and a note are already on the kitchen table.

I have a couple of sleepless nights ahead of me, knowing she's nearly naked in my bed, by herself. Maybe touching herself as she thinks about me. God knows I'm going to be touching myself. I shift as I walk, hoping she doesn't take *too* long.

I hear the front door open. Sammie must be taking another load down to the—

"Rick!"

I stop, my hand inches from the closet doorknob. The son of a bitch is back. Early.

Every inch of my body screams to march in there right now and punch the douchebag. But acting like some uncivilized freak will just chase Sammie away. So I don't. My arm tightens, wanting that punch, but I won't.

"What are you doing?" I hear a male voice. He sounds more annoyed than angry.

"You texted me, not your booty call last week, Rick." Sammie sounds strong, not frightened.

"So?"

I turn around. I can't be in the hallway, with her alone with him.

"What did you think I was going to do?" But her voice is strong and she's holding it together. I feel a rush of pride, though I know I don't have a right to.

Rick drops something onto the floor and a boom reverberates through the loft. "I don't know. Ask to join us?"

I stomp down the hall. Even if I don't punch him, he needs to know I'm here.

"Who'd you bring in here?"

"None of your business, Rick." Fear is creeping into her voice.

"It's my business who you bring into *my* place, you little bitch."

"Little bitch?" Sammie sounds shocked. "Have I always been a *little bitch* to you?"

"You're surprised? And here I thought you liked it."

When I round the corner, he's standing over her, his posture dominant and threatening. He's muscular like an athlete, but I'm bigger.

"Leave her alone," I growl.

Rick looks up, his eyes narrow. "I'm not the only one with some side action, huh?" He steps away from Sammie.

She's shaking. I walk to her, my gaze not leaving Rick, and pull her against my side.

The need to punch him—punch *anything*—makes my shoulders tense.

Sammie steps in front of me, her back against my chest, like she's protecting *me*.

When she speaks, her voice is low. "He's a million times a better man than you, Rick."

She's against me and I feel her shaking grow. She can't be here anymore. I curl my arms around her waist. She doesn't need him cutting her down.

"Let's go," I whisper.

Her arms fold over mine. "He's a million times a better person than me."

Rick snorts. "*Everyone* is a better person than you, sweetheart."

He's glaring at her, not looking at me, and I think that if she'd come here alone, he would have hit her. Her breath hitches.

"Don't listen to him." I want to tell her the truth—that she has a beautiful heart and wonderful mind and that I'm falling in love with her. That she's worth so much more than how this asshole makes her feel. "You're my muse," I whisper.

Sammie turns in my arms, her eyes huge, but she doesn't speak. A tear appears on her lashes and all I want to do is to kiss it away. All I want right now is to pick her up and take her out of here.

I look over her shoulder, right at the son of a bitch. I'm trying not to yell, but it comes out loud anyway. "You're a fucking idiot."

I pull Sammie closer.

Rick laughs. "Sure thing, bro."

If she hadn't been between us, I would have hit him. But she holds onto me and she's more important. Much more important.

She doesn't turn around. "Do not contact me again, Rick."

He pulls his wallet out of his pocket and tosses it onto the table. "Get out, you little skank. If I find anything of yours left behind, I'm burning it."

He flips us off and walks away, into the living room.

And I all but carry Sammie out of there.

CHAPTER 14

Samantha

Tom slams the back of his truck. On my lap, Mickles circles inside his carrier and lets out a frightened little whimper.

I don't blame the kitty. I want to whimper, too.

Tom's taking me to his place. He refused to let me go back up to the loft after putting Mickles in the carrier. He went in by himself to get my grandmother's lamp. I sat in the truck for an agonizing fifteen minutes, terrified that he and Rick would get into a fight and Tom would end up in jail because of me. But he appeared again, the lamp in one hand and the bag of cat litter in the other, and finished packing the truck.

He opens the driver's side door and stands there, looking at me with more concern on his face than I've ever seen from a boyfriend. "Are you going to be alright?"

My own thought buzzes in my head. *Boyfriend.* I obviously mean more to him than just a fuck buddy. A lot more. A million times more.

"Honey, are you okay?" He crawls in but doesn't start the truck.

I nod *yes*. "Thank you."

Tom leans across the shift and gently kisses my cheek. "You *are* my muse. Please believe that."

My mouth opens and I suck in my breath. What's going to happen when he realizes I'm not as good a person as he is? Will he kick me out, too?

The truck starts and he pulls out onto the street. We head back to his place, silent except for Mickles's meowing.

"Everything he said is bullshit, Sammie." He's watching traffic and not me. "I am not a million times better than you. Him? Fuck, yeah. But you? No." Tom throws me one of his disarming grins.

This handsome man wants me to be his muse. He wants me to live with him and be his friend and his lover. But mostly he wants me to be happy.

My breath hitches but I hold in the tears. I'm a fucking mess.

"Tell you what. I'll stop and we'll get a pint of that extra thick, extra chocolaty ice cream and call it dinner, okay?" Another disarming grin comes my way.

I laugh. I can't help myself. "You said no bad food." He's trying so hard to make everything better. It's working, too.

"Since when is chocolate bad food? It's therapy." He winks. "At least that's what I see all my female relatives say on social media."

I laugh again. How can he make me feel so much better so fast? It's like he's magic.

Which, I'm beginning to suspect, he is. If I found some sort of supernatural being when I first saw him as a freshman. "Did you put a spell on me all those years ago when you drew that first picture?"

Now Tom laughs. "Why yes, m'lady, I did. And the only way to break it is to eat ice cream with me." He glances over again as he pulls into the grocery store parking lot. "You, my beautiful Sammie, are about to be treated to a good meal. One I cook special for you."

"Oh?" He has that happy look to him again, like when he gave me the first drawing. He's put what happened with Rick behind him, even if I haven't yet.

"Your new life awaits and I intend to celebrate." He rolls down the windows. "So that neither you nor Mickles become uncomfortable while I'm inside purchasing secret ingredients for our special meal."

Opening the door, he hops out. "I shall return to you momentarily, my sweet."

As I watch him walk into the store, I breathe deep for the first time since we left the loft, and I realize Tom rescued me. Not during the altercation with Rick—that, he let me handle myself. I needed to handle it myself. I needed to see just how much Rick didn't care.

But Tom does. And just now, here, in his truck, he offered me another a life preserver so I don't drown in the residue of the hell I just left behind. The hell of my own making that I've been wallowing in.

I scratch Mickles's fur through the door of his carrier. "What do you think, my fluffy friend?"

The cat answers with a questioning meow.

"Yeah, I think you're right. I think I better not screw this up." I sit up straight in the seat. I'm leaving the fucked-up me behind, in the loft, with Rick. Tom's right—I need to own not just my libido but all my wants and desires. And right now, I want my lover to also be my friend.

I want intimacy with my sex. I want to wake up with the sun.

I want Tom.

Tom went all out. The whole meal smelled as good as it looked. The steak was the best I've tasted in a long time, as were the potatoes and the salad and the wine. He even managed to coax Mickles out from under the bed for his dinner.

We ate on the floor again, next to his easel, with one of my boxes between us acting as a table.

I sit back, watching him. I feel relaxed, floating in a warm wine buzz. I hold up the tumbler for a bit more. "We need to get you some proper stemware."

"Hmm..." He takes another sip.

I tap the box. "And you need a table."

"Sounds like we need to go shopping." The *we* rolls off his tongue, accented lightly by his baritone, and he smiles.

He's beyond handsome. My body has been responding to his gaze and his touch all evening and it's been driving me insane. Everything tightens. My mouth waters and I feel new moisture between my thighs.

It's different this time. My desire for him feels deeper, as if it's coming from everywhere and not just from my erogenous zones.

But if I'm honest with myself, I'll admit that it *isn't* different. I'm just admitting it for the first time. He's caused this reaction from me since the first moment I met him and up until now, I didn't want to think about it.

Because I didn't think it was real. No man who saw only my tits would laugh and smile with me, or comfort me the way he has, or would have rescued my cat, too. Or want to take me shopping for housewares.

He helped me unpack, made dinner, even served the ice cream first. We talked about work and our favorite movies and how we're going to get him into a gallery.

He'd stood still for a long moment, watching me, the most wonderful grin on his face.

The same way he's looking at me right now.

I'm his muse.

"I'd like to go shopping with you," I whisper.

His smile widens. For the first time, I see what Tom looks like when he's truly happy.

My heart feels as if it's going to burst out of my chest.

"Tomorrow?" He stands and picks up our dirty dishes.

I follow him into the little kitchen, watching his flawlessly proportioned backside. I'd rather spend my Sunday rubbing my hands over his ass again while nibbling on his little line of body hair descending from his navel to his oh-so-perfect cock, but shopping could be fun, too.

We chat about what he needs for his apartment as he washes and I dry the dishes. Twice, he leans over and kisses my cheek. By the time the last dish returns to the cupboard, we have all of Sunday planned.

It feels good. He wants to be with me, not just fuck me, and for once in my life I feel wanted.

He pulls me tight to his chest. "I'm happy you're here, Sammie. I'm happy you decided to stay with me and not with someone else."

Under my hands, his lower back feels strong and powerful. Against my cheek, his heart beats strong and comforting. Stubble rubs against my hair but it's nice. He smells of cooking and washing dishes and the afternoon's work, but it's good. It's life with him.

Once again, I feel luckier than I deserve. I kiss his jaw, hoping he understands how much I want to be with him. All of him is hard against me—his abdomen, his arms, the bulge in his pants. He strokes my back sensuously as he buries his face in my hair.

But he pulls away. "Mickles and I will sleep in the living room tonight." Tom waves his hand before grasping mine. "So you can settle in."

I blink. The hunger in his eyes mirrors the hunger I feel, but he's not taking advantage. He's not pulling me into the bedroom.

And I don't know what to say.

CHAPTER 15

Thomas

Sammie doesn't say much as she unpacks her stuff in the bathroom. I hear clinks and clatters as items fill up the countertop and appear in my shower. Her toothbrush whirs and the water runs before she steps out again, wearing an old pair of sweats and a worn t-shirt.

With her hair down, her face fresh, she's more beautiful than I've ever seen her before. Her skin glows. The t-shirt hugs her breasts and I want to pick her up and back her against the wall. I want to rip off the shirt with my teeth.

But she needs to feel that I want her here for more reasons than the promise of great sex. No matter how I feel, no matter what I say, I know I need to demonstrate my intentions. And I need her to demonstrate hers.

It'll kill me to get into a relationship with her only to find out six months down the road she never really wanted one in the first place. I can't lose my heart. Not like Dan did.

I fluff my pillow and the small and uncomfortable air mattress squeaks. "Good night, Sammie."

She watches me with her big eyes for a long moment, then nods. Before I know it, she's down the hall. The lights go out in the bedroom.

I turn off the lights in the living room. The room is still bright—I haven't closed the curtains. Nor will I. The moon is full tonight and fills the sky with a silver sheen. If I'm to lay here on my brother's squeaky air mattress, at least the heavens can keep me company.

Mickles appears next to my head, purring. I scratch his ears until he seems satisfied and walks away, down the hall. Looks like the kitty sleeps with Sammie, even if I don't.

My mind wanders to memories of her moaning under me, her cheeks and lips flushed, her nipples tight nubs. Damn, she felt exquisite. So soft against my cock.

My hand finds my lengthening shaft. I could go in there. I could go into the bedroom and pull back the blankets. Strip off her sweats right now. Suck her clit into my mouth. Flick it with my tongue. Make her scream my name.

I want *her* rubbing me right now. I want to make her understand how much I want her.

From the other room, I hear the bed groan. My hand freezes.

Mickles meows.

I sit up and pull the blanket over my erection when I hear her walk down the hall. The last thing I want is for her to feel obliged. I know she likes sex—I like sex, especially with her—but it can't be just sex. Not with her.

Sammie stops in a pool of moonlight, shimmering as if she'd descended from heaven. She's more beautiful than any angel with her hair flowing over her shoulders and her skin glowing in the silver light. I blink, staring at her, unable to speak.

"Tom?" She shuffles slightly and I hear her bare feet on the carpet.

She took off the sweats. She's standing in my hallway wearing only the t-shirt and her panties, my muse. My goddess.

I groan. I don't mean to, but it escapes.

Her foot slides over the carpet again. "Thank you for being a gentleman." Her hand grips the corner where the hallway meets the living room wall. "You've given me something no man has ever given me before—I feel valued."

Her hand smooths across her belly and the t-shirt hitches up along her hip. I see her tiny panties and her lovely skin. But mostly I see her body language. I see the trust she's giving me.

"Part of my head is screaming I don't deserve you. But I don't want to fall victim to that any longer. Because that's what's been happening. A part of me used to think Rick was right."

"No, Sammie—"

She holds up her hand, silencing me. "But you're telling me something completely different. It feels good, Tom. It feels healthy and so much better. I feel right with you. Happy. And..." A small sniffle pops between her words. "And I want to see you happy. I *want* to be your muse."

She steps forward and her feet move out of the pool of silver. The light travels up her long legs, over her torso, and across her breasts. And when she stops, I see her face clearly.

She's looking at me with more affection than I've ever seen from a woman. More caring. More desire to make this work than I could ever hope for. And more genuine desire for me.

Her hand extends and she reaches. For me. "Please come to bed."

I'm off the damned air mattress and in her arms before either of us can take a breath. I scoop her up.

"Sammie," I whisper. Her breath tickles my neck as she wraps her legs and arms around me. I grip her backside, holding her up as I back her against the wall.

I kiss her with everything I feel, on her lips, her cheeks, her neck.

She moans, gasping, and pulls me in for a deeper kiss. Our lips dance, our tongues touching, mingling. She tastes of mint and femininity; smells of sweet soap and sex.

My beautiful Sammie tangles her fingers in my hair and I feel the fire of her skin, the hard buttons of her nipples, the heat of her body pressing against my cock.

And I want her so much I grind against her belly as I hold her to the wall. It's too much. I'm going insane.

"Take off the t-shirt." She moans again as she paws at the fabric covering my torso.

I lean back enough for her to pull it up. Wiggling one arm out, I switch the hand gripping her ass and she pulls the shirt over my head and down my shoulder.

A low growl rolls from her throat when she runs her fingers over my biceps. "Damn, you are *gorgeous*."

I chuckle and nip her earlobe. "I'm going to fuck you unconscious."

The low, stuttered breath of a response almost sends me over the edge. Right here, with me holding her on the wall and rubbing against her through my flannel pajamas and her damned panties.

I drop her legs to the floor.

She holds tight to my neck, refusing to let go. "Tom! Now. Please." Her mouth works across my chest and she scrapes her teeth first across one nipple, then the other.

I don't usually like such play but when she does it, it feels like she's setting off a volcano under my skin.

"Damn, woman." I pull her t-shirt over her head, stopping for a moment when the fabric curls around her wrists. Her breasts thrust out at me, wonderfully etched by the moon's shadows, and I drop my mouth to her left nipple.

"Don't stop." She's breathing heavy now, almost panting.

I tongue her nipple, suckling and biting. She shudders under my touch and I barely hold it together. I need to be in her. Now. But first I'm going to prove to her that she made the right choice.

Her t-shirt drops to the floor as I drop to my knees in front of her. I hook the lace of her panties and yank, pulling them down her thighs.

The last time when I went down on her she tasted sweet, and I want more. I grind the heel of my palm into her clit and she moans again. Her fingers tangle deeper into my hair and flex against my scalp.

I lick.

"Oh my God the real you is a thousand times better than any fantasy." Her fingers flex again.

Surprised, I stop tonguing her beautiful, sweet pussy. "What?"

Sammie blinks, her face saying what she doesn't vocalize: *Oh, shit.*

"You fantasize about me?" My inner teenager is dancing around yelling *That's right, baby!* and *Oh hell yeah!* Sammie thinks about me when she gets off. Not that douchebag and not some movie star. *Me.*

"For four years."

I blink up at her, stunned. Four years? That means... "Since you saw me on campus? When I drew the first picture of you?"

She nods.

The stupidest thought possible parades through my head: *I win.* I won before I even met her. I won the lotto four years ago and I'm just now finding out.

I must be smiling like an idiot because she is smiling at me, her beautiful face warm and happy. She tugs on my shoulders and this time I don't argue. I stand, taking her in a new, deep kiss.

"I think..." I'm kissing her so hard, she can barely speak. "...I've always..." I pinch her nipple. She shudders and I pull her breath from her with another kiss. "...known it would be you."

She feels right against me, holding me, wanting me. And I think, finally, all the ugliness that asshole made her feel has vanished. She's here with me. Completely, totally with *me.*

"I'm falling in love with you, Tom."

CHAPTER 16

Samantha

He didn't let go when I said it. He didn't drop me or pull away or run. He picked me up again.

My wonderful Tom, his eyes as silver and beautiful as the moonlight spilling in through the balcony door, holds the naked me against his rock hard body, his face buried against my neck and his stubble rubbing the delicate skin of my shoulder.

"Promise me you'll stay." I barely hear his whisper. "Promise me you're not going to decide in a year and a half that you're bored."

What am I supposed to say? I would never—

The realization of what he means drops on me like a cascade of rocks. This is about his brother's divorce.

He might be holding me in the air, his arms curled around my body and his hands gripping my bottom, but he's the vulnerable one, not me. If I'm careless, I'll rip his heart to shreds.

I will never be careless with this man.

"You are not boring." I kiss along his hairline. "You are the opposite of boring."

He chuckles against my neck and his deep baritone vibrates over my skin. I moan, feeling an orgasm build out here in the hallway, in this pool of moonlight.

I've found what I've been missing all these years. What I've been looking for but never thought I deserved. "I'm the luckiest woman alive." I found Tom.

"Sammie," he whispers.

I kiss him with everything he's given me. "You are better than any fantasy and I really do love you." With everything I have.

I drown in his next kiss. How can I be so lucky? He's with me, around me, and I so very much need him inside me.

"Please, Tom. Now. Don't tease me anymore."

"Tease you?" He's growl-chuckling in my ear. "You wear a matching indigo bra and skirt and you accuse *me* of teasing?"

He paid enough attention to *notice*? "I want you *right now*, Thomas! Now! Damn it—"

I drop toward the floor, fast. He's flipped me and I'm about to skid on the carpet, but he slows my descent. I land with the most beautiful man on the planet looking down at me, his face intense and fierce and showing just how much he wants to be with me.

"Tom!" I'd rather die than hurt him. He's everything. My soul.

"Sammie." He frees himself from his flannel sleep pants and the next thing I know the head of his hard shaft is pressing against my opening.

My nails dig into his buttocks. He moves into me slowly, sliding carefully, making sure he's not hurting me. His lips glide over to my ear. He kisses, his breath hot and full of desire.

"Sammie, I love you." He pumps, filling me completely, and I slide along the carpet, my back heating.

I'm with him. Where I should be, in a splash of moonlight under an open window. With my Tom. "I love you, too," I say, loud and clear. "I love you."

He pulls almost completely out. I feel the head of his cock rub around my opening and then he's inside me again, burying himself all the way to his hilt.

I almost scream, he feels so good. I've never had a man so deep before, never so intense. He fits inside me perfectly, stretching me almost to the point it hurts, but not quite. Tom holds me just before the pleasure becomes pain.

My back arches when he pumps into me again and I moan, shuddering. His mouth descends to mine and all my breath leaves me, lifted away by the god who takes me hard, right now, on the carpet in the hallway of his tiny apartment.

"Tom," I whisper. His name is all I can say.

His gaze never leaves my face. He thrusts and I moan and I don't want this to end.

No man other than Tom will ever touch me again. No man could possibly match what he does to me.

My orgasm knocks me back and I lose all sense of the world. I feel only Tom's body pressing into mine, hear only his ragged groans. It floods me but I know he's building toward his own climax. He doesn't stop and I don't want him to. I want him to come inside me. I want to see his face in ecstasy.

He kisses me again, breathing into my mouth. His breath is hot, full of desire. Full of passion. And I kiss him back.

Groaning, his back arches. His orgasm rocks through his body and I feel myself responding, another taking me. They reverberate between us, and we both gasp, holding tight to each other.

Tom is beautiful, his handsome face full of happiness and life. Tom, my lover. Tom, my love.

He drops on top of me, his strength spent. But I don't push him off. I pull him closer.

We lay on the floor, curled around each other. His body regains its center and he smiles, his blue-green eyes warm and happy. His fingers trace my cheek.

I'm happy for the first time in years.

"So much for taking it slow." He kisses the bridge of my nose.

I grin, my fingers tracing his cheek. "I think I like being a cougar."

Tom laughs and his cock bobs inside me. It's one of the most wonderful sensations I've ever felt.

His face takes on an expression of mock seriousness. "You liked that, didn't you?" Seriousness and hunger.

I can't stop a moan from escaping. My younger lover isn't going to let me rest. Smiling, I run my hands up and down his spine. His eyes flutter and his shoulders release. Tom drops again, his full weight pressing down on me.

"*You* liked *that*, didn't you?" I'm just as mock serious.

Grinning, he kisses me again. "I don't want to sleep on the air mattress tonight."

He's never sleeping anywhere except next to me. Not tonight. Not tomorrow night. Not any night.

When we stand in the moonlight, I curl into his embrace. I run my palm over his arms, his solid shoulders, and up onto his head. I wrap my fingers in his hair.

Tom kisses me with more passion, more real desire than any man ever before has and I know this is right. This is perfect.

The moon glides across the sky. When we finally sleep, he lies next to me, sated, his arm over my belly.

I kiss his forehead, just as sated.

And finally, after all this time, happy.

CHAPTER 17

Thomas

Andy hands me a glass of champagne. Like Sammie, he's far too smart to be working in Campaign Relations but he waves his hand in the air and says some cliché about "house payments" any time someone brings it up.

Except when Sammie asked for his help after she took on repping my work. He spent a full hour looking at my paintings and drawings and by the end of the day he'd called five of his contacts.

That was seven months ago. Now, when he's not fetching booze, he mingles with the guests at my first gallery show.

"So, you two set a date yet?" He points with his champagne flute at the life-sized painting of my fiancé. In it, Sammie leans back, one leg dipped into a lake and the other propped up, her luscious body covered only in a black bikini bottom. One arm covers her breasts. But the true beauty of the painting isn't her form, it's the happiness I captured in her face. The golds, oranges, and reds of the sunset cascade over her skin, but she's looking at me. And she's smiling.

"We're thinking spring." I'd marry her right now but her family in Grand Forks will never forgive her if they can't plan the whole affair.

To my surprise, they don't seem all that put off by the number of nudes she has sat for, though her father, who's already consumed three full glasses of champagne, has spent the entire evening blushing.

Andy nods. "If you two elope, I will never forgive you." He frowns and nods toward an older couple I don't recognize. "Your adoring fans want an *event*."

I chuckle. Without Sammie's communications work and Andy's contacts, none of this would have been possible.

Andy pats my arm. "Off I go to sell, sell, sell!" Winking, he walks away.

I hear a little boy's hushed voice and I turn around, instinctively kneeling.

"Uncle Tommy!" Bart, dressed in a tuxedo t-shirt and black pants, one of his action figures gripped by its leg, runs into my arms.

I hoist him up. "Aren't you up past your bedtime?"

He stares at the painting. He's been talking nonstop about the show for two months. Dan and I had a long talk about a five-year-old and naked lady paintings, especially when that naked lady was going to be his new aunt, but we both agreed he'd never forgive us if we left him out. So I made sure Andy set out a couple of my portraits of him, and also some of his drawings of his toys, in the special "Bart" corner.

Dan sat him down and told him exactly how he was to act and that he was to stay out of the main gallery unless either Dan or I was with him. And the difference between paintings and photos. Plus a few other things. He's been an exceptional little man all evening, listening and following directions, and charmed many guests with his ever-widening understanding of art.

Bart leans close to my ear. "Sammie is pretty."

I laugh. Yep, my nephew is most definitely a Quidell man.

He looks over my shoulder. "Ms. Frasier is prettier." He's developed quite the crush on his art teacher.

"Well, at least I know you won't be stealing Sammie from me."

"Uncle Tommy!" Bart pushes his fists into his hips when I set him down. "Stealing is bad."

Dan rounds a display, the pretty Ms. Frasier next to him. Bart, making a show of behaving, walks stiffly to his father.

Dan hoists him up. "I think someone is tired."

Bart yawns. "I'm not tired."

Camille—Ms. Frasier—nods to me as she takes Bart from Dan. "Well done, Tom." Bart snuggles in, obviously happy his favorite teacher came along to keep him company.

I nod back. "Thank you."

"Dinner tomorrow?" Dan sticks his hands in his pockets. My poor brother looks uncomfortable in his suit, though I've noticed he's upped his grooming game these past few weeks.

I glance at Camille again. She's talking with Bart, giving him her full attention. Dan runs his fingers through his hair, watching them too, and he looks happy.

"Dinner it is, then. But no mac and cheese this time, okay?"

Bart giggles. "I *like* mac and cheese."

Sammie appears, gliding around the same display. Her indigo dress hugs her curves and she's as luminescent in real life as she is in the painting. Smiling, she pats Camille's arm and ruffs Bart's hair. "Someone looks tired."

Bart yawns again. "I'm not *tired.*"

Sammie laughs and kisses my nephew's cheek. "You have been a very good Quidell tonight. We are all proud of you, young man."

Bart beams.

"We will see you tomorrow for dinner, okay?" Sammie musses his hair again.

My little nephew nods. "Okay, Auntie Sammie."

She blinks, backing toward me. This is the first time Bart has called her "Auntie." I take her hand, squeezing. My beautiful Sammie beams as much as Bart, and, I do believe, she is just as happy.

We watch them go. Sammie leans against my shoulder, her cheek pressed against my arm. Her soft floral perfume wraps around me, adding an extra touch of femininity to her already perfect female form.

She squeezes my hand. "The first time he asks Camille to sit for him, your brother's going to freak out."

"Probably." I kiss the top of her head. "But I bet he'll draw a spectacular picture."

She looks up, smiling. "Andy says we can leave, if you want to."

"Oh?" Her dress is loose at the neckline and I have an exceptional view of her cleavage. Leaving sounds like just what I need right now.

"But first I want you to come down the street with me." Sammie tugs on my hand, leading me out the door.

It's too cold to be out without our coats and the sidewalk is slick, but she laughs and pulls me into the night air. The city feels alive tonight. People bustle by, most looking at Sammie and her bare arms, some laughing. Our breath freezes and Sammie snuggles close. I loop my arm over her shoulder.

The shops all brim with shoppers and the skyline twinkles. Music blasts from the restaurant down the street, along with the smell of burgers and fries. The cold air makes the blues bluer and the reds crisper, and I think, when we get home, I'll paint my Sammie in her dress under the winter night sky.

A block down, she produces a key from her clutch and pulls me into a dark stairwell. Shadows fall over us, but she shines, and lifting her against the wall would add a wonderful cap to the evening.

But she's laughing and up the stairs, out of sight, before I can yank up her skirt.

"Sammie?" I hear her heels clinking on a wood floor.

The lights are off but I see the space clearly. It's huge, with one full wall of floor-to-ceiling windows. The city lights pour in, flooding the entire wide area with golds and silvers and the reflected red and green of a neon sign across the street.

To one side, an open bookcase blocks the view of an old desk that has been pushed against the wall, and between the shelves I see Sammie's blue dress.

I stare at her for a moment, through the shelves, realizing that even though we aren't in a library, this moment is very much like her school fantasy. The one she's described for me now. Several brilliant times.

I'm immediately hard. I step out from behind the case. Sammie leans back on the desk and my palms find her breasts. I rub, watching her bite her lip. "Let me see." It's cold in here but her skin feels volcanic. I hitch up her skirt. "I want to see."

She's not wearing panties. All night, my exquisite Sammie has been walking around my gallery opening in her bright blue, clinging dress without panties.

I stare at the v between her legs, my mind totally lost.

Sammie smiles and undoes my belt. Is she going to suck me off? I want to be in her. I want to kiss her while I fuck her. My beautiful Sammie.

"You want to see?" she whispers into my mouth.

"I want *you*."

She gasps when I pound into her. Damn, she feels tight. I hold her legs and she screams my name and when we both come, I collapse on top of her. She's given us both that perfect end to a perfect evening.

Sammie wraps her legs around my hamstrings and holds me inside her. "What do you think of this space?"

"Hmm?" She smells good and I'm not thinking anymore. She's intoxicated me.

"It's nice, isn't it?" She kisses my cheek and wiggles.

I pull out even though I don't want to.

"I thought you'd like the windows."

I glance around once I've readjusted my clothes. It is a beautiful space. During the day, the light coming in would be perfect for painting.

"With both our salaries, we can afford it." She's watching my face as she readjusts her dress. "It's zoned residential. We could renovate. Live here."

My beautiful Sammie found this place with its open view and its wide spaces. She found it for *us*. "It's available?"

"I thought maybe we could paint that wall orange." She points to a little jut-out next to the windows. "If you don't think it will bother you while you're painting." Sammie skips into the red and green light thrown by the sign across the street. "This whole area here should be your studio!"

Her dress swirls around her legs as she turns in a circle, her arms out, like a ballerina. She dances in the red and the green, my muse in blue.

All I want—all I will ever want, from this moment forward—is to see her the way she is now. Happy and alive and spinning in the moonlight, for me. The light I will never block from her life. "I love you, Ms. Samantha Singleton, Sammie for short."

I scoop up the woman I love. The woman who makes everything worthwhile.

Sammie laughs and kisses me with all the passion in her soul. All the warmth and the joy she's always had. And can now express.

"I love you too, Mr. Thomas, Tom Quidell." She snuggles against my chest. "I love you very much."

The Story continues
in book two, **Daniel's Fire**

Ex-firefighter Dan Quidell fights to hold his life together after a divorce and career-ending injury. Then he meets Camille Frasier....

DANIEL'S FIRE

Book 2

CHAPTER 1

Daniel

My truck's service indicator winks on as I pull into the lot of my son's daycare. Frowning, I park outside the big Community Center building and stare at the little blue wrench and the letter-number combo on my dash. It's one of the expensive service reminders. One involving every filter and hose attached to my truck's engine, and from my last check, it probably means new tires as well.

I pull the key and sit back, mentally adding "take in the truck" to the cloud of nag inside my head. Most people would call it a mental to-do list. To me, it's a massing zombie scene: I'm on the rooftop and each time I tick something off the list, I get an undead kill shot.

Most days, I get more of them than they get bites out of me.

It's a violent way to keep a to-do list, I know. But visualization is one of the techniques they taught me while I laid on my back in that damned hospital recovering after the doctors inserted pins into my shoulder. And my thigh. And layered on the skin grafts. My doc told me if popping the heads off slow, lumbering zombies helps decrease my stress level, then by all means I should pop away.

Both my brothers think it's hilarious. Some guys have stacks of porn on the top shelves of their bedroom closets. I have stacks of shitty movies because my little brother Rob buys every idiotic zombie DVD he finds.

I glance up at the wide steel and concrete expanse of the Community Center's boxlike, early nineties architecture. My kid's in there right now, laughing and playing with the other four-year-olds, and I can't help but think that I need to up my game. Life's got too many shitty zombies. I have a boy to protect.

I look at the sun, feeling its warmth for a second, and breathe in. The air smells fresh, though the highway is on the other side of the hill and the road noise hums through the lot. A summer breeze blows and the occasional cloud keeps it from getting too hot. It's a nice day.

I count, because it's another technique the doc at the hospital taught me. To understand the moment. To see what's really here. And to live.

Sometimes it's hard. But I do it. I have a kid.

Bart's daycare teacher—the amazing Ms. Cunningham, who used to teach high school English before "retiring" to organize and run the community-based daycare—set up a strawberry picking field trip for all the kids at the Center. She called me personally, claiming I was one of her favorite students back in the day, and asked if I would like to come along.

Who am I to say no to Ms. Cunningham? Besides, I get to spend time with my kid *and* watch the pretty young teachers sticking out their sweet round asses while they bend over to pick berries.

I may not have stacks of porn in my closet, but I'm still a man. Even if my scars and my life have shut down dating.

I slam the truck door and lean against the front fender, stretching my hamstring. I changed into cargo shorts and a long-sleeved t-shirt before driving over. At the time, I didn't notice that the scar on my leg was visible.

My brothers tell me not to be so self-conscious. But, like seeing what's really here, sometimes it's hard.

I walk toward the Community Center door. The aches are bad

today, even with the nice weather. Maybe the flavor of fresh berries on the tongue and the laughter of little kids will ease at least some of it.

I can hope.

⚜

Camille

FORTY PRE-KINDERGARTENERS, SIX TEACHERS AND AIDES, AND EIGHT parents. That's three kids per adult. I hand over a bright green t-shirt and the corresponding green kids' shirts to Ms. Selby, the pregnant parent standing in front of my table, in the middle of the Community Center lobby. She's pretty. Wearing designer yoga maternity wear, too. Her perfume smells like an expensive field of handcrafted French lavender. Or how I imagine a field of expensive Old World lavender tended only by the most artisanal hands would smell. The closest I'll ever get to France is downloaded movies and the occasional glass of fine wine.

"I'm supposed to put this on?" Smiling, though she's obviously annoyed by the chaotic green of the shirt, she holds it like she would a pair of stinky workout shoes.

"It's so your group can easily identify you. And you, them." I point to the three little kid shirts and her assigned list before pointing toward the room she's with.

Nodding, she takes the shirts and walks down the hall, her designer sandals snapping against the floor.

I watch her go. Sandy—Ms. Cunningham to all the parents—is wrangling her room of little ones, as are the other teachers. I don't get my own room until next week—I'm teaching pull-out art classes—so I'm wrangling the parents.

When I hear the Community Center's door whoosh open I look up, expecting another neighborhood mom to saunter in, or the second dad. We have two today. The first guy, a tech from one of the local computer businesses, walked in early, blinking like he'd never seen the sun before, and went about following directions as well as the best of our students. He waits now in his bright yellow t-shirt in his daughter's room helping the other kids with theirs.

The second one is little Bart's father. Sandy's eyebrow arched just a tad bit when she said his name, and her lips rounded for a fraction of a second. The man has a reputation—a *good* reputation.

I remember the news reports. How Bart's father and another fire-fighter got a family out of an apartment building before it collapsed. How they'd both been injured. Dan Quidell is a hero.

I've seen Bart's file. Hell, all the teachers have seen his file. We need to know when kids have non-custodial parents who might cause problems and sadly, little Bart is one such kid. So I know what his dad looks like, as I do his ex-wife. Her photo in the file is a six year old snapshot. His, a slightly blurry cell phone snap. Mr. Quidell holds Bart but he's turning away, like he doesn't want his photo taken. Bart, though, is mugging for the photographer, as Bart tends to do.

There'd been the snickers in the break room this morning when Sandy went over the parent list. "Hug a Teacher" mugs held high and the calls to make sure that when Dan Quidell changes into his neon colored parent t-shirt, he does it out in the open, where they all can see.

I rolled my eyes. Because, I'm sure, the man *likes* being considered a piece of meat. The disrespect left a sour taste.

But when the Community Center doors whoosh open and the road noise rolls in, when I see one Mr. Daniel Quidell in the flesh for the first time, only two words echo through my head. Two very unteacher-like words. Two words that sum up the halting physical grace before me: *Holy fuck.*

The sun backlights his body, so I can't immediately see his face, but I see his shape. Like a lot of tall men, he does the slight head duck as he walks across the threshold into the main lobby, even though he has plenty of clearance. He twists too, angling in one broad shoulder before the other.

He moves like the dancers I used to date, gliding on strong, sure legs. But I see the snagging of his joints, and, I suspect, some aches, and I'm sure not all his injuries healed right.

His scars from his firefighter days must still cause him pain.

Stopping just inside the door, under the full glory of the lobby's huge skylight, he curls one sculpted bicep as he reaches to pull off his sunglasses.

The tingle doesn't creep up from my belly or between my legs or from any other part of my body. It manifests from every one of my cells as if I'm standing between two static electricity generators. Two of those huge sparking monstrosities from old movies, the ones Dr. Frankenstein used to bring his monster to life.

I look at the big, gorgeous man framed by the Community Center's entrance, at his well-proportioned chest and arms, his flat abs and his strong, centered-though-pained gait as he walks toward me, and my entire body suddenly has a mind of its own. Or half a mind. It most certainly has *desire*.

Holy fuck bounces through my head again. I want to rub those shoulders. Soothe those aches. Stretch and loosen that body. I want to give him relief in *every* way possible.

He hooks one temple of his sunglasses over the collar of his long-sleeved t-shirt as he glances around. A smile appears as he notices my table. And me.

I hope I'm not blushing. God, I feel like I'm blushing. My skin feels hot and my nipples tingle and I swear if he asks, I'll sneak off to a supply closet with him just so I can suck him off.

Which is unprofessional of me. *Very* unprofessional. For goodness sake, I teach his little boy.

But the smiling Mr. Quidell, with his short chocolate brown hair and his incredible blue-green eyes, is beyond gorgeous.

He extends his hand. "Dan Quidell," he says, his voice washing over me in a wave of warm, deep tones. Damn it, he sounds as good as he looks.

One side of his mouth curls up higher than the other. Just a little, and it gives him a hint of devilishness. He's got a swashbuckling air to him, but in a leader kind of way, like he's the head pirate.

I inhale and stand up straight, determined to be professional. I will not embarrass myself and I most definitely will not embarrass a parent. I like my new job, even if I need to find a second one to pay my rent and my school loans. Losing the job I have because I'm an idiot is out of the question.

I take his hand, shaking once. His fingers are roughly smooth, with that thicker texture testosterone gives a man's skin, and they engulf mine.

I inhale again.

"Ms. Frasier." He nods toward my name tag and I swear his eyes are lingering on my chest. "You're new?" Oh, his voice really is like sonic velvet.

When he releases my hand, I almost sigh. His gaze does the unconscious dance over my breasts and my hips that straight men's eyes do, and it takes all my effort not to wiggle where I stand.

The man is too damned distracting.

But I think he's trying to be professional, too. Because I'm one of his kid's teachers.

"Started this week." I smile as I pretend to look for his name on the list. "I'll be teaching pull-out art classes as soon as my room is set up."

"Bart will like that."

I look up again. He's still smiling, but now the muscles of his face have taken on a deeper pull. His stance changed, too. I can't put my finger on it, but I'm sure, all the way to my bones, that this man loves his son.

And I want to sigh again, but I don't. I dig through the pile and pull out a neon pink, size medium t-shirt. "I have your t-shirt right here."

No way is it going to fit.

Mr. Quidell laughs when he holds it up. "We match."

He's right. I hadn't thought about it, but the store only had six colors, so there's doubling. Each teacher got a color and Sandy put one parent with most of us.

And I got Mr. Quidell.

I *am* blushing. I must be the same color as our shirts.

He's making a face and yanking on the seams of the shirt, like he's trying to stretch it. "Is this the biggest you have?"

"No one warned me about your big broad shoulders," I blurt out.

Oh hell, I think, and curl my lips into a thin line. I almost slap a hand over my mouth, but that would just make things worse.

He laughs again and that crooked smirk reappears—and my stray thought about vanishing into a supply closet with him for a quickie jumps back into my head.

Why am I thinking this way? I know how to keep my libido in check. I'm not some young freshman with a crush on the senior quarterback. Or a hero-worshipping fangirl.

The last thing he needs is to think that I'm some firefighter bunny.

His brow crinkles. His gaze drops away and he steps back, holding the t-shirt up between us like a screen. "I'll make do." When he lowers the t-shirt, he's looking down the hall. "Should I go to Bart's room?"

Did I make some unfriendly facial tic? Did he pick up something from my body language? I stiffen, thinking my ogling made him uncomfortable. He's a parent of one of my students. Damn it, I need to be professional.

Kids are so much easier to deal with than men.

I hand him his group's pink t-shirts and his list. "We'll be lining up in a couple of minutes. Will you be riding on the bus with us?"

He glances at the names before answering. "Had an indicator light come on as I was parking, so it looks like it." A frown jumps across his face before he flashes another friendly-but-distant smile.

I make a show of marking my sheet. Dan Quidell nods one more time, watching me for a longer moment than I expected, then walks away, toward his son.

CHAPTER 2

Daniel

We're in the second bus, bouncing down a county road not far out of town. Bart stares out the window, wide eyed, watching the fields go by. The kids are loud and the bus smells more like rotting milk than the old vinyl seats I remember from my time on school buses. The seats are smaller, too. My other two young charges sit in front of us, because, it seems, my "big broad shoulders" take up a lot of room.

One of the kids, a little girl named Emma, occasionally peeks over the top of her seat. She blinks a few times, her eyes big like she wants to ask me something, then she turns around and sits again.

I'm trying to be attentive. I am. But the new teacher with the soulful dark eyes whose name is Ms. Frasier sits two seats up, and right now she's tucking a strand of her glossy, lovely, I-want-to-wrap-my-fingers-in-it black hair behind her ear. It's up in a ponytail or bun or whatever women call that knot they put on the back of their heads, and the nape of her neck is visible.

There's a slight of sheen of sweat on her skin. She glistens.

God damn, Ms. Frasier is *glistening*.

"Daddy, look!" Bart taps my arm and bounces on the seat. "Horses!"

Sure enough, we pass a pasture with three horses gnawing on grass and swishing their tails, and every kid on our side of the bus rushes the windows. I'm surprised we don't roll.

In the seat in front of us, Emma crawls over her little friend, Mandy. "Horsies!" they squeal in unison.

The pretty Ms. Frasier laughs as she lifts the little one next to her onto her lap and points, and I wonder why Bart's mother couldn't be like that. Then I catch myself. Dwelling helps no one.

And I don't even know Ms. Frasier's first name. When she made a hard face in the lobby—that particular way women move their cheeks and lips when they're closing themselves off to talking to a man—I knew I'd better step back.

Not that it matters. Bart's my priority. He was four years ago when I pulled myself up onto my fucking crutches and out of my hospital bed to face my bitch of an ex-wife in that damned courtroom. Thank the Lord for my lawyer—and the support of my station and my family. Bart's safe now.

But I still wish he had a mom.

Bart smiles and bounces again. "Take a picture, Daddy!" He points at the horses. "Please?"

I quickly pull out my phone and snap a few as we pass more horses.

"Let me see!" He grabs my phone and swipes through the photos. "They're blurry." Frowning, his big blue eyes sad, he hands it back.

"Sorry, little man." I tuck the phone into my pocket.

Bart pats my elbow. "That's okay, Daddy. I'll draw a picture so we both remember." He nods once like he *knows* he's taking care of his thick-headed daddy and returns to looking out the window.

Grinning, I muss his hair, and thank the whole wide world for my great kid.

Emma is watching me again. Her little eyes stare over the top of the seat. "Are you a superhero?" she whispers. "You look like a superhero."

Next to her, I hear another little whisper. "Superheroes aren't *real*, Emma! My mommy said so."

Bart beams. I lean close. "What do I say, Doctor Bartman, sir? Do I tell them about our lair? Minion One wants to know."

Emma screeches.

Two seats up, the lovely Ms. Frasier leans over her seat. "Sit down, you two." She cocks an eyebrow and waves a finger at me. "And you, Minion One, behave. Or I'm revoking your Minion status."

The two girls giggle. Bart presses his fists into his waist. The beautiful Ms. Frasier watches me with just enough mock in her sternness to make wonderful memories for all the kids.

And just enough of a grin to make a wonderful memory for me.

❦

I TIE THE PINK T-SHIRT AROUND MY HEAD, LAWRENCE OF ARABIA style. It's either that or over my shoulders like a cape, and I rather the kids stop with the superhero stuff. As, it seems, would the lovely Ms. Frasier. A couple of the other teachers glare at me because I broke protocol and a rash of t-shirt tying imitation swept the group, but I'd rip the seams of the thing if I put it on.

And no one needs to see me change. The kids don't need to see my scars.

I take my little group out into the field, Bart in front, the girls in the middle, and me following behind. They each carry a plastic basket to collect their berries, but I suspect more will go straight into mouths than into the containers. They're so excited they all but run into the rows of low bushy plants. They fall into parallel picking, very much like they would fall into parallel play, the way the many parenting books I read while recovering said they would.

The field smells like Bart's favorite juice boxes, but real. Dots of bright red berries peek out from under all the deep green leaves. My feet sink into the dirt, but not too far. Walking behind the kids is comfortable, considering.

The pretty Ms. Frasier herds her group in front of ours and when she bends over to help a student, I get a spectacular view of her perfect, round backside. No flab there, just one smoothly curved ass. Great for grabbing onto.

Bart tugs on my shorts. "Are you going back to work after, Daddy?" He filled his basket already and is looking up at me with his most plaintive face.

My settlement money went into the house and a good nest egg for Bart's college, and it means I have savings, so I can't go on disability. So I work. Last year, I went out on my own doing inspections and fire system design consulting. I'm doing well, but businesses take time to grow. Today, I'm working with a new builder. A company that, if I'm lucky, might lead to a major contract in a few months. "Sorry, little man. I have a meeting this afternoon."

Bart frowns. "Oh." He holds up his berries. "Will Uncle Tommy be home?"

My brother used to live with us, to help out, but he moved out over the weekend. Bart's bummed. So am I, to be honest. And I no longer have help at home.

Maybe I should ask Ms. Cunningham if she knows anyone. Bart's too important to leave with any old babysitter.

"Uncle Tommy moved to his own place, remember?" I take Bart's hand. "I'll be back when all your classes are done, just like yesterday. Remember that, too?"

"I remember." He points at the main building. "Can we go now?"

The girls are getting tired, as well. Adrenaline wears off fast when you're four. "Depends on what Ms. Frasier says, right?" I call.

She rubs her hands on her pink t-shirt and it pulls tight over her not-too-big and not-too-small breasts.

The woman is freakin' hot. Lusciously lickable and smokin' hot. Curved perfectly to hold up against a wall, level of hot.

Parts of my body I thought I'd locked down and put into storage want out. For a second, I remember how good a woman's fingers feel when they dig into my shoulders, when she's close to coming and she can't stop herself. How incredible her breath will feel on my neck. How intoxicating it is to hear her whisper my name.

I blink and look away from the luscious Ms. Frasier's incredibly hot body. I need to remember who my priority is. And it ain't my cock.

"We tired?" Ms. Frasier asks.

I look over again, determined to be a good dad. I mock yawn and slump my shoulders. "I need a nap."

The girls giggle. Bart, though, rolls his four-year-old eyes. "Daddy! Act like a grown-up!"

Ms. Frasier laughs, and for a moment that hard teacher-parent line evaporates. She's a woman and I'm a man, and we're sharing this moment with the kids. And damn it, it makes her even more beautiful.

"Okay, everyone, line up!" She glances around, doing the teacher counting thing where she instantly knows the exact location of every child. It's impressive.

Smiling again, she shoos me toward the buses. When her group runs by me, she yells, and they slow, falling in line with Bart, Emma, and Mandy. Three paces ahead, they pair off and hold hands, each with their baskets firmly grasped in their other fists.

Ms. Frasier falls in line with me and before I realize it, I'm reaching for her hand, to mimic the kids.

But when my fingers graze her wrist, she looks up, her eyes wide with surprise.

"Sorry!" I jam my hands into my pockets. What am I doing?

She grins and tucks a stray strand of her jet black hair behind her ear. "The pink hat suits you."

We both laugh. The tension eases and I grin, too. "What's your name? If I'm going to accidently hold your hand, I should at least know your first name."

In front of us, the kids take up their places by the school buses. Ms. Cunningham counts them off and sends them in by color groups.

"Camille," my comrade in neon says.

"Camille," I say. A beautiful name for a beautiful woman. "It's nice to meet you."

CHAPTER 3

Camille

One month after the strawberry picking field trip, Bart's taken to spending as much of his days in my room drawing and painting as he's allowed. Getting him to do any other activity takes effort—he's not all that interested in reading or numbers or playing ball. Just colors and lines. But we work at it, and I'm getting him to hold his attention on a few books.

Dan often stays later than the other parents when he comes to pick up Bart. We talk about Bart and his talent, and how the art gene jumped from his father, right over Dan, to Bart. And, it seems, to Dan's brother, Tom.

Two months after the field trip, autumn cools the weather. Bart's now in long sleeves every day, like his dad.

Dan still stays longer, standing in the middle of my room, often close enough we brush elbows, Bart on his hip, smiling his most wonderful smile. He asks questions about my career goals and hopes for the future. He's always attentive, always focused on our conversation, watching me with his mesmerizing eyes. But mostly we talk about the movies we like and the ones we think might be fun for Bart to watch.

By the fourth month, I've learned a lot about running a small business specializing in fire disaster prevention. By the fifth, I also know all about Uncle Tommy's new fiancé and the coming gallery show of his drawings and paintings. About how Uncle Robby is in grad school in a different state and how Bart misses him.

The holidays come. We make special ornament keepsakes, little plastic globes filled with memories from the year. Bart proudly gives his to his father, and Dan, smiling, hands me a lovely apple tied with a gorgeous, intricate bow. "For Bart's best teacher," he says, holding it out. When I take it from his hand, his fingers sweep over mine and that same tingle I felt the first time I saw him jolts through my body like static electricity.

And it becomes oh so very difficult to be professional around Dan Quidell.

By the sixth month after the field trip, I know all about Bart's upcoming fifth birthday party. Uncle Rob will be home this coming weekend to help celebrate. The Quidells are having a family celebration.

Turns out Dan's brother Tom used to live with them, to help with Bart. But he moved out about the time I started at the Community Center daycare and now Dan's handling everything himself.

I can tell. Each day he looks more exhausted than the day before.

And he's been late to pick up Bart a couple of times, when he's driving from the south side of The Cities and hits bad traffic.

Like today.

Dan staggers in, his white button-down shirt wrinkled and his chin covered with what looks like an uncomfortably itchy five o'clock shadow. Bart's resting on a mat, bored, hungry, and half asleep, his backpack next to him.

"I'm sorry." Dan looks around. Bart's the last one out. Again. Dan takes the new artwork from me when I hold it out and looks at it, and his face crinkles up like he's in pain. Which he might be. I know the changing weather makes aches worse.

I asked my mom, a physical therapist, about it. She went on for almost an hour about scars and pulling and old injuries. Now I know every time Dan hitches his hip it must be because his leg hurts. All I want to do is sit him down and rub the muscle until it loosens.

Then straddle his lap, rubbing other, just as hard parts.

I glance away. We both behave professionally because professional is the way we need to behave. Bart's growth and happiness is both our goals.

Even though I think, sometimes, while we stand between the kids' easels, Dan wants to touch me as much as I want to touch him.

But business is business.

Dan looks at Bart's latest puppy picture like he can't decide if he should make a joke about it, feel proud of his son's talent, or just set it down and curl up on the mat with his boy.

"New contract. It's a forty-five minute drive on a good day." He glances at the window. "Traffic's terrible."

"Could your brother pick him up on days you're late?" Dan needs relief. Running your own business is hard enough, but to do it as a single parent, as well? I don't know how he's still conscious by the end of the week. His weekend evenings are probably consumed by account work and balancing checkbooks, as it is.

Fear flashes through Dan's eyes. Fear like he'd just opened a cabin door to find the movie monster shambling toward him. Like his zombies just caught up.

"No, no, no we're not kicking out Bart. Don't worry." I touch his elbow and my fingers glide over the cotton of his shirt. I know I shouldn't. But my hand reaches anyway, fingers meaning to give reassurance.

Dan nods and I realize I've never seen him in short sleeves. Not even when it was blisteringly hot outside. His shirt feels rough, like no one ever taught him how to care for laundry and keep his clothes soft.

He glances at the mat.

Bart sits up and stretches. "I'm hungry."

Dan's eyes close and I swear he's counting. His shoulders roll back, and when he opens his eyes again, he smiles and holds his arms out to his son. "Come here, little man."

Bart runs to his father and Dan hoists him up. Bart's thumb moves into his mouth and he sucks on it for two quick pulls, then seems to realize what he's doing. His hand vanishes around his daddy's neck.

I want to take Bart and give him a hug. Damn it, I want to give *Dan* a hug. I want to stroke his hair and whisper to him that it's okay. He can rest.

"Are you still looking for help? Sandy said a while ago you were looking for a babysitter. I'm available." The words roll out of my mouth on their own. But damn it, Dan needs help. And honestly, I still need that second job. I nod toward Bart, doing my best to be professional. "I can bring him home on the nights you're running late. *We'll* make dinner. Right?"

Bart nods, but he's too tired and his thumb makes its way into his mouth again.

I can't read what's flitting over Dan's face. Concern? Relief? Disbelief? He looks shocked. He hugs Bart to his shoulder. "My schedule isn't always set."

"That's fine." I tap Bart's arm. "Would that be okay with you? We could paint some more."

He smiles as he nods.

"I'll pay what you need."

I look up at Dan Quidell's handsome face and all I see is hope. And thankfulness. He's looking at me like a man chased by monsters who believes he's about to get eaten. He can't believe I just offered an escape. "As long as I have enough to pay my rent and my school loans and still eat, I'm good."

The disbelief turns into a big smile and he turns to his son. "I gotta put you down for a second, buddy. Okay?"

Bart nods and Dan sets him on his feet before digging in his back pocket for his wallet. "Do you have a pen?"

I grab one off my desk.

"Thanks." Dan pulls out a business card and flips it over. "Address. My cell number's on the front. Can you come by tonight? After work?"

I take the card. They live three miles away. "I'll be by in an hour."

Dan, smiling, hoists up Bart again. "Should we make Ms. Frasier dinner, little man?"

Bart blinks. "Mac and cheese?"

I laugh. "I like mac and cheese, too!"

"Dinner it is." Dan extends his hand to shake.

His palm feels strong and warm, his skin wonderfully male, and the tingle moves from my fingers up my arm. Six months of talking every day, of sharing about Bart, of me silently and unprofessionally lusting for this fantastic man, and this will be the first time we see each other outside of work.

"Thank you." Dan grips Bart, smiling again.

"You're welcome," I say, as I watch Dan carry his son through the whooshing door. They're gone, into the evening's setting sun, but I still feel Dan's hand on mine.

CHAPTER 4

Daniel

I hand a plate to Bart. "Set it on the table, buddy."

He nods and walks slowly out of our open kitchen toward the dining area. Next to the table, just outside the patio door, snow covers the deck I added as part of my therapy. Doc told me to keep moving, so I kept moving. There's something meditative about swinging a hammer.

I almost sold the house and all the memories of my ex when I received the settlement, but I didn't want to give her that satisfaction. So I remodeled instead. It's an open floor plan, with stairs to the second floor next to the front door and a walkout basement tucked underneath. This floor is mostly kitchen and living room.

Now it's ours, Bart and me. I built him a nice home. And my ex-wife is somewhere, presumably living in the woods in one of the big square states out west with her newest boyfriend. The farther she is from sane people, the better the world will function.

Bart grips the plate as he shuffles along the hardwood into the dining area and to Camille. She watches, letting him set the table one plate and spoon at a time, and smiles every time he looks over the table's edge at his work. He's doing his "arranging" thing again, making the plates and the silverware into pictures.

When he makes a smiley face with his plate, a spoon, and two strawberries from the fridge, she claps and gives him a hug.

And all I can do is hope I can pay her well enough to make watching Bart worth her time.

I carry the dish of mac and cheese to the table. I made spinach salads too, with some other strawberries, and a vinaigrette. Bart thought I was crazy for putting berries on *spinach*.

Camille watches me as I sit down. My leg hurts more than usual today. My shoulder, as well. I should probably put heat on them after she leaves, though I wonder how her fingers massaging the tightness away would feel. Rubbing across my shoulders, her breasts pressed against my back.

I force the thoughts away. This is not a business relationship I'm going to mess up no matter how beautiful she is. Bart's too important.

Camille eats her mac and cheese, commenting on how good it is, and says she likes the salad. Bart, proud, launches into a detailed description of how he took out the vinegar and the shaker and helped measure *and* pour, though he still refuses to try the salad, instead sticking to dipping his strawberries into his whipped topping.

After dinner, Camille helps me get him into bed, even reading him his bedtime story. We both tuck him in and he cuddles in safe wearing his superhero jammies holding his superhero beanie toys.

I close down his door.

"I'll help clean up." Camille points down the stairs before jamming her hands into her pockets.

She'll stay a little longer. I grin and follow her down to the kitchen, letting myself watch her walk, knowing she can't see me appreciating the luscious curve of her lower back.

She's average height, the top of her head coming in under my chin, and she's smoothly round. Her teacher-clothes hide her shape, but it's still obvious. And it's nice.

At least I'll get to look at a pretty woman when I come home from work, even if touching will be out of the question.

"Do you work out?" After six months of chatting every day, I know a lot about her life, except her exercise habits. The question, though, slips out of my mouth before I realize I have no right to ask. And that it makes it obvious I've been looking at her ass.

So I try to climb out of the hole I just dug. "I mean, if helping out interferes with your routine. I have equipment here. It's downstairs. I got it because my doctors and therapists said I should and when Bart was a baby I couldn't go to a gym. I'd put him in his playpen and he'd watch. Usually demanding I take him out. You're welcome to use it."

From over her shoulder, I see Camille grinning. She's probably wondering why I keep talking. *I* don't know why I keep talking.

At the bottom of the stairs, she's still grinning. "My apartment complex has this crappy little workout room and there's usually some creepy guy in there." She rolls her eyes. "The Community Center is too expensive. So yeah, that'd be nice."

Her eyes are the richest, most vibrant dark brown I have ever seen. They're like melted chocolate. I nod and look away, absently rubbing at my neck. I drop my hand when I realize what I'm doing.

Camille frowns. "Is it bad tonight?"

"What?" Is she asking about my workout equipment? I must be making a weird face because she chuckles.

"I can tell when you hurt. It shows in how you move." She points at my shoulder. "I used to dance. When I was in school." Shrugging, she walks into the living room. "It's obvious."

She's a dancer? No wonder she moves with such grace. And has such a nice ass.

"Sit down." A hint of commanding teacher rolls out in her voice when she points at the chair.

What am I supposed to do? She's Ms. Frasier and I have to do what she says. I drop into the chair with the low back Tom placed next to the couch. My brother stood in my living room when he moved in, staring at my hand-me-down furniture, and said if I'm going to live with Dad's cast-offs, I should at least not arrange them exactly the way he had.

I hadn't realized.

Now, Camille moves behind the chair I'm dutifully sitting in, and dances her fingers over my shoulder muscles.

Her touch is firm through my shirt and a little cool, as if her hands are cold. I want to grasp them between my own. Give her my warmth.

"You have an asymmetry here, in your neck muscles." Her fingers press and for the briefest moment, her breasts brush against the back of my head. "Let's try this."

I want to pull her over my shoulder and onto my lap. I want her to smooth those dexterous fingers over my chest before she wraps her arms around my head and rubs her hands over my neck and my back. I want to feel her fingers in my hair. On my scalp. To breathe in her scent, a warm mixture of brightly-colored art supplies and sweet woman. Sweet, like she uses a natural shampoo and soap, ones with a fruit scent.

If I lick between her breasts, will I taste it?

Her fingers skip up the sides of my neck, then down again, before thumbs press into my flesh.

In just the right spot. With just the right pressure.

My thoughts flip from wanting her touch to feeling all its brilliance. My entire neck releases and a wave of relief flows down my spine. Rolls down and through my hips until it pools in my groin. Her breasts brush against my head again and I hear her feet reposition on the carpet. She's going to press into my neck again.

"You're an angel." She is. One perfect and wonderful angel. Six months quietly trying to learn everything I could about her life and I never, not once, caught a hint of this particular skill.

Now I'm wondering what else I don't know.

I *want* to know.

Camille chuckles and presses again, this time on my deltoids. "My mom is a physical therapist. I was considering going into it, but I like to teach. Watching the kids paint and draw is its own magic." She presses again. "I do wish there were more art therapy jobs."

More tension releases and that feeling I had when I first saw her, when I went on the field trip with Bart's class, follows the leaving aches. The joy that comes with seeing beauty, that moment of understanding I'm in the presence of someone special, flows into my body. It's warm and crackling, like a campfire. It pushes out all the pains and I sigh.

Me, Daniel Quidell, ex-firefighter, lets out a less-than-manly sigh of relief.

Her hands fold over my shoulders and it's not just her fingers on my body anymore. Her palms lay flat against my shirt.

I want to pull off the collar around my neck. Tear off the fabric over my shoulders. To have her skin against mine—*all* of her skin—would prove once and for all that she is the angel I think she is.

But my scars might scare her away and she's the best thing that could possibly have happened to Bart.

"How much does it hurt?" The teacher tones of her voice have fallen away and she's replaced them with sympathy. Or maybe, I wonder, if what I'm hearing is empathy. She's almost whispering.

Could I be so lucky to hear empathy? "I'm conscious of it most of the time." There's really no other way to describe it. The aches and the pains don't leave. They're always there.

"They're background." I shrug. "You know how when it's cold outside and your joints seem to slow down and you can't ignore it completely? Like what should flow smoothly is clogged up by slush and you have to wait longer than you expect to get through? It's like that. When my shoulder pings, I know it's there."

One of her hands lifts off my shoulder and she moves around to the front of the chair. The other hand slides along my skin and my shirt bunches up under her fingers.

For a second, she looks at her fingers and not my face. "The massage helps?"

More than she knows. More than I can verbalize. Her touch, even through the fabric, is warm and soothing and better than any of my therapists'.

She must have read my relief from my body because a smile lights up her beautiful face. She's got a golden tone to her and the loveliest skin I have ever seen.

"Before I go, we're going to make sure you sleep well tonight." Her hand lifts off my shoulder as she nods toward the kitchen. "Do you have avocado oil?"

"Avocados have oil?" We eat healthy but Bart hates avocados so I stick with olive oil.

Camille grins and shakes her head. "It'll help with the massage."

"Oh." That means she wants me to take off my shirt. *Maybe I can get her to take off hers*, I think. Then I realize what that means. If this gets weird, she might not want to help anymore, and I can't do that to Bart.

And she'll see my scars.

Her head tips to the side. "You look conflicted."

The light filtering in from the kitchen halos around her head until she drops onto the couch.

I swear she's carried the light with her. That it's still there, in her hair, and on her fingers. Camille's surrounded by angelfire.

God damn, she's beautiful.

"I'm sorry," she whispers, her face suddenly as pained as my back felt. "I just thought that maybe I could help you as well. Not just Bart." She pats her thigh and smiles. "Tell you what. Let's make arrangements for Monday. You said you have another late meeting, right?"

All I want is to kiss her. To lay her down on the couch and press kisses over every inch of her skin. The lovely sweep of her neck. The exceptional roundness of her breasts. I want to take the wonder of her touch and give it right back to her as gentle rubs and hard thrusts.

I don't dare stand up. I feel my heart beating and my cock is pulsing right along with it.

"Late meeting," I say. Only those two words will leave my mouth. If I don't shut it right now, my lips are going to be nibbling on her earlobe.

"Do you want me to bring Bart home? We'll make dinner." She smiles again and I swear the halo has returned. The squiggles covering her loose-fitting blouse draw my attention but I can't stare at her chest. I know those buttons will pop right off the fabric if I rip it from her body. Pop like little corn kernels and bounce across the living room.

Nodding, she stands. "I have the key you gave me before dinner and the extra booster seat in my car. Bart and I have the routine down."

She rubs her hands over her belly the way she did on the field trip and I almost scoop her up. I'd make it up the stairs and into the bedroom before I got winded. I can still pass all the state firefighter requirements.

Except for the metal in my bones and the scars on my skin.

"If you want me to do your pressure points again, just ask." Camille tips her head again and her face is intense, the way I imagine she watches a student who is upset. She's gauging what she needs to do to calm me down.

And I don't know what to do. Bart needs her. So I better not mess this up.

I stand slowly and slide my fists into my pockets to disguise my rock hard cock as best I can. "Next week, then."

She glances at my crotch and I swear her eyebrows arch in approval.

If only I could be so lucky. But she hasn't actually seen my shoulder yet.

Camille nods before picking up her purse. At the door, she smiles again, and I lean against the frame.

"Good night, Dan." With that, she walks to her little compact car waiting at the end of my driveway.

I close the door. The house suddenly feels worn. My furniture isn't mine. It's no one's, to be honest. Except the kid's art table and easel, in the corner. And the two boxes full of action figures. And the stacks of cartoon DVDs.

But when Bart's asleep, there's not a lot here.

I stand straight. This is the world I've built, and I should be proud of it. My son has a bright future.

I'll count in and count out, forcing my libido to calm the fuck down. I'll stand in the damned shower and take care of it myself. Though this time, I suspect my mind is going to wander to a real woman.

But I won't let it. I can't interfere with what I mean to provide my son. Because everything's for Bart.

＼

CHAPTER 5

Camille

Why the hell did I just stand up and leave like that? And now I'm driving home. Down the dark suburban streets toward my apartment building. Alone.

Again, that most unteacher-like word reverberates through my head: *Fuck*.

The raw need on Dan's face alone almost brought on an orgasm. When has a man ever reacted to me like that? I touched his shoulders and he was instantly hard. Hard enough his erection clearly wanted release.

His *huge* erection.

Maybe I imagined the whole damned thing. But I couldn't let his neck hurt him like that. But I wasn't expecting that response. He's a parent. A *gorgeous* parent.

I slap the steering wheel of my pathetic little hatchback. Damn it, I just wanted to help.

My head's spinning. I park in my building's lot and stare at the crummy entrance of my low rent apartment. Babysitting will help me make ends meet. I have to remember that.

And, I think, that's why Dan didn't touch. Business is business. He sees me as someone trustworthy with his boy.

I close my eyes, fighting my body's need to cry. I feel a tear anyway. Why am I reacting this way?

But I know. A man with a heart as good as Dan's deserves the most respect and the best treatment I have to offer.

And he's going to get it.

WHEN DAN DROPS OFF BART MONDAY MORNING, WE CHAT SOME. He stands an extra foot or so away, as if he's afraid I'll jump into his arms. Or that, maybe, he'll throw me down on top of my desk, both our jobs be damned. I can't tell. But his gaze makes my skin heat. It's hard not to fan myself like some belle.

He tells me he needs to grocery shop, but there's leftover mac and cheese, and fruit on the counter. And that he will be home about nine or nine-thirty.

I watch him dodge incoming kids and exercise class participants as he strides toward the Community Center exit. He spends more time watching me than where he's walking.

Bart spends the day extra chatty and happy as he moves back and forth between Sandy's room and mine. By the end of the day, all the kids know that I'm his new babysitter. I field question after question about why Bart gets a teacher babysitter and the other kids don't.

A couple of the teachers seem annoyed.

It's not against the rules to babysit outside of work hours. I think they're more upset about who I'm sitting for, not that I'm doing the work.

Dan seems oblivious. Not once in the past six months have I seen his eyes roam over any of the other teachers or moms, or any of the women in their tight workout clothes who take the fitness classes on the other side of the Community Center. He's focused on Bart. And chatting with me.

At ten after five, the last of my other kids leaves with his mom, and it's just Bart and me. He bounces over, his big blue eyes wide, and takes my hand. "I ride in your car tonight! Daddy's truck is *big*."

A lot about Dan Quidell is big. But I can't think about the hard lines of his big body right now. I have a room to tidy.

I kneel down so I'm eye-to-eye with Bart. "We need to clean up first. Will you help me?"

Bart's little arms wrap around my neck and I'm suddenly gripped tightly by a wonderful Quidell man. "You're pretty," he says.

I pick him up, hugging him just as tightly as he's hugging me. "And you are quite a handsome young man."

When I put him down, he helps me clean up by putting all the papers into the recycling. And when we leave, he holds tight to my hand, his superhero backpack over his arms, and together, we go home.

⚜

BART'S DETERMINED TO STAY AWAKE FOR HIS DAD. HE CUDDLES against my side on the couch in his superhero pajamas, one of his superhero action figures in his hand, and we settle in to watch super-hero cartoons. Garishness pops and giggles from the television but he's asleep within fifteen minutes.

His little head smells like kid's shampoo. He'd been so good all evening, doing his chores and following me around the house, to make sure I knew where all the dishes went, where the towels were, and what temperature his bath was supposed to be. He lined up all his superheroes on the lip of the tub, talking to each in turn, and washed his hair all by himself.

The beautiful child leaning against me trusts me enough to fall asleep on my arm. I hoist him up carefully and he mumbles a word.

A word that sounds faintly like "Mommy."

But he couldn't have said "Mommy." He doesn't see her. Hell, from the file, I doubt he even knows what she looks like.

Bart wraps his legs around my waist and I carry him upstairs. He's getting big, but I manage. In his room, I tuck him in and set his nightlight.

The door creaks as I close it, and suddenly I'm alone in the Quidell house. Downstairs, the refrigerator clunks to life. The television is on mute, but light reflecting up the steps jumps and jitters with the still-playing cartoon characters. Their house smells clean but also like men live here. There's no subtle hint of flowers, or sweetness.

I breathe in. Sandalwood.

The door to Dan's bedroom is half closed and I stare from my spot in front of Bart's. I see the outline of a messy bed, but no overt signs of clutter. Or clothes on the floor.

I turn away, to go downstairs. It's not my business.

Besides, Dan should be home soon.

My foot hits the landing at the bottom of the stairs just as I hear the garage door open. Dan's headlights arch across the front window as he pulls into the driveway, and for a second they overtake the flashing from the cartoon on the television. I click it off and walk toward the kitchen, and the entrance from the garage.

The lock tumbler clicks over and the door opens. Dan swings into the kitchen, glancing around, as if looking for Bart.

"He's asleep," I say, as I come around the corner.

His keys drop onto the counter next to the paper sack he sets down. He blinks his beautiful blue-green eyes, smiling his most wonderful smile, and the next thing I know, he twirls me around in the center of the kitchen. "I got the new account."

"New account?" He didn't say anything about tonight's meeting being a big deal. Only that he'd be late.

"I didn't say anything because I didn't want to jinx it. But I think you're my good luck charm and from now on I'll always tell you. Promise." For a second, he looks like he wants to kiss me.

Then again, he usually looks like he wants to kiss me. Unless I'm imagining that, too.

"Spill it, big guy." I've known Dan Quidell for six months and this is the first time I've seen him not-Bart-associated happy. Real, adult man happy, not just parent happy.

I swear he's standing his full six three-and-a-half height, with his shoulders more square and strong than I've seen before. It suits him.

I like it.

That wonderful swashbuckling smirk of his reappears and I almost sigh. I *am* like some freshman with a crush on the senior quarterback. But this is business, and we're friends, and I won't ruin it—or the evening—for Dan.

He drops his jacket on a chair in the breakfast nook and strides back to the sack on the counter, still smiling. "I got a chardonnay, a pinot noir, and a malbec. Don't know what you like." He holds out all three bottles, two in one hand and the third gripped in the other.

The wines look expensive. "I've never had malbec."

Dan glances at the back of the bottle. "Well, it says here that we will celebrate my new contract with the 'rich splendor of a smooth-but-intense, full of hints of blackberry, Argentinian grape.'"

He winks once before setting down the bottles. "You hungry? I bought cheese." He pulls out a block of equally expensive-looking cheese. "And bread." An artisan loaf follows.

It's like a picnic on the Seine, but with South American wine instead of a French Bordeaux.

"And chocolate." He's grinning like Bart now, as he lifts half a pound of chocolate perfection from the bag. The candy in his hand probably cost as much as the wine.

And he wants to share it with me. "Don't keep secrets, Dan." I'm smiling as much as he is. "Tell me!"

He pulls a couple of glasses out of a cupboard and a nice wooden cutting board from a lower cabinet. After a moment of digging, he pulls a corkscrew from a drawer. "Haven't used this in a while."

I set the cheese on the board. It's soft under its wax coating. There's French on the label. He really did go all out. "Are you going to tell me or not?" I set the bread next to it.

The cork pops from the bottle. Holding the glasses and chocolate in one of his big hands and the bottle in the other, he walks backward toward the living room, still grinning.

I drop onto the couch next to him and set the board on the coffee table. It's an old thing and kind of rickety. I get the impression he doesn't care all that much about the furnishings. Making sure Bart is comfortable seems to take priority.

Dan pours the wine. "It's with a major hotel chain. They're

upgrading seven of their buildings here in The Cities and the firm brought me on for the duration of the contract."

"That's wonderful!" He's been in business on his own for a year and he's already making good.

"There's more." He takes a sip before slicing us each some cheese and bread.

I take a sip. The wine is smooth and rich, like he described, and has a wonderful layered depth missing from the cheap stuff. "This is good."

"Try this." He holds out a piece of cheese he's set on a small bit of bread.

I lean forward and wrap my lips around the food, taking it from his fingers with my teeth.

Dan's face changes. The little boy exuberance suddenly contracts. His focus is completely on me.

It feels wonderful. He watches my mouth and raw need winks through his features again, the way it did last night.

I want to push him against the couch cushions and lay kisses across the stubble coating his jaw. To run my hands over the biceps straining the fabric of his wrinkled button-down. I want so very much to feel him thrusting into me with what I whole-heartedly suspect is a cock worthy of his big, gorgeous body.

I look away. I can't think of him that way. He is, technically, my boss, even if he's the hottest boss on the planet and a man who wants to celebrate his accomplishments with me.

"Turns out the firm doing the remodel has offices in seven other states. If they do well here, there's a good chance the contract will go national, and me with it."

"That's great!" Not hugging him takes considerable effort. I take another sip of my wine.

His smile fades as he slices us more cheese. It's as smooth as the wine, and perfect with the bread. Perfect, like Mr. Dan Quidell.

"It'll mean more time away from Bart. More late nights. And travel." He taps the edge of the cutting board, and doesn't look up.

He can't think like that. He's an excellent father.

I touch his arm, so he'll look at me. "Do you want the extended contract?"

Dan's eyes widen. He nods and his smile returns. "Yes."

"Then you work for it. Bart will be fine. He's a bright kid. Besides, it won't be long before he's in kindergarten. It'll get easier. I promise."

Dan breathes in and out and his shoulders straighten as if I just lifted off the weight of the world. "You're right." Sipping his wine, he sits back. "I worry too much."

"Yes, you do." I sit back as well. The cheese isn't slowing down the alcohol from hitting my bloodstream and a buzz starts. "I better wait before driving home." I wave my hand at my glass. "I don't drink often and I'm a lightweight."

"A lightweight with a beautiful soul." Dan laughs and hands me another piece of cheese. "With beautiful eyes to match."

I don't know what to say. He's watching me the way he was earlier. If he puts the same focus on his work, he'll be unstoppable. No wonder they chose him for the contract.

"I inherited them from my Maori grandmother."

His surprise quickly turns to admiration and he raises his glass to me. "A Norse king, at least one Highlander family, and a rumored Brazilian professional wrestler. Don't know for sure." The swashbuckling grin returns.

I laugh. "No wonder you're big and broad."

"And no wonder you're lovely." His gaze feels like he's physically touching me. I want to moan.

It's almost too much and I look away. "I had an ex tell me I look like a demon because they're so dark." I roll my eyes.

"Jerk *and* an idiot." Dan frowns again, but this time, the focus remains. If my ex was here, I suspect Dan would have punched him.

"Oh." My lips round and I think I'm blinking. Dan is wonderful. And handsome. And intense. And...

Maybe it's the wine. Or maybe he makes me a little drunk. But I lean in and kiss his cheek.

CHAPTER 6

Camille

The raw need returns to Dan's face, but this time I feel it
vibrate from the strong fingers he curls around my elbows.
He won't let me pull away.

His kiss bends me back. He pulls my bottom lip between his, then
my top, as if he's tasting me the way he tasted the wine. My body stops
everything—breathing, thinking, moving—so it can concentrate on the
feel of his mouth and the touch of his fingers.

One hand moves up and cups my shoulder, pulling me closer. The
other moves to the side of my rib cage, next to my breast. He doesn't
grope or cop a feel, but his thumb is right there, ready, perfectly posi-
tioned to sweep over my nipple.

He pulls back just enough for me to inhale, then his mouth is on
mine again, working across my lips from one corner to the other. He
tastes like the wine and a little like the cheese, but mostly I sense *Dan*,
his strength and his masculine hardness. And I want more.

A lot more. Every muscle of his body moving against mine.
Every kiss.

His forehead touches my cheek before he pulls back. "I'm sorry. I —" His face crinkles up. "It's been a while since—" His mouth closes into a thin line.

"You're worrying too much again."

The next kiss drops me onto the cushions. Dan's lips work along my jaw, down my neck, and back up to my earlobe. His breath fills my ear, warm and strong, like him.

I wiggle, curling my legs around his waist, and pull him close enough his erection rubs against my belly.

A quiet moan rolls from his chest and he pushes up, off my body. On one arm. He's planking on the couch, over me, using one arm, and looking at my face as if he's completely unconscious of his body's effort.

"*Ohhhh...* you are so strong." I run my hands over his chest, wiggling again. I won't run this time. I know he worries and I know I should too, but I have to have him. Even if it's only once. "I'm on the pill and I had all the tests after that jerk told me I had demon eyes."

Dan runs his free hand over my breasts, staring like he's never touched nipples before. Staring with utter joy and exuberance. For me.

I yank his shirt out and push my hands up under the fabric, feeling the ripples of his abs. I have to see. I *need* to see. "Take off your shirt."

He sits up before I finish the sentence, but he's not pulling off his shirt. He sits back.

"What's wrong?" Did I move too fast? Does his shoulder hurt from holding himself up? I reach for him but he catches my hand.

Dan closes his eyes as he pulls my fingers to his lips. Slowly, gently, he kisses my knuckles, his lips reverent as they explore my skin, and my body aches for him. But I see the tension in his shoulders again.

"Do you hurt? Do you—"

His next kiss silences my questions. I melt against his chest, all my thoughts folded up and set aside by his embrace. But he pulls back again.

He looks down as he unbuttons the first button of his shirt. The second button releases and I fumble with the one at the bottom, working up as he works down. His chest over his heart appears first and I see a gentle sweep of hair. Under my fingers, his abs tighten and release as he works his shirt. His skin and his muscles are shadowed, but I see the definition.

He truly is gorgeous.

With the last one, I tug at the fabric, my need to feel his skin too much. I want him *now*. I want to be on top so I can rub his abs and kiss his chest. I want to feel his large hands cup my breasts as I ride his cock.

I want, more than anything, to be with Dan not as his son's babysitter. Not as a teacher. As a woman.

He holds my wrists again. Softly, but he doesn't want me to push back his shirt. "I have scars, Camille. From the fire and the operations."

My brow crinkles and I bite my lip. How bad can they be? He has use of his shoulder and leg, even if it's diminished. "Dan, I don't care. Unless you're all furry like a werewolf. And bark. I don't like guys who bark."

He chuckles and quickly kisses me on the lips. The shirt slips off his shoulders.

I see what he's been hiding. And I see why I've never seen him in a short sleeved shirt.

The skin across his shoulder looks pock-marked, as if someone punched hole after hole into his deltoid. A big v-shaped surgical scar caps his shoulder and pulls the marks like someone had played connect-the-dot. Down his arm, the scar takes on a more hamburger-like texture just above his elbow. Along either side of the joint are two more long surgical scars.

The scars from what must have been skin grafts extend onto his chest and probably onto his back. He turns slightly, showing me his side. The grafts halt as he moves, not stretching. Dan has an inflexible quilt from his collarbone to his shoulder, down the side of his chest, and a narrow band running down his hip. The patch vanishes under his waistband and I suspect it doesn't end until it reaches his knee.

"Three pins here." He points to his shoulder and his elbow. "And two here." His finger moved to his thigh. "My friend Jason hauled me out. He ended up with pretty bad nerve damage. Ended his career, too."

The scars feel bumpy and areas don't feel quite alive. Like they're rubber. But they're not. They may block part of his life, but they're part of the man in front of me.

"Dan." I pull him to me, kissing his neck and his chin.

He responds immediately, yanking my shirt up and over my head. A deep, throaty growl rolls from him the moment he sees my black lacy bra. I don't have nice clothes, but sometimes I buy sexy underwear.

I put some on this morning, hoping. Dan does not disappoint.

He buries his face in my cleavage and makes little yipping noises, like he's a werewolf puppy. Laughing, I unhook my bra, freeing my breasts.

The other men I've been with always seemed to ignore my chest. I'm not huge, but I'm not small, either. They seemed to look at my boobs, nod, and get on to the business that interested them the most.

Not Dan. He palms my breasts and sucks a nipple into his mouth, humming the entire time. The vibration feels wonderful and I release a growl just as throaty as his.

"You are heavenly." I barely hear him. He scoots down and nips at the skin on the underside of my breasts.

I'm panting. He has me *panting* and we're still half dressed.

Maybe he'll be the one. I don't orgasm easily. Never have, no matter how much I want a guy. But Dan's incredible. The electricity is back and it's sparking across my skin every time he sweeps his fingers over my belly or his lips over my nipples.

I pull on his shoulders. "Kiss me."

The look on Dan's face is, I think, the happiest I've ever seen a man during sex. He immediately covers my mouth with his, but he's careful. Slow. And his big, strong arms curl under my back, lifting me off the couch.

He wants this to last. He *wants* to kiss me, like it's important.

"Dan..." I manage to get his name out between our lips. He's holding me off the couch, up toward his body, and I feel like I'm floating. Oh God, Dan makes me float.

It might happen. He might be the one to do it.

"I've wanted to kiss you every day for the last six months." His muscles hum under my hands.

Six months and I've wanted much more than to kiss him. I reach for the fly of his pants because I need him *right now*. Every muscle in my body shudders the way my nipples did when he curled his tongue around them. I see only the beautiful man kneeling between my legs. Hear only his steady breathing and the wonderful sound of first the button of his pants releasing, then the zipper.

But he stops and his eyes narrow. A hand cups a breast again. This time, he's not gentle. This time, he pinches. "Take off your pants."

I immediately unzip my jeans and wiggle them down my hips, revealing my matching little black lace panties. Dan growls again and before I have my jeans off my thighs, he grabs the fabric and yanks them down and off my legs. They snap against the wall next to the television, knocking one of his brother's lovely paintings, but Dan doesn't notice. He kneads my hips, his thumbs rubbing over the lace covering my pussy, his face focused and very, very intense.

A thumb sweeps under the fabric. "God damn you are *wet*."

I feel the tingle that happens before an orgasm. The fluttering and the overload like I just put something in my mouth that's more flavorful than my tongue can handle. I suck in my breath and Dan is on me, covering me completely with his big, hard body.

His next kiss takes away all the breath I just pulled in. He takes it and gives it back, his fingers curling into my hair, his hand gripping the side of my head. "My angel," he whispers.

I can't speak. Words don't form. My panties snap across the room, following my jeans, and Dan grunts, his shoulders twisting and contorting.

He's pulling off his pants.

Time all but stops. I hear the dull clinking of his zipper against his belt buckle. The fabric of his chinos wisps. The waistband of his boxers snap against his skin and another grunt pops from his throat and against the skin of my neck.

How can it take so long to get off a pair of—

He pushes into me faster and harder than I expect, his face still against my shoulder. I buck against his thrust, overwhelmed by his size. I rake my nails over his shoulders, stuttered whimpers lifting from my throat. His thrust hurts but it doesn't *hurt*. It fills. Dan fills me all the way to my spine.

He stops moving, his big body frozen like he's been encased in a block of ice. Like that slush he talked about Friday night, the cold that makes his joints hurt, suddenly solidified around his entire body.

"Did I hurt you?" His beautiful eyes show more concern than I've ever seen from a lover. He still doesn't move. "It's been—"

I kiss him the way he kissed me—deeply, our lips bruising, our breath mingling.

He moans into my mouth as he thrusts again. Just once. And stops. Again.

He lifts himself up just enough we can see each other clearly.

The men I've been with controlled their facial expressions, and right now I see Dan trying to do the same thing. I see the *I'm cool* and the *Fuck yeah* that guys think they're supposed to show. But I see something else, too. Something intense. And I can't tell if it's joy or need or thankfulness. Or maybe it's all three.

Then it's gone as if he's burying it in snow. It washes out into the *I'm cool* and damn it, I want it back. I don't know why, but I do. Because deep inside, I know it's special.

He moves deeper and I feel the same extra physical intensity I feel when a man blindfolds me during sex. That same extra enhancement of every little sound, every little flavor on a man's lips or the tip of his cock. Every extra wave of electricity through every single nerve-ending brushing the surface of my skin.

Whatever his look meant, whatever the emotion he's feeling that he thinks he needs to cover up, makes *me* feel alive.

"Dan," I whisper. I curl my fingers into the muscles of his strong backside, my nails digging in just a little. Just enough to pull his attention to his own skin. And I move my hands a little up, then a little down, in the rhythm I like.

Because I think he's the one who's going to do it. "I want you to come inside me," I rasp.

His eyes close and his mouth opens. A shiver moves through his entire body. "Holy hell," he groans. His abs lift off me as he curls his body so he can kiss my neck.

He's not pumping. He pushes in gradually, his hips swirling in a just as slow, just as careful corkscrew motion and it's almost too much. I feel the head of his cock pulse with each slide in, and the pull of the suction caused by each slide out.

It's magic.

"What are you doing to me?" I'm panting again. I haven't been with a lot of guys, but enough to get a sense of what they like. And to learn a few tricks to heighten sensation enough so I can come. But most of my ex-boyfriends just liked to fuck.

Dan stops moving again. He's deep enough not to break the internal vacuum he's created, but he's just barely inside me.

The electric feeling he caused with his gaze snaps across my abdomen, this time created by his cock.

"I..." His tongue traces my lips when he kisses me, and his teeth glide over my cheek like he wants to bite, but he doesn't move his cock deeper. "You don't like it?"

A micro-expression flashes over his face so fast I don't know if I truly see it. Maybe I'm picking up something else from his body. But I swear I see *Oh shit I'm doing it wrong.*

"This is the best sex I have ever had," I blurt out. "And you just started. Oh my God." My head tilts back and I moan. "I like it a lot."

His eyes and his mouth round into perfect circles but the new expression vanishes as fast as the one before it.

And I'm drowning in a new kiss.

A deep, wonderful, intense kiss that flows through his neck to his shoulder muscles under my gripping hands. I run my fingers down his spine, feeling the joy I feel on his lips work through his body and loosen all the knots along his backbone.

The dancing emotions resurface across his face. The skin around his eyes tightens and loosens, pulls and releases. His cheeks do the same. He's trying to control his expressions, but he's not good at it.

For a second, I wonder how much practice he's had.

He presses his forehead against my temple. "I want to be with you."

His words come out fast, their tone tightening and loosening like his expression. Like he's been fighting their escape. But they're out now, between us.

"You're with me right now." I kiss the bridge of his nose.

Deep inside my heart, in that same place where I know what his expressions mean, I hear a little voice: *I want it to always be like this.*

The rounding of his eyes and mouth happen again, until it vanishes into his next kiss. Slowly, he moves into me again. I think he's testing to see how deep he can thrust. How much of him I can take. I rock my hips and with each push I stretch a little more. And each time, a new shiver rolls through Dan.

"If I move faster, I'll..." He groans into my ear. "I haven't done this in..." Another groan. "You feel so damned *good*."

The electricity fires through me again and I think it might happen. He's not actively rubbing my clit. Just pressing his pelvis against it so excruciatingly slowly.

I need more.

"Do it." I want this to last but I want him to pound me. I want his fingers gripping my shoulder and I want to see him on the edge. I want his body hitting mine *just right*.

He stops again, but this time he looks puzzled.

"Please." I pant again. I want every single inch, every single kiss Dan has to offer. I rock my hips against his.

When he whispers my name, my world implodes. I feel the living warmth of his healthy skin, and the cool shell of his scars. I feel him watching me carefully and adjusting how he holds his hips to pull the most moans from my throat. But mostly I feel Dan letting go.

The wonderful man—the brilliant, caring man—pumping into me becomes everything, and I kiss him with all that flows through me.

I weave my fingers into his hair, holding tight as his speed increases. He fucks wonderfully—absolutely, incredibly *wonderfully*. Hard, smooth. Shifting, he rises up and slams against my clitoris.

My moan surprises me. I always need fingers, slaps. A vibrator. But the moan starts in my belly and rips with lightning speed up my spine and out through my open mouth.

I immediately realize how loud I am and I slap my hand over my mouth, quelling the sound.

But I still feel that need. I'm so close. On the edge.

Dan stops thrusting but stays buried in me, and kisses along my fingers, grinning like he won best in show.

"Don't stop." Damn it, I need everything he's got.

His next thrust pushes me up the pillow under my back.

"I don't always orgasm," I whisper.

Dan stops again. "What?"

"Dan! You're *excruciating*!" I dig my nails into his backside.

Another hard thrust slams me into the pillows. "Good excruciating or bad excruciating?" His eyes say his question is serious.

"Good... good... but I need more."

He smirks his pirate smile. "Tell me what you need."

I kiss him and he stops chuckling. His gaze stays locked to mine, his face still intense. Still focused.

"What you're doing. Don't stop." I want to come at the same time as *this* man. No one else. Him.

He rolls his hips in a way I didn't know possible when he thrusts and I want to yelp again. I want to shout and yell and make sure he knows how intense he feels. How deep he's inside me.

I tighten my lower abs and we arch together; clench together. Dan responds with a shudder and another moan, and a deeper, harder thrust.

His back tightens under my palms. His abs curl and his arms quake. He presses his face against my neck, his mouth locked against my skin, and I feel his deep baritone more than hear it. His cock pulses sharply and I feel it through my hips.

"I..." he whispers. "*Oh*..."

I feel his frenzy ebbing away as his lips dance over mine. His body's relaxing.

"Could you..." I wiggle under him. "I need a little..."

Dan grabs my hips as he sits up, keeping my pussy against his pelvis and his cock deep inside me.

The pad of his thumb taps around my opening. He's looking for my clit.

When he finds it, my back arches.

"There?" Each new rub carries more pressure. "Tell me when it's right." He watches my pussy—watches his not-yet soft cock glide slowly in and out with each of twirl of his thumb—like he's looking at the most beautiful work of art in the world.

His look alone is enough. The muscles of my pelvis and my belly contract. And another loud moan rips from my throat.

"*Fuck.*" Dan falls on top of me. He manages to keep his thumb between us somehow.

Another wave of the orgasm rocks up my spine.

"That work?" he asks.

"Ummm...." I can't get out an answer. Not as words.

He tries to move off me but I keep him where he is.

I kiss his temple. The shoulders of the beautiful man kissing my neck feel calm under my fingers. The tension that had been under my hands has been replaced by an easy looseness.

I kiss his forehead, holding onto this incredible man.

More happiness shows in Dan's eyes than I've ever seen from a man after sex. More calm. And, I think, joy. His kisses show it too, as his lips travel over my chin and jaw, down the side of my neck, onto my shoulder. He's so gentle.

I release my legs' hold around his hips and scoot up under him, moving my back against the arm of the couch. His kisses move down to my collarbone as I wiggle, until he dips his head and kisses my nipples, first the left, then the right.

"Today is a good day." His lips next to my ear feel as warm and soft as they were against my nipples. "One very fine day, indeed."

"Hmmm...." Maybe if I wiggle enough, he won't stop the kisses. Or the tickle strokes he's brushing across my bellybutton. "Yes, one *very* good day."

Dan chuckles but holds himself off me again, planking on the couch as he looks down at my face.

He doesn't speak. His face says it all even though, once again, he's trying to cover it up with the *I'm cool* expression. I see joy and just the right amount of pride. But I also see worry.

"How do we handle this?" he says.

All I want is to take his hand and walk up the stairs to his bed. To sleep for the rest of the night against his side and climb on his cock the moment the sun peeks over the horizon. But he had to ask that question and reality roars back into our world.

And it's not just us anymore.

CHAPTER 7

Daniel

I don't want to move. Seven years with my ex-wife—high school through her pretending to go to college up until my injury—and she never, not once, reacted to me the way Camille does. Not once did she tell me what she needed. Not once did she curl around me the way my angel curls around me now. Not once.

Not once since my injury have I shown a woman my scars. Not any of the three whole dates I've been on. None of them made me feel the way Camille makes me feel.

The way she's made me feel since the strawberry picking field trip. The way I've felt every morning when she greets us at the Community Center and every evening when I pick up Bart.

Not once while I was with my ex, Lori, did I realize wanting to hold a woman, wanting to be close and to kiss and to stay in her—to have her *want* me to stay inside her—was how it should be. Like this. Like it is right now.

With the most beautiful woman I've ever met, much less touched. Who didn't push me away because of how my skin feels. Who, I am pretty sure, likes what I have to offer.

Lori never looked happy during sex. Camille's fingers rub circles across my shoulders and I feel better than I have since the moment I first held Bart. Better maybe, because she'll hold Bart, too.

She kisses my forehead and I don't want this to end. Not tonight. Not tomorrow. I want to wake up with her. To see her in the sun. To love her again like this.

I kiss along her cheekbone, to the bridge of her nose. "How do we handle this?" I whisper. I want her here, with me. I want her here this weekend, when my family comes to celebrate Bart's birthday. *Let me hold your hand while my son blows out his candles*, I think.

Camille presses on my shoulders and I flip onto my back on the couch, taking her with me, my feet propped up on the arm and my angel straddling my hips. She gazes down with her soulful eyes when I pull the throw off the back of the couch and wrap it around her shoulders.

"You've been alone since the accident?" She sweeps a finger across my chest, stopping at the edge of my scars.

I frown. I don't really want to talk about it. What I'd like to do is to put an end to my stunted love life.

So I distract her instead. "You wanna do it again?" I accent my words with a small thrust up with my still-firm cock. She says go and I'll go.

Maybe I shouldn't have shut down this part of my life. But when Bart was a baby, it seemed like the best thing to do. No complications. No explanations about the accident. No pity.

No woman rolling over when we're done, like I don't matter.

Maybe Camille will stay tonight. Maybe she'll sleep next to me, instead of on the far edge of the bed.

I sit up but keep her straddling my lap. The need to distract her from her questions is suddenly subsumed by my own set of questions. About what this means. About "handling" this. About the look of teacherly concern she's giving me right now.

And suddenly I'm wondering if she feels the same strength of connection I feel.

"Hmmmm." But she's biting her lip like she wants to stay. Her hips sway just a little against mine.

I kiss her. It's all I can do. She looks at me with her teacher face and all I want to do is replace it with the ecstasy I saw while we made love. The ecstasy I gave her, and she gave me.

Because it's there. Damn it, it was there.

She sighs and tucks her head into the crook of my neck. Her fingers dance over my scars, touching but not probing. She's careful. Considerate. "How do you feel?" she asks.

Wonderful, I think. But I choose my words carefully. "Half a year of slowly getting to know you and it finally happened." I feel my smile work through all my face—my cheeks and my eyes. My mouth. She's incredibly beautiful.

She blinks. A little shiver runs through her body. And I remember what I said: *I want to be with you.*

I do. But I dance back from the edge of these emotions because I know it's too early to admit they're there, much less talk about them.

"You sound like you planned this." She's grinning. I feel her cheek tighten where she presses her face against my neck.

Plan isn't the right word. Hoped for. Wished would happen. Wanted oh so very much but didn't think possible because, mostly, of that horde of zombie nags inside my head. "I resigned myself to waiting until Bart started kindergarten before asking you out."

I hadn't realized how much I missed having a woman pressed against me. How good soft hips and breasts feel as they rub across the skin of my chest and thighs. How nice a woman smells. Or how calming the sound of her breathing is.

Now I have the loveliest, most caring angel I know caressing my arms with her fingers and I need to be careful or I'll lose the brilliant bit of luck I've got.

So I know I probably shouldn't ask. I probably should see if Tom will watch Bart for a night and ask Camille on a real date. But she's here and she's beyond beautiful. She's wrapped around me and I do not want to be without her. "Stay tonight."

"Oh, Dan," she whispers. For a glorious moment, her arms tighten around my chest, but she pulls away. And sits up. "It's Monday."

"Uh-huh." I grin, palming her sweet breast. It's exactly the right size to hold in one hand and her nipples are little perfect buds. "You are incredible. Blazing hot kind of incredible."

Camille chuckles and looks away, over the back of the couch. "How is this going to affect Bart?"

Nothing would make my son happier than to see his dad with the woman he's taken a liking to. But I don't say it. I don't say *Stay and we'll all talk about it tomorrow over breakfast.*

"I need to be careful." She looks around like she's trying to find her clothes.

Careful? I drop my legs over the side of the couch when she scoots off my lap. "Why?"

She strokes my chest and her fingertips trail over the top of my abs. Her tongue flicks out to wet her lips as if she's considering licking my midsection. I almost flip her on her back again.

"With work. This, with us, isn't against the rules, but I think it's frowned on." Her forehead crinkles. "Some of the other teachers don't seem to like that I'm... sitting for you."

My calm turns to indignation. Why the fuck should they care? Why the fuck should *she* care? It's not like it's interfering with her job. But then I remember: She's new. And not making much. And needs to pay school loans.

My first inclination is to say *Quit. Live with us and quit your job and be here for Bart. And me.* But then I realize what it is that I'm thinking and how caveman it is.

I dance back from this set of emotions too and don't say anything at all.

"I want Bart to be okay," she whispers.

I pull her to my chest and kiss her forehead. My body is screaming *protect* while my brain whirls around in a storm of *what-ifs.* What if she gets fired? What if something goes wrong and Bart can't handle it? What if *I* can't handle it?

"I need to be at work at seven and I don't have a toothbrush here, much less clothes." But she's not moving away.

I have to believe that for once, a part of my life isn't going to degenerate into taking out one lumbering undead must-do after another. That my to-do, must-fight-off unending list of zombies won't invade here, with her.

Monsters that don't die. Monsters that stalk my family with little frowns and admonishments. With the slow wag of a finger because I can't possibly be a good dad and a good lover at the same time. I can't be a man because there's too much that must be done and I don't have the time.

I nod. And I let go.

I don't want to. I just had the best sex of my life with a woman who told me it was good for her too and now we're dancing around emotions and consequences like we made love inside a minefield.

Why the hell can't it be simple for once?

"I think," she says, her face taking on her teacher look again, "that being with you is the best place I can be." She smiles.

For a second, the what-ifs look friendly. Camille, still naked and still beautiful, kisses my chin. "When do you need me next?"

I snort. "Right now." She needs to know the truth of how much having her here means to me, even if reality is crashing down around us. And boxing me in. Again.

She throws me a mock stern look. "To bring home Bart, silly."

She said *bring home*, like she thinks of here as her home. I stroke her shoulder, feeling the silky smoothness of her skin. "Tomorrow." I'll be done by four-thirty and can pick him up early, but I want her here.

"Okay." She kisses me again. "I'll see you in the morning?"

I nod.

"We'll figure it out." She stands up. "I'll bring him home at five and we'll see you soon after?" She's picking up her panties and bra and I want to snatch them from her hands. And carry her upstairs.

I nod instead.

She dresses and we stand together in front of my door, her arms around my waist and mine around hers. She smells sweet and faintly like fruit, and like sex.

And I feel a new herd of zombies creeping up on me—the divorced dad monsters. My brain tosses around every manner of problem it can think of and I see momentary blips of the courtroom. Legal documents. Of car payments and school registration forms.

Why do these things have to invade? Why can't Camille stay and stroke away my tension and let me do the same for her? I'm beginning to wonder if such a thing is possible. Or feasible, no matter how strong the love is.

Camille presses against me and I know, for sure, the strength of what I am feeling. I've been here before. I know. The tingling in my fingers. The very strong desire to touch her all the time. To stroke her skin and ask about her day. The desire to pick her up and set her within the circle of my home.

But I'm not my brother Tom who had nothing to lose by taking a chance and moving a woman into his house right out of the gate. And the woman in my arms has much to lose as well.

Her kiss silences all the real world thoughts, if only for the moment. Her lips feel warm and soft. I want to taste more, to touch more. To see every inch of her skin and to completely map her body. And all her responses.

But she's going home.

"I'll see you in the morning," she says against my lips.

"Tomorrow."

And she's off, gone, leaving me alone in the house I built. I cork the wine and put away the cheese. Standing in the kitchen, alone, I stare at the chocolate in my hand.

She went back to her place. We had sex and she left me alone. But, damn it, I understand why.

My hand tightens around the candy. Understanding doesn't mean I have to like it.

It's not going to happen again.

CHAPTER 8

Camille

This morning, when Dan walks through the Community
Center's doors, he's holding Bart's hand. His son skips along
with his backpack over his shoulders, trying to keep up, but
his daddy is watching the other teachers, not him. Or me.

Dan's stride is tense and borderline belligerent the way I'd expect a
man who's about to get into a fight to walk. He wears a light blue
button down shirt today, one that's just as wrinkled and uncomfortable
looking as all his clothes.

His shoes slap hard against the Center's granite tiles and the sound
stops when I walk over. His focus immediately snaps to me and his
face softens. "Hi." A small smile lights up his face.

Bart pulls on his hand. He seems happy this morning, bright-eyed
and energetic. He's going to be talkative, for sure. "Bye, Daddy." He
wants to run off to Sandy's room.

Dan kneels down. "You be good today. Okay, little man?"

Bart nods. "I will!" Then he's off, into Sandy's room, to his cubby.

I step forward a little, so I can see Bart as he hangs his pack on his hook. When I see Sandy acknowledge him, she waves, and I turn back to Dan.

He's less than a foot from me and his gaze is steady on my chest.

"Dan!" I step back, glancing around.

No one seems to have noticed. Dan's bluster is back, but it's not aimed at me. It's clearly aimed outward, toward the world.

"Please don't." I step back again. "We talked about this. We need to be careful. At least for now. Okay?"

He blinks when he looks at my face. His hand twitches as if he wants to take mine, and he frowns. "I don't like it." His lower lip wiggles and I very clearly see where Bart gets his adorable pout.

Chuckling, I would like to take his hand too, but he can't do this. Glancing around again, seeing that it is all clear, I step closer—but not too close—and lower my voice. "You're as spoiled as your son, you know that? And just as cute."

His shoulders relax. The brightness of his smile surprises me. He looks as happy as he did last night, after he told me his good news. And after we had sex.

Absolutely amazing sex. I feel the need to press my thighs together, but I can't do that in the Community Center lobby. And I cannot, at all, be flirting with a parent.

Or have a parent flirt with me.

Still, part of me is kicking myself for leaving. But there are steps to a relationship. And he has a son, so this isn't just about us.

"I want to do this right." I blurt it out the way I swear I blurt out half my words around him. What is he doing to me to make me act this way? It's like my subconscious absolutely *has* to tell him things my conscientious, logical brain thinks I shouldn't. At least not yet.

Dan's lips part but he presses them together as if his logical brain just caught something *he* shouldn't say. Yet.

"It's pizza night tonight." He glances around and stuffs his hands in his pockets. "I downloaded that new kid's movie. The one that's supposed to be funny. Do you want to stay for dinner and watch a little of it with us?"

It's not a date, but I think he's trying. "Are you asking me on a family fun night, Daniel Quidell?"

The grin he gives me is just as swashbuckling and just as devastating as any I've seen from him and I almost melt right here in the lobby. In front of everyone. I want to take his hand and drag him off to the supply closet and kiss my job goodbye for a brilliant quickie with my gorgeous new boyfriend.

Dan nods affirmative, but he suddenly stands up straight. One of the other teachers is watching us from her doorway. Mary Beth. She's not much older than me, and pretty, and had been the most vocal about having Dan take off his shirt during the strawberry picking fieldtrip.

She and I don't get along, though we're cordial. But now I'm wondering. "It'll be good for you to pick him up tonight." We shouldn't be seen leaving at the same time.

Dan nods and points at the door. "Bye, Ms. Frasier," he says loudly, and turns away.

I can't help but watch his perfect backside as he walks toward the door, knowing full well the other teachers can't either, and suddenly I understand Dan's antagonism.

Slowly, I breathe in and out, counting.

There has to be a better way to handle this. Fighting the world won't work. The world always wins.

❦

BART TELLS ME IN FULL DETAIL ABOUT HIS FAVORITE CHARACTER IN the movie and how Daddy lets him watch half an hour before he has to get ready for bed and how he's going to watch the whole movie on Friday because he doesn't have to take a bath unless he's stinky.

He's been monopolizing my time since I arrived, holding my hand as he takes me around the living room to show me the little scenes he built with his action figures. They all seem to be connected somehow, the scenes, but I'm not quite sure how. He piled all sorts of similar toys at each spot—blocks and markers, a couple of toy cars, and at one, an apple he must have taken from the refrigerator.

"The world needs red!" Bart does a brilliant superhero pose before picking up his favorite figure and running into the kitchen.

So he's saving the colors from the bad guys. I shake my head, knowing I shouldn't be surprised at what Bart comes up with. But sometimes he understands a lot more than he should at his age.

I sip my malbec, feeling it warm my throat, happy that Dan saved the rest of the bottle, as I follow Bart back into the kitchen.

"I like pepperoni." He says it with great certainty, like a young man who has sampled many pizzas and found all other meat and cheese combinations wanting.

I kneel and lean close as if sharing a valuable state secret. "I like pepperoni, too."

Bart presses his fists into his hips and looks up at his father. "I *told* you she would like *my* favorite *better*."

"Bart!" Dan frowns at his boy. "Be polite."

Bart frowns right back at his father and stalks off toward the living room and the line of action figures he set up on the coffee table. He mutters to each in turn, but I can't make out what he's saying.

"I don't know what's gotten into him." Dan watches his son as wipes his hands on a kitchen towel. Absently, he rubs his neck. It must hurt tonight. The oven timer beeps and he nods over his shoulder. "Pizza's ready."

He walks away to prep our dinner before I have a chance to rub away his pain. Out in the living room, Bart bangs his toys on the table, and I'm pretty sure that the Quidell men are fighting over me. But how did Bart figure it out?

I step into the kitchen, where he can't see me. "Did you say something about us to Bart?" I wish Dan had waited until we figured out a game plan.

Dan sets the pizza on top of the stove. "No." His lips bunch up as he gets out a cutter.

I set down my wine. "He's too perceptive for his own good."

Dan snorts. "Just like Rob."

Dan's youngest brother, the one in grad school. From the look on Dan's face, I suspect being "just like Rob" isn't necessarily a good thing.

"Bart is still a little kid, Dan. Which means he doesn't have the vocabulary to express how he feels." Out in the living room, Bart tosses one of his action figures onto the couch. "And I think he doesn't understand sharing me with you. Or you with me. Life has its silos, when you are four."

Dan won't look at me. He doesn't say anything, either. He just kisses my temple and steps out where Bart can see him. "Dinner, little man!"

Bart walks toward us, an action figure in each hand, talking to his make-believe friends more than paying attention to his father.

Dan squats so he's at eye level with his son. He balances on the tips of his toes, his arms resting on his thighs, like he's a superhero watching over a city from the edge of a rooftop.

"Doctor Bartman," he says, one eyebrow cocked. He steeples his hands even though he's still squatting. Dan's doing a Minion One yoga pose.

I don't know why, but it warms my heart. And other parts of my body. He's so incredibly good with Bart. "That hurt your leg?" But he shouldn't be doing it if it hurts.

"Stretches my hips." Dan winks at me.

He's flirting *and* playing with his son. Damn, the man is amazing.

Bart saunters up, his chin up like a good superhero. "Yes?" He presses his fists into his waist.

"There's a grocery bag on the floor next to the shoes." Dan points toward the front door. "Will you get it, please? Before we eat."

Bart's eyes narrow. "Why?"

"Because I got you something special today."

Bart drops his action figures into his daddy's hands and bursts back toward the door as fast as his almost-five-year-old legs will carry him.

"No running in the house!" Dan yells, but he's smiling. When he stands, he runs his hand over the back of his head. "It's silly stuff. I found them in the Christmas clearance bin." His swashbuckling grin reappears.

"What did you get?" I'm as bad as Bart. But Dan's enthusiasm is contagious.

He just grins some more and waits for Bart to reappear.

Bart fishes around inside the plastic and I hear little jingles like he's got a small Santa in there. His face crinkles up when he sees what his fingers found. "Daddy!"

Bart pulls a pair of superhero-covered slipper-socks from the bag. White ones with the knitted-in face of Bart's current favorite hero all over them. Little high bell sounds twinkle off their pointy toes.

Dan bought superhero elf socks.

I try to stifle my laugh but end up almost snorting wine out my nose. Full-bodied South American grapes aren't all that comfortable in the sinuses. I set my glass on the kitchen counter.

Dan's obviously trying not to laugh too, but one escapes when he points at the bag. "Show Camille what else is in there."

Bart frowns and pulls out another pair of superhero elf socks. The second pair is bright green with a different hero face all over them, and are much bigger.

Big enough for Dan. Bart looks shocked.

I can't hold the laughter anymore. I double over, giggling uncontrollably.

"Show her the other pair."

Bart dutifully pulls out the last pair. They're bright red and smaller than Dan's, but bigger than Bart's.

"Are those for me?" Dan bought me hero elf socks, too?

Both Dan and Bart smile the most wonderful, beautiful smiles.

"Does that mean I'm Minion Two?" I'm a Minion.

And it feels better than when I graduated from college. Or when I got my first job. It's as good as the feeling I had after seeing Dan's relief when I offered him help with Bart. It's as good as every hug from every kid at the Community Center.

Bart scratches his head, frowning. "Uncle Tommy is Minion Two." Then he stands up straight and holds out the socks to me. "You will be Minion Two and Uncle Tommy will be Minion Two-Two!"

Dan and I both back into the kitchen counters when we double over laughing.

"Why Two-Two, buddy?" Dan's rubbing at his eye, he's laughing so hard.

"Because I can't take away his job. Uncle Tommy will be sad." Bart sets the jingling heap of socks on the table.

I lean against Dan and press my ear against his big, broad shoulder. He wraps his arm around me, still laughing. Still watching Bart more than me. It's an unconscious gesture and it feels just as right as being Minion Two.

"We should eat before the pizza gets cold." Moving away takes a lot of effort. I'd stay next to him all night like this, if I could.

Which I can. And I think, tonight, maybe I will.

We eat, and Bart seems happy. He chews his pepperoni. After he's in his pajamas and it's time to watch the movie, he plops between us, alternating leaning against Dan and me. By the time we get a half hour into watching the dancing computer-generated animals and their musical numbers, he's already fast asleep against my side, his arm around my waist and his head against my breast.

Dan carries him up to his bed and he hugs his dad the entire way. When I tuck him in, he mumbles something about his birthday and becoming a big boy.

I want to pull him to me and hug him tight. But I place my hand on his back instead, letting this little man sleep.

Dan, holding a handful of action figures, watches me from the door. Quietly, he sets each small protector of the city and the world in a line on Bart's table and they throw a long set of hero shadows onto Bart's pillow.

We close down his door. Dan touches my hand, my elbow, my cheek. We stand in the open space between his son's bedroom door and his own.

The yellow glow of the street light outside filters in through the window over his front door that's visible from the top of the stairs. A long line of bright light falls over each step, and across Dan's feet. Downstairs, the appliances hum. Outside, a neighbor slams a car door. The house smells like pizza and suburbia and...

...and family.

It frightens me. Just a little bit. It feels like the extra stretch—the extra strain—when I stretch my arms too far apart. Like two parts of me want to go in completely different directions.

I open my eyes. Next to me, standing in the open space between his boy's bedroom and his own, is the most luscious man I have ever seen.

Or touched. I feel naughty, looking at the huge, hard male in front of me and thinking about how damned good he feels. How tense and utterly fuckable he is. Because there's a lot more to Dan Quidell than how well he uses his body.

I'm against Dan's broad chest, holding tight, feeling his strength encircle me. How are we going to deal with work and making sure Bart is okay? Dan feels real under my arms—warm and strong and everything I want. He smells like cooking and a long day and I know his shoulder hurts.

All I want to do is to release the pain in his muscles. "I don't want to think about the world or how we—"

His kiss pulls all my worries from my body. He's here—I'm here, with him, in his home. It feels right. I take his hand. And I lead him toward his bedroom.

It's cleaner than I expected, and larger. A king-size bed waits opposite a big window covered with black-out curtains. His dresser lacks the typical man-clutter of combs and wallets and deodorant, though he's got a fabric-covered bin full of random stuff sitting on the floor next to his closet and a basket of what looks like clean clothes. The bed looks freshly made, like he changed the sheets this morning.

Grinning, I stand on my toes to kiss the stubble covering his cheek. "You're wonderful, you know that? Truly wonderful."

The happiness brightening his face reminds me of Bart's joy when he's proud of a drawing. He'll hold it up, his body erect, and loudly declare "Look what I made!"

I have the feeling no one has ever thanked Dan for the little things. For his steady work and his caring.

"I bought jo-jo oil. Or I think it's called jo-jo oil. The clerk at the health food store said it was the best for scars." Dan points at the dresser top. "She said ylang ylang is good too. It smells nice and it reminded me of you, so I bought candles."

Jojoba oil and aromatherapy candles. I pick up one of the pillars and breathe in deeply. The rich, almost jasmine-like scent fills my senses. Ylang ylang carries deep notes that make me hungry, like I smell the preparations of a sweet feast. Not the food itself, but the promise of food. I glance at Dan. And the promise of a great tactile feast.

His skin is a wonder. Yes, his scars pull and rub, but what isn't damaged is healthy and warm and when I touch, I want to touch all of him. I want to taste the saltiness of his stubble and feel the softness of his chest hair. I want to run my fingers over his biceps and watch his face slacken because it makes him feel so, so good.

"Sit down." I motion to the edge of the bed. "And take off the shirt, gorgeous."

Dan curls an arm around my waist and pulls me toward him as he sits. Hands roaming, he stares at my breasts as he strokes my back, my hips, my waist. "Hmmm..." A kiss lands over my heart. "*You're* gorgeous."

"If I'm going to massage your shoulder, you'll need let go of me so I can reach the oil." But I don't want him to let go. I don't ever want him to let go.

"Don't want to." He buries his face in my cleavage. "Have woman."

I can't help but laugh. He's grinning against my breastbone and just knowing he feels good enough to crack jokes brings all my joy to the surface. "Shirt off, man. I don't want your neck locking up during sex and having you fall on top of me. You're *huge* and weigh what? Two-twenty?"

"Two-twenty-eight. I'm down from my full carry-equipment-up-three-flights-of-stairs days."

I moan and my fingers grip his huge arms tighter than I mean to as memories of him holding himself up over me fill my mind's eye.

Dan's eyebrow lifts. "You like?"

I nod, grinning the way he was earlier, like a little kid who just received the best toy *ever*.

"That look is all the motivation a man needs to work out." His kiss steals all my breath.

But he's going to wait because I know his shoulder still hurts.

So I pull away.

CHAPTER 9

Daniel

I light the candles before stripping off my shirt. Her gaze lands on my shoulder scar and for a second I have to fight the need to pull the shirt back on.

But she strokes her hand over my collarbone. "Looks like you might have a knot here." A finger presses on a spot at the base of my neck.

The pressure she applies isn't all that much but I already feel the difference radiating down my arm. "I'm keeping you." Damn it, I am too. She doesn't care about the scars and her touch is magic. And she's the best thing to ever happen to Bart.

When she steps back, I'm entranced by her smile. If I have to beg to get her to stay tonight, I will. I'll drop onto my knees and wrap my arms around her waist and beg like a child.

Though that's probably not a good idea. I smirk, trying not to look too much like a dumbass.

Camille shakes her head. "Now I know where your boy gets his charm."

My smirk turns to a grin and she chuckles as she closes her eyes, breathing in the scent of the candles. I think I made a good choice. She seems to like them. Her body's tension melts away with each deep breath. The candles are a natural beeswax color and they spread a golden glow over my bedroom and over the beautiful woman standing at the foot of my bed.

Just looking at her makes me happy. Seeing the curves of her breasts and hips, and the lines of her jaw and arms.

I reach for her again but she steps back, watching my face, and strips off her blouse and jeans. The bra and panties match again. Some dark red shade. Not that I notice—how they hug the sweep of her hips and push together her breasts is all I care about.

I'm the man who gets to touch the woman in front of me. To kiss and lick and roll her nipples between my tongue and the roof of my mouth. Because she picked me. The angel picked scarred-up old *me*.

It's been too long since I've felt this way. Too long since sex was something available, much less allowed. Camille watches, her face showing the same hunger for me as I feel for her and damn it, it makes me want to throw her down and fuck her blind.

The massage can wait. My cock didn't ease into hardness tonight— it decided the moment Camille pulled me into the bedroom that it wanted her as much as the rest of my body. The pressure from my fly rubs and my entire length aches.

Freeing myself from my trousers and boxers takes a moment and when I pull them off, my cock springs against my lower abs, fully at attention and waiting impatiently for Camille's caresses.

She sighs as she looks me up and down. "Why did I wait six months to kiss you?"

This time when I grab for her waist, she dances out of my grasp and scoops the oil off the dresser. Kneeling on the bed, she points and I sit again. The oil spreads over her palms and she rubs her hands together, warming before she caresses. It smells slightly sweet, like it has a hint of the candles to it.

Leaning back, I press my hips and cock up and pout at her over my shoulder. "I need a massage all over, Ms. Frasier."

Camille responds by nipping the top of my ear. Her teeth flick over my skin, her tongue just touching, and I shiver.

I didn't know the attentions of a woman could be like this. Lori and I started dating young and I never wandered. And after...

Camille's hands move across my shoulders as she nips and the oil between her palms glides like silk over my skin.

...After, I thought no woman would want to take a chance with me. And I put parts of my soul—and my mind and body—in the freezer, thinking I'd never need them again.

Camille's angelic fire is thawing me out.

She rubs gently at first, stroking her hand over the scars, but her fingers probe. She's looking for knots. When she finds one, her thumb presses in and down, forcing the muscle to lengthen along its axis.

Once again, my entire back lets go. I groan, the tingle working down my arms to my fingers, and I turn around on the edge of the bed. Her luscious breasts are right there. Right in front of me, and I yank on her just-covering-her-nipples bra, releasing what I want most.

Camille's head drops back as I tongue first her left nipple, then her right.

"Dan," she breathes, weaving her fingers into my hair.

The desire in her voice makes me harder. So hard my cock aches more than my muscles or my skin. More than the pins in my bones. It pulses to my spine and overrides all the bad pain with good.

I hook my thumbs into her panties and yank them down her thighs where she kneels. I could throw her onto her back and pull them off, but she's insanely sexy with her bra pushed off her nipples and her panties around her knees. Gorgeous and intense.

I drop flat on my back, pausing to take in the splendor of the underside of her breasts. Slowly, she unhooks her bra. Her breasts fall free of the cups, two perfect round wonders of sweet, tender softness, each capped by nipples hard and waiting. For me. For my mouth.

I see the line of her ribcage from this vantage point, and the smooth curve of her belly. Her hips sweep out in perfect proportion to her breasts and I think, for a moment, that I understand what "art" is. What "beauty" means. I'm looking at the underside of its breasts.

She wiggles slightly, inching the panties lower, but I reach over my head and grip her hips. I stroke my thumbs over her hipbones, feeling the smoothness of her body. Slowly, I pull her across the bed. She slides on the sheets, her panties rolling down off her thighs, under her knees and shins. The sheets and the lace crinkle. The sound blends with the popping of the candles on the dresser.

Flickering candle flames aren't the only things blazing right now. So is my woman.

"I want to have sex with you every day." She sounds dreamy. "Every *hour*." She moans as she runs her hands over my arms.

All I know is the sweet, female musk of her pussy. I let go of her hip with one hand. My fingers need to find her clit so I can make her come like I did last night. Now.

She bucks against my hand, slick and pink. Flawless. I lick.

The moan accompanying her full-body shudder makes me wonder if she did, in fact, just come.

Holy shit, I think. She said sometimes it's difficult for her. But the way she responds makes me think I'm doing something right.

I want to fuck her right now. Flip her over and fuck her and make her come while I'm deep inside her. I want to feel her pussy contracting around my shaft. To see her face slack with pleasure.

She drops forward. Her mouth descends onto my cock and the next thing I know I'm pressing against the back of her throat.

I groan into her pussy when she forms a tight seal around my shaft. Her head moves up and down as she vacuums. One of her hands cups my balls as the other holds tight to my hip. I try not to thrust. I try to relax and twirl her clit with my tongue as she works me. But the hand on my hip pulls up each time she takes me deep.

I groan again as I flick my tongue across and around her clit—and Camille quakes as my baritone moves across her pussy. I hum. She sucks and shivers. God, my *voice* gets her off.

Another deep pull on my cock makes *me* shiver. I need to be in her. Now.

I push her up and her mouth comes off my cock with an audible pop. She sits up, still riding my face, and I lick one more time before flipping over fast.

"Did it happen?" I need to know. Damn, this is amazing.

Her tongue traces her lips. "Yes," she breathes, her eyes closing. "God, Dan, *yes*."

I throw her down on the pillows and yank on her hips as she drops. Her ass is on my thighs before she hits, her legs spread and pussy open, her mouth slack.

"Do it hard like you did it last night. Pound me." She pinches her nipples, rubbing her breasts, urging me to fuck her.

I scoop my strong arm under her hips and pull her toward me as I guide my cock into her opening with my other. I'm in, deep, and I feel her clench around me. She's tight and hot and slick. I pull almost all the way out before thrusting again.

"Is it always going to be this good?" I'm barely able to ask the question.

A guttural moan erupts from Camille when I bottom out, hitting her deepest parts, and I can't go deeper.

"Hold my wrists." She lifts her arms and crosses her hands in front of her face, the insides of her wrists pressing together.

I'll have to let go of her hips. But she asked.

I wrap my hand around the top of her clasped fingers. Leaning a little forward, I hold her ass on my thighs with my other hand, and continue to pound into her.

"Lower. Around my wrists. Squeeze." Her mouth is open and she's breathing hard.

Damn it, I don't want to have to think about balancing while I'm fucking.

I must have made a face because she pulls back her hands and pinches her nipples again. "Keep doing what you're doing." It bursts out of her fast, between two thrusts. "*Ah...*"

I can't talk any more. But I can finger her while I pound her senseless. Carefully, I find what I want, and jitter the pad of my thumb against her clit.

A loud, high-pitched yelp rolls out of her throat.

Fuck yeah, I think. I lean forward and take my weight on my arms. I want to *feel* her yell. My kiss quells the next yelp and Camille laughs against my mouth.

I pound her hard. She rocks with me, clenching her abs as I slide in and out, tightening her already unbelievable pussy. My balls slap against her ass and my whole body feels just as heavy and tender.

My orgasm is like the rush after the sting of a pinch or the pulling off of a bandage. Every nerve in my body makes a brilliant cocktail of endorphins and chemicals and fires a lightning storm through my senses. I *hear* my cock releasing. I swear I'm bathed in fire.

She locks her legs around my waist and refuses to let me move off her, even though I weigh two-twenty-eight. I'm still inside her and it's wonderful. Beautiful. My Camille smiles and strokes my cheek and, I think, for the first time since the accident, I fully relax.

"You seem happy." Camille kisses my shoulder. "Feel better?"

She lets go enough I can roll off, but I take her with me, pulling her close, keeping her tight against my body. Her forehead feels warm against my neck, but her fingers feel cool when she runs them through my chest hair.

I pull her hand to my lips and gently kiss each of her knuckles, one at a time. "A lot better."

I feel her smile against my skin.

"Did you come a second time when you yelled?" I want her to feel as good as she makes me feel. Better, if I can.

"Almost." She twirls her fingers in my chest hair. "You are amazing."

Part of me can't help but feel a little miffed. I don't have practice with women other than my ex and Camille but I should be better than "almost." And what kind of sex is she having if "almost" is "amazing?"

"I'll do better next time." I pull the sheet and blanket up and cuddle with her, inside the warmth.

Camille chuckles but doesn't say anything.

"Will you stay?" I whisper. She'll need to go to work in the morning but I have to ask. "I'll set the alarm early. We'll eat toaster pastries and all go to the Community Center together."

Camille smiles and gently kisses my lips. "Toaster pastries?"

I'm about ready to do the begging I know I shouldn't. "Bart will be okay. We have all week to talk about it. Rob flies in Thursday night and Bart's party is Sunday. He'll be fine by then."

My arms tighten around her even though I should probably give her space, but I can't. "You taking an interest in teaching him, and helping us, and..." I close my eyes.

I feel Camille push up on her elbow. She doesn't say anything.

When I open my eyes, she's watching me carefully. Like I'm going to break. "I think you've been alone too long," she whispers.

Shit, flits through my head. What am I doing? Am I scaring her? For the first time in my life I'm in a good relationship and all I want is to make it real.

"Dan." Camille kisses me as gently as I had kissed her hand. "I brought my toothbrush."

She's staying. She's going to sleep here, with me. I'm going to wake up tomorrow and she's going to be here and we'll get it all squared away with Bart.

I touch her face. I don't remember moving my hand but she's kissing my palm and I'm happier than I should be.

"Sometimes," she says as she lays her head on my shoulder again, "I wonder about your ex. About how she treated you and Bart." She looks up again. "I read the file."

I close my eyes again. My calm starts to drain away and the zombies start massing. Lori is the last person I want to talk about.

"It's okay." Camille kisses my cheek. "I'm sorry I said anything."

"No, no." I roll on my side and force away the unease. That part of my life is done. Lori's gone and she's never coming back. "I'd rather talk about you."

Camille and I are flush against each other, chest to chest, belly to belly. She scoots closer and wiggles a leg between mine. It's beautiful and warm and better than any time with my ex.

Every time with my ex.

Camille kisses my chest. "You're going to be like this all the time, aren't you? Asking me to stay."

Until you move in, I think. "Uh-huh."

"Because you want wake-up sex. Admit it." She strokes my chest again.

I feel how much Camille cares in how she strokes my arm. In how she cuddles against me. She's perfect and I don't think before I open my mouth. I don't censor myself or hold it back because this is right. I hold her close and kiss her hair and what I feel rolls out of my mouth. "Are you promising me a morning of passion with the woman I love?"

Camille stiffens. Right here, right now, in my arms, she stiffens like she's gone cold. Her heart speeds up and pounds against my chest and she's not looking at me. Not doing anything.

And I feel the slush return to my veins. I'm cold again and I can't move fast enough to get away from the zombies.

"Dan..."

Why did I open my mouth? It slipped out.

"Dan!" She kisses me. Not the sexy, horny kisses of earlier. This one's different. It's slow and her lips press against mine but it's sweet. And it's distant. "You *have* been alone too long."

I snort. It should have been a laugh or a chuckle or some sort of suave noise but no, I flat out snort like a St. Bernard.

Camille sits up. Her teacher face returns and she watches me for a long moment. I can't tell what she's feeling. I've never been able to read women well. If I could, I would have ended it with Lori before she killed our marriage.

But I can tell what Camille is about to say.

"I don't think I should stay tonight."

I totally fucked up. Work's been good. The kid's good. I have an incredible girlfriend and I just fucked it up because I'm lonely.

I might as well admit it. *Lonely* is me and I am it. And it looks like we're going to continue to be conjoined, lonely and me. Together, always.

I should have kept my mouth shut.

"I think we need to slow down, that's all." She kisses me all sweet and distant again. "*You* need to be sure. We both need to be sure. For Bart, at least."

I nod. I want to throw the pillow at the window and rip down the curtains. Get dressed and go for a run and punch a brick wall somewhere. Go into the basement and lift until my elbows pop and every muscle in my body burns.

I need to find some way to get a little heat back into my veins.

"I am not breaking up with you, Daniel Quidell."

I glance at Camille. I know she's assessing my mood and that she thinks I'm acting like a little kid. That, right now, I'm no better than Bart was at dinner, when he stomped off.

Maybe she's right.

Her brow pinches together and I swear she's going to poke her fists into her waist the way Bart does when he's mad. "Say something."

"I'm sorry?" What the hell else am I supposed to say?

She swings her feet over the side of the bed. A small shiver runs up her spine when she turns her back to me. I hear a sigh, too. A small one, like she's trying to be strong.

Not picking her up and pulling her back into the bed takes all my concentration. I don't think about what she's saying. I see only that she's upset.

"Camille..." Gently, I touch her back. She feels cool again, like the air pumped out by the furnace isn't keeping her warm. Like she needs to be against me.

Her back straightens but she doesn't turn around. "You know, I do like toaster pastries. The blueberry kind without the extra icing."

Why did I have to scare her like that? "Bart likes cherry."

She glances over her shoulder. "I'll see you tomorrow morning?"

I nod. I'm an idiot.

Camille gathers her clothes. The candlelight flickers over her lovely skin, the heat crackling, and I can't help but wonder if I'm dreaming. If, perhaps, my brain has had enough of my six months of wanting to be near her and I've finally snapped. If the last few days have been a dream meant to force myself into admitting I'm in love.

And that, perhaps, I moved too *slow*, after the field trip. That by *not* asking her out I signaled I wasn't serious.

So now I have to think about it. Be sure. Because if I was sure, I would have figured it out before the leaves fell from the trees and the slush moved into the world.

I roll off the side of the bed and pull on my clothes and follow her down the stairs to the living room.

She stands in front of the door for a long moment, her bag in her hand and her knit cap pulled down over her ears, ready for the cold outside. The house buzzes and clicks, reminding me how empty it's going to feel the moment she walks out my door. But she thinks I need to think, so there's not much I can do about it.

At least tonight.

Camille digs around inside her bag. Smiling, she pulls out another, smaller bag. It's bright green and quilted and, I suspect, holds her toothbrush. "Will you put this in the bathroom upstairs for me?"

I take the little bag. My fingers wrap around the scratching, polyester fabric, and I feel little bottles and brushes move around inside. "I'll clean out a drawer." Grinning, I set the bag on the steps, so I remember to take it up.

When I turn around, she hugs me tight, and the pom-pom on her hat brushes against my chin. It tickles and a shiver flows across my jaw.

"I'll see you in the morning." The shiver is followed by a kiss. A sweet, warm kiss from a woman who's leaving her toothbrush here, but not sleeping in my bed.

I nod and let go.

"You're quiet." She grasps the door handle but doesn't open the door. She just watches me with her teacher eyes.

If I start talking, she'll run away. Probably forever. "I don't know what to say."

Camille looks at her feet. "We'll talk tomorrow. Make a plan. Okay?"

I want to kiss her. I want to pick her up and carry her back up the stairs and go to sleep happy for once in my life. Happy and feeling like I conquered the zombies instead of them eating my limbs while I watched.

But not tonight.

When she leaves, I watch from the window until I see her headlights vanish around the corner. I'll see her in the morning.

And I'll have a plan. Because I'm going to fix my mistakes. I may have taken it too slow before, and too fast now, but starting tomorrow, it'll be just right.

CHAPTER 10

Camille

Dan and Bart are late this morning. I pace in the Community Center lobby under the bright skylight, listening to the kids yell and the front desk staff laugh and smelling the bad coffee they brew every morning for the gym crowd. What if I scared Dan away last night? What if he thinks I'm some kind of ice queen or something?

I *had* to leave. I had to. I had to pull on my clothes and pick up my bag and walk out the front door. I didn't have a choice.

That teenaged part of my brain screamed *Yes!* when he said "the woman I love." I wanted to pull Dan on top of me and kiss him deeply and watch his beautiful eyes light up with all that joy he shows when we're together.

I feel it in his fingers. In the way he touches. I taste it in his kisses. I hear it in the smoothness of his voice. He's not lying.

Dan Quidell loves me.

But another part of my head was screaming *What did that bitch do to him?* What, exactly, did his ex-wife do that made him so lonely?

Because I don't think it was anyone else. He hasn't said, but I think I might be the first woman he's been with since his divorce.

Which means I'm the rebound. I pace again inside the big white glare thrown through the skylight. I'll need to go in soon. All the other kids are here. Everyone but Bart.

I pull out my phone. Should I call?

But how can I be the rebound if it's been almost six years? What if he's *settling*?

When I close my eyes, I see orange and green after images from my phone. And from the pool of sunlight. Maybe from all my fretting.

How the hell did Dan go with no girlfriend for six years? Hot, handsome, fun Dan?

Sandy ducks her head out of her room. "You okay?"

I stop pacing. "Bart's not here."

She opens and closes her mouth, but doesn't say anything. She just nods before returning to her room.

Shit, I think, careful not to say it out loud. At work, I try not to even think swear words, in case one slips out, but sometimes it's difficult.

I know why Dan's gone for so long without a girlfriend. The surgeries. The scars. And, I think, expectations. Men like Dan—gorgeous men—are expected to be interested in only sex. I know how the other teachers react when he's around.

That's not Dan.

And he's in love with *me*.

I'm smiling. I'm fretting but I'm smiling. But I won't admit how I feel. I won't do anything that, in the long run, causes him pain. I won't let him charge headlong into a relationship because he *does* deserve all the respect I can give him.

And if I admit it to myself, I'll jump into his arms when he finally does come through those doors.

And he'll sweep me up into his big, strong arms.

Maybe I should.

No. Both Dan and Bart need rational, not weird and fawning. He needs to be sure.

The doors swoosh open and I look up from my phone's screen. Dan strolls in carrying a big, flat box, Bart next to him.

Bart immediately runs for me and the next thing I know, he's hugging my legs. "We're going to the zoo on Thursday! Do you want to go to the zoo? Daddy says you can come. I want you to come, too."

I stuff my phone in my pocket as Dan walks up. He's in a t-shirt and his work boots, so he must have a more hands-on day ahead. The t-shirt hangs loose around his midsection but its long sleeves do nothing to disguise his biceps.

A sudden ping of jealousy—or maybe it's possessiveness—flits through my gut and I glance over my shoulder, making sure none of the other teachers are watching my man. It happens so fast I surprise myself.

When I glance back at Dan, he's watching me with a raised eyebrow. "No toaster pastries at the donut shop." But he smiles and nods to the box.

"Is that why you're late?" The box is full of every kind of donuty goodness the shop has to offer. The sweet smell of sugar and fat leaks out every time Dan jostles it, too.

The cocked eyebrow turns into a frown. "We wanted to get you a peace offering."

"You didn't need to do that." I touch his elbow before I realize I probably shouldn't out here in the open, but I don't think I care anymore. We may need to be careful and slow and rational, but seeing him frown makes me rash, fast, and decidedly irrational. "I was worried."

Dan blinks. "Oh. Sorry." He looks like he's about to drop the box and lift me up for a good strong kiss. One of his mesmerizingly intense lip massages that, by themselves, are so damned good I almost come.

Because I want to be with him that much.

Bart tugs on my shirt. "Are you coming to the zoo? Please?"

"Thursday is your day off." Dan shifts the donuts to his other hand. "Rob's flight comes in at five so I thought we could go to the zoo during the day and then I'll pick up Minion Three while the little man here gets his pajamas on. That is, if you can stay for a while on Thursday evening. I'd like to introduce you to Rob."

I work ten hour days four days a week, with Thursdays and the weekends off. "You don't have meetings on Thursday?" He's been working so hard, though. He needs a day off.

"Moved them. Tom's gallery opening is next Tuesday so I thought I should concentrate on what's important for a couple of days." Dan musses Bart's hair but he's looking right at me.

I see worry flash across his face, like he's afraid that the time off will catch up with him and bite him in the ass. Or that his peace offering won't be accepted.

"Please, Ms. Frasier!" Bart tugs on my shirt again.

"Bart, what did I say in the truck?" When I look back at Dan's face, I can tell he's counting as he breathes out. That all this—Bart begging, him doing his best to present himself as a cool and calm boyfriend bearing gifts, the party this weekend, his youngest brother coming into town—is stressful. I don't think he has a lot of reserves to dealing with it all.

Frowning, Bart looks up at his father. "Be respectful."

"Are you being respectful?"

Bart tugs on the straps of his superhero backpack and stomps his foot. "I was asking!"

I tap Bart's shoulder and point to Sandy's room. "Why don't you go on into Ms. Cunningham's room so I can talk to your daddy, okay? We'll get it all figured out."

He huffs but does as I say, scuffling across the concrete floor.

"My first pull-out is in a couple of minutes so I don't have a lot of time." I reach for the donuts. "I'll put these in the break room."

"I know it's not a date but Tom can't really help right now because of his show so I thought maybe spending the day with both of us would be okay."

I tuck my hand under the donut box, intending to lift it from Dan's grip. But our fingers touch. We stand for a second, fingertip to fingertip, and the electricity flashes through my body again. It curls from my knuckles to my wrist and all the way up my arm. The tingle touches my shoulder the way his lips touch my skin. It strokes my back the way he kisses my spine.

And under the box, I sneak my hand into his. "You're worrying too much again."

We stand for a moment, palm flush against palm, a box of sugary treats balanced over our wrists. Dan smiles. And I see some of the stress drain away.

"I'm sorry if I came on too strong last night." Dan glances around. "I just—"

He stops talking when I squeeze his hand. Carefully, I let go and take the box. "What time should I be at your place Thursday morning?"

Dan blinks and I see more of the stress drain away. "We could pick you up."

They could. "I'd like to have my car."

He pouts more than frowns. "Oh."

"So there's a car at your place when you're picking up your brother." I shake my head. "You *do* worry too much."

His pirate smirk appears and he tucks his hands into his pockets. "If you're over by nine, we can be at the zoo by ten."

"Okay." The Community Center's big clock dings. "I gotta go." I don't think. I just do. I lean close and kiss his cheek.

Dan opens his mouth to say something but slams it shut and steps back. "Bye, Ms. Frasier."

Blinking, still smiling, he rubs the back of his head as he walks away, toward the door.

When I turn around I see why he responded the way he did. Mary Beth is standing in her door with my morning pull-out students, frowning.

CHAPTER 11

Daniel

Bart's bouncing like one of the prairie dogs in the exhibit along the Northern Trail. "I'm cold."

We rode the monorail over the outdoor animals but Bart wanted to see the tigers up close. At first, he was too excited to notice the temperature, but now that he's seen the tigers, he wants to go inside.

I swing him up into my arms. "We're almost there, buddy."

Camille rubs her hands together and her breath curls around her face like a little cloud. The day smells clean and fresh, and we pretty much have the run of the place, except for the many wandering groups of school kids.

The trail loops through the trees and we walk along, listening to the other kids and the calls of the zoo's many birds as we make our way back to the main building.

Camille rubs Bart's back when he leans his head against my shoulder. He's excited, but he's also beginning to tire.

"Do you still want to see the fish?" she asks. "It's warm and you can rest."

"Oh!" Bart bounces in my arms again.

"Hold still, buddy. I'm carrying you, here." He's going to be too big pretty soon. He's already almost too big for Camille.

Bart ignores me and bounces anyway. "Will we see sharks? I want to see a shark."

"We'll see sharks." Camille pulled her hair into a ponytail today. Her face looked different this morning when I opened the door and it took me a while to figure out that she's not wearing make-up. I just thought she looked fresh and dewy. Her skin glows more.

She tasted fresh, too, when I kissed her in the kitchen. A little like coffee, but clean, like the winter air. I think I like make-up free.

All I want to do is lay on the couch with her snuggled in next to me. Spend the day kissing and making love. Breathing in her scent and tasting her skin. Letting her presence center my mind and her body soothe my aches. But she wants to do this right.

Which is wise.

But I'm as impatient as my son. And I have a plan.

We did the trails first, focusing on the tigers and the giraffes. I gave Bart my phone and he snapped pictures until he was satisfied, so he has "references for his drawings." He sounds just like his Uncle Tommy when he says it.

When we hit the Tropics Trail, he strips off his coat but he still wants to be carried. The brightly colored birds chirp and the komodo dragons flick their tails, but more than anything, I think Bart wants to sit on the carpeted step in front of the zoo's big aquarium wall.

It's a long, dark hallway down to see the fish. I set Bart down and he skips along ahead of us, his excitement returning. "How many sharks are there? Can we get a shark, Daddy? I want a shark."

Camille leans her head against my shoulder. "I suspect he'll be drawing sharks for at least three weeks."

"Fluffy kitty-sharks with tabby markings." I weave my fingers through hers as we walk.

The aquarium wall is a good fifty feet long and at least ten tall. Bart presses his nose against the glass and watches the fish swim by. Camille snaps a few photos of him with her phone while I sit on the carpeted step behind where he camps out.

My hip hurts. I think Bart might have to walk for a while. I rub at it absently, watching Bart point at all the little fish.

Camille sits next to me, enjoying a rest while my son enjoys the exhibit. It smells like aquarium water and people in here, but we're mostly alone, at least for the moment.

When she leans against my shoulder, I wrap my arm around her waist. She wiggles closer. For a second, I wonder if I can sneak a real kiss, but I behave like a gentleman and weave my fingers into hers again instead.

It's quiet here. No random group of fourth graders around.

I think now is the time to put my plan into action.

"I've been thinking a lot about what you said." I have been, too. "About moving too fast and doing this right."

Camille doesn't pull away. She snuggles closer. "Oh?"

In front of us, Bart's mesmerized by a shark that's taken up position directly in front of him. The blues of the water play over his face and hand, and when he laughs, it mixes with the piped-in sounds of the water lapping against the glass.

"I want to explain myself." Give some perspective. "I decided last night to give you a reason why I said what I said."

Telling her how I feel is telling her the truth. I have too many lumbering nag zombies and thinking about how every single word I say may be screwing up my relationship is just making them bite harder.

So I suppose I'm being selfish.

Bart laughs and splays his fingers over the glass. He's not tapping, which means at least he's listening to Camille's instructions, even if I'm not. I'm done thinking about it. I splay my fingers over her hip.

But a small part of me is frowning and stomping his feet because I never get to be selfish and maybe this once I can because this is something important.

Camille is important. Extremely important.

She moves so she can see my face better.

Even in the low blue glow of the aquarium, I see her attentiveness. All her focus is on me, except for the little constant bit she keeps on Bart.

"For the past six months, I *have* been planning. Every morning, I plan what to ask you about when I drop off Bart. Every evening, when I pick him up, I plan a follow up question. Because I've been trying to get to know you."

I grin and sniff. "Though you're good at redirecting and getting me to talk about myself."

Camille grins, too. Gently, she draws little circles on my thigh with her finger. "You're interesting." She leans against my shoulder again. "I never thought about fire prevention and structural engineering issues before."

"I've learned a lot about you." I kiss her temple. "And each piece of information I gathered made me want to be with you more than I did the day before."

Against my shoulder, she inhales sharply and I can't help but pull her closer. We sit huddled together on the scratchy zoo carpet, watching Bart watch the fish. And, I hope, solidifying what I should have tried to solidify months ago.

I breathe in the scent of her hair. "I know when your birthday is. I know your favorite color and your favorite flower. And I know you want to visit France someday." *Maybe that someday will be our honeymoon*, I think. "Plus a lot more I'm not going to say right now."

"Daddy!" Bart stands up and points into the tank. "A diver!"

I look up. They must be feeding the sharks.

I pull my arm out from around Camille. "I guess it's time to take more pictures."

"How do you know all that?" She looks confused.

Chuckling, I nod toward my boy. "Doctor Bartman likes to talk about his favorite teacher. Something I wholeheartedly encourage."

Her mouth opens and closes as we stand. I pull my phone out of my pocket.

"I just don't want you to feel like you're..." Her lips thin and she twists to move to Bart's side.

I grip my phone, hoping I made sense. "Feel like I'm what, *Camille?*"

She blinks, but looks up at my face. "I want you to be *sure*, not just settling for any old relationship. You deserve better than that."

"You think I'm settling for *you?*" I don't know how else to describe how I'm feeling other than shocked. Flat out stunned and shocked.

Because she's stunning in every way a woman can be stunning. "I thought you were settling for *me.*"

I think, maybe, I embarrassed her a bit. She won't look at me but she's smiling.

But I can't help but joke. "You know, since I'm 'almost amazing.'"

"Dan!" Camille throws me one of her mock-stern looks. "My mom taught me to never settle for less than the best."

I kiss her gently before snapping a picture of the woman I am in no way "settling" for. Sometimes I can't believe how beautiful she is.

Or that she's my girlfriend.

When we leave, Bart walks between us holding both our hands. He talks nonstop about the diver and the sharks and the tigers he saw earlier. Camille smiles the entire time.

And I think she's glowing more than she was before.

We have lunch and hit the gift shop before heading home. Bart falls asleep in his booster seat but is wide awake by the time we pull into the garage, chatting about the animals and his new zoo toys and insisting that he's going to wear his new zoo-themed pajamas for Uncle Robby.

"Can we have pizza tonight?" Bart stands in the middle of the kitchen and stuffs a cookie in his mouth as he asks.

Camille shoos him toward the table. "Sit down while you eat your snack."

He nods and climbs up onto his chair, his cookie in one hand and a juice box in the other.

I pull Camille close and kiss her cheek. Bart watches like it's the most normal thing in the world. "I think he's okay with this. With us."

She nods, watching him more than me. The kiss she gives me is warm and wonderful and I feel that maybe we're okay. That we're moving in the direction we need to move.

And maybe she's seeing me as a man who has already gotten to know her. Maybe I'm no longer conjoined with *lonely*.

"Go get your brother." Camille kisses me again. "We'll be here when you get back."

CHAPTER 12

Daniel

I'm going to introduce Camille to Rob tonight. I'll introduce her to Tom and his fiancé, Sammie, at Bart's birthday party. Maybe a little of Sammie will rub off on Camille. Sammie was living with Tom a week after they met.

I can only hope.

I smile to myself and tap my steering wheel. Tom's always been better with women than me. He handled his relationship with Sammie well right from the beginning. Unlike me.

Still, Camille seems to have forgiven me.

Rob, on the other hand, is a little shit. It's not his fault. Our mom and sister's deaths did a number on him. It did a number on *all* of us, me included. Rob is smart enough he should have figured out that he's a little shit and stopped his shitty behavior a long time ago. But he's managed, somehow, to continue in his ways through college and now, I bet, at his new graduate school.

I inch down the freeway toward the airport to retrieve my shit of a brother for a weekend home. He can't stay for Tom's opening even though it's Tuesday. He's got a midterm. But we're going to video chat it for him and Bart's excited.

I've seen some of the paintings my middle brother is showing. We had a talk about Bart seeing naked ladies, especially when the naked lady is Sammie. But we have a plan, and Bart is so excited he's drawing special pictures for his special no-nudes corner of the gallery.

The truck slowly moves along and I watch the brake lights in front of me flash on and off. Rob's waiting by the airport pick-up doors and texting me every five minutes asking where I am.

Driving, I text back, which I do when traffic stops. *Stop texting me you idiot.*

My little brother is an impatient brat.

If my brothers and I are the Norse superheroes in Bart's action figure collection, Rob is the skinny, dark-haired, evil one. The clever evil one. He's way too smart for his own good.

But I love my brother. He reminds me of our mother.

When I pull up to the gate, Rob tosses his bag into the back of my truck before climbing into the passenger seat. He looks as bohemian as most college students—stubble, worn clothes, but with expensive earphones around his neck and the latest must-have phone in his hand.

"You smell like coffee," I say.

He pulls across his seatbelt and settles in. "Love you too, asshole. About time you showed up."

I give him the finger.

Rob laughs. "Someone needs to get laid."

I snort and pull the truck into the traffic lane. At this rate, it'll be nine by the time we get home and Bart will be in bed already. And I won't have any time with Camille.

"Well, well." Rob's eyebrow arches. "How long you been banging the nanny?"

I glare at him. How the hell did he figure out I was in a relationship with Camille? Then again, she's the only woman I talk about. "Do *not* make her feel uncomfortable."

Rob throws his hands into the air. "Sorry. Not going well?" He pulls out his phone and swipes at it a couple of times.

"It's going just fine. You taking notes?" He might be. He's always aware of the shit going on around everyone. He likes figuring out social systems the way normal people like to solve puzzles. Which is why he's in graduate school and I'm walking around with my high school diploma and a few college courses under my belt.

"Of course. I'm trying to figure out how you and Tom attract the hotties." He glances over before shoving the phone back into his pocket. "And manage to keep them around."

Except my ex-wife had issues I was too stupid to see at the time and my new hottie wants to take it slow.

Rob puts on his best mocking face. "Turn that frown upside down, young man, before we get back to your place. The boy's going to wonder what his uncle did to his daddy." Rob nods to the traffic. "It's going to be all Uncle Robby! Uncle Robby! Daddy's fucking my nanny and I want a puppy!"

I roll my eyes. But I can't help but chuckle. "He wants a kitten, not a puppy."

Rob laughs. "Tom said something about Bart taking a shine to his girlfriend's cat." He takes out his phone again. "That woman is freakin' hot. How the hell did he get her to move in with him after knowing her for what, a week? Two? I need to learn his secrets." Rob swipes again, then tucks away the device. "Research purposes only. God knows I don't want a woman leaving her yogurt in my fridge and her tampons in my bathroom."

"Tom and I are going to step back and watch the ladies snip off your balls." Traffic's loosened and I turn onto the main north-south artery. Looks like we'll be making good time after all. Which is just fine. My brother is an annoying little shit.

Now Rob gives me the finger. But his voice drops low when he speaks again. "They're serious, aren't they? Tom and Sammie?"

I glance over. His face has that faraway look he gets sometimes when he goes all wistful. "He gave her a ring, didn't he?" A bright little sapphire because, for some reason, indigo holds a special meaning for them.

They have an ease to their relationship I hope to build with Camille.

Rob asks about Bart and tells me about his classes as we drive home, obviously not wanting to talk about women anymore. I have him text the pizza place and put in an order for dinner, and that seems to shut him up.

Though I can't shake the feeling my smartass little brother has something on his mind.

⚜

CAMILLE AND BART ARE COLORING AT THE KITCHEN TABLE WHEN WE come in. Bart's in his zoo pajamas, all clean and ready for bed—and also wearing his new Christmas socks. He screeches and jingles his way to his uncle, and I set the pizzas on the kitchen counter.

Camille watches Rob for a long moment, her deep eyes searching. She smiles but I can tell she doesn't know what to do.

She's wearing her Christmas socks.

My first instinct is to scoop her up and lay a massive kiss on her perfect lips right here, for my brother and my son to see. But I don't want to embarrass her, so I squeeze her fingers instead.

Before Rob sets down Bart, he gives Camille a friendly hug, smiling too, but doesn't say anything other than pleasantries and comments about the jingle toes when Bart does a little dance.

Over dinner, Camille quizzes Rob about school and his studies.

"Cultural Anthropology." Rob sits back in his chair and takes a sip of his beer, watching Camille. "I will be job-free and homeless the day I finish my dissertation." He winks at me. "Guess it'll be me living in your basement instead of Tom."

Bart points at his uncle. "Uncle Tommy makes better mac and cheese!" Then he leans toward Camille. "Ms. Frasier makes the *best* mac and cheese."

Rob gives me one of his *oh, boy* expressions but all I want to do is crawl over the table and lean against Camille, too. When I feel her toe stroke my shin under the table, I smile.

"Dan tells me you enjoy French cooking." Rob whistles at Bart and directs him back to eating his pizza.

"My parents gave me a new cookbook for Christmas." Camille and Rob drop into a long conversation about France and French culture.

Bart bounces in his chair and holds up his foot. "Are there super-heroes in France?"

Camille laughs and rubs his hair. "Maybe you should ask your uncle. He knows all about all the different places in the world."

Bart grins as he stuffs his pepperoni and extra cheese pizza in his mouth, quiet now that his mouth is full.

Rob drinks his beer, watching.

After dinner, Rob takes Bart into the living room. "Show me your army, buddy." He winks at me over his shoulder.

Camille chuckles. I pull her into the kitchen.

"Hmmm..." I hoist her off the floor, my arms under her sweet back-side, and set her on the kitchen counter. "Looks like we get a moment."

Up on the counter, she's close to eye-to-eye with me. She bounces her slippered feet. Her heels tap the cabinet door making rhythmic *thump twinkle thump twinkle* sounds.

It's unbelievably sexy. Or maybe it's the luscious pout she's giving me. I don't know. But I think I want moments like this to keep happening.

"You know something?" Camille strokes a finger across my chest. "I like being with you. I like talking to you. I even like your brother." She glances around me and listens to Rob and Bart playing in the living room. "He's funny and good with Bart."

"Hmmm..." I'm too busy kissing up her neck to her earlobe to pay all that much attention.

Smiling, she kisses my cheek. "It's not just the incredible sex."

There's genuine caring in her eyes. It's as deep as the caring I see when she looks at Bart. Different, though, but I don't know how.

I move close, curling my arms around her waist, feeling this beautiful woman and her wonderful, soothing touch. "Will you stay tonight?" I kiss her neck, her jaw. "Rob's not a problem." The next kiss I lay on her lips. She tastes fresh, even though we just ate. "Please."

Concern works across her cheeks. "Don't you want time with your brother? I don't want to be in the way."

"Daddy!" Bart runs into the kitchen waving a piece of paper in his hand. "I drew Uncle Robby's ph—"

My son stops cold when he sees my arms around Camille and I can't tell if he's shocked or happy.

But then he runs for us, his arms wide. "Hugs!" he yells, and jumps for us both.

Camille jumps down and laughs when I lift him high, kissing his cheek.

Bart snuggles in close. "I like hugs."

"I like hugs, too," she says. She watches me as she says it, not my son. Me.

And all I want to do is pull them both close. Kiss them both. But my brother is watching from the dining area.

Camille kisses my lips this time. "I'll get him ready for bed." She walks past Rob, nodding once, and disappears around the corner with Bart. "Story first, buddy?" I hear her say, then the sounds of Bart pulling books off the shelf under the DVD player.

Rob watches them until I hear them settle into the couch. I drop a plate into the dishwasher.

My brother walks into the kitchen. "When's the wedding?"

Out in the living room, Camille reads Bart a story. He reads along, sounding out words. She's going to have him reading novels before he starts kindergarten.

"Tom and Sammie are thinking late spring." I drop another plate in the dishwasher. "I told him they should go to Vegas."

Rob looks me up and down and rolls his eyes as he pulls a beer out of the fridge. He's looking at the floor and not me. Then my brother suddenly smiles and slaps his leg. "Women are impossible."

This isn't about Tom and Sammie. Or about me and Camille. "You were a douchebag to a woman again, weren't you? What's her name?"

Rob sniffs but doesn't answer my question. I peer down the hallway. Bart's drawing a picture of Camille on the big pad of paper thrown over his bright green kid's-easel. She's sitting on the edge of the couch, both her legs to one side and her chin up, like she's a mermaid.

My son stands tall and sticks up his thumb, peering around it at the woman who is better to him than, I think, even me. Who is better to *me* than I am to me. Wonderful, caring Camille.

But what if it doesn't work out? What if I end up more like Rob than Tom? Bart couldn't handle it if he lost her.

I tap the kitchen counter. Bart would be devastated.

Rob watches me watch them. "That bitch Lori is gone and your arms and legs work." He takes a pull on the bottle. "I like Camille. I suspect Tom will as well."

Rob shakes his head. "Dad always says the best thing you can do for a son is to love his mother." He snorts and takes one last sip.

But the sadness hasn't left Rob's face and I *know* this isn't about my delicate sensibilities. "You didn't do anything illegal, did you?"

Rob blinks and his eyes narrow. "You are pathetic, you know that?" He shakes his head as he drops his empty into the recycling. "You're like a goddamned puppy, the way you look at her."

With that, my brother walks away, into the living room.

After a long second, I hear Camille laugh and Bart fuss about brushing his teeth and I lean against the sink, wondering what it is that has me worried.

Because I'm not like Rob. I'll do all the necessary work needed to hold together my relationship.

CHAPTER 13

Camille

The streetlight in front of Dan's house buzzes in the cold evening air. Snow floats down, the crinkly kind, and tiny sparkling ice crystals pelt the world. Somewhere down the street, a dog barks. My boots crunch through the crust of the new snow and my breath hazes the air between me and my car door.

It's time to go home.

Not because I want to. Dan asked me to stay but I told him he needs time with his family. And me time to get used to what happened today.

Not so much the speed, because Dan's right. We've known each other long enough for a serious relationship. But today, at the zoo, it dawned on me that I am, in fact, in a serious relationship. With the man I've wanted for half a year.

Somewhere deep inside, a part of me doesn't think it's real.

Dan doesn't think I have demon eyes. And he's fun. And responsible. And damned hot.

I allow myself a full, deep sigh, out here in the cold, my car keys in my hand and my breath curling around my face.

I hear the front door. Rob had been sitting on the couch when I pulled my coat out of the closet. Dan stood next to me, first looking at his brother, then at me, then back to his brother.

Rob, for his part, gave Dan a "you're a fucking idiot" eye roll and went back to watching some awful reality television show on some random awful channel, a beer in one hand and his phone in the other.

I had expected Dan to plop on the couch next to his brother, not follow me outside, but he dashes down the steps, careful of the snow. When he stops, he zips his jacket and stuffs his hands in his pockets. "It's cold tonight."

"It is." I yank the flaps of my hat low over my ears. "What time should I be here for the party?"

Dan blinks his gorgeous eyes and they look more silver—like the snow—than their usual ocean-like blue-green. I'm in the presence of Jack Frost, except this Mr. Frost only looks cold because he burns with a blue flame.

His pirate smirk flickers for a second and I know what he's thinking: *Right now. Come back inside.* "Tom and Sammie will be here at noon."

I nod. "I'll text before I come." Stepping close, I give him a quick kiss. "I'll see you tomorrow."

"Meeting you was the best thing that has ever happened to me. And to Bart." He waves at the house and again I see what he wants to say in his eyes.

"Oh, Dan." I wrap my arms around his chest and lay my cheek over his heart. The zipper of his jacket rubs my skin but it doesn't matter. I'm safe in the arms of this wonderful man.

"After you leave, the house feels wrong. Because you're missing." He rubs his face against the knit of my hat.

When I look up, his eyes say everything.

The words we've been circling around, the words I should *not* say now because we're being rational and taking the correct amount of time, just pop out of my mouth like they have a life of their own.

And I just say it. "Are you asking me to spend the night with the man I love?"

I say it.

The shock on Dan's face quickly turns into the bright, intense joy I saw the first time we made love. He lifts me high, even on the snow, and his kiss steals all my fears. It warms all the cold shivering my bones. And it convinces me that he loves me as much as I love him.

"Come inside. Please." I barely hear him, he's kissing me so deeply. His next kiss is as strong and as wonderful as the first.

I can't go back to my silent apartment. Not after admitting how I feel. I pull him toward the house.

I'm in his arms again, kissing his jaw and neck. We fall through the door, laughing and touching, Dan stroking my arms and my shoulders. His fingers grip, but gently, and his eyes all but gleam silver in the evening's light.

And completely unaware of Rob until he throws a pillow at Dan's head.

"Get a room, you crazy kids." Fake frowning at us, Rob turns off the television. "I'm going to bed so keep it down."

Leaning against Dan's shoulder, I watch the youngest Quidell brother whistle as he strolls toward the lower level, leaving us alone.

Dan weaves the fingers of both his hands around mine and tugs me up the stairs. He walks backward two steps above me, his grand and obvious erection right there in front of my eyes.

Oh, the wonders of this man. Of his smile. His touch. And his kissable wondrous abs.

The look on his face shows half concern over what we *should* do—sit down on the steps and talk—and what he so very obviously *wants* to do—be naughty. Right here. Because I'm staying and he doesn't have to worry about asking again.

Which half do I indulge? Which kind of assertive should I be?

I run my finger over the bulge in his pants. The fabric of his jeans feels thick and taut, like what's under it. Dan closes his eyes and his face turns toward the ceiling. A low, stifled moan makes it past his tightly closed lips. The fingers of his hand grip the handrail and the wood creaks under the pressure. His other hand splays over the wall, palm flat. If he's not careful, he'll poke his fingers through the wallboard.

I glance over my shoulder, listening for Rob. I hear him shuffle around in the lower level, then the click of a door as he goes into the guest room to sleep.

Dan, too, glances over his shoulder, listening. Making sure Bart's asleep. When he looks back at me, he's grinning again.

"You have no idea what your pirate smirk does to me," I whisper.

He blinks for half a second, but then he exaggerates his grin and leans closer. "So I be pillaging ye tonight, aye?" he whispers back.

I'm tingling. I run my hands over my breasts and down between my thighs, squeezing and pinching my own flesh. Playful Dan makes me want to suck his cock right here. Right now.

The pirate grin changes into Dan's look of raw hunger. Backlit by the light over the steps, I see the outline of his shoulders. His muscles contract and his arms just get bigger and harder. I could rub myself against his bicep and come a thousand times.

The handrail groans again, and this time, so does the wall. Dan mouths two words: *Do it.* The electricity fires through my body, brought on by the intensity of his face alone.

You gonna pound me? I mouth, though I know the answer. I like it when he borders on losing control and he's slamming me with all the strength of his incredible body.

His eyes narrow and another low growl makes it past his closed lips. *Arrgh, matey.*

A snort I can't stifle bursts out and Dan laughs, doing his best to stifle his own sounds. He totally blocks the stairs with his big body, not moving, not reaching for me or grabbing my hair or doing anything... planned. But that's not quite the right word. More like expected of him. He got beyond "ask Camille to stay" on his evening checklist and I rewarded him for his hard work by telling him the truth of how I feel. And now he wants to play.

He's happy. Carefree, I think, for the first time since I met him.

I watch his face slacken as I rub my palm over his cock. He looks as if the simple act of touching him solves all the world's problems and seeing his joy makes me happy, too. Happy and horny as hell.

I loosen his belt, working carefully and as quietly as possible. He glances up the stairs again, then twists his head, also listening for Rob. When he's satisfied, he gives me a quick nod.

I undo his fly, slowly unzipping his jeans, more to tease than to keep quiet. Impatience hums off his body and I'm surprised he doesn't make the stairs groan from the vibrations. I half expect the walls to bow out from the sheer pressure of his desire alone.

All his heat focuses on me. "Aye, the mast is up, me lovely pirate lady," he whispers, winking while he exaggerates his grin again.

"You going to tie me to it, good sir?" Now might be a good night to introduce some of the naughty tricks I've learned. I don't think he's got toys, but we can improvise.

Keeping quiet's going to be difficult, I'm certain.

I work my fingers into the fly of his boxers and rub my thumb and forefinger up and down his shaft as I loosen the button.

His body quakes under my touch, his cock solid and hot in my hand. I haven't released him yet. Haven't worked him through the fly of his boxers. I grip him under the fabric and run my thumb up and down the underside of his shaft.

"You be a fierce and terrible creature, one brimmin' with the fire of angels." His lip curls and I see on his face what he's not saying: *Suck me already.*

I twist my hand around and stroke his balls. The quake turns into a shiver and his hand comes off the wall. Dan grabs my ponytail, curling my hair around his hand, and stares down at me.

The fabric of his boxers pulls and stretches as I lift the elastic waistband over the head of his cock, down his shaft, and under his balls. It's not comfortable. I can tell by his grimace. But it should heighten the pleasure of the experience.

I run the pad of my thumb over the head of his cock, spreading a bead of pre-cum. Dan tastes not-quite-salty. Not sweet, either. I don't think it's a flavor, but it is hard and living and hot. He feels so very good in my mouth.

I feel his hips wanting to buck. He wants to thrust. I suck hard, pulling him deeper with only the force of my throat.

"God damn." Dan's voice is smoky, deep, barely capable of making words.

I pull off him but I keep my hand around his shaft. "Are you going to give as good as you get, pirate man?"

He swings around me, rubbing his cock against my breasts as he moves to the steps below. Roughly, he grabs my ass and pushes me up the stairs. His other hand works under my shirt as we move, under the band of my bra, and around my breast. Having his wrist between my bra and my skin makes the elastic dig into my ribcage but the sting only intensifies the pleasure when he pinches my nipple.

The hand on my ass moves between my legs as he pushes me up the stairs. He turns his palm sideways like he's making a gun, thumb up and pointer finger extended, and rubs my pussy. Behind me, he uses his teeth to pull up my shirt.

At the top of the stairs, he pushes me down on the landing, belly to the floor and ass hanging over the first step. The hand on my breast pulls out of my bra. The band snaps hard and I moan. Dan chuckles as both his hands work my jeans, unbuttoning, unzipping, and yanking them down my hips to my knees.

I'm wearing a sweet pink boy-cut thong tonight. One with a wide band of lace around my hips but not a lot else. The growl it elicits from Dan is loud enough Rob probably heard it downstairs. I don't think Dan cares anymore.

He bends over me, his knees outside mine on the first step. He grips the handrail and his shoulder pulls back, but I feel the weight of his body. And his hard cock against the cleft of my ass. "Hmmm, fair maiden," he whispers in my ear. "You bring nothing but joy to this pirate's heart."

His fingers grind into my ass and he pulls away enough to maneuver his cock into the tight space between my denim-constricted thighs. "So I will offer you a boon. Fucked..." He thrusts against the outside of my pussy, his cock rubbing over the just-barely-there lace. "... or licked." A finger follows his thrust.

Dan very quickly, expertly, finds my clit.

My growl is as loud as his.

"Bedroom, bedroom, bedroom," I beg. We need to shut the door. I can't be quiet. God, not with him.

Dan hoists my legs onto the landing and I crawl across the floor, my jeans around my knees and his fingers in my pussy, into the bedroom. The door swings shut fast, about to slam, but Dan catches it and carefully pushes until the latch clicks.

I stretch up, still on my knees, and yank my top over my head. Dan presses me against the wall behind the door before I can unhook my bra and his mouth latches onto the nape of my neck. The full length of his hard body presses against my back. His cock rubs fire hot against the curve of my lower back and his hand moves down my belly, under the lace around my hips.

Slowly, his fingers work into my pussy. "You haven't answered."

I can't. I can barely breathe. His pointer finger rubs my clit and his middle and ring fingers circle around my opening. He can't do much more, with my jeans around my knees.

I move his free hand to my breast. "Pinch." Just the little extra should be enough.

Dan yanks down the cup of my bra and flicks my nipple like he's flicking away a bug.

The orgasm shudders through my belly and down into my thighs with lightning speed. It thunders into my breasts and across my nipples, up into my neck and throat and to the spot just below my ear where Dan breathes on my skin. A loud whimper flows from me and my muscles lose their cohesion. I flop backward, against Dan's front, and every inch of my body chimes.

A *heh* finds my ear. He's proud of himself.

"Pillaging pirate," I moan.

He undoes the clasp on my bra and pushes the straps off my shoulders, kissing each inch of skin the elastic slides off of. "I'm happy you're staying."

Behind me, he pulls off his t-shirt. I feel his hard abs against my back, his hard cock against my ass. Slowly, he lifts me to standing, but he keeps my jeans where they are, on the floor. I step out of the fabric, feeling his hands roam over my hips. Feeling his fingers hook into the lace of my panties and pull them down, too. I stand naked, still facing the wall, listening to Dan remove his jeans and his boxers.

I close my eyes, seeing in my mind the perfection of the man behind me. His balance. His strength. The wonder of his healthy skin and his intense, focused need for me. The curve of his cock and the tightening of his neck muscles that happens every time I stroke him with a firm grip.

Dan spins me around.

CHAPTER 14

Daniel

I'm not greedy. I don't demand, but I need her kiss. My tongue dances into her mouth, then darts back. Hers traces the outside of my teeth.

I cup her breasts, one in each hand, and massage with great care. My thumbs rub her nipples and I swear I feel the tingling heat she feels. I swear it fires into my hand and up my arm. I can only hope I make her feel this good. The way she makes me feel.

Her neck tastes sweet. Fresh, like the rest of her. She moans and I lift her off the floor, arms under her backside, and hold her high enough I need to tip back my head to kiss her again.

Camille curls her arms around my head, kissing my lips and my forehead. Her fingers trace my ears, touch my temples. Her hands stroke my neck.

Our gazes lock. I hold her in the air for a long moment, watching the desire and the love in her eyes. It's there. For me. And I kiss her again.

I slide one foot back, then the other, until we reach the bed. My hands move on her sweet round ass and my forearms tense. Her weight feels good on my muscles. My back, my chest, my arms all tighten, all ready to respond.

I widen her legs.

Camille wiggles, helping my cock find her opening. When I sit on the edge of the bed, I thrust all the way in.

"Oh my God," she breathes. She's straddling my lap, riding my cock. I grip her hips, to keep her from sliding off. And to work her tight pussy up and down my shaft.

I move slow, or else I'll be in a frenzy. She's set my entire body on fire, and I want it to last.

I lift up until I'm almost completely out, then down again until I'm buried deep. "Do that clenching thing you do," I whisper. Her pussy contracts and changes shape and I don't pretend to understand, but it's something only an angel can do.

She tightens her lower abs as I pull her up. "Like that?"

It's magic. Hot, smooth, bright-white magic wrapped around my cock and pulsing into my abdomen and my chest. And all the way up into my head.

I groan, my eyes half closed. "Jesus, Camille." I slide her down and she circles her hips.

She can't leave. Not anymore. Something new opened between us tonight and it's weaving itself through my entire body, up my spine, into my legs. It's knitting me back together.

It's as if I physically feel the net she's made for me, to stop me if I fall. Camille's here now and I won't drown in the cold slush.

I want to give it back to her. Make the same intensity, the same connection, and do it right so she'll always understand.

"Tomorrow." I pull her up, moving faster than before. "I'm going to love you in the morning. In the sun."

Every morning, before we go to work. I'm going to do this again with her lips pressed against my neck and her breasts against my chest. Feel this with her, knowing she's here.

"Dan." She plants her knees along my thighs and takes some of the task, pumping on me.

Up, then down, I slide in, then out. Each time, I fill her farther, deeper. How can she do this to me? How can she be so intense, so exacting, and make every fiber of my body quake?

I loosen my grip on her hips and I roam my hands over her ass, her back. I kiss her breasts, her neck, knowing my breath is as hot and as demanding as my cock.

But I need to say it as much as I need to feel it. And my arms tighten around her waist.

I press my face against her collarbone. "I love you."

I love this magnificent woman.

"I love you, too." She whispers her words into my ear and her full-body, bright-white angelfire takes over.

I flip her on her back. I use my thumb on her clit like I did before, but this time I don't think about what I'm doing. Not pumping takes all my concentration, but I want to feel her come before me. While I'm on the edge and buried inside her.

I circle my hips so that the head of my cock hits every point inside Camille I think will make her scream. Her eyes roll back and I kiss her, taking into my mouth her loud, stuttered moan.

My spine doesn't know if it should arch or curl when my abs flutter like I'm swimming. But I'm not drowning. I breathe in rhythm with the woman under me and this is right. With her it's right.

She's here. She's given me back my strength and I don't feel the weight of the world anymore.

I can't finger her anymore. I can't be slow. I lean into her, kissing her again, and pound her so hard she slides upward on the bed. Our bodies hit and the mattress groans, but I don't care. Her fire is burning away the slush in my veins.

When I come, the world blanks out. I see only her beautiful eyes and hear only her heart beating, and it's perfect.

Camille curls her fingers around mine. "Hmm, pirate man, you plunder well."

I try not to laugh but she smiles. She's righted the ship of my life. I kiss her gently, dancing my lips across her cheeks and her chin. With one hand, I caress her shoulder. With the forearm of the other, I hold myself up. "Did it happen twice this time?" I'm going to make it happen.

"Almost." She wiggles but doesn't move out from under me.

"Almost?" Again? I frown.

"I tell the kids all the time that it's good to have goals." Camille's eyes look brighter than usual. "Almost" must not be all that bad. She wisps her fingers over my lower back.

The tickle makes me wiggle. I forget my irritation.

"I'll bring over my toys." Another wisp of her fingers makes me chuckle.

I slowly lower myself as I kiss her neck and shoulders. "Hmm..." At this point, sleep is more interesting than talk of "toys."

My life's coming together. I have all I need: A beautiful girlfriend who cares about me. A company that's doing well. And a brilliant son who loves her as much as I do.

I roll off. We cuddle under the blankets, wrapped around each other. She rests with her head on my shoulder and runs her finger through my chest hair.

"That tickles." But it feels good. *She* feels good.

"You know I'm going to have to go back to my place sometime tomorrow. I need clean clothes. And to get the toys." Absently, she runs her hand over my scarred shoulder.

I kiss her forehead. It doesn't matter. She'll be here in the morning.

And tonight, I sleep well.

CHAPTER 15

Camille

I straighten my blouse and ponytail when I hear the doorbell. Today is my first encounter with Tom and Sammie. Dan said she models for most of Tom's paintings and I can't help but feel intimidated.

Dan's ex was model-worthy, too. The Quidell men seem to like their woman beautiful.

It's dumb, I know. But I did have a guy tell me I have demon eyes.

Bart pulls me toward the front door. "Uncle Tommy is here!"

When Dan swings open the door, Bart lunges for his uncle. "Did you bring me a present? Uncle Robby brought me a present but he won't let me open it and it's small." He scrunches up his face. "Did you bring Mr. Pickles?"

Tom hoists up his nephew and strides through the door, doing the same duck and twist Dan does when crossing thresholds. He's not quite as tall, but he's just as broad, with lighter hair and the same brilliant blue-green eyes.

"Kitties don't like the cold, remember?" Tom winks at his nephew.

Bart frowns. "I remember. I want a kitty. And a shark!" He thrusts his fists into his waist again.

"Shark?" Tom grins and offers me his big, beefy hand. "Tom. Sammie's coming with the little man's birthday tribute." He nods over his shoulder. "You must be Camille."

I shake, standing as tall as I can. "Nice to meet you."

Behind us, Rob helps Sammie with a big package and a few smaller ones, and I immediately see why Tom paints so many pictures of her. She's taller than me, with auburn hair and striking eyes. But it's how she walks, and how she watches the world, that telegraphs her assuredness. Capturing her composure would make any painting special.

Dan takes Bart's birthday haul and sets it against the coffee table, with Bart's other gifts. The rest of the afternoon is a whirlwind of family stories, birthday cake, and the tearing of gift wrap. Three new superhero costumes from Dan, a special pad of artist's paper from Tom and Sammie, a new action figure playset from me, soon rest as a giant heap of Bart-ness on the coffee table.

Bart's favorite, at least for the afternoon, is Rob's gift of a special little kid's camera. It downloads wirelessly to Dan's tablet computer. Bart strides through the house with the camera strap looped around his wrist, taking picture after picture, while Dan and Rob follow behind holding the tablet so Bart can instantly see his work.

I spend much of the time chatting with Sammie, asking questions about Tom's show. She has an entrepreneurial streak and when I mention that Dan could use some help her eyes light up. The next thing I know, she sits Tom and Dan down to discuss logos and business plans.

When the doorbell rings, Dan and Tom are deep into "company branding" and I pat Dan's arm. "I'll get it."

He squeezes my fingers and kisses my cheek. "Thanks, honey."

I like being in an official relationship. As I walk to the door, I think I like it so much I might bring up moving in some of my clothes. And maybe my easel, so Bart and I can paint together on the weekends.

I peer through the peephole and see only the back of a woman's head. Expecting a charity looking for donations, or someone wanting to share their faith, I pull open the door, ready to politely send her on her way.

But I recognize her the same moment the winter chill hits my face. Blonde, taller than me, ice blue eyes. Gorgeous. I see why the teenaged Dan fell for her.

My first reaction is to step outside even though I'm in my t-shirt. Even though the night is chilly. But this woman cannot see Bart and Bart cannot see her. I close the door, leaving only a gap wide enough for me to slip my arm through if I need to.

The former Mrs. Quidell wears a nice but thin blouse under her open leather jacket, and I see her glaringly yellow camisole. Her hair is swept up into a loose but smooth ponytail. And she grasps the handles of a bright, clown-themed gift bag with expensive looking gloves.

"I have a gift for Bartholomew." She holds out the bag. The laughing clown design is appropriate for a toddler, not a five-year-old boy with art and superhero fixations. "Is he here?"

My gut tightens up so much I want to throw-up, but I don't show it. Why would she appear now? Like this? But it's obvious. She means to passive-aggressively cause as many problems for the Quidell family as she can.

I don't answer. Instead, I glance past the door into the living room, hoping to catch someone's eye. Situations like this are best handled by two people, for reports and support.

Dan says something about "angelfire in the logo" and I hear Sammie's clear, high approval. Then Rob's warm baritone rolls through the house. But none of them are close enough to see me.

I look Lori Taylor-Quidell straight in the eye. "You need to leave. If you wish contact, this isn't the time or place to do it." She's non-custodial and Dan told me she needs written permission from him and a social worker, as well as supervision, to see her son.

I shiver and rub my elbows. I won't let this woman near Bart. Or Dan. I think talking about his ex-wife drags up memories he doesn't want to re-experience. Dan and Bart don't need her ruining the evening. Defusing this situation without raising alarms is something I can do for them.

I hear Rob again. He sounds closer, so I quickly duck my head through the door.

He's sauntering toward the stairs, his phone in his hands and his eyes glued to the screen.

"Rob!"

He looks up.

"I need a witness to back me up."

Immediately, he sees who stands on the front step and his surprise turns to anger. I watch his shoulders take on the same tense hardness Dan's do when he's upset and Rob's stride also takes on the same semi-belligerent swagger.

Rob swings open the door and very quickly steps between me and Dan's ex. He doesn't ask or acknowledge that I have this under control, or that I asked him to show support, not to take over.

He's not as big and broad as Dan or Tom, but he's still taller than most men, and he easily blocks my view of the other woman. I see him swipe something on his phone.

"State your reason for violating the terms of the divorce and custody trials, Lori." Rob's recording her every move.

"I don't give you permission to have that thing on!" From around Rob's shoulder I see Lori's shocked expression.

"Dan gave me blanket permission to film on his property for all reasons I deem valid, including but not limited to matters of security." Rob sounds like a cop. He's authoritative and dispassionate, the way you're supposed to respond to a potentially threatening individual.

He shifts when I do, to stay between us. "Camille, as the other witness here, do you give me permission to film this event?" He holds his phone over his shoulder so it picks up my face.

"Yes, I do," I say into the phone's camera. At least we will have documentation.

"Thank you." Rob returns to holding the phone so Lori is squarely in the center of the frame.

Lori's face hardens. She holds out the gift bag again. "I have a birthday gift for my son."

He's not your son, I think. *He's Dan's son and he's much better off because of it.*

"The terms of the custody agreement clearly state that you are not to be within three hundred feet of Bart without the permission of a social worker and the child's father. You do not have that permission today."

Rob holds the phone over his shoulder again. "Camille, are you aware of any attempt by this woman to contact Dan?"

"No," I say, as clearly as possible.

"How the hell would *she* know?" Lori points a finger at my face.

Rob shifts again and completely cuts off all sightlines between us. "You are well within the three hundred foot limit. You leave *now*, Lori."

"Is she fucking him? In the same house with *my child?*" She screeches the last two words.

I hear rustling. Tom yells something from inside. Chairs scrape and I hear Dan hand Bart over to Sammie.

Rob takes a step toward Lori. "Camille, please dial 911."

Jabbing her finger at his phone, Lori backs down the steps. "You can't use that in court, you goddamned ape! I don't give you permission!"

I slide the screen on my phone so it lights up and hold it out, for Lori to see.

"Go inside, Camille." Rob waves his hand over his shoulder. "Keep Dan away."

I step back into the doorframe.

Tom appears first. "What—" His face turns the same hard, angry menace I just witnessed from Rob and he pushes by me, out onto the step. "Shit."

Lori drops the bag on the concrete of the walk and fumbles open the door of her rental. Rob immediately snaps photos of the car and the license plate. When she gives him the finger, he snaps a photo of that, too.

Like Rob, Tom looms between me and the car, a giant mountain of male protectiveness. Why do they both act like I can't handle myself? I'm trained for situations like this.

The door swings fully open and Dan pulls me into the house. "Why is she back?" His tension hums off his muscles and his face turns hard and cold.

Tom glances over his shoulder and his brows knit together when he sees the anxiety on his brother's face. "Stay inside, Dan. We've got this."

Rob picks up the bag and walks toward the house when Lori pulls out of the driveway.

The cold finally bites into my skin and I shiver, rubbing my arms. "I didn't need either of you blocking her from me."

Rob glances at Tom before looking at Dan. His eyes narrow just like Tom's, and he fiddles with the video he just took.

Tom nods, looking me up and down. "Sorry. Reflex. But you be careful around her."

Dan wraps his arms around me as I step into the warmth of the living room. "I could have handled her." He tenses again and his arms tighten around my waist.

"It's Bart's birthday. You don't need her shit today any more than he does." Tom pushes by.

Rob stands in the door for a moment, watching the street. "Camille, did you call the cops?"

Dan's watching Rob over my shoulder. "Did she threaten Bart again?"

I didn't call the cops. I only held up my phone. "I haven't called yet."

Dan turns me around. His grip on my arms is strong enough it actually hurts. "Did she threaten *you?*"

I read the file. Lori Taylor-Quidell threatened to steal Bart when the custody hearing came back in Dan's favor. The judge responded by restricting her contact to supervised visits, and only with specific permission.

Then she disappeared out West, with a new boyfriend. Dan hasn't seen her for two and half years.

Until today. "Is she violent?" The file only says she is non-custodial with no contact.

Dan glances at Rob again. "Someone vandalized Rob's car when he was an undergraduate. No proof it was her."

Tom paces and rubs the top of his head with his hand. "I had items stolen. A music player. A laptop. Again, no proof."

Dan lets go. "Goddamn it." He steps away. "I'll call the non-emergency number. We need to file a report."

When he and Tom walk away, Rob holds the door. "I'm sorry I offended you earlier." He nods toward the street.

Down the hall, Sammie works with Bart at the dining room table. She's pointing at something he's drawing. He laughs, happy, and holds out the paper for her to see.

Rob stops next to my side. He glances down with eyes clear of all the menace I saw earlier. "I know *her.* She fucked with Dan's head pretty bad when he was at his lowest, lying in his hospital bed hopped up on pain meds. Told him everything that happened was his fault because he's boring and can't make good decisions."

"He believed her?" I glance down the hall as Dan dials the land line.

Rob sniffs. "She ripped at him the entire time they were married, but in small ways. Saying things Tom and I didn't realize were causing him pain. That stuff accumulates."

He watches the street for a moment, then shuts the door. "I think the stealing and the damage was revenge on Tom and me because we won't let her near Dan anymore."

"Will she come back?" My gut reaction of keeping her away from Dan was right. He doesn't need to see her again. That part of his life is done.

Rob swipes at his phone. "Maybe. Her tolerance for work is low, even working at making someone else's life hell, so I don't know."

I squeeze his arm. "Thank you."

Rob scratches the top of his head in very much the same way Dan does when he's perplexed. "Just be alert, okay? I'll be damned if she causes harm to the only woman who has ever given my brother joy."

Nodding once, not looking me in the eye, Robert Quidell walks away, toward his family.

CHAPTER 16

Daniel

Bart became quite excited when the cops showed up to his birthday party—once I explained that nothing bad happened, just that Daddy and Uncle Rob needed to report an unwanted visitor.

Uncle Tommy had already cleaned him up and gotten him into his pajamas when the two officers pulled up in their cruisers. Bart stood in the front window watching, his eyes wide and his mouth an open circle, as the officers looked over the front entrance area and the driveway.

When the younger officer, a squat kid with a military buzz cut, waved at my son before his partner came inside, Bart all but wet his jammies. So Sammie bundled him up and carried him out to see the cop cars, three of his superhero action figures gripped tightly in his mittens.

The officer who waved let him sit in the back after taking a minute to play with him and his toys before he, too, came inside.

Bart asked his new friend if he could take a photo with his birthday camera so he could draw a good picture. The young officer set his hat on his hair stubble and did a fine cop pose. I got his email, promising to send him a copy of the picture when it's done.

At least my son had the good type of "memorable" evening. Me, I'm fidgeting. I want to pace. But reports need filing. So reports get filed.

The older officer, a tiny woman with a graying ponytail named McMillian, talked with everyone one at a time, starting with Camille. When Rob took his place at the table, he hooked his phone to the cruiser's laptop and downloaded the video. When my turn came, I handed Bart over to Camille. His excitement had worn off and he tried very hard not to suck his thumb.

Camille squeezes my fingers before carrying him toward his room. "Time for bed, little man."

"Two and a half years?" Officer McMillian asks me.

"Yes. She vanished without leaving a forwarding address or phone number." I had hoped we'd never see her again.

When Camille walks away, McMillian returns her gaze to her laptop. But she doesn't ask another question right away. "I remember when you were injured. I remember all the hoopla, too. You doing okay now?"

I nod. The support the city gave me—and in particular the police and my station house—was what got me through my injuries and my court battles. For a while, when Bart was an infant and before Tom moved in, six police and firefighter families cooked my meals and helped care for my son.

But that all stopped when my therapy dropped from "recovery" to "maintenance."

"It's good. I have a big contract with a hotel chain." I lean back in my chair, smiling.

McMillian nods. "Good. You don't need any more shit. So let's do a thorough job documenting, here."

She taps at her laptop. "Your brothers both seem to think she's caused damage to their property in the past. Do you believe this as well?"

"Yes. No proof, though. No charges." I look over my shoulder. Tom and Sammie speak to the other officer as they prepare to leave. His gallery show opens on Tuesday and they still need to stop by the space tonight.

I wave. "We're all taking extra precautions."

McMillian nods. "Did you see the incident on the front step?"

"I was in the kitchen." Camille had tried to spare me from facing my psycho ex. I feel a frown try to harden my face, but I fight it.

On the one hand, I'm thankful. And thrilled she handled it as if she's part of the family. But on the other, I'm terrified Lori might come after her.

After a few more questions, McMillian closes her laptop. "We're done here." Her little portable printer spits out a hard copy of the report. She also transfers an electronic copy to a thumb drive for me. "I suggest you inform your son's school immediately that his birth mother is in town."

"I will."

Camille turns the corner, having come back down the stairs. Bart must be asleep.

"My girlfriend is one of the teachers at the Community Center. She's there all day," I say.

McMillian sets all her police-issued electronics into their case and closes the lid. For a long moment, she watches Camille. "Several of us do security work up there on our off hours. I'll get the word out."

We shake hands when she stands. "Thank you."

After she leaves, I still want to pace. I still want to throw shit at the walls and punch a hole in a door. I can hold it together when the cops are around.

But McMillian's gone.

And that bitch Lori poked her nose back into my life.

Why can't I calm down? But I know why. This is Lori's M.O. Hurt in small ways then run off and let it fester.

Still, I won't take the chance that she might come back tonight. I stand with Camille in the front entrance for a long moment, holding her tightly against my front. "I don't think you should go back to your apartment at all this evening." I want her here, where I know she's safe. "I know you can handle yourself, but I'd feel better if you didn't go."

"I need a few things." But she nods against my chest. "Will you come with me? Follow behind. We can fit a lot of my stuff into your truck."

She's more than staying tonight. I think, maybe, she wants, at least partially, to move in.

With me. With Bart. My happiness must be obvious because she's smiling, too.

"Don't get a big head, pirate man. We still have a lot to talk about." Camille reaches for her bag.

From the kitchen, Rob raises a glass of water in salute. "I'm not going anywhere. Until tomorrow." He shrugs and walks toward the television. Picking up the remote, he clicks it on and drops his ass on my couch. Using his full arm, he clears an open area in Bart's accumulated toys, and props his feet up on my coffee table.

Camille weaves her fingers into mine and pulls me toward the door.

CHAPTER 17

Daniel

Camille's apartment is a cramped space with rickety windows and worn, cheap carpet. The building smells faintly of old deep-fry grease, and the paint in the hallway to her apartment has a sticky texture.

I don't like it. I tap along the hallway wall, listening for the studs. It should have cinderblock firewalls between every other unit at a minimum, but the building looks—and sounds—hollow. Even with the old fire codes, the inspector should have done a better job.

"This place is a deathtrap." I sniff and tap the worn door to her apartment. It's thinner than it should be and sounds filled as opposed to solid. There's a gap under it, as well. One perfect for drafting in smoke.

I can't tell if she's amused by my statement or annoyed. Either way, she's out of here tonight.

"The rent's cheap." She pushes her key into the lock and wiggles it because it sticks. When she pushes it open, I follow her inside.

Like most apartments, hers has a galley kitchen off a small living area and a bath and bedroom off a short hallway. I feel a cold breeze moving through the room from the windows over her couch. I bet they whistle when it's windy.

"What's your lease say about giving notice?" The less rent she needs to pay, the faster we can pay off her school loans.

She doesn't have a lot of stuff. The furniture we can sell or put downstairs. I have room for all the books. And I've already had an artist living with me, so I know where to set up her easel downstairs.

We can have her out of here by Monday morning.

Camille drops her keys on her kitchen counter and turns slowly. "Sounds like someone's made up his mind about what he wants."

I've made some shitty decisions in my life. Marrying Lori, for one. Not sticking with college. But Bart's happy and I think that even with our rocky start, I'm doing well with Camille.

Lori showing up isn't going to ruin what we're building. I won't let it. I've got a good thing going.

And all those to-do zombies? For the first time in my life, I feel like I have them under control.

That my actions won't breed more.

"I don't want to waste any more time."

Camille watches my face the entire time I step toward her, but she doesn't look upset. Or annoyed. And I think maybe she's made up her mind, too.

"I wasted six months because I didn't know what to do." I used to worry about what Lori wanted. Was I making enough money? Were my brothers okay? Someone had to pay attention.

But I don't feel that way with Camille. I feel like she's got my back. Like my decisions are right.

Slowly, she runs her finger over my belly. "I think you knew what to do. I think you just didn't trust yourself to do it."

I'm in her arms before she finishes her sentence. Up close, her subtle yet sweet scent fills my senses and I want to rub my palm over her breasts. It's as if my brain recognizes the few moments alone we have and immediately wants to take advantage.

"Rob told me how she used to tear you down."

I blink, my attention pulled away from thoughts of nibbling on her nipples. "I don't want to talk about Lori." I'm done thinking about my ex. I wrap my hands around Camille's waist to pull her closer. We're in a child-free environment.

And I suddenly very much want to lift her onto the counter and fuck her right here, in her kitchen. Slowly. With her beautiful eyes lighting up with joy and pleasure. With her lips on my ear and her breath whispering what I need to hear: *Love you.*

"Dan." Camille pulls my hands off her hips and laces her fingers into mine. "I want to tell you something."

Shit pops into my head. What did I do now? "I thought you wanted to move in." Maybe I don't have all my zombies in a row. Maybe—

"Dan!" Camille curls her arms around my neck and pulls my head down for a long, deep kiss. One hand strokes the back of my head. The other drops and smooths over my ass. Her mouth lingers on mine, touching, feeling, expressing.

And I stop wondering how I've screwed up again.

One last little kiss lands on my chin. "You worry *way* too much."

I'm grinning like a little kid. Like Bart when he wins a game. I don't need to worry anymore. "Maybe I need to burn off some energy." I nibble on her neck at the same time I brush my fingers over her breasts.

She tucks her head against my neck. "I see the same ability to read a situation in you that I see in your brothers." A new kiss lands on my chin. "Tom sees. Rob, I think, hears. And you..." A hug tightens around my waist. "I think you feel. Cold or hot. Tense or loose. It's in your body."

She must read that I'm not following by the look on my face. Camille laughs. "I haven't been with a lot of men. You're the fourth. But I will tell you this, gorgeous: I trust you infinitely more than I trusted any of them. With my life. With my *body*."

So she trusts me to get beyond the "almost." I like this idea.

She tugs on my hand. "Come with me."

Her bedroom is blander than I expected. Old furniture, dull colors. I barely register anything beyond the bed. I swing her up and drop her on her back at the same time I yank up her t-shirt. "Want," I growl.

"Hold on, mister pirate man." She pushes me off. "There are a couple of things we can do that will help me get where we want me to be." As she sits up, she leans over the side of the bed and pulls out a trunk.

Ah, yes, "the toys." This should be interesting.

"I think the reason I never got there with any other man is because I didn't trust them as much as I trust you." She flips open the lid. "What you do already is amazing and I think that with a little extra the sex is going to be—"

Inside the trunk I see a lot of long, black things. Things that cause pain.

I'm off her, kneeling on the edge of the bed. "You're into that? Why didn't you tell me?"

Camille's mouth rounds to a perfect circle. "I thought since you like playing that maybe we could try a few things."

Not this. "Not with what's in there." I point at the trunk. Not with things that hurt.

She looks at the toys, then up at me as she sits up. "Um, okay." She looks at the toys again, but I can see her disappointment. It's that same disappointment Lori showed when she was making her *Why didn't I wait and marry someone better?* face.

Like she thinks she's settling.

Camille frowns. "I've never had more than one orgasm at a time. Before you, everything was just a tickle, except when a guy used the toys."

She slams the trunk lid when I don't respond, but her face changes like she's had an idea. "Maybe the vibrator?"

I nod, but turn around. The light in the parking lot streams through her living room window and throws a pool of glare onto her couch. I walk out and drop into its center, blinking.

Shit, flits through my head again. I shouldn't freak out. She's not Lori. I don't even know what she's asking. But I know what I will and won't do.

But maybe I don't. Lori told me I was boring. She pointed her finger at my chest and said because I like to be on top and I like to kiss that I'm boring and I get what I deserve.

So I deserved her cheating on me. I deserved having to take that paternity test.

Camille sits on the couch but not close enough to touch. "Is this about—"

I know what she's going to say. "No." It's not. She might be spinning in my head but this isn't about her.

"Oh." She reaches to touch my arm but pulls back her fingers. "Was there someone else? Because I'm not into—"

"I've been with two women, okay? You and her."

Her frown works from her face to her shoulders and her chest. Camille slumps and sets her hands on her lap.

"That's how my life worked out. When Mom and Jeanie died, Dad gave up. Someone had to work. Tom and Rob needed me. So I tried to go to college and work full time but I couldn't handle it. I married Lori and I worked because I was at least good at being a firefighter."

Camille doesn't move. She doesn't ask questions, either. But the frown vanishes.

I rub my face. "The night of my injury, the police were already at the building when it blew. They'd been called on a domestic. Jason and I carried the mom and her two toddlers out. She'd been beaten pretty bad."

"Dan..." Her face takes on a completely different look and I wonder if maybe we can get through this.

But I'm not sure. "I've seen what violence does. So I won't hurt you, Camille. Even if you ask me to."

"That's not what it's about." She moves closer, but still doesn't touch.

I miss her fingers on my arm. I miss the closeness and the caring. And it's gone.

"We don't have to—"

I stand up. I need to pace. Move somehow. "I know stuff like this is a deal breaker. You're not going to want to stay with someone who's... boring. You shouldn't settle."

Camille stands, too. "Did I say that?" The frown reappears. "Why would I *ever* choose a box full of toys over *you*?"

For a moment, I'm silent. She might think that now, but women change their minds. They get bored. "I rather you told me now instead of a couple years into a marriage. I don't want to go through that again."

"That's not going to happen!" Camille twirls around. "Will you listen to me, please? You need to get beyond Lori. If you need to find someone to talk—"

"This is *not* about Lori!" I feel like punching the wall. But I won't.

"Some of it is. Obviously." Even my truncated ability to read women can see that she's angry. I see it in how she's standing.

"I will *not* hit you." Or tie her up. Or dominate her. "If it's a deal breaker I want to know *now*. Because I can't handle another six years of trying to heal."

"It's *not* a deal breaker! There are other things we can do." Camille's entire body slumps. "Can we talk about it? Please?"

I feel the zombies massing. They're familiar: Change this little bit of myself for a woman. Give up another area of my life so she's happy.

Sex with a woman I love makes *me* happy. Sex that's slow and genuine. And now pain wants to slither in.

"I'm going home." I need to think.

"Why?" I see tears. Her cheeks quiver. She's crying.

"I can't do pain anymore, Camille." I walk to the door.

"Dan!"

But I let the cheap door of her apartment close behind me.

I let it close off this part of my life.

⚜

I DROP MY KEYS AND MY PHONE ON THE KITCHEN COUNTER BEFORE I lock the door to the garage. I'm home. Alone.

Rob rounds the corner from the living room and stops in the open arch leading into the kitchen. "Where's Camille?"

I don't answer. I get two beers out of the fridge instead, and hand one to my annoying younger brother.

"What happened?" Rob flicks his cap onto the opposite counter, over the cabinet with the garbage can.

"We had a fight." I don't open my beer and it sits on the counter, mocking me.

Rob takes a pull at his. "What'd you do?"

"What did *I* do? Why is it always what *I* do?" Why do I always get what I deserve?

"Hey." Rob sets down his bottle and pats my back the way he pats Bart when he's upset. "Talk, brother."

What the hell am I supposed to say? It's not like he'd understand. That kind of shit doesn't bother him.

His sophomore year, he got into the kinky stuff for a while. Did a few things that raised my eyebrows. Sometimes I don't care if his high school years sucked. Sometimes I think he does shit like that to play it up and prove he's a "misunderstood bad boy."

He steps back. "She's got *toy* toys, doesn't she?"

My finger taps the counter, then the side of my beer, then the counter again, all on its own. Like it needs to be restrained. "*Fuck.*"

"It's not the end of the world." Rob rolls his eyes. "If she was into the lifestyle, she would have told you already. So they're exactly what she said they are—playthings."

I step away from the counter into the middle of the damned kitchen, where I can't touch anything. "I don't like it."

Rob rolls his eyes again. "Oh for God's sake! It's all the rage with the kids these days. It's like those damned vegan vampires of a couple of years ago—it's not nearly as potent as the real thing. It's sparkly spanking."

"I'm not doing that." I'm pacing. My body feels cold and I need to keep moving. "You know why."

Rob takes a long pull on his beer as he watches me walk two strides toward the dining area, then two strides back. "*Me* knowing why isn't important. You need to tell *her*."

I stop. "I told her." Maybe I should open that beer. Bart's asleep. But it takes more than one beer to get a buzz going for me. I burn it off faster than it accumulates.

Except drinking never solved any problems.

"*All* the whys?" Rob doesn't get much of a buzz, either. So he's rational. Or at least as rational as my evil little brother can be.

"The ones that count."

He rolls his eyes again.

My phone buzzes. Rob's closer to it than me. He glances down as he takes another swig. "You should answer that."

I don't move. I need time to think. Hell, *she* needs time to think. If it's a deal breaker, then the deal needs to be broken.

Rob scoops up my phone and presses *accept* before I can stop him. "He's sorry and he's an overreacting idiot." His eyes narrow as he stares at me. "Right?"

I don't respond. How can I? I should be sorry. I'm screwing this up. But I can't do pain.

I can't.

Rob blinks and his eyebrows scrunch together. "Hey, listen Camille. He's home safe. We'll get it sorted."

Camille's indistinct voice pops from the phone, a flat, static-filled version of the woman I love. Because she's not here. She's far away.

I want to bang my head against the refrigerator until both it and door are well dented.

Rob says something else. Something about his flight out tomorrow. Then he hangs up. "You're thinking that if she likes the spanking and the tethers, she's lying if she tells you she will live without them." He sets his now empty bottle next to my phone. "Correct?"

I nod. Rob understands. "Lying to me and to herself."

Rob frowns. "Yes. As I have experienced."

"See? You know why." I'm pacing again. Why can't I hold still?

My brother grasps my shoulder. "Since when are my fucked-up girlfriends an example you should be looking to for dealing with your *not* fucked-up woman? Talk to Tom. Ask *Sammie*. Seriously. She's got a good head on her shoulders."

He's concerned. Actually, I believe, honestly concerned. I stand up straight. "I'm okay," I say. I shoulder the burdens of the world every day. How is this different?

"Anger isn't going to help, Dan."

Anger? "I'm not angry." Disappointed. Shocked. Maybe scared. But not angry. "I'll be angry if I get caught up in another lie."

He takes his hand off my shoulder. "I need to finish packing. You need sleep."

He flies out tomorrow morning at nine. "Be ready by six. I need to drop off Bart before taking you to the airport."

I won't have a moment to talk to Camille.

Rob nods and walks away, toward the guest bedroom, leaving me alone in my kitchen with my buzzing appliances and my buzzing life. Why don't I see this shit coming?

Why can't I read women better?

I turn off the lights and head to bed, knowing full well that I won't sleep tonight.

CHAPTER 18

Camille

I'm hoping Dan will at least talk to me this morning. I wasn't expecting what happened last night. At all. He's playful and I thought…

I stop pacing and sigh, pressing my fingers into my forehead. Most of the kids bounce and yell in their main rooms right now and my first pull-out starts in fifteen minutes.

Bart's not here. Again. Dan didn't call him in this morning, either.

I know he needs to take Rob to the airport but I think he's avoiding me.

The doors whoosh open. Bart skips in, his pack on his back, followed by Rob.

Not Dan. Rob.

Bart hugs my legs. "Are you coming home tonight?"

It takes all my effort to keep from sobbing right here in the Community Center lobby in front of the laughing front desk staff and my boyfriend's not-so-little younger brother.

I squat down to give Bart a hug. "I don't know."

Bart won't let go. "I miss you."

I was only gone this morning. I rub his shoulder as I watch his face. He looks genuinely upset.

I give him another hug. "Off to your room."

"Can I spend the whole day with you?" He hugs my legs again.

"We'll need to ask Ms. Cunningham."

Bart nods and runs off toward Sandy's room.

I watch him go. He picks up way more than a five-year-old should.

Next to me, Rob rubs the back of his head. He's not wearing a winter jacket—I don't think he brought one—and looks cold.

He stands with his feet planted too, his body angled like he has something to say. To my surprise, his phone stays in his pocket.

He watches Bart hang his pack in his cubby hook. "When we were kids, our father used to bring us up here at least once a week to the play area." He nods over to the large slide and ball pit that takes up a good chunk of space off the lobby.

"When Tom started middle school, after Mom and Jeanie died, Dan would bring us after school to play ball in the gym." He nodded to the other side of the building. "He took care of us."

"Dan told me how your mom passed. Said it was a car accident." Like Lori, he doesn't talk about it much.

Rob rubs his head again. "Tom and I are eighteen months apart." He shrugs. "Dan's six years older than Tom. Jeanie was in between." A smile flits across his face. "My sister and my oldest brother were almost exactly three years apart. Dan was in high school when the crash happened. Dad took it hard. Tom and I did not respond well to Dad's depression."

I'd been surprised when Dan told me their father wasn't flying in from Sedona for Bart's party. Or Tom's opening. "Is that why he's not around?"

Rob nods and leans closer. "I got Tom to promise to live-blog tomorrow night, mostly so I can share it with Dad."

Dan's bad boy brother doesn't seem all that naughty.

Quickly, I give him a hug. He blinks but quickly squeezes before stepping back.

"He told you what happened last night, didn't he?" I ask. "What should I do, Rob?" It pops out like so many other words have popped out over the last few days. Maybe all the Quidell men make me speak the truth, even if it's awkward.

He crosses his arms and watches Sandy's room, not me. "Dan had a good scholarship to a good college. He wanted to study structural engineering. Work big construction. Do you know why he became a firefighter?"

Because someone needed to work. "Your family needed the income."

"The crash happened two blocks from our house. Dan was the second person there." Rob's lips thin. "He saw the good first responders can do."

"I didn't know." Yet another bit of his life I didn't understand. "I figured he'd tell me when he was ready."

Rob nods toward the rooms. "He married Lori two weeks after they graduated."

Mary Beth is watching us from her room. I can't tell if she's frowning but I bet her eyes are narrow and her fists nice and tight.

Damn it, I think. *I don't need this right now.* And neither does Dan. We both need a little support. A little bit of compassion.

"I don't understand why he left last night." And why he refuses to talk to me. "Is he here, Rob? Will he come in? I can't go out. My class is about to start." I point at the door. Maybe I should go out anyway, the hell with my job.

"I think he feels boxed in." Rob's entire body shakes as if someone ran a finger up his spine. "Hell, Camille, I think he's *always* felt boxed in. Then you came along and let him out and he breathed for the first time in over a decade."

But Lori showing up and me bringing up something he thinks he'll need to accommodate because he *has* too, all produced the perfect storm of Dan worry. "Last night... reminded him of his box," I breathe. *Shit.*

The big clock over the Community Center door chimes. "I need to go." I squeeze Rob's arm and shuffle backward toward the rooms, even though I'm still confused. Still ready to sob. Still kicking myself for something that I think I should have seen coming.

But how could I have? Pain takes time to reveal. A man, even one as strong as Dan, can only handle so much at a time, no matter how much love and trust he feels. And Dan hadn't worked up to telling me what Rob just did.

I wave to Rob. "Tell him that when he's ready to talk, I very much want to talk."

"I will, Camille." Rob smiles as he, too, walks backward. He points and winks. "Think outside the box!"

Then he's gone, out the doors, on his way back to graduate school.

CHAPTER 19

Daniel

I feel numb this morning. Not angry. Not sad. Not depressed or frantic or anything else. Just numb. So I sent Rob into the Community Center with Bart instead of going in myself.

Thankfully, Rob avoided calling me names. Or accusing me of acting like a child. If I want to take a little time, I can take a little time.

I'm going to need to get over her sooner or later, anyway.

Bart didn't say much this morning. Though he did spend a lot of time hugging Uncle Robby and asking him when he'll be home again.

I rub my hand over my face and tap the fingers of my other hand on the steering wheel of my truck as I wait for Rob to come back out. He's been in there long enough already. I tap the steering wheel again.

Maybe he's talking some sense into Camille. The man knows how to sweet talk women. God knows it's gotten him in enough trouble over the past decade. The moment he decided girl cooties were something he *wanted*, no woman's been safe from his charms.

Rob has more than made up for my lack of field playing.

He's smiling when he saunters out the Community Center door

and I think my heart skips a beat and spikes right through the numbness.

Rob slams the door of my truck and the vehicle's entire frame rattles. He buckles in before picking up the coffee he made me go through the inconvenient and narrow drive-thru three blocks from the Community Center to get. The coffee smells like cinnamon and makes me hungry even though food is the last thing on my mind right now.

"I have fixed your problem." Rob pulls his phone out of his pocket and holds it up so I can see the screen. "Plane. Hour and a half. Security. Drive."

I start the truck. "What did you do?"

Rob shrugs. "Like I said, I fixed your problem." He swipes at his phone, ignoring me.

When we're on the freeway, halting and starting in morning traffic, I can't take the silence anymore. I need to know. "How?"

Rob shrugs again. "You know, you're acting the same way you acted when you had to haul your broken ass into the courtroom for the custody hearings. All 'man against the world' stoic hero. No tears shed. No emotion displayed. Because it gets in the way of your open can of whoop-ass."

"So? Bart's my priority. He needs stability." The brake lights of the car in front of us come on and I stomp a bit too hard. Rob slams against his seatbelt.

"Careful, bro. Got a test tomorrow. Don't need brain damage."

I glance at him. He sniffs at me as he takes a sip of his coffee. Quickly, he returns it to the cup holder before we hit another slowdown.

"What did you say to her?" A part of me wants to go all manic monster and rip shit down. Another part wants to crawl into bed and do whatever Camille wants so she won't leave.

I don't like either part.

"I gave her enough background I think she now understands your projection issues." He strokes his chin. "Or maybe you have a dissociation going on. I slept through Psych 101 so I don't know onto which page of the DSM of Mental Disorders you fall, my issue-filled brother."

"You aren't helping." More brake lights. More stomping.

Rob frowns and his coffee sloshes. "When she asks you to stop freaking the fuck out so the two of you can talk, you stop freaking the fuck out and sit down with her, okay?"

Of course I will. I owe it to her and to Bart to at least try. But I don't say anything more. I don't need Rob psychoanalyzing me.

Rob's phone, once again, appears. And, once again, his finger swipes.

I'd glare at him if I didn't need to watch the traffic. "Why don't you try living in the moment and not on your phone."

My little brother tucks away the device. He sips his coffee, his face stern the way mine is when I want Bart to listen. "What would I do 'in the moment,' Daniel?" This time, he slurps from his cup.

My hospital therapist's voice rings through my head: *See the world. Understand what's real and what's in your head.*

God damn it, my inner voices are ganging up on me and echoing my youngest brother.

I frown. Traffic picks up when we get around the curve and the sun's no longer in everyone's faces. I push my sunglasses up my nose. Rob returns to swiping at his phone.

At the airport, I pull up to the drop-off and put the truck in park. Traffic crawls by as other people look for a place to swing in. The ubiquitous airport information voice pipes from the speakers over the door, telling us all not to leave our bags unattended.

Rob unhooks his seatbelt. "Her name's Isolde, by the way."

"What?" Her name is Camille. He's not making sense—

The light dawns. Isolde must be his latest conquest. The one he didn't want to talk about when I picked him up. "What did you do this time, Robert?"

Absently, he taps his fingers on my truck's dash. "She's Mack's sister."

"You're fucking around with your roommate's sister?" I roll my eyes. "Is that why you're checking your phone all the time? To see if your roommate's kicked you out?"

The rawness of the pain on my little brother's face hits me hard in the gut. I almost reach for his arm, give his elbow a brotherly squeeze, but his look vanishes as fast as it appeared. "It's complicated." He points at me. "More complicated than your pathetic issues, dumbass."

"Of course." My little brother isn't a man who shies away from dating. Usually a new woman every week. "With you, it's always complicated."

The pain flits across his face again. "Unlike you, the life I've built lacks a solid reputation. My house, at least according to the female half of the human race, is not one of stability and emotional safety." Now Rob rolls his eyes.

We fall silent for a moment, both of us listening to the roar of the planes and the whoosh of the traffic. Two Quidell men, sitting by ourselves because it's the world against us.

Rob slaps his seat. "Time to go. Got a plane to catch."

I give him a quick back slap before he hops out. "Don't flunk your courses."

Rob walks to the back of the truck and pulls out his bag. When he comes around, he waves. "Don't spoil your son!"

My youngest brother strides through the sliding doors into the airport, his head low and his phone in his hand once again.

I pull out into traffic, also alone again, and head back to my life.

CHAPTER 20

Daniel

Through the speaker of my phone, I hear Tom's corporate desk chair squeak. I managed to catch him before he left his office for lunch. "Rob's right, you know."

"I don't know what to say to her." The parking lot of the fast food place I stopped at smells like old grease and engine oil. I glance at the burger in my hand, realizing it tastes the same, except with a coating of sugary red ketchup. I set it on the driver's seat, careful to keep it and all its toppings within the confines of its wrapper and the bag it sits on.

I'm outside so I can stretch my hamstring, even though it's too damned cold today. Winter better hurry up and go away.

"No, you don't." I hear Tom's keys jingle and his desk chair slide in. He's about to leave to meet Sammie. "If you did, you wouldn't be whining about it right now, would you? You'd take care of it like you always do."

I swing my shoulder. It's tightened up again, without Camille's touch to tame it. "You're more of an ass than Rob." Which I didn't think was possible.

Yet his words sound familiar. Then I remember: Rob said almost exactly the same thing. That I shoulder the burdens of the world.

Maybe I do. Maybe that's my role. But maybe my shoulders are full. Maybe I can't take shit sneaking up on me anymore. Maybe this one little thing that looks little to everyone else is just heavy enough I finally dropped to my knees. Which means my zombie list will catch up.

I scratch at my itchy stubble. How can I need help and fear the burdens help brings all at the same time? Because that's what this is. My fucking shoulders are full and I feel like the one person who might lift away some of the burdens is balancing on my forearm so she can reach. The weight's shifting, but I'm still carrying it. Now it's on my front instead of my back.

Or maybe I'm just being stupid and scared.

Not a great role model for my boy, that's for sure.

"I'm not ready to talk to her yet. Not out in the open like that, at the Community Center," I say into my phone. "I got shit in my own head to work out."

Tom snorts. "Yes, you do." He moves again and I hear muffled voices. "Sammie's here." I hear more talk. "She wants to know if you want us to pick up Bart tonight."

They'd do that? "What about the set-up at the gallery?"

I hear Sammie say something about not worrying.

"We're good. We're taking the day off tomorrow," Tom says.

I hear Sammie: "If you're anything like Tom, you'll have it all figured out by the time you see Camille at the gallery tomorrow night."

But I'm not like Tom. My brother isn't selfish. He's the one who sacrificed to move in with me after my injury because I needed the help.

"Listen," Tom says. "We'll meet you at your place around dinner time. You need us, just text. I mean it." My brother says good-bye and cuts the call.

I set my phone next to the chewy, now-cold burger. It sits on my seat, wrapped up so it doesn't stain my upholstery. Standing in the cold, my foot on the truck's running board as I un-cinch my leg muscles, I close my eyes, counting the way I'm supposed to, when the world gets out of control. Taking that deep breath to calm my body because, as the docs said, the first step to regaining your strength is to silence the nag-zombies in your head.

What if it's too late? What if...

I rub my face again. What if, when I'm ready to talk to her, she doesn't want to talk to me ever again?

Shit.

Am I moving too fast again? Too slow? What if she feels like *she's* settling?

I see zombies everywhere. Or maybe Bart's sharks. But I know I'm not one of his superheroes.

Or the pirate Camille wants.

Or, right at this moment, the good independent contractor my contacts want. I rub my leg again. God knows being a good firefighter again is out of the question.

Father. Lover. I thought, too, if my luck held, maybe a husband again.

I don't know who I am. I throw the burger and the equally cold fries in the trash and drop my ass in front of my steering wheel.

Or what I should be.

CHAPTER 21

Camille

I wrap my hair into a loose French knot and pin it up, carefully leaving tendrils around my face. Smoky eye makeup follows. My shimmering ocean green shawl covers my shoulders and I wear a dark blue long sleeved dress and nice boots, because it's darned cold tonight.

It's time for Tom's gallery opening.

Tom said to give Dan his space when he and Sammy picked up Bart yesterday, so I've let him have his space. Dan didn't bring him in this morning. His call to the Center said something about helping Tom and Sammie finish their gallery set-up.

So I didn't text Dan. Or call, even though I *know* set-up is done.

I know because Sammie volunteered Monday evening to help me "think outside the box." I figured if anyone could help, it would be Dan's brother's communications-genius fiancé.

At first, I was embarrassed asking her for sex tips. But it turns out that Sammie knows a thing or two. We spent a good two hours discussing our big, beautiful men and I'm sure Tom had a wonderful night because if it.

222

Tempted as I was to give myself a little relief, I'm wrapping my horniness up in my nice dress and boots, just for Dan.

The drive to the gallery takes longer than I thought it would, with the ice. I concentrate on the road, welcoming it as a distraction from Dan as much as cursing it for making my little car skid around corners. When I see Dan's gigantic red truck, I maneuver into the tight space in front of it, thinking about the tight spaces I can get into with Dan.

Tight spaces made accessible by all the oil I'm going to massage into his skin.

A tap on my window startles me so much I gasp, and it pulls me from my revelry. Sammie stands in the street in a beautiful indigo dress with what looks like Tom's coat over her shoulders.

I roll down my window. "What are you doing out here? Get back inside before you freeze to death."

"You're here!" Sammie bounces on her high heels. "They're inside. Bart's drawing pictures for the guests and Tom has Dan walking around the gallery with his phone on video chat so Rob can see." She smiles. "I think everyone at his school is watching. Don't tell Tom. He's nervous enough as it is."

I somehow suspect it's not just Rob's classmates who are watching.

"I have something I want to show you before we go in." She's grinning like the world's all rainbows and kittens.

"Okay." I really just want to go in and find Dan, but Sammie's excitement is contagious.

"Won't take long. I promise." She grips my arm after I shut my door so neither of us slips on the icy sidewalk.

I nod. We help each other over the snow on the curb. Sammie rubs her hands together and stomps her feet.

"We need to go inside before you turn into an indigo popsicle." I tug on her arm. We can have our girl talk where it's warm.

"This way." Sammie's grin returns and she pulls me down the street. "I need your opinion before I show Tom." She stops at a door and pulls a key out of her clutch. "I think it's perfect, but I want to know what you think first, as another artist."

Inside, we climb the stairs to the upper level. It's a wide open and spacious space, with huge windows facing the skyline. Some old furniture sits in a corner and I think the loft must have been an office at one time.

"It's gorgeous," I say. "Beautiful view. I bet it has incredible light during the day."

Sammie twirls around. "I think he's going to like it."

I haven't known Tom long enough to know for sure, but I think so. *I'd* like it. "If he doesn't, I'll move in with you."

Light from the signs outside, on the street, flood the loft. Sammie stands in the middle of a puddle of red and blue, watching me the way I watch my students.

Her relationship with Tom took a very different course from mine and Dan's. Like with a lot of his painting's subjects, Tom immediately saw in Sammie what she needed illuminated.

I wish I'd seen what I needed to see with Dan a lot earlier. None of this would have happened.

Sammie pats my arm. "Tom's told me how rough Dan's injury and divorce were on him. On the whole family, really."

She waves and I take the stairs first. Her heels click as we walk toward the door. "I think Dan feels he needs to keep the world in order, or everything will fall apart."

"You're right." He does. "But I need to know *he's* not going to fall apart."

Sammie squeezes my hand. "You know, when I met Tom, I didn't think I deserved someone as good as him. He opened up the path I needed to walk in order to see that I do."

I don't know if she's referring to me or to Dan. Right now, the path is flooded and the cold water is freezing my feet.

And Dan's, too.

"He deserves so much more than he's allowing himself," I say. Dan's good at his work. He's brilliant with his son. And he's always there for his family.

Sammie takes my hand and pulls me down the street, toward the gallery. "Did you know you're the only person he talks about? Not his contracts or how well his business is doing. It never dawned on him to ask for logo design help because for the last six months, whenever Tom and I visit and it's Ms. Frasier this, Ms. Frasier that. How happy Bart is. How wonderful you are to both of them. He's been in love with you for a lot longer than you think."

We stop just outside the gallery door. Light pours through the wide plate glass front window, around the stylish, bold lettering of the gallery name. Inside, a crowd mills about, with knots of people gathering in front of several large, colorful paintings, all of Sammie.

I don't know what to say. I feel my chest tighten and a new hiccup force its way into the back of my throat.

"Hey, hey." Sammie takes my hands again. "Do you want me to send him out? My friend Andy and I will watch Bart if you want to take him down the street. Get coffee."

I shake my head. "It's Tom's special night. Both Dan and Bart want to be here." I give her a hug. "I do, too."

Sammie opens the door and a sweet chiming fills the gallery entrance. "We better go in before the boys miss us."

I nod, following her inside.

⁂

DAN'S EYES GROW BIG WHEN HE SEES ME. "YOU CAME?" HE LOOKS around before holding up his phone. "Rob wants to say hi."

On the screen, Rob waves. A cute blonde woman leans in and waves too.

"Hi, Rob," I say.

He gives me the thumbs up.

"Hold on." Dan and Rob chat for a moment, then Dan slips the phone into his pocket. "Seems his friend wants to get ice cream."

I want to push him into the corner and poke my finger into his chest all while yelling "What the *fuck* do you think you're doing, mister!" Then rip off his suit so he lets loose all his pent-up anger and frustration with hard thrusts and breath-stealing kisses.

But that's not going to happen.

"Do you want me to take your coat? There's a place set aside in the back." He points to a dark hallway leading away from the little corner set up for Bart.

Behind Dan, in a small, cordoned off area, a handsome dark haired man sits at a low table next to Bart, coloring in a picture of a puppy. The cubby is separated from Sammie's nudes, and contains several drawings of Bart and his action figures, plus a couple done by the little master himself, including two he did in class, for me.

I pull off my coat and hand it over. "Thanks."

Dan's face takes on an impressive expression of awe as I adjust my dress and shawl. I realize this is the first time he's seen me in non-work make-up and clothes. And most likely the first time in a dress.

"You look stunning." He reaches out to touch my hand but stops. Then his fingers vanish under the folds of my coat.

His suit's nice, cut well, and I wonder if it originally started as court attire. My poor boyfriend looks quite uncomfortable. "You look every inch the handsome man you are, Dan Quidell."

I'm going to do something about this.

"I'll drop your coat." Dan walks backward for a few steps, watching me. "Are you staying?"

"Yes."

He looks impassive. And maybe a little afraid. "So we can talk?"

He wants to talk. Finally. "Yes."

When he walks by the table, he whistles to Bart and points.

"Hey, little man!" I kneel with my arms wide open, waiting for Bart to notice me.

"Ms. Frasier is here!" Bart all but leaps into my arms and hugs me with all his five-year-old strength.

The man at the table stands and offers his hand. "I'm Andy, Sammie's friend. You must be Camille."

"Yes." We shake. "Nice to meet you."

Bart tugs on my hand and I lean down. "Mr. Andy's not a good drawer but don't tell him because he's nice and he will be sad."

Andy swallows a guffaw. "From the mouths of babes."

Bart leans against my hip. "Are you coming home tonight? I miss you."

"I miss you, too." More than I realized.

He clutches my legs. "I want you to come home."

"I'm here now." I hoist him up but the strain hurts my back. The slight heel on my boots aren't helping. "I can't carry you for long, okay? You're too big."

Bart wiggles. "It's okay." He hugs me again and pats my shoulder as if he's the teacher and I'm the student. "I can walk."

I set him down. "You *are* a big boy and I'm very proud of you for behaving so well, and for showing your pictures alongside your uncle's."

Bart stands proud as he sticks out his thumb the way he does when he's painting. "Look!" He pulls me to one of the display walls.

One of Tom's pencils of Dan and Bart catches my eye first. Both father and son lounge in a kiddie pool, in Dan's backyard. Both dressed as superheroes, splashing away. Dan's long sleeved shirt sticks to his sculpted torso, but Tom hinted at the scars underneath. The edges of the drawing give a sense of the terrible world beyond the pool, but the world need not fear. Doctor Bartman and Minion One will save the day.

Right next to the pencil is one of Bart's drawings. One I've never seen before. It's his dad, and him. And me.

And we're happy.

"I made that one for you." Bart points. "I want you to come home."

The hiccup makes it past my lips. I cover my lips with one hand and hug Bart close with the other.

All my thoughts of seducing Dan vanish. He needs love tonight more than he needs sex, no matter how much I want him to know how horny he makes me.

Andy takes Bart's hand. He nods toward the hallway. "Dan's taking his time back there. Why don't you go check on him? Doctor Bartman and I have this under control, don't we, buddy?"

Bart nods. "I'll draw you a new picture."

When Bart tugs on Andy's hand, Sammie's friend winks. I stifle a frown. Does everyone know? But at least they're looking out for us.

I run my hands down the front of my dress. Time for a talk.

I tiptoe down the hallway as best I can in my boots. Shadows slide across the bare-brick walls, cast by a lone light I suspect is coming from the coat room.

The sounds of the gallery diminish the deeper I go, as much, I suspect, from my own awareness of my heartbeat as from the walls' muffling. My heels click. My dress rustles. My body remembers how good Dan feels against my skin. And how warm and alive his cock tastes in my mouth.

I stop and close my eyes for a second. I need to get my horniness in check. Dan's my priority.

I hear Dan brush against the doorframe ahead of me. The light goes out. He's about to come out of the coat room.

When I step in front of him, he shivers, surprised. "Camille."

Quickly, I splay my fingers over his chest. He looks delicious in his suit. I give him a shove backward. "We have a moment. I'd like to take advantage of it."

Dan frowns but slides his feet back into the coat room. It's dark and I can't make out anything but a couple of piles of jackets, a desk, and a high counter against the back wall. Artwork covers all surfaces, but I can't make out colors. And it smells like donuts.

My mouth waters.

"I don't know if this is—" Dan stops talking when I curl my arms around his neck.

"When I said that I would *never* choose a box of toys over you, I meant it." I press my entire body against his.

"Maybe now. But what happens in six months? A year? When the new wears off and you want more." He's arguing but he's not stepping back. His hands drop to my waist and his fingers grip my hips.

"What about you, huh? In six months when the new wears off, are you going to start noticing how other women look at you? Because they do. Are you going to wonder about what you've missed?" It's not Dan's personality to play the field, but I need to make a point.

It's not *my* personality to push him away.

His frown deepens. "*No.* Why would I do that? I'm not an idiot."

"Then why would you think *I* would? Learning how to make love with you is an opportunity. A wonderful, brilliant opportunity I won't pass up."

CHAPTER 22

Daniel

Camille's scent fills my senses. It's ylang ylang. Like the candles. Like the night I said *the woman I love*.

She's right here, pressed against me and more gorgeous than I thought possible.

And she wants me. I rub my thumb over her hip. I don't feel lace under the clingy fabric of her dress, but I do feel it when I rub my palm over the top of her thigh.

Stockings. And no panties.

"An opportunity?" I ask.

"To learn. To build something special that's only between us." She gently kisses my chin.

"But—"

Camille lays a finger on my lips. "I worry too, Dan. I worry about what your family thinks of me. I worry about my job and I worry about not making enough money. I worry about Bart because I know it's going to be difficult to get him interested in math. And I worry about you working too hard. And about you worrying too much."

My body tightens on its own. My arms wrap around her waist. My shoulders drop down. And I bury my face against her neck. "I'm sorry," I whisper.

Camille moves us a step to the side. She leans against the counter along the back wall and I hoist her up, setting her bottom on the smooth surface.

My back straightens. She's high enough I no longer need to stoop. I can stand tall.

She kisses my cheeks, my chin, my lips. "This isn't about the toys, or settling in our relationship, or, I think, the stress of your current life."

I don't know what to say. She's right. It isn't. I have an inkling about a deeper problem, but I don't know what it is. Like Tom told me, if I did, I would have taken care of it a long time ago.

"I want to be with you, Daniel Quidell. I'm not giving you up without a fight." Her kiss is strong and warm. Loving.

I bury my face in her neck again. "I'm sorry." It's the only thing I can say.

"You can talk to me." She kisses my temple again. "You could talk to a therapist if you want. Someone who's on the outside. It's up to you."

What is happening here? How did I get to this place? I'm stuck in the slush of my life and I think Camille might be offering me a lifeline.

All I want is to let her warm my cold bones.

"I want you to know that Sammie and I had a talk last night. We discussed our Quidell men." Her fingers stroke my neck and my arms.

I chuckle as I imagine them comparing notes. "Now I have to worry about living up to Tom." The suggestive tone in her voice distracts me from my internal whining.

Or maybe I just don't want to think about it anymore.

She leans in. "We talked because I want you to enjoy sex with me as much as I enjoy it with you." One hand works into my hair. The other roams over my crotch. "I think you will like what I learned."

My cock is suddenly very much alive. And very much not worrying about the world anymore. "Right now? Here? Someone might come in."

Camille leans back. Her body quickly disengages from mine, and cool air fills the void between us. I frown.

She touches my cheek. "I love you, Dan. I trust you. I *want* you. I don't think you accept how insanely sexy and wonderful you are. I want to show you. Prove it to your skeptical mind. But I do need one thing before we move forward."

A good pounding? I think.

I must have smirked because she kisses the bridge of my nose. But she's not smiling.

Shit, flits through my head. What else could there be? "What?"

"I need to know that you want to deal with the worrying." She looks at me with her teacher face, gauging my reactions.

"I *am* dealing with the worrying." Every goddamned moment of my life I deal with the worrying.

"Dan." Her kiss is intense. But the desire I feel isn't the desire I was expecting. Her body tenses. Her brow pulls together. "Please. It's like you're keeping your soul in a box under the bed."

I'm not horny anymore. I'm confused.

"At the zoo, you put a lot of effort into keeping me. You put insane amounts of effort into your business and your family. Promise me you'll put the same determination into *yourself*."

I hear a couple of people shuffling down the hall. The owner must be bringing patrons back to pick up their coats.

Quickly, I lift Camille off the counter and set her next to me. She smooths her dress and runs her fingers over her hair. "Where's the light switch?" she calls. "It's dark in here."

I grasp her hand before I realize what I'm doing. When the light flicks on, we're staggering toward the door. "On our way out."

I smile my best smile and we push by, all but running down the hallway.

Before we round the corner, Camille tugs on my hand. We stop, standing together in the dim light, my family in front of us and the intrusions of the world behind.

"Please think about what I said. Maybe we can talk again later this week?"

She's not coming home with me. Though I don't know why she would.

I hoped that she would always have my back, no matter how stupid I act or how much pressure being with her adds to my burdens.

But her eyes don't say *adding*. Her eyes say *subtracting*.

Maybe she has my back in ways I don't understand.

The light in the coat room goes off again. "We need to go." I tug on her hand.

Together, we walk into the gallery.

And I need to find a way to make that *together* as real as the concern I see in her eyes. Because at this point, I know that burden's completely mine.

❧

I watch Camille pull away. Her hatchback sputters and it takes a significant amount of effort for me not to call her back. But she's right—I need to think. My need for her pulls at my gut and, deep inside, it's not all that different than when I lost Mom and Jeanie. But I think that's part of the problem.

I glance at the gallery when I hear the sing-songy chime go off because someone swung open the door. Sammie glides out into the cold, laughing, her shoulders bare, Tom right after her. They hurry down the sidewalk hand in hand without noticing me. I watch them go. Tom curls his arm around his fiancé, protective of her skin.

She laughs again.

I walk back to the truck. Bart's leaning his head against the seat, half asleep and bundled up in his winter coat and hat. He only stirs a little when I open the door. Outside, Tom and Sammie stop at another door, their heads close together.

Even from this distance, I see how Tom watches her. It shows in his paintings, too. Tom always sees the essence of a situation. And the essence of people.

Bart stirs. "I'm cold." But he closes his eyes again and returns to leaning his head against the seat.

"Sorry, buddy." I start the truck, flicking on the heater, and watch

Tom and Sammie enter the other building. They close the door behind them just as a blast of still-chilly air washes over Bart and me.

No heat until the engine warms up. The engine has to do what the engine has to do before the fire can take hold.

I pull the truck out onto the street and head home, my to-do list popping into my mind as I drive, the same as it always does. What's left to get Bart ready for school tomorrow? Am I prepared for my meetings next week? Do I need to shovel the walk again?

Just like an engine, I don't seem capable of changing, unlike my artist brother. Out on the freeway, I remember Rob asking me what Tom's secret was. How he solidified his relationship with Sammie so quickly.

My brother Tom reads the moment, not the demands laid on him. He sees what needs seeing, not checklists. Or threats of terrible futures.

Is that what Camille meant about putting effort into myself? Does she think I don't keep myself safe?

Or maybe *too* safe.

I wish I knew.

But tonight made me sure of one thing: I need Camille in my life.

And if that means I need to push through things that make me upset, then I'm going to take a chance, even if the shit might hit the fan.

I'm going to do what she needs me to do.

CHAPTER 23

Camille

The morning after Tom's gallery opening, Bart runs in, hugs my leg, and bounces into Sandy's room. I half expect Dan to do the same thing but he stops in front of me in his wrinkled button-down and chinos.

"You look happier." He's happy like he's come to a conclusion. My heart thumps. "Do you feel better?" I want to jump into his arms. Give him a big kiss right here, in front of all the other teachers.

Dan clasps his hands behind his back but doesn't stand like a college professor, the way Rob does. He squares his shoulders and pirate smirks where he stands in the bright sunlight spilling from the skylights, not saying anything.

My heart skips a beat. "Dan, don't keep secrets." What is he up to? His hair is messier than usual today, and I don't think he shaved.

My heart skips a beat again and I feel like bouncing, too.

He shakes his head and holds a finger to his lips. His foot slides back. He's walking away. "I'm working too hard." But he winks.

"Dan!" The clock chimes and I look over my shoulder. When I look back, he's waving as he dashes through the door.

Damn it. I almost text Sammie. Maybe I should text her. See if Dan said anything to Tom. Or maybe I should text Tom.

Sandy walks up, watching the door more than me. "Class time," she says. "Got everything worked out with Dan?" She nods toward the door.

"How did you know we were having issues?" It's not like I talk to my coworkers about my relationship. They're not exactly supportive.

Sandy chuckles. "All the kids keep asking me why Ms. Frasier is mopey. And Bart's been sad. Acting out in my room, though I suspect he's been extra good for you, hasn't he?"

I didn't know. "Why didn't you say something? I could have talked to him." He's usually such a good kid. "What's he been doing?"

Sandy shrugs. "Normal mad child behaviors. Not doing what he's asked to do. Taking toys from the other kids." She nods at the door. "Frowning a lot, like you and his daddy."

No matter how hard I tried, my Dan problem spilled over into work.

Sandy pats my arm. "Let's go. The little ones await."

I follow her back to the rooms, listening to the volume and pitch of the kids as they play, in case there's a problem. Or if someone needs a hug.

I glance over my shoulder again, hoping, maybe, Dan will come running back in, because I think a hug right now is what we both need.

DURING THE THREE O'CLOCK SNACK BREAK, ALL MY KIDS RETURN TO their main rooms, Bart included. On Fridays the teachers always do a theme—today is spring rain showers—and I painted rainbows on everyone's cheeks. They're all excited to show off their colors. I walk them down the hall, the six little artists who spend their time after lunch with me, dropping them off one by one with their teachers and their aides.

Bart's the last to drop off. He holds my hand, skipping along next to me, a rainbow on each of his cheeks. "When will the snow melt?" he asks.

He's been asking all sorts of weather-related questions today. When will it rain? Can I build a mudman the way I build a snowman? Why can't you touch rainbows? Why do you plant flowers? My daddy doesn't plant *anything* and there are flowers all over my yard.

"The flowers are yellow!" Bart says. "Some are purple. I like the purple ones the best." He skips along. "Will you come for pizza tonight?"

At Sandy's door, he hugs my waist. "Daddy misses you too."

Sandy appears in the door before I can answer Bart's question. Grinning, she leans down to Bart. "Your uncle is here."

I look down the hall and into the atrium. "Dan's not picking up Bart today?" I was going to make him stay and talk.

Tom and Sammie sit at one of the far tables, behind a planter, out of sight of my room. They're dressed for work, both in their corporate attire, as if they'd just come from the office. When they see me notice them, they both get up, waving.

"Uncle Tommy!" Bart jumps up and down. "Auntie Sammie!"

When they're close enough, Bart looks up at Sandy for permission to run to his uncle.

"Go on," she says.

Bart takes off, leaping for his uncle like a little superhero. Sandy pats my arm. "No more pull outs today. You go on, too."

"What?" She's telling me to leave early?

Sammie pulls an envelope out of her purse as they get close. Sandy winks and backs away, into her room.

"You all packed for your big weekend, buddy?" Tom glides Bart through the air and Bart stretches out, arms straight in front, legs back, laughing.

"Hey, Minion Two-Two, concrete floor." I point at the ground.

Tom frowns and spins Bart up onto his hip. "Ms. Frasier's a buzzkill, Doctor Bartman."

Bart screeches when Tom tickles his belly.

I glance at Sammie. "Weekend? It's Wednesday."

She smiles. "We're taking the rest of the week off and Doctor Bartman's staying with us, isn't that right, buddy?"

Bart screeches again. "Can we go to the zoo?"

Sammie pats his back. "Of course we can." She hands over the envelope. "We're supposed to give you this."

I take it. Across the front, in Dan's blocky and masculine hand, is "To m'lady, Ms. Frasier."

Bart points at the door. "Did you bring Mr. Pickles?"

Tom chuckles. "The kitty is at home, buddy."

Bart frowns. "Oh. Did you bring juice boxes?"

Now Sammie chuckles. "We'll have him home before bedtime Sunday."

They're taking him through the weekend?

Tom puts Bart down. "Go get your stuff." He shoos Bart toward Sandy's room. "And don't distract the other kids, Doctor Bartman. You're incognito, remember?"

Bart puts his finger to his lips and makes a shushing sound before tiptoeing into the room.

I watch him go. "He knows what 'incognito' means?"

Tom shrugs. "Of course he does. He's a superhero." He walks by, toward Sandy's door, following Bart.

Sammie leans close. "Dan called Tom this morning. Said the two of you needed time alone." A knowing smile brightens her face. "I want *all* the details. Every single one." Her hug surprises me, but only a little. "Time to see Mr. Pickles, Doctor Bartman!" She winks and helps Bart zip his jacket when he reappears.

Tom waits, Bart's bag in his big hand. "Dan is still confused, Camille. But he's trying." They walk out the door together, Bart between Tom and Sammie, on the way to a kid-filled weekend.

My fingers jitter when I look down at the envelope in my hand. What's Dan doing? My stomach's flip-flopping because...

Because I'm happy. He's trying and it makes me happy.

I open the envelope.

Inside, on a white index card, are three words: "Meet me outside." That's it. Just "Meet me outside."

I run for the door, not returning to my room to fetch my purse. Not to clean up. Not even to get my coat.

Because Dan's here. And he's waiting.

CHAPTER 24

Camille

The cold hits me hard when I run through the door. It's warmer today, but my breath still steams in the air. The sun shines, but a breeze kicks up the nippiness.

I don't care. Dan's here, somewhere.

Sammie waves as she closes the passenger door of Tom's big red truck. Bart's in his booster, tucked into the corner seat behind her. Their truck rumbles to life and Tom pulls out of the lot.

I don't see Dan's truck. It's the newer model of Tom's and just as big. And just as red. Both trucks stand out. It's not like Dan could hide it. I look around again. Am I on the wrong side of the building?

I stomp my feet, wondering if I should get my jacket. Where's Dan?

Not far from the Community Center entrance where I stand, the driver's side door of a big, shiny, silver car swings open. It's one of those sleek, fast German sedans, the expensive ones.

Dan's head appears over the top of the door and he leans against the car's frame. With one gloved hand, he points at the car's passenger side. "Are you going to get in?"

The car stands at attention and guarding its parking space like a good dog. Or a cheetah.

"Where's your truck?"

Dan grins as he saunters up the steps, leaving the car wide open. "At home."

"Did you buy that thing?" I point at the car.

"Rental. For the week." He curls his arm around me and I immediately warm. Even through his jacket, he gives off enough heat to stop any hypothermia creeping into my bones. "A gorgeous woman deserves a gorgeous ride."

"Dan!" I shiver as he unzips his jacket and pulls me inside. Damn, the man is warm. And hard. And my head fits perfectly against his neck when I wrap my arms around his chest.

"Will you forgive me for being an idiot?" He nuzzles the top of my head.

"You're not an idiot. You're overworked and you've had too much shit go wrong in your life and you just need to learn ways to deal with it that won't drive me insane."

Dan glances around. He watches a middle-aged woman in workout clothes walk by before saying anything. "You know, when you put it that way, it makes sense."

I poke his chest. "I don't always know what to say! My therapy expertise is in art."

"You're damned good at the physical, too." Dan watches a mom pushing a stroller walk by. "In the car." He nods toward the sedan. "Please."

I step around his big body and walk down the steps to the car's passenger side door, doing as he asks. It glides open like it floats on fairy dust. "Your car is distracting."

Dan chuckles and twists his big frame into the driver's seat. He barely fits. "No to-do list for the week, though I did make several reservations."

The car all but swallows me whole when I get in. It doesn't smell at all. Not even a whiff of cleaner. It's like the Germans managed to engineer a bright spring day into the ventilation. And I've never in my life sat in a seat with such perfect lumbar support. I buckle in and lean my head against the buttery leather.

Dan starts up the car. It purrs to life, the dash lighting up and all the indicators pinging their welcome. Even its flickers and chimes scream luxury.

"You went all out, didn't you?"

He doesn't take it out of park. He does, though, start the heater. "Got a hot date with a hot woman. Doing my best to impress. Because, starting today, I'm going to work less. Relax more. And try new things."

Dan shifts as best he can in the seat, to angle his body toward mine. "It's time to stop fearing the worst. So I thought we could go back to your apartment for a while."

I see his chest tighten.

My reaction blurts out uncensored. "We will not!" I slap the dash. "You don't *want* to! It's obvious in your shoulders that you don't want to! We will *not* dive right into something that makes you uncomfortable."

"But..."

"How is setting aside a belief that is obviously important to you because you think I will leave, *not* you settling?" Why can't he see what he's doing?

Dan blinks and his cheeks tighten. "Then tell me what I am supposed—" Dan flings open his door.

"What?" But I see her. Lori stalks toward the car from the same rented sedan she had the night of Bart's birthday party.

"Stay in the car, Camille." Dan slams his door.

I think several unteacher-like words. Lori would show up now, wouldn't she? Ruin what otherwise is turning out to be a spectacular day.

Not this time. I get out, slam the passenger door and walk around the car, standing between her and Dan. I'm cold again, but I don't care. She's not going to cause Dan's already too high stress level to shoot through the roof or take up our entire weekend making us file police reports.

"The Community Center daycare has the right to restrict access to the grounds of any non-custodial parent. You are not to enter the building or the parking lot. Get back in your car and leave." I'm between her and Dan before she gets half way across the lot.

Lori Taylor-Quidell glares over my shoulder, at Dan. "Since when can you afford a car like that?" she yells. "Did you hide something during the settlement? Tell me the truth, you pathetic worthless little man!"

"*Little?*" She's crazier than I thought. I hold up my hand. "Don't talk to her, Dan. Don't—"

"Why are you here, Lori?" Dan slaps the top of his rented German sedan. "Because you don't give a shit about your son. You never have."

Lori pokes at the air like she's trying to blind Dan with the tip of her finger. "I want what's mine!"

"You got yours when the judge sent you packing!" Dan flips her off.

"Oh, really? I put up with the whiny Quidell boys for *seven years*! Tom's the only one of you to grow a pair after your mother died! Living with you and all your tight-assed workaholic moping damaged me!"

I open and close my mouth, stunned silent. "Did she just say that?"

Anger reddens Dan's neck. "I swear she wasn't this crazy when we were married."

Lori thrusts her fists into her waist in very much the same way as Bart does when he's upset. "You owe me! And now you're driving around in a car like *that*?"

"You checking up on me?" Dan walks around me but stops several feet from Lori.

Around us, several people stop to watch. A few others continue into the Center.

Now Dan points at Lori. "*Owe* you? I worked my fingers to the bone for you! I stuffed my life into a box because I needed your help with my brothers and I was too damned immature to realize..."

Dan pivots. He turns around completely where he stands on the asphalt, his face a mask of shock. "...what it was doing to me. When my injury happened the box got smaller and I couldn't breathe anymore. Which is why I freaked out the first time the person I love— the person who loves and wants to help *me*—said something I thought would make my box that much tighter."

I'm in his arms before he stops speaking.

"I didn't hear what you said. I heard what I feared." Dan folds his jacket around me. "I'm sorry I didn't trust you, Camille."

"I've always trusted you," I whisper. "I trusted you'd figure this out."

Dan stiffens. He's not looking at me. He's looking at the Community Center entrance.

"I didn't do anything!" Lori screeches.

I look over my shoulder. The Community Center is two blocks from the city's police station and main fire house. We get uniformed officers coming in and out all day, usually stopping to pick up a cup of coffee. Sometimes they stay and play ball with the kids. We also usually have one or two off duty, out-of-uniform officers on the grounds most afternoons, in the Center's workout facilities.

Like today.

Mary Beth, the other teacher who's been giving me dirty looks since the strawberry picking field trip, stands on the step, shivering. Behind her, Sandy opens the entrance door. Mary Beth points at Lori as our uniformed officer strides through, his eyes on Lori and only Lori.

Another officer walks out into the cold—the woman named McMillian who took our statements the first time Lori showed up—and pats her face with the corner of her t-shirt. She must have been in the gym.

The uniformed officer walks by, nodding once. "You!" He points at Lori. "State your name."

"Why?" Lori backs away.

Up on the step, Mary Beth calls out. "Her name is Lori Taylor-Quidell."

The officer looks at Dan, who nods.

The officer continues walking toward Dan's ex. "The on-duty teachers and the staff of the Community Center have informed me that, by court order, you are not allowed on the premises."

"We want to file a complaint!" Mary Beth calls. When she looks at me, her expression says it all: *I'm sorry.*

"You need to come with me." The uniformed officer pulls out his cuffs.

"But... but..." Lori holds perfectly still when the officer takes her arm.

Dan's big chest presses against my back, blocking the cold. "An arrest will get her to leave us alone," he whispers. "The first time she disappeared was right after the judge ordered her to put in effort to see Bart."

I look up. His gaze moves from watching the officer haul away Lori to the other teachers on the steps, and back again.

I turn in his arms. His lists are surfacing again, even if he's finally broken out of his box. I feel them in the tightness of his lower back and see them in the sadness around his eyes. He thinks he's going to have to take care of Lori's intrusion. Be there for all the report filings. Make sure Tom and Sammie know. I'm pretty sure he thinks his life just killed all the joy he'd hoped to generate this weekend, with me.

"Hey." I kiss his jaw. "Look at me."

Dan blinks, but smiles when he looks down into my eyes.

"I'll get my coat. And I'll be right back. Okay?"

He kisses my forehead before he nods. His arms release and my wonderful boyfriend takes a step back.

I run up the steps to Sandy and McMillian. Stomping my feet, I rub my arms. "Do you need us? I mean really, truly need us here?"

McMillian looks over my shoulder at Dan. Her cheeks are red and she steps side-to-side the way someone who just stopped a run does. "Big plans?"

"Dan needs a break." A real break. One from the weight of his life. "She can't ruin the weekend for him." For *us*.

Sandy pulls her sweater tight around her middle. She catches Mary Beth's gaze and for a second, it looks as if the other two teachers are communicating telepathically. "He does need a break. So do you." She nods toward me. "He worries too much and you shoulder too much of the world."

I snort. It's not pretty, but it's how my body reacts. "*I* shoulder too much of the world?"

Sandy rolls her eyes and pats my arm.

I return my attention to McMillian, hoping maybe I have a little of that teacher telepathy, as well. All I can think is *please please please let us go. Please*. World shouldering or not, Lori can't ruin this moment for Dan. Or me.

In the lot, Lori yells something at the officer.

"Oh, resisting arrest." McMillian sniffs. "Not smart."

Mary Beth shakes her head when Lori pulls her wrists away from the officer. "We'll file the complaint."

"You two will need to file witness reports on Monday." But McMillian's grin tells me all I need to know.

"Thank you!" I'd hug her but she's a cop.

She smiles though, and gives Dan a thumbs-up.

And I run for my coat and purse.

༻✦༺

DAN'S HUMMING. HIS FACE IS BURIED IN MY CLEAVAGE AND HE'S humming like a happy little kid.

Somehow, he managed to find a secluded spot surrounded by a dense wall of trees fifteen minutes from the Community Center. How we made it this far, I don't know. I almost went down on him while he drove, but we're in the police's good graces right now and I didn't want to chance it.

When I told him what I was thinking, it opened the spout on *his* fantasies. I started tingling listening to him describe what he's going to do to me in the backseat of our rented wonder of precision German engineering.

Warm light spills through the sunroof and the windows. And I'm never letting this man go.

The humming turns throaty. "What did you say?"

"What?" I'm lost in the sensations caused by his roaming tongue.

"So we could leave?" Dan dances his fingers over the soft leather seat and smiles the same exact smile I see on his son when Bart's happily engaged in the moment. When he's creating something new and he knows his teacher has his back. That right now, he doesn't have to clean his cubby or pick up his paints.

He can enjoy being who he is.

"Only the truth," I say. Outside, the trees glisten and the world leaves us in peace. Which is what it needs to do, right now.

Dan hums again, his lips roaming across the upper edges of my bra's cups. "You still like me even though I'm dense?"

"You just need an education, Minion One."

"Yes, Ms. Frasier." Dan chuckles as he yanks down a cup, exposing a nipple. "I'll do everything you say, Ms. Frasier."

The way he suckles and flicks sends intense waves of pleasure through my breasts. The car is off and the cold is sneaking in, but my man has lit a fire in my soul.

And my body.

He moves against my pelvis, all hunched over in the back seat of the sedan in the cooling, turned-off-car air, rubbing his thigh against my still-covered pussy and humming against my frantically sensitive nipples.

"We have five days just for us?" I'm panting. I want to see his gorgeous chest and torso but I can't because we're in a car.

Dan yanks down the other cup of my bra and moves his efforts to my other breast. "Uh-huh."

"You took five days off? It's not going to be a problem?" Bart's in good hands, but I can't help worry about his business.

Dan looks up. An eyebrow pops up and his pirate smirk surfaces. "You worry too much."

"So we have five days of you doing *exactly* what you are doing right now?" No man has ever wanted to fuck me the way Dan does. It's not just sex. He wants to be close. To kiss.

To have his mouth on mine the same way it's on my nipples right now. His lips demanding all my attention while his fingers touch and stroke and express just how much he wants me.

Dan drops his mouth back to my nipple and hums his response.

Five days of loving this man.

"I will do *anything* you ask me to, Dan." I don't care what he wants. "I trust you more than I trust myself."

Dan comes up for air. "You're going to orgasm when I'm pounding you. It's going to be at the same time I come. I'm going to be in you and I'm going to see your beautiful eyes and feel your fingers in my hair. I'm going to feel your pussy tighten around my cock while I black out from the orgasm you give me because I love you."

No irony shows on his face. He's not playing. He's totally, completely serious.

"*Oh*..." I breathe. "We're going to do it in a way that makes both of us happy, aren't we?"

Dan's pirate smirk reappears. "Uh-huh."

When he returns his attention to my breasts, my back arches.

Because I love—and trust—this man to figure out what needs to be done.

And to do it right.

CHAPTER 25

Camille

"Mommy!" Bart walks carefully up the path from the dock toward the cabin's porch. He's wearing only his swim trunks, and a couple of mosquitos buzz around his head. His nose twitches like he wants to swat at them, but he's holding Isolde's—Isa, Rob calls her—big digital camera and he's doing a very nice job of not dropping it.

I set down my not-quite lemon-flavored water and swing my legs off the lounger. I think I'll stick to the non-flavored stuff but Sammie offered and I thought I'd try it. She's down on the dock with Tom, Rob, and Isa, talking about lighting over the lake and sunsets and appropriate amounts of art generation to write off our family vacation as work.

The steps creak when Bart takes them one at a time. "Smile!" he says when he crests the top one. The camera rises to his eye and he snaps a photo.

Part of me wonders why Isa is letting a five-year-old run around with one of her digital single lens reflex cameras, but the other part fully understands. My soon-to-be stepson's talents include all types of picture rendering. We've spent many weekends painting together, and working with photos in a couple of different editing programs.

"You're being careful with her camera?" I pat the lounger so he'll sit next to me. He's grown so much since his birthday I'm beginning to wonder if he'll be taller than me before he's out of elementary school. "Did you put on sunscreen?" I look over his young Norse King-slash-Highlander shoulders. "Don't get a sunburn."

"I did." Bart gives me one of his *Whatever, Mom* looks. "Stop worrying."

I chuckle and mess his hair. "Can't help that I love you."

Bart smiles and leans against my shoulder. "Uncle Robby and Isa want to go for a walk. Isa is bringing her other camera and she's going to show me how to take pictures the right way." He holds up the one strapped around his neck. "Uncle Tommy and Auntie Sammie are coming with. Can I go?"

I glance down at the dock. Sammie raises her water bottle and winks. She knows Dan and I haven't had a lot of alone time since we arrived on Wednesday night.

I wave a thank you.

"Sure. But put on a shirt and long pants, okay? And wear your sneakers. No flip flops on the trail." I rub his head again.

"Okay!" He kisses my cheek. "Thanks, Mommy."

I watch him carefully hold the camera as he wiggles through the screen door. From inside, I hear him tell his dad how he wants to take a picture of a moose.

Dan chuckles when he pushes through the door. He stops for a moment in the shade of the porch, his own water bottle in his hand, watching his brothers on the dock. "Rob's semi-girlfriend seems to have taken to Bart, even if they're still friend-zoning each other." He nods toward the water.

Isa leans her head toward Sammie and the sun glints off her blonde hair. I stand and lean against Dan and he hooks his thumb through the side of my bikini bottom.

"You took off the t-shirt." He's been wearing long-sleeved tees all weekend even though it's in the nineties, I think mostly because of

Rob's not-quite-girlfriend. But now I cuddle skin-to-skin against his broad chest.

"It's warm. No slush in the bones today." He shrugs. "Isa's nice."

I'm glad he feels comfortable enough to not worry about it. "She is. So are you." I kiss the edge of his sweep of chest hair. "Hot *and* sexy."

Dan takes a sip of his water. "Me or her?"

"Hmm." I glance at the dock. "Should I go blonde?" Could be fun.

Dan's eyes narrow. "Are there any Maori goddesses with pale hair?"

I chuckle. He's always looking for ways to get me worked up. Little scenarios. Ways to tempt me into using my imagination. We've developed quite a lot of coded looks and language. By the time we get Bart into bed, I'm usually ready to scream.

Once he figured out that's what I need, he's been unstoppable.

Sometimes I think he spends his bi-weekly sessions quizzing his therapist on conditioning techniques to use on me instead of taking the time to work on himself.

Same with his physical therapist.

Not that I'm complaining. He's happy and healthy. The man next to me is a joy to live with.

"So they're taking Bart for a walk, huh?" Another finger floats over my skin and into my bikini bottom.

"That's the plan."

"How long will they be gone?" He's watching the dock and I can tell he's holding in his pirate smirk.

Bart bounds out the screen door dressed appropriately for a walk, except his shoes are untied. The camera's strap loops around his neck, but it's twisted and doesn't look comfortable. "Taking pictures!" He holds up the camera.

"You be careful with that thing." Dan points his water bottle at Bart's chest.

Bart rolls his eyes. He stopped sticking his fists into his waist about a month ago and now makes faces instead. "Yes, Daddy."

"And tie your shoes." Dan points at Bart's feet.

Bart rolls his eyes again but bends carefully, maneuvering the camera around his knees, and ties his shoes. Then he's off, down the path, toward his uncles. They walk away along the lake's beach pebbles, two Quidell couples and their young nephew.

I like the lake. The cabin has been in the Quidell family since the fifties and has a quaint charm, though we'll need to build on as the family grows. The kitchen needs upgrading, anyway. "You and Tom talk about adding studio space?" The men spent a good deal of time discussing options yesterday.

Dan drops his water bottle on the lounger and scoops me up. My legs swing into the air and he lifts me over his shoulder in a firefighter's carry, and I screech like Bart when one of his uncles swings him around.

"That be a fine backside you have there, Ms. Frasier." His free hand works completely into my bottoms and he grips my ass with quite a lot of determination. "Think I'll pilfer it for me own."

Dan nibbles on my hip.

"Put me down." But I don't mean it. His shoulder feels rock hard against my breasts and I have a nice view of the muscular v of his lower back.

"Aye, matey." Dan swings open the door, twisting expertly to carry me in without knocking my head or knees or ass. "The waters be calm. And I do say I be tossin' a lovely maiden down on me bunk."

"Down. Oh God yes." I nibble on his shoulder blade and watch as Dan kicks his foot back, hooks the door to our bedroom, and slams it shut without turning around.

We're alone in our little room surrounded by suitcases and Bart's toys. It smells like the woods—moist and alive—and a cool breeze moves through the open windows. The plaid curtains rustle but the room's bright and cheery in the middle of the day.

"The massage oil is in my bag." I point at the floor, under the window.

Dan grunts and strips my bottoms off before he drops me onto our bed. The box spring groans and creaks and I bounce up, a good couple of inches of air between me and the bedding.

Twenty feet from the porch into the bedroom and he's already hard enough he's straining his cargo shorts.

"I think you fancy a roll in the sheets, my good sir." I reach for the zipper on his fly but he pushes me down on the bed, bending over me, a palm on each breast.

"I think you should wear your bikini instead of a wedding dress." Dan yanks the cups of my top to the side and immediately rolls first one nipple along his tongue, then the other. "The past two days watching you on the dock and in that lounger wearing only black triangles over my favorite parts has been murder, woman. My will power is at its end."

His kisses trail down my chest to the edge of my rib cage. When I breathe in, he licks my bellybutton.

"You going to tie me up with my bikini, pirate man? Revenge is yours."

Dan grunts again, frowning. His fingers make quick work of untying my top and he pulls it out, looking at the cups like he's got no idea what to do. "The straps are too flimsy." Frowning again, he props himself up on his elbows and fiddles with the top's ties. An eyebrow arches and he snorts. "Won't get enough force on the pressure points on your wrists. It'll bite into your skin and not do what it's supposed to do."

The pout on his handsome lips causes a full-body sigh from me. Dan's engineering-oriented brain produced some unexpected benefits and I have proof in our trove of "improved" toys.

Which I forgot to bring. But I have Dan. I pull him down on top of me. "Then to hell with it."

My top flies across the room.

I breathe in his ear. A shudder runs through his magnificent body.

"Take off the shorts, gorgeous," I whisper.

Dan grunts again. The fabric of his shorts rubs against my hips. I feel him work his way out of his boxers and hear the cotton wisp against the bedding as it drops to the floor.

"Give me what I want," I breathe.

He's not careful and damn, it feels *good*. Dan moves up along my body so he pounds against my clit. I pant, taking him deeply. He slams me hard, hunching against my body, and I slowly scoot upward on the mattress with each hit, into a patch of warm sunlight. Gold covers my eyes but I still see Dan. I see the clear joy in his eyes. And his love.

"I love you, Daniel Quidell." I feel his cock's rhythmic pulses inside me and I yelp when he crashes into me one last time, groaning.

Dan pulls us to the pillows. "I love you, too, Camille Frasier," he says, his lips on my ear.

We lay together in the warm summer air, both happy. Both in the moment.

And I will never have it any other way.

The Story continues
in book three, **Robert's Soul**

Bad boy graduate student Robert Quidell meets his match when his roommate's sister moves into their apartment....

ROBERT'S SOUL

Book 3

CHAPTER 1

Robert

"Astopwatch was used to measure the interval of perambulation through the pre-determined social interaction area..."

I rub my glove's scratchy palm over my face. It's fifteen degrees outside and the bus's heater is busted, but at least I had the ride to read journal articles about the culturally anthropological implications of leisurely walks.

I rub my face again. Who the hell uses the verb *perambulate?*

The bus takes the last corner before my stop. I grip the side of the seat as I attempt to counter the inevitable sway. The moment the bus stops and my boots hit the concrete, I'm scampering my ass through the bus fumes to my drafty but warm apartment.

The University bus drops off seven blocks from home. I could wait the fifteen minutes for the city bus. Or I could trot the sidewalks with a laptop and twenty-five pounds of textbooks on my back, toasty warm from the effort and fully deserving of the beer awaiting me in my fridge.

The better choice, I do believe.

I stuff the article into my backpack before yanking the flaps of my prize yellow-and-black-striped, pointy-tipped winter hat over my ears. When one has a gift-bearing, almost-five-year-old nephew, one must wear one's badge of uncle-hood with pride. Which I do. Every day. And will continue to do so, until spring comes and the wind chill goes away.

Some days I wonder if I should have chosen a graduate school in a warmer climate. But I like it here, even if the weather is too much like home. This university offers a fresh start.

The bus groans and shudders as it pulls up to my stop. I jog down the steps to the cold concrete, and breathe in the crisp night air. I'm already halfway up the block when the bus rumbles away.

The stop is on the very edge of the university property, just beyond two old and huge dorms. The energy of academia wanes out here, off campus. We all sleep away from the grand and imposing structures of the University, but we don't *live* here. We live in our labs and offices, in our buildings and student unions. The beds are for sleep and sex.

More sleep than sex, at least for me.

New city, new school. A new reputation of seriousness and depth. Yet my dates continue to find the wonders of my undergrad years on the internet. I'm fully aware that I'm a "bad boy." And that women have expectations for how I am to express my badness.

Sometimes social media has its... drawbacks.

Cold air dances over my lips, to my cheeks, and then onto my eyeballs. The chill makes the buildings and the streets look cleaner, as if I'm looking through blue ice at a dust-free world. All the moisture in the air froze out and nothing floats on the wind anymore. The world stopped being human-built and is a faery-land cleansed of all the grit and grime.

Or my corneas crystalized and I'm too fucking cold to realize it.

I stuff my hands into the pockets of my jacket. The cold makes me thirsty and I focus on my awaiting beer.

The books in my bag press the slab of my laptop against my back and I wish I didn't have to carry the entire contents of my PhD program every time I go into campus. Plus today, I'm also carrying the twenty-three student assignments I need to grade over the weekend.

The teaching assistant gig pays tuition and fees, and nets me enough to pay rent and to eat. It's fun, too. Most undergrads take Intro to Cultural Anthropology to fulfill distribution requirements, making it a class they choose, so we don't get a lot of whining. At least my section didn't last semester. On the other hand, Mack, my roommate, told me stories: A drug arrest his first semester, a student who plagiarized and got off because his daddy's a big shot lawyer, the creepy male student who stalked the woman who TA'ed before me.

On the road next to the sidewalk, a car drifts by, obviously looking for an address. My breath clouds the air and I feel a little warmer now that I'm moving, so I push my bumblebee hat back, to get a better look at the world around me.

A musical beat bounces down the street. I hear faint and distant laughter.

Mack said something about a party tonight. I'd declined his invite, citing the contents of my backpack as my reason.

But mostly I'm trying not to meet women at parties anymore.

A new life needs new ways of living. And I no longer want alcohol to be a factor in how women assess what I have to offer.

My phone chimes. I try not to have it out in the open while I walk because there've been a few snatch and grabs around campus. Last week, a woman got held up at knife-point. So I glance around before pulling it out.

I pull off my glove and sweep my finger across my phone to unlock the screen. *Left the party. Headache*, pops up.

Mack must have just left the party. I immediately glance around again because my brain thinks it might see him leave. Except the apartment is a block west and on the other side of the party house.

My sister stayed, appears.

I stare at the message for a moment. Sister?

Then I remember: The photographer.

Isolde

MY TWIN BROTHER ONCE ASKED ME WHAT I SEE WHEN I LOOK AT

the world. We were kids playing in the woods, me in front and Mack following, climbing over fallen logs and dancing around holes and hollows. The trees smelled summer fresh and the sunlight flickered over leaves and vines and our upturned faces.

Before I answered, I turned my face to the sky, my eyes closed. Warmth smoothed over my skin. Clean air tasted as good as the water from a cool, bubbling fountain. I stood perfectly still, a child with her toes in the moss and her twin brother an arm's length away, weak before the truth: I don't see the truth.

The world is so much more than my eyes telling me "Don't trip on that," or "Watch out for the spider!" I don't *see* because what's around me is much more beautiful than my sorry eyes can measure.

Which is why I take pictures.

I'm not an artist. I'm a scientist. I take readings with my lenses and I run analyses with my processing software. I can't resist digging in and uncovering the truth. The pull to know—to experience—is too powerful.

So when my dear twin brother tells me to put away my brand-spanking-new, ultra-high-resolution, megapixel camera phone and "enjoy the party" I tell him to go away.

He stands close because bad pop music thumps through the house and if his lips were more than a foot away I wouldn't be able to hear him. Which, when I think about it, might be preferable.

"Isa, come on." Mack pushes his wire-rims up his nose and gives me one of his narrow, one-eyebrow-cocked eye rolls. It's meant to convey annoyance but mostly it shows condescension.

"You better not give that look to your students or you're going to get a ton of bad evaluations." I poke at his nose with my camera phone. Winter semester started last week and the party is supposed to be some sort "welcome back from break" celebration.

His look changes to one of perplexity as he leans closer. "What?"

Now I roll my eyes, knowing full well my face looks identical to his. Same muscle pulls. Same eyebrow arch. Same dirty blue eyes under the same dirty blonde hair. At least on him, the "dirty" looks more like verdigris in his eyes and copper in his hair. It makes him handsome under his glasses. Under mine, I just look like every other semi-chubby boring chick with a phone in her hand.

My dear brother rubs his forehead and his fingers shadow his face. The party's lights are low, with most of the house's illumination coming from the multitude of twinkling fairy lights woven through banisters, stapled up along the house's crown molding, and thrown over the random fifties art hanging on the walls.

The house must have been built in the thirties. The rooms circle the central stairwell and are all separated by grand double doors. Leaded glass panels top all the windows. I need to get a few shots of the moonlight through the bevels before I go.

"Why don't you talk to someone?" Mack waves his beer bottle. It's the same random microbrew I'm drinking and the stuff smells like piss.

Mack takes a sip out of his bottle and makes a *this is gross* face. "It's not an undergrad party, you know. They're all adults. Some have jobs."

I know a few people here. I come and go from this part of the world, and right now I'm in town for three days before I'm off to Namibia for my next shoot. It's a big deal—I'm assisting one of the best photojournalists working in the field and every time I think about the gig my stomach does flip-flops. Which is why Mack dragged me to this party. To take my mind off business.

But for me, my upcoming shoot is as much graduate school as Mack's current road toward a PhD. He's in cultural anthropology. I'm documenting "the cultural" for the anthropologists and the magazines.

It was nice of him, though, to store my stuff on such short notice during the month I'll be gone. One should have a permanent address, even if one is permanently not at home.

I had my fill of our mother's house when her new boyfriend moved in. Codependency is not my cup of tea. I'd rather be out in the world falling victim to my need to see instead of locked down in California.

I don't know what Mack told his roommate, though. Mack says he's a first-year student in his department. Called him "the new kid" and said he's charming. His name's Rob or Bob or maybe Cob. I don't remember, but I do remember the slight tick moving across Mack's cheek when he said "charming."

The twitch means the same thing now as it did in high school and our undergraduate years: Stay away, sister. We've got a player on our hands.

Not that players pay attention to me. I'm not their type, with the glasses and the ubiquitous camera equipment and the general roundness to my hips and breasts. I glance down at my chest. My knit top's a little tight and my chosen-for-comfort-while-traveling black skirt and tights show more of my roundness than I generally like. Half a month in the wilds of Africa might just be what I need to finish thinning out. I dropped thirty pounds the last time I was overseas.

Not that I need thinning, really. Sometimes I wonder why my brain still thinks these thoughts.

Mack rubs his forehead again.

I touch his arm, drawing his attention. "One's starting, isn't it?"

Migraines began for my brother less than a week after we turned thirteen. They were pretty bad in high school, and it took him vomiting in the nurse's office to get him to admit something was wrong. I dragged him home and made Mom sober up enough to take him to the doctor.

He's been on meds ever since. Once we got into college, the headaches lessened, and he's been doing well lately, but I can tell when one starts.

If he goes home now, takes a med, and sleeps, he'll be fine tomorrow.

He nods yes.

"Do you want me to walk with you back to the apartment?" The party house is about five blocks from Mack's place. I stowed my stuff this afternoon, taking the key he gave me, before he dragged me here to see old friends and introduce me to his new ones.

Except the roommate. Rob-Bob-Cob was off somewhere. Mack said studying.

Mack waves me off before setting his bad beer on a low table against a wall. "No use you leaving as well. You haven't seen your friends in ages." He nods toward the living room. "I'll walk my own sorry ass home. The fresh air will do me good. The headache will clear up before I get back to the apartment. I promise."

He waves at the party again. "Just be quiet when you come in, okay? If you find Rob passed out on the couch, don't poke him. He has bad breath."

I snicker. So the player has his flaws.

But I can't abandon my brother. "I don't need to stay."

Mack pinches the bridge of his nose. "You want to get some more shots with that wonder of digital precision, don't you?" He points at my camera phone. "I know you do."

I do. I'm as fascinated by the new and developing language of social media photography as I am by the wilds of the planet and the cultures of humanity. It's another property of the world that needs documenting, measuring, and analyzing.

Mack nods over his shoulder. "Lisa was asking about you. She's in the living room. Go say hi."

I squeeze his hand. "Are you sure?" We all went to the same college in our undergraduate days and Lisa also came to this university with Mack. It'd be nice to talk to her.

Mack squeezes back. "Promise me you'll be careful walking back to the apartment, okay? See if someone will walk with you."

I frown. I can handle myself. You need skills if you're going to do fieldwork.

Mack frowns back at me. "Please."

"Yes, Dad."

He chuckles, but stops when it obviously hurts.

"Text me the moment you get home." I pat his arm. "I want to make sure you're okay."

My poor twin brother nods one last time. He pulls out his phone, swiping at the screen, and the sudden blue haze lights up his face. He waves the device in my general direction and makes his way toward the door, leaving me to fend for myself in the cultural jungle of a grad student party.

CHAPTER 2

Robert

I stare at Mack's text. We now have a semi-permanent house guest. Permanent in that she's technically moving in, but semi in that she rarely sets foot in the United States.

When he asked if she could crash in our apartment, I just shrugged and returned my nose to reading articles and grading papers. Mack's sister can sleep on the floor if she wants. Who am I to say no?

The screen fogs around my grip and an extra hint of blue creeps out from under my fingertips. And up my flesh. I stuff my hand into my pocket as I watch the texts from Mack roll in.

I need a pair of touchscreen gloves. Otherwise I'm going to lose a digit to frostbite before the winter's over. I pull my hand from my pocket again. *Does she have someone to walk her home?* I text. Five blocks in the cold by herself isn't likely to cause problems, but still.

She said she'd find someone.

The party is a block up and one over. I wasn't planning on walking by it, but I could. *Do you want me to ask her?*

Mack doesn't respond for a long moment. I stuff my ungloved hand into my pocket again and resume walking. But I dodge up the side street, knowing I'm going to end up at that party, no matter what he says.

Took my med. Off to sleep. She'll frown but don't let her walk home alone.

Okay, I text back, feeling more relieved than I probably should. It's not my place to butt into his family, or to swoop in, but I'd hate for something to happen.

Especially since we haven't yet been introduced.

Shit, I think. He showed me pictures a couple of nights ago. She's his twin sister, and I'll be looking for a sweeter, prettier version of Mack.

A nice, lovely Wellington whose first name I don't remember.

Send me a photo, I text. *What's her name again?*

I stuff my phone into my pocket and pull on my glove, hoping my roommate hasn't gone off to bed yet.

But he still hasn't answered by the time I round the fence into the front yard of the party house.

It's a semi-rundown place, like all the other student-rented houses around campus. The concrete front steps settled a long time ago and are now uneven. The porch sags and needs painting. But, like the apartment I share with Mack, the rent's probably cheap.

Music thumps through the hallway of the big house full of partying grad students. It shakes my eyeballs and my perception of people talking in tight huddles, causing a slight visual bump, making it difficult to distinguish faces in the too-dim light.

I press into the crowd and slowly make my way toward the back of the house.

Mack's photos of his sister were from their early undergrad years. In every single one, she was slightly out of the frame, or slightly blurry, or slightly behind something. None of the photos gave me a good sense of her features, her hair, how she stands, what her smile looks like.

I push into the back room of the house and sling my pack off my back. The hostess is a socially-oriented person, a woman aptly named Sunnie, who'd put a cruise ship entertainment director to shame. She wouldn't appreciate me smacking around her guests with twenty-five pounds of textbooks. Sunnie is a fellow grad student's wife and in the process of starting her own social media public relations company. No one was surprised when they learned she'd already landed three big clients.

A week into my first semester, one of her parties landed Mara in my bed. Then Olivia, a couple weeks later. Neither relationship lasted more than two weeks.

I met my brother Tom's hot new woman over winter break. Looked at all his new paintings, many of which were studies of her graceful curves and the lovely line of her jaw.

They smiled at each other. I watched them hold hands without realizing they were holding hands. And I wondered if a woman could see me that way.

Not that I'm jealous. I'm not. Both my brothers are better at commitment. I learned to accept my little relationship-deficit issue a long time ago, but I don't need to feed it right now. Which is why I stopped going to parties.

New town. New standing with the female half of the human race. At least I keep telling myself that.

I rub my face as I walk through the dim halls of the grad-student-filled house, wondering about building that new reputation.

I used to bring one or two, maybe three, brilliant evenings to as many women as I could. I'm their nova, their bright point of physical pleasure, the memory they use to make their long-term committed boyfriend feel inadequate.

I took my job seriously. Or so I like to tell myself.

I don't do that anymore. Maybe it's boring now. Maybe I'm worried about finishing my degree. Or maybe somewhere in the back of my mind I'm irritated that my brother, who wasn't dating, is now engaged to a woman he swears is the love of his life.

I circle through the house's dining area, scouting the crowd as I make my way toward the dining room. The house twinkles tonight. Layers and layers of tiny lights cover the ceiling and every surface in the interior. At least six or seven strands wind around the bar, making it look like an ice giant puked on the booze. I push in and lean on the counter.

The bar is an add-on to the house and probably put in by a former owner sometime in the seventies. The counter top is an ugly orange-tinted laminate full of pot marks and scratches. The tiny fridge underneath is probably the same age as my father. And the five bar stools are sticky black vinyl numbers that feel like they came from a dollar store.

Sunnie, our hostess, leans forward, her elbow on the bar, and her ample bosom flattens against her chest. She's a lovely woman, slightly older than me, with a sweet round face and a wit she normally keeps to herself. Says "commentary" doesn't help keep the clients.

"Nice to see ya, handsome." Sunnie winks as she wipes the counter with a rag, playing up her hostess-slash-bartender role. "Why you wearing the buzz cap and carrying your books?" She points at the bee stripes pulled over my hair.

"Just walking by on my way home from the library." I hold up the bag. "Studying."

She's not watching the bag. She's watching my bicep. I stifle a head shake. It's not like she can see anything under my jacket, so I don't know what she's actually thinking. But I can guess. I get a lot of looks like that.

"Ah..." Sunnie smiles and hands me a beer. "I'll keep the bag back here if you want to relax a little."

I grin but keep the tight hold on the straps. "Mack asked me to walk his sister home."

Sunnie nods toward the crowd. "She's probably in the living room." A bottle appears.

I take it, adhering to the student motto of never passing up free beer, and lean closer. "Do you, by chance, remember her name?"

Sunnie laughs and wipes down the bar again. "Sadly, not this time, handsome. Sorry."

I toss my hostess a salute before turning back to the crowd. I take a sip of the beer. *Chilled* is about all it is. Frowning, I stare for a long moment at the amber liquid in the bottle gripped by my fingers. Not all microbrews make the grade.

I take another sip anyway, and scan the crowd.

A knot of three women stand off to the side, in a corner. They laugh, and one I recognize—Mack's friend Lisa—touches the arm of one I don't.

The new woman looks up from her phone and the lenses of her glasses momentarily mirror the blue light of her screen.

But it highlights her face.

The party blanks out. Lisa and the other woman laugh but I don't pay attention. I don't care that one pushes a strand of hair behind her ear or that the other sips at her wine. I see only the set of the new woman's shoulders. The lush roundness of her hips and how they balance her two mounds of female perfection on her chest.

I notice her ease with the tech in her hand. But mostly I wonder how that sweep of her finger would feel on my skin. I want to know if her voice is as smooth as her body. If I'll hear the same layers of brilliance I see.

I want to know what color her eyes are. If her lips are dark and rosy, or light and pink. I want to see her smile.

My head tips to the side, my brain wanting to see around the glare bouncing off the glasses hiding her eyes.

And I finally recognize my mystery lady.

CHAPTER 3

Isolde

Mack's old friend Lisa leans closer. They dated for a year before grad school. Now they're buds. "Have you met Rob yet?" she says.

Robert Quidell. It took Lisa and her friend Anne to nail down his name, along with a few other traits my brother's roommate seems to possess.

"Not yet," I say, and take a sip of my beer. It's weak and bitter, and tastes more like what I used to drink out of a plastic cup in high school.

Anne sighs and nods her head like she's in the know. "He's God's gift, by the way."

Lisa laughs and touches my arm. "So you're warned. For when you do meet him. Best to know what to expect."

Anne laughs.

I watch them both, marveling at the similarity of expression on the faces of these two very different women. Lisa is tall, thin, and more blonde than me. Anne is short but also thin, and dark. But their lips both curl into the same sardonic, knowing grin.

I snap a photo and glance down at my phone. This new camera is doing a pretty good job in the low light. Though I wish I had fill flash.

"God's gift?" I ask, making conversation.

Anne nods. "He's easy on the eyes."

Lisa laughs again. "And other parts."

I look up at her face, shocked. Lisa's not the sleeping around type. She laughs again. "Or so I've heard."

I think they've both had too much to drink. "I'm not looking for a relationship." I'll be leaving town in a couple of weeks.

"No one said anything about a relationship." Anne sips at her beer.

I roll my eyes. I try not to, but it happens anyway. "Dear Penthouse Letters," I say. "I never thought it would happen to me. But when I walked into my brother's apartment—"

A warm baritone flows over me from behind. A wonderful voice, one more musical and resonant than the song blaring from the speakers in the corner. "Hello, ladies," the mystery man says.

I turn around and look up at a textbook handsome face topped off by the most ridiculous hat I've ever seen. It's yellow and black, with a pointed top and two earflaps that look suspiciously like bee wings, and it makes his pale eyes all but glow.

The new guy grins and points at his head. "Nephew gave it to me." A look of pure joy flashes over his face as if thinking about his nephew makes him happier than anything else in the world.

But the look of joy vanishes quickly. And I think that I just glimpsed something most other people aren't allowed to see.

Or don't see, because they don't look beyond the perfection of his strong, square features and his shadow of stubble. I glance at Lisa and Anne. Neither of them seemed to have noticed his expression. They're both staring at the new guy with eyes full of dismissive lust. As if they see only the wonderfully masculine jaw exactly proportioned to balance the broadness of his shoulders. He's not particularly big, or extra tall, though he's tall enough I need to tilt up my head when I look at him.

When I glance back, he's looking at Lisa and Anne. And I think he looks faintly disappointed.

My body skips a beat. Not just my heart, but my entire body. How could they have missed the happiness he flashed when he mentioned his nephew?

I want to touch his face to make sure the muscle movements I saw dart across his cheeks were real. A part of me wants to push my fingers under the bumblebee hat and run my fingers through the dark hair poking out under its edge. It's the part that saunters onto a scene and often does exactly what it wants to, no matter what my responsible brain says. But listening to the *Bad idea!* thoughts often gets me shitty pictures.

Warm and slick creeps between my thighs. I want to nuzzle my face against his neck and breathe in his skin, smell its scent, feel its softness. My tongue wakes up too and somewhere in my head I hear *Lick his abs.*

God damn, I'm a freak.

Deep in my brain a little voice is saying *see* this one. There's more to that look. More than Anne and Lisa give him credit for. I want to understand this man's world. His body. How he moves. The things my cameras can't capture. Get a full sensory understanding of what's right in front of me.

He's watching me. Not Anne, who is arguably the prettiest of the three of us, or Lisa, the thinnest. He's looking at me.

"Rob," he says, and holds out his hand.

I blink. My mouth must be open. I don't shake back even though I know I should be friendly. But *goddamn* this man is magnetic and I don't dare touch him.

"No you don't, Robert. Shoo." Lisa waves her hand at him.

He smiles and his pale eyes twinkle. I almost melt. What the hell is wrong with me?

"Are you Mack's sister?" He holds out his hand again and his gaze stays glued to me.

His name's Robert. Rob. He's the mysterious roommate.

"Yes," I say. I take his offered hand this time, unable to resist the need to feel his skin. To know if his touch is as focused as his gaze.

His fingers glide first over the tips of mine. A tingle fires into the tight array of small muscles and tendons holding together my joints. When his grip tightens and his fingers press into the flesh of my wrist, I feel his electricity merge into my bones and flow through my veins.

And realize that his hand is ice cold. Startled, I let go, and wave my fingers in the air. "Did you just come in from outside?"

Rob laughs and stuffs his hand into his pocket. "Sorry. Texting with your brother. Don't have good gloves."

I swear his eyes twinkle again.

He leans close. "What's your name?"

Lisa and Anne look at each other and I see a plan forming. A slightly mean plan, as if they think, for some reason, that he needs a lesson.

Part of me thinks the undeniably hot guy smiling at me right now probably doesn't deserve to be played. But another part of me gets a thrill. If he has to figure out my name, his attention will stay on me.

"We are not giving you *any* information, Robert Quidell." Anne pokes his shoulder. "No name. No likes and dislikes. Nothing. Now go find someone else to charm."

He doesn't look at my friends. He watches me, assessing. Mapping, I think, every angle my body twists into as a response to his presence. Looking for patterns in my small movements, my twitches. He's reading me the way he'd read a book.

I feel the same twinge I do when I peel back the shadows and photograph a truth. When I find a moment, a small point in the universe, and I document what is truly there. When I know what's in front of me isn't simply a picture.

Robert Quidell is as real and alive and full of the pushes and pulls of the universe as any subject who has ever crossed through the focal plane of my lens.

He knows it, too. "I provide only an opportunity to be charmed," he says, his face open yet sardonic, his posture friendly yet cocky.

The man in front of me is no idiot.

I laugh and shake my head, wishing I had enough light to see the true color of his eyes. His irises glimmer and I wonder if I'm looking at reflected starlight.

I grin. He's too delicious an opportunity to pass up, even if he is my brother's bad boy roommate. "Hmmm... I'm sensing a... reputation?"

Rob laughs. But his face falls a bit too, and the laugh seems to be more to cover what I suspect is, for him, a sore spot. I said "reputation" and his shoulders slumped like a fugitive who'd just been caught by the FBI. Rob Quidell stands in front of me, a man carrying the weight of his sins.

Or it seems so to me.

My thighs press together and I wiggle where I stand. My neck and cheeks heat and I thank all that's good in the universe for the low lighting. My nipples tighten and my breasts feel as if he's already dancing those exquisite fingers over my flesh.

Am I feeling empathy? I don't know. But I do, deep inside, think this man needs a second chance.

CHAPTER 4

Robert

Lisa and Anne must have warned Mack's sister about me because
the moment she figured out who I am, her posture changed.

If the music wasn't so loud, I suspect I'd be hearing a
little voice in the back of my head whispering sentences like *Feel that
drop in your stomach? Your rep turns every new encounter into the same old,
same old.* And *This is what you get for being an ass.*

But I'm not an ass. I'm honest about what I have to give and I
always give what I promise.

Yet that little whisper jabbing its fingers into the back sides of my
eyeballs yells *The women just delineated, laid out, highlighted, and bullet-
pointed for Mack's sister the schema you built yourself, dumbass.*

The look I see on my roommate's sister's face is exactly the same
look I see on every woman's face. It's the same *Oh, I know your type.*

I suppose I shouldn't be surprised.

I grin though, and laugh, when she mentions my "reputation."
What else am I to do? This script's been written. Welcome to the new
episode of *Educating Rob Quidell*, everyone's favorite sitcom.

It takes energy to break through a woman's walls and, honestly, I'm tired. And she's Mack's sister, so it really doesn't matter. Let the ladies have their moment of poking at little old me, because it gives Lisa and Anne a sense of power.

It's funny how it's always the ones I don't sleep with who play the mean games.

I don't frown. I control the tics and the twitches. And I watch Mack's sister do her best not to be affected by the promised lust my reputation carries with it. But she squirms.

Because she knows my type.

So we all fall into the game we're expected to play, because the game is what we all expect. Me included.

"Living life nameless must be tough." I grin again and nod, doing my best to say *I understand the game*, as I set down my tasteless beer on the table to the side of Mack's sister's hip. Her skirt's short and I can't help but stare at the hem of the dark fabric brushing her thigh. She's beautifully proportioned.

I twist a little, angling my chest toward her body, and make a show of looking at her ass.

But her grin looks more open than I expect.

Lisa and Anne vanish from my perception. I stand straight and relaxed, focusing on the woman in front of me. The drop in my stomach eases as I look at the lovely planes of her face. I see the same bone structure as Mack, but softer and feminine. Exquisite. Her glasses don't hide the intelligence in her eyes, or her obvious ability to perceive the world around her.

I doubt anything is lost on this woman. My gut does a little dance, but not to push off the costume Lisa and Anne placed on my shoulders, or to stop feeling sorry for myself. It dances because I'm in the presence of brilliance.

Nothing is sexier than a mind as agile as the body.

I don't think I will have a problem walking my roommate's twin sister home tonight.

"You have one of the new ultra-pixel phones?" I point at the small bag strapped around her shoulder. She'd dropped her gadget into it when I walked up. "I have one." I pull mine from my pocket. "No clue how to use the camera."

She blinks and shivers a little, as if I surprised her. When she turns her back on Lisa and Anne, aligning with me, I almost smirk at the other women. But I don't need to be the bad boy they think I am.

I drop my lips close to Mack's sister's ear. "Did you see the stained glass window on the porch? The moon is shining through it. I'd like to take a picture."

The smile she gives me is wonderful and beautiful and beyond any I could imagine. The game, for the moment, vanishes.

When she reaches for my phone, I don't touch her again. I don't know why. I usually stroke a woman's elbow or her shoulder. Small movements to make her comfortable with me. But with Mack's sister, for some reason, it feels disingenuous.

Maybe because I've touched so many women so many times I don't believe I'd feel her skin, her body, under my fingers. I'd feel all the other elbows and shoulders the way I feel every steering wheel in my hands whenever I drive a new car.

It's never the moment I'm in. It's always all the moments where I've been.

But I want to touch. I want to be somewhere I can hear her clearly. Someplace with fresh air so I know it's her scent, her perfume I smell, and not Lisa's.

The porch should give us a moment to recalibrate.

And maybe I can get her to tell me her name.

She grins and holds up my phone, looking at the screen. "I'm still learning the limits of mine." She tilts it side to side like it's one of those sloshing water toys that makes new images when you wiggle it.

I step back and hoist my backpack onto my shoulders. She picks up the coat that's sitting next to her on the table where we dropped our tasteless beers, and I shepherd her into the crowd. Lisa throws me a dirty look, one meant to say *I'm telling Mack*, but my roommate will know I've made friends with his sister soon enough. The desire to make kissy lips at Lisa almost overcomes my control. Instead, I wave and walk into the crowd with the beautiful woman whose name I don't remember, on our way to a moment of privacy.

And I can no longer keep my fingers away.

CHAPTER 5

Isolde

Rob spreads his fingers over my lower back, his palm resting where my spine curves out toward my ass, as he guides me through the crowded hallway toward the house's front door.

His hand's no longer cold. Warmth flows through the fabric of my shirt, to my flesh, and up my backbone. His fingers press but don't dig, and his hand flows with the movements of my body.

He's learning. I see it on his face when I look up, too. He's watching and adjusting and figuring out how to understand the best way to interact with me.

Like I'm a puzzle.

I hold his phone in my hand. I feel, strangely, as if this man handed over part of his soul. That allowing me to touch the device I grip between my fingers and my palm—and allowing me to carry it—symbolizes something. I just don't know what.

Or maybe I'm reading more into it than there is. Maybe I'm reading a whole lot of what I want into a whole lot of nothing. My body is attracted, for sure. How could it not be? He's spectacularly gorgeous. Firm and well-angled, with a nice shadow of stubble on his chin. Where I should be behind the camera, he should be in front of it. But I've been around beautiful men before. Fashion shoots tend to be flooded with beautiful men.

Shoots have production plans. Scripts, basically, of the story that needs to be told via the produced visuals. Perhaps my brain is making up a script for the pretty bad boy with the bee hat and a hand on my back.

Rob leans close so that I can hear him over the music. His breath dances over the top curve of my ear, across the sensitive inner folds, shifting the few strands of my hair that have fallen from my ponytail.

I close my eyes for a moment, letting the sensation wash over me, and allow him to escort me through the crowd toward a place without distractions.

The responsible part of my brain wants to stop this game right now. But we have five blocks until we reach the apartment and, damn it, I want to enjoy his touches while I can.

"What should I call you? Since I'm barred from learning your real name." he asks, his lips still only inches from my ear.

He could nibble, if he wanted. Right here in full view of all the partygoers. Nibble on my ear and work his hand under my shirt and I don't think I'd stop him no matter how annoyed my Responsible Brain got.

"What do you want to call me?" I say. We're playing a game, so a game we will play.

Rob chuckles as he pushes some drunk guy out of the way. Grad students, for the most part, behave better than undergrads, but parties are still parties.

The drunk guy blinks and gives Rob the finger.

We both chuckle as we fall out onto the front porch. The music drops to just the *thump thump* of the beat. I slip on my jacket, transferring his phone from one hand to the other, as the cold air hits. The world takes on the real colors of night—the soft shadows of pinks and greens that the twinkling electric fairy lights hid. The moon shines in the sky, surrounded by a spray of clouds, and the streetlights throw pools along the sidewalk leading away from the party.

It's as crisp and blue as the chill in the air.

"The window is over there." Rob points off to the side, where the porch takes a turn and wraps around the side of the house, to another door, on the side. I think it used to be a servant entrance.

He tips his head as if trying to see around the corner, and smiles as he takes my hand. He pulls me toward the promised stained glass window.

The tug moves me forward, but his grip flows up my arm. All I see, all I feel, is the strength of his arms. How it's *there*; how it's part of him. It's not a feature he scrubs clean or plays up because he wants to attract women. He doesn't present it to the world as a part of his uniform.

It's in his bones.

It's what I need to photograph.

We turn the corner and blocks of colored moonglow dance over his face. He smiles, pointing at his phone, which I still hold. "What do I do?"

He's playing. He understands how to use the camera. I can tell the moment he unlocks the screen for me. When I turn toward the window, he moves behind me, watching over my shoulder. I half expect him to stroke my arms the way a tennis pro would while whispering things like "Your grip needs to be firmer."

I must be smirking because he chuckles in my ear. "I think I shall call you Diana, goddess of the moon."

The tone in his voice carries the perfect amount of wry humor. A big hearty laugh rolls from my belly and I bend over, giggling. "You are a freak, you know that, Rob Quidell? A total freak of nature."

He laughs too, and his pale eyes glimmer in the colored light, still brilliantly intelligent and still hiding their true color from me. "I promised your brother that I'd walk you to the apartment, so hopefully I'm not *too* freaky."

I snap a picture of the window and hold up his phone so he can see. "If you set it like this..." I swipe my finger over the screen. "...and use this filter..." I swipe again. "...you'll get a nice image."

Rob nods. "Ah."

Yeah, I'm pretty sure he knew exactly how to take a good photo with his camera phone. "Mack asked you to walk me home?" I snap another one for him, framing the window just right to get a nice image of the moon.

"I volunteered. I was walking by anyway." He reaches over his head and pats his backpack.

An image of him making the exact same move, but shirtless, flickers through my mind's eye. I see the wonderful elongation and tightening of a man's abdomen that happens when he curls a bicep and holds an arm next to his ear.

Something must have flickered across my face because Rob smirks.

My shoulders tighten. "You didn't need to stop. I can handle myself." The words snap from my mouth a little tighter and a little higher pitched than I meant them to. The last remnants of the terrible beer must be messing with my head.

Either that, or I'm embarrassed about ogling him.

His mouth rounds and he steps back. He looks a little shocked. "Sorry if I offended."

"No offense." My responses to him confound me. I'm not used to feeling this way. So I smile. "So you're my knight in shining bumblebee armor?"

I flick through the filters on his phone, looking for something that will get me a good image. Not of the moonlight flowing through the window, but of Rob standing here with the window's reds and blues dancing over his skin, a beautiful boy draped under a blanket of beautiful colors, topped off by a ridiculous hat.

He's much more interesting than the moon and I might as well concentrate on photographing the wonder standing next to me than on how he makes me feel.

He doesn't answer. No stupid crack about knights or armor or slaying dragons falls out of his luscious mouth. He just grins and I swear his eyes soften.

Maybe it's a trick of the light. Maybe, like before, I don't see what I think I do. But I swear, for a second, I see a very different desire in his eyes than what he expects me to see.

I snap a picture.

He blinks, stunned, and the look disappears underneath his façade. I check the image, hoping.

I didn't catch it. His eyes are in the process of hardening. The tilt of his head is changing to add distance. I missed it by a microsecond.

"Damn," I whisper.

"What?" He leans closer. "My nostrils too big?"

Chuckling, I hand over his phone. "You going to walk me home, pretty boy?"

"Nice to know the photographer thinks I'm pretty enough to photograph." Rob nods in a way that says *uh-huh* and crosses his arms. "Are you going to tell me your name?"

My brother and this man have been living in the same apartment for a semester, so I *know* Mack has told him my name. It's his problem he doesn't remember, not mine.

"Do you have a middle name?" I ask. For some reason, I'm expecting something ridiculous and elaborate, like Maximillian or Rachenthrall. Probably because of the ridiculous and elaborate hat.

Rob narrows his eyes. "Why?"

I shrug. "Just wondering."

"What's yours?" He takes my hand again as if it's the most natural gesture ever and tugs me toward the side exit off the porch.

I only grin.

We round the front of the house, Rob still holding my hand. Out on the sidewalk, we walk toward the apartment. Rob unconsciously falls into a stride matching mine, one that seems a little too short for him, but not uncomfortable.

Maybe this isn't such a bad game. Touching and being touched isn't bad. He's my brother's roommate and, I think, a man worth knowing.

So I breathe. I let myself feel the tingling again, wondering about that air mattress Mack inflated and tossed on the floor of their "den" before we left for the party. That squishy, crinkly, baggie-full-of-air that I will be sleeping on for the next three nights.

Then I remember the tingle in my hand and arm when Rob took my hand. It resurfaces and fires across my shoulders and to my breasts.

And I wonder if Rob's bed is more comfortable.

He smirks and stuffs his phone into his pocket. Leaning back, he makes a show of checking out my ass again, then looks up at the sky. "This bumblebee says you are as lovely as a spring day." He leans close, his head turning as if he's about to kiss my neck, but he breathes in deeply instead. "Fresh scented and sweetly hued."

Rob's smirk widens into a full-on, smartass grin. "I think your middle name is Daffodil, like the flower." He smoothes his hand over his bee hat. "Daffy, for short."

I smack his arm. Not hard, but I can't help myself. I'm laughing too hard. "Mack should have warned me that you're a brat." Though Lisa did warn me about his charm.

"I thought I was a freak of nature." Rob and I walk along, him on the outside, between me and the street, his pack on his back.

Out here in the yellow glow of the streetlights, when we both pull on our gloves, I notice the black leather cord tied with what looks like an old, tight knot circling his left wrist. It's worn and I wonder how long he's kept it close to his skin.

His flawless, warm skin. Gorgeous, healthy, clean and fresh-smelling, lovely skin that is as perfect on his neck and jaw and forehead as it is on his arms. And it's all topped off by what I suspect is a mop of wrap-my-fingers-in black hair.

I skip ahead so I'm not looking at him anymore. I think my brain—responsible and not-so-responsible parts—needs a break from his scrumptiousness. It's causing me to need to fan myself.

A step or two ahead of Mr. Robert Quidell, I'm out in the open again, looking at the world. My fingers want to pull out my new camera toy and snap a few images. Stuff I'll look at later to see if I can manipulate it into moody, flowing wonders. Pieces that, by virtue of showing the sameness of this street with all other streets, might give some insight into what's *not* the same here. What's different in the world of the image-taker.

Like the man who's next to me again, less than an elbow away. Rob strides along, grinning and pointing out buildings so he has an excuse to touch my back. It feels like both a conscious and an unconscious effort on his part, as if he's learned how to play *my* game, and now he's an expert. He stopped thinking about it ages ago and now he's fallen into an easy automatic looseness.

He's Mack's height and he doesn't tower over me, which I like. He's probably six feet, maybe a fraction under, but his shoulders are broader than I'd expect for a guy his size. Not that he's over-muscled—I hate that—just that his bones look big.

The sense of strength returns. I see it in the power of his stride and the mesmerizing cords of his neck.

"So no Daffy?" Rob smiles a real smile, not the player smirk from earlier. He walks parallel with me, his eyes forward, except for the occasional glance down the front of my shirt.

My body reacts the way I suspect he engineered his attentions to make it respond: A blush rises across my neck and cheeks, and across my chest. I feel hot, even in the cold air. My belly tingles. And I suspect my hips sway more than my usual walk.

Perhaps I should admit to myself how desired I feel. How his ease and his smile make me think he doesn't have the shallow definitions of beauty I've encountered with many of the men who work in my field. The guys who allow their image aesthetics to shape their three dimensional world.

The irony of having this gorgeous man make me feel this way makes me smirk. Perhaps I drank more beer than I realized. Looking at him makes me feel a little drunk.

I push my glasses up my nose, to better see his face. "Perhaps I should call you Goofy."

I still can't tell the color of his eyes.

Rob laughs again. "Call me Pluto, Lord of the underworld. My Diana, goddess of the moon." He flicks his hand at the sky.

His eyes flash. Their silver tones burst with the moonlight and for a moment I wonder who the real moon god is. It's certainly not me.

He's enjoying himself and, I think, he wants me to enjoy myself too. I'm a puzzle. He's a puzzle. We're having fun. Even if I do call him on his bad memory when we return to the apartment, I think I'll play along for a little longer.

"The moon is my strobe, Lord Hades."

Another, heartier laugh rolls from Rob. "Where have you been all my life?"

I shake my head. But when his hand glides over my back again, his fingers moving slowly up from the low curve of my spine toward the spot just below my shoulder blades—and just below the clasp of my bra

—I find myself leaning toward him. My hips twist slightly as I walk. And the next thing I know, Rob Quidell has his arm around my waist as we walk.

His fingers glide over my hip and settle into a gentle hold. Is he acting possessive? Is he telling me with the pressure of his fingertips what he wants? I don't know.

But he smiles and I feel safe even though I just met him. Literally just met this man with a reputation of making women feel good without the guilt of attachment and I feel my not-so-Responsible Brain roll through all sorts of excuses: *Mack will protect me if Rob turns out to be an asshole.* And *He's freakin' gorgeous. When have you been with a freakin' gorgeous guy? You might work with them but they ignore you.*

"Home." Rob points at the apartment and his hand moves up my side to just under my breast. A quick, barely perceptible squeeze presses through my jacket before his hand lifts away.

I want it back. I'm not often on the receiving end of touches. Gentle, strong, firm, light, it doesn't matter. I'm behind the camera—behind a wall—and I'm not to be touched. And now I have a desirable man touching me.

I like it. I like it a lot.

And my not-so-Responsible Brain kicks out the ultimate rationalization: *You're leaving in three days. What difference does it make?*

His hand trails across my back before stroking my opposite elbow. He's watching my arm, not my face, as if seeing his fingers perform this dance makes him as happy as the sensations the skin on skin contact creates.

I don't breathe and I hold perfectly still. His gloved fingers make a soft, smooth sound as they glide down my arm toward my palm and I think of rain in moonlight. He blinks slowly. The glow of his eyes vanishes, but not the gentleness of his touch. The electricity. The cool fire of our nerve endings brushing against each other.

He's a magician. Beautiful beyond words or images and I don't think I dare photograph him again unless I know I'm capable of creating images that capture him in three dimensions. Because he's popping out of the background for me. Taking all my attention with his fingers. And everything else suddenly, completely flattens out.

When his hand settles into mine again, I'm lost. Hypnotized. I feel my fretting drop away. Right here on the concrete steps to the apartment I would have been sleeping in anyway, I decide this game is more important than good citizenship and appropriate behavior.

"You make me feel naughty, Lord Hades," I whisper. It's juvenile. But something tells me Rob Quidell understands "juvenile" better than any other adult I've ever met. That he knows what to do come morning, when we're staring at each other over our cereal and coffee. That he'll smile and wink and tell me he's happy he could be of service.

And that what we are about to do might feel naughty, but isn't. Feeling naughty only makes it more fun.

Hunger works from Rob's cheeks up to the muscles around his eyes and down to his jaw and neck. He tightens, but not in an angry way. In an "I'm about to pounce" way. And I think I gasp.

Out here, on the steps up to the building, the glow from the street-light twenty feet away reflects off the concrete under our feet, and I'm sure that this time he sees the heat creeping from under my coat's collar and up my neck. And the blush deepening the color of my lips. Maybe also the lust building in my eyes, even behind my glasses.

I'm positive he sees it in how I wriggle. Or how my breasts involuntarily thrust out toward his chest. Or how my hip wants so very much to rub against his crotch.

He leans forward, his gaze tight on mine, as if measuring and re-measuring my consent with each heartbeat thundering inside my head. Each moment. Each of his warm, mint-scented breaths.

"I am at your service, my goddess," he whispers as his lips graze my cheek.

CHAPTER 6

Robert

I think she's been waiting for a "You must be tired from running through my mind all night" line or perhaps a straight-up "let's fuck" since we walked out of the party.

The little voice in the back of my head that presses its fists into its waist and frowns before yelling *Charming women is bad!* has been waving its arms since we walked off the porch, poking at me, saying it's my own damned fault I get treated the way I do. If I hadn't bedded every woman I met since I was a teenager, I wouldn't have the rep.

And maybe Mack's sister wouldn't be eyeing me as if my services are the begin-all end-all of my role in this world. The way she's been the entire time we've walked home.

When I took her hand, the game slid from my fingers to the delicate skin of her wrist the way the sheets will slide on my bed when I lay her down naked and flushed.

And I won.

Her invitation is right in front of me in the looseness of her cheeks and her half-closed eyelids. She moves closer and brushes against my front. Even through our coats, I know her nipples harden to little buds. I know she's wet, wanting me.

I could slide her tights off the perfect curve of her hips and down her legs. Maybe use them to tie her ankles together. Or maybe tie her legs wide open, spread for me, slick and waiting.

I could press my fingers into her breasts. Breathe in the warm bronze sheen to the full waves of her hair. See the secret depths of her eyes.

Because I won.

Part of me didn't want to win. Part of me wanted the schema dictating how a woman sees me to disintegrate and let the two of us play by a different set of expectations. Hell, I think I wanted *her* to win. Just this once, I wanted a woman to play by her rules. I wanted to open my eyes to a new way of seeing the world.

But it seems we both took the easy route.

I breathe in the curls of her breath and the cold makes her scent all the warmer.

She gives me a brilliant come-hither look. "I think we should go inside."

Am I disappointed? Am I angry? But why do I want to kiss her so much even though this was too easy? Even though she's my roommate's sister and should be, by all measures, off limits?

But I think "off limits" might be what's fueling my win. I'm the inaccessible bad boy. The male she's never allowed to touch. I represent all the men she's not supposed to play with.

So exactly whose rules are we playing by?

"You realize Mack will not be happy with either of us, don't you?" I say. Perhaps pointing out the obvious will break us out of this path we've both stepped onto.

"He's a big boy. I'm a big girl." She grins. "I'm here for three days. Then I'm gone."

Or reaffirm my suspicions.

Back on the porch, I thought maybe we were connecting at a level deeper than the expectations Lisa fed into her head. But now I'm back to being a woman's bright point of physical fun.

Yet I shouldn't want to kiss her as much as I do. I don't kiss my nova-ing stars, my lovely moon goddesses. It seems too personal, too blinding, too close to their brightness. But Mack's sister tips back her head, her lush, moist lips parting slightly. Her tongue appears for a fleeting microsecond, then vanishes again into her mouth. And I lose all sense of the game.

Her scent intoxicates me. Her touch more so. I don't want to think about the inevitable embarrassed laughter and sucked-up handshake coming tomorrow morning, when we eat breakfast across from each other, Mack scowling at us for our immaturity.

I whisper the word I've been thinking since I saw her standing with Mack's friends: *goddess*.

She's my goddess tonight.

My lips graze hers. I touch with pressure only gentle enough to let her know how much I want to lift the hem of her skirt and cup her ass, but not enough to demand. It's her choice. I may have won, but the rules are hers.

She glances around as if embarrassed by public displays of attraction. Or tempted by them.

"There's an alcove off the entryway," I nod toward the dark, glassed-in front of the building, "if you don't want to go upstairs."

Her eyes and mouth round. If she wants a bad boy, I'll play the bad boy and fuck her against the scratchy brick wall of the back of the alcove, my jeans around my ankles and her skirt yanked over her face. Mack will never need to know.

My cock responds, itching for attention. It knows the drill. The game. We fuck; it feels good. The itch is scratched. Then I go about my life the way I always do.

The fatigue I felt when she first indicated she knows of my "reputation" filters in. Fucking will happen. Gripping her ass is going to be glorious no matter if I take the path of least resistance and play to her expectations or if I try harder. If I take her under the stairs, or take her to my room and my bed. If I do what's expected, or if I become someone beyond a woman's expectations.

I know the rewards of expectation. I don't know the prizes of extra effort and diligence. Right now, my cock doesn't think it's worth the effort to figure it out.

"What if we get caught?" She stares at the door but she presses her ass against my crotch.

I feel myself slide into old habits as if I recorded all this and I'm watching a playback. Automatic desire tells my hand where to sit on her back, my lips the correct pressure to apply to the top edge of her ear. It tells my cock to stand at attention because I'm likely to get a quality blowjob tonight.

My habits feel comfortable. Warm and secure. This isn't a relationship—it can't be a relationship—so what difference does it make if I fall down to expectations? What difference does it make if I let my reputation give a woman a couple hours of joy?

So why is my back tightening up? She wants this.

"We won't get caught." The alcove is well-hidden.

"Are you going to take off the hat?" She takes my hand and pulls me toward the apartment vestibule.

We run up the steps and to the front of the creaking glass door. She pulls the extra key out of her little bag but fumbles it with her gloves. "Oh!"

My hand swings around her waist and I catch the key before it hits the ground. My chest is pressed firmly against her shoulder blades. My other hand splays over her belly. And carefully, gently, I press my erection against her ass.

She shivers. The cold exaggerates the vibration running from her hips to her breasts and up into her jaw, but it's the promise I press into her back that's making her moan.

"Here." I brush my lips against her ear. "Let me."

Slowly, I slide the key into the lock, mirroring the pressure I give the metal with the same force of my palm across her hip bone. She responds by wiggling her ass against my erection. I pull her against my front and yank open the door. Quickly, I roll us both in.

The vestibule of the apartment building is a dim, gray space full of mailboxes and creaky stairs. Sometime in the past, someone thought it a good idea to add a short wall blocking the sight lines to an empty space under the stairs. It's full of ladders and paint supplies now, and closed off by a mesh door, so no one can get in.

Unless you know the lock combo, which I do. I helped the super one day with a plumbing problem. He didn't think to change the numbers afterward.

I move her toward the stairs and around the short wall to the wire of the alcove door. Her fingers weave into the mesh and when she moans, the door rattles.

I don't turn her around. Don't demand a kiss. If we're playing the game this way, I'll play by the conventional rules. So I thread my hand under her jacket and slowly wiggle her shirt up underneath.

"I want to take pictures of you." Her voice is breathy. She leans into me, her back arching, and looks up at my face.

I want to spin her around. I want to taste those lovely lips. But that's not the game. "Now?"

Somewhere in the back of my head, my reputation is grinning like the cocky son of a bitch it is. What's a little more amateur porn going to hurt? My face isn't visible in any video that's online now. I know how to make sure it won't be this time, either.

It'll do her more harm than me.

She flips around and presses her back into the wire mesh. Her hands run over my chest and she rubs her lower belly against my cock. But her eyes narrow. "When I say I want pictures."

Oh, she's good. I grin. "With or without the hat?"

She answers by pulling off her gloves, unzipping my jacket and curling her fingers around my belt buckle.

CHAPTER 7

Isolde

Rob pulls my hands off his belt. His fingers stroke tiny circles on my hand before his skin lifts completely off mine and for a brief moment, all my perception zeroes in on my wrist. He touches just the right spot with just the exact amount of wispy pressure to set every single nerve ending in my body on fire.

My lips part and a minuscule, hitched breath passes over my tongue. Rob presses me against the cage and all I want to do is drop to my knees and find his cock under all the layers of jackets and clothes between us.

"Wait." Both his hands move away and he fiddles with the lock on the cage. The mechanism pops open and the door rocks under my weight.

Rob wraps his arm under my bottom and half-hoists, half-drags me to the side so he can open the door. It whines as it swings wide, so loud I think it's going to catch attention, but Rob doesn't seem to notice. He wiggles us inside, between two ladders leaning against the wall and a stack of what looks like industrial paint buckets.

A tarp spread over a stack of cans twists when his backpack drags over it. Rob frowns and closes the door, dropping his pack in front of it. We're trapped in here, behind a fence guarded by his books.

Only the dim light from the entrance area filters in. The paint smells astringent, with a little grease mixed in. A wheeled toolbox rattles when Rob pushes it against the wall opposite the ladders and he turns me around again, leaning me over its top.

His hands roam over my stuck-out ass, pinching and kneading, before he grabs my coat and pulls it off my shoulders. I hear it drop onto his backpack, followed by more rustling. He must be taking off his.

"Leave on the hat," I breathe. It makes this ridiculous moment all the more ridiculous. I'm about to fuck my brother's roommate. A man who doesn't know my name. A guy I'm going to be living with, if only randomly and temporarily.

A man with layers I want to see. But whose body is way, way too distracting.

So I'm letting this happen. I am, I think, getting it out of the way. Because if I don't, fucking him is all I'm going to think about as I lie on my air mattress staring at the ceiling. How he's one room over lying naked on his belly, his arm over the side of the bed, snoring softly instead of awake and hard and going down on me.

His roaming hands feel incredible. His touch is better than any other man's. And even if there's no relationship here, at least I've had a sample of what a gorgeous man has to offer. At least, for once in my life, I feel desired.

Rob chuckles but doesn't speak. He moves away for a second and I hear his backpack zipper open. Cellophane crinkles, then a strip of condoms appears on a step of the ladder next to my face.

Not one condom. Three.

My entire body quakes like I'm about to orgasm. Oh my god, what is he promising me? I turn around. His jacket lies on top of mine. He wears a dark-colored t-shirt that's tight around his chest but loose around his middle. He's backlit by the low light filtering in from the overhead globe in the entryway but his biceps pop. As do his forearms.

The arms of this man alone spark every single one of my deep, primal needs. A part of me wants to fight it, to dig for those special looks, but I want this, too.

I want both.

"Tomorrow at breakfast, we talk like adults, okay?" I say.

Rob chuckles again. "I aim only to please my goddess," he purrs.

He hoists me up onto the tool case, flicking my skirt at the same time so I'm not sitting on it. The fabric fans out over the cool metal and my perch rocks, but Rob presses his knees into it, holding it still. He's between my legs looking down like his cock is going to burst from his jeans on its own. As if my presence has set free his personal monster.

He works both hands under my skirt and up between the waistband and my tights. His fingers search for the elastic and when he finds the edge, his fingertips curl against my skin. But he doesn't yank them down. Not yet.

"Undo my belt," he says.

I immediately fumble with the leather, yanking as I try to work in the gloom of the alcove. His buckle rattles. Rob grins, fighting my pulls, and rubs small circles with the fingers he slid between my waistband and my skin.

The belt loosens and slides out of the buckle. The denim of his jeans feels softer than I expected, as does the cloth-covered waistband of the underwear peeking out the top. I close my eyes and work my fingers between the fabric and his skin, drinking in the lusciousness of this man's hard, firm muscles.

"Button and zipper," Rob sounds as if he's stalking me, playing with his prize. I'm the best he's ever caught and damn it, he's going to savor his toy.

I'm so wet I can barely think. I'll come the moment he flicks my clit with the pad of his thumb.

All I want is his cock. Fucking my pussy, fucking my mouth. Hell, pumping between my tits or my ass cheeks. I don't care. I just want to feel him lose control and come and come again.

I release the button on his jeans. His eyes half close. His mouth opens just a bit. And I slowly unzip his fly.

His fingers yank down my waistband at the same time, at the same speed. His thumbs flare out, pressing on my mound, and as the zipper of his jeans parts, his thumbs do their own opening. They curl down and inward, and stroke the edges of my inner lips.

"Oh, fuck," I groan. My head drops back but my hands rub his cock through the fabric of his boxer-briefs.

Rob leans into me and presses his thumbs together just below my clit, and he pinches closed my labia.

I moan and he chuckles into my ear. "You are freakin' sexy," he whispers. "I'm going to fuck you every night you're here. Every goddamned night."

He thinks I'm sexy? I pull back a little, and look at his wonderfully masculine face. Is he lying because we're hooking up? Does he mean what he's saying?

I can't tell in the low light. All I know is that his long, thick cock is rock hard and separated from my grip by too much fabric.

"You say that to all the girls, don't you?" I nip at his neck right along the collar of his shirt.

"Only the freakin' sexy ones." His lips press into the skin just below my earlobe. "And you are the by far the sexiest of the freaks."

His thumbs pull apart and I feel my pussy spread for him, even though my tights still strangle my hips.

But there's something off about how he's speaking. His face shifts a little again and he looks like he wants to kiss me. Or maybe he's disappointed that he can't. Or that he's saying weird, player things to me.

Because he's supposed to.

And I realize I still can't see the color of his eyes.

"Are you ready to do this?" Again, something is off about the pitch of his baritone. The way he speaks reminds me of how Mack talks to students.

Impersonal. Explicit. There's not to be any corner or point or fold of this encounter left open to interpretation. We may behave like juveniles, but he knows how to play the game.

Right now, looking up at his face, I wonder how ready *he* is to do this.

And I don't feel horny anymore.

Why are we here, like this? Why did I let—*lead*—this man into a dark corner so I can satisfy some primal need for hot sex? Because he's perfectly formed and excellently muscled? Because he's obviously a good person, even if he allows behaviors like what we are about to do? Because he has a reputation and I won't have to take any responsibility for my own lust?

"Are you?" I ask.

His thumbs pull away from my pussy. His fingers release my tights. He steps back. And the man I saw at the party resurfaces, if only for a brief flicker.

But it's gone. "Yes," he says. But he watches me with the semi-stern face of a soldier waiting for explicit confirmation of orders.

He won't proceed unless I make it clear I understand exactly what's happening. And I think the bit of Rob I saw earlier has been submerged into this other, sexual part. When his reputation took over, he became a different person, or an actor playing a role, or drummer keeping the beat.

I wonder what this means to him. And I wonder if I give in and feed my lust, what it will do to his soul, because I'm wondering about the slippery grains of his reputation. I'm wondering if I'll be the pebble that starts the final spill and if he'll ever be able to dig himself out from under it. From under what my selfishness might do to him.

The look that flashed across his face at the party can't get buried. I can't be the woman who starts the avalanche he can't escape from. No matter how weak I am, I won't do that to this man.

"How many times have you done this?" I ask.

CHAPTER 8

Robert

If only she knew how often women have asked me "how many times." What number am I? What notch am I on your belt? Have you fucked enough women to know how to do me right?

Or enough to leave me in peace tomorrow morning?

Mack's sister pulls her thighs together and drops off the cart. She runs her hand down the front of her shirt and stands up straight. Hitching up her skirt, she yanks her tights back where they should be. When she tips her head to the side, I see the frown on her lips.

I stand in front of her with my jeans open, but my auto anti-lust response kicks in and dampens my horniness. My cock presses painfully against the teeth of my fly as I zip up, irritated even through the cotton of my boxer-briefs, but with a little effort I can will away the discomfort. I have control. I can make my body behave.

The alcove takes on definition again and I see the ladders and the paint buckets. I smell the industrial chemicals instead of her incredible sexiness. I may want to rip those tights right off her hips and lick her to the best damned orgasm she's ever experienced just to prove to her she's made a mistake turning me down, but that's not going to happen.

If she changes her mind in this moment, then she changes her mind. And I need to change mine, too.

No sex for Robert tonight, though there ain't no harm in telling her exactly what she's going to miss. "You ever come twice while fucked?" I run my hand up the outside of her thigh. "Because I'll get you there. And a third, licked."

I'll find the right spot inside. The point which takes a thrust and gives back the shudders and the moans. The place where the friction makes a woman lose control and beg for more. I'll pound it just right.

"I'm sorry," she whispers. "I'm sorry I listened to Lisa and Anne and not what you were telling me."

Telling her? The only thing I told her was that I'll give her the orgasm she needs to make her life worth remembering.

"When did your nephew give you that hat?" She points at my head.

The edges of the earflaps rest just outside my perception but I know they're there. My preposterous hat. The symbol of family and connection I wouldn't trade for anything. And I was going to fuck a woman whose name I don't know while wearing it.

I close my eyes and take another step back.

"Last Christmas, when I was still an undergrad." I lived off campus then as well, the way I do here. At the time, my middle brother, Tom, was living with Dan, my oldest, and Dan's boy, my nephew Bart. The kid who gave me the hat because "Cold ears are bad, Uncle Robby."

Tom's out of Dan's basement now, and employed. And engaged. My brothers, the two responsible adults of our family.

The mood's gone and it didn't take the metal teeth of my zipper to do it, either.

I rebuckle my belt. My balls ache and the tiny, immature part of my brain screams *It's not fair! She's mean!*

Mack's sister touches my elbow. "I'm sorry. I just don't think either of us really wants this."

She's watching me the way she did on the porch, under the moonlight, when she snapped that photo of my nostrils. Watching me more like she's a therapist than a photographer.

It's weird and I look away. "We should go upstairs."

Time to sleep in the same apartment with the woman who just

cockblocked me because she's more in tune with my psyche than I am. Because she's right. I don't really want this. But a game is a game and you can't change the rules right in the middle.

But she did. Ripped them like short-and-curlies right off my balls. Why?

She picks up her coat and drapes it over her arm. Watching me still, she swipes it with the palm of her hand. The fabric makes the same sound as the tarp did, when we groped each other in the alcove.

She brushes around me, doing her best not to touch, but I still feel the pressure of her body move across my abdomen. I still smell faint hints of that bad beer from the party, but also the dry, sterile smell of airplanes and airports. She's probably just as tired and loopy from traveling all day as I am from my epic ten-hour study-fit on campus.

So maybe she saw me as a way to release tension. I snort and reach to pick up my twenty-five pounds of backpack. That's me, the talking vibrator who cracks jokes.

She presses open the cage door, moving it slowly to minimize the squeaking, and her fingers curl into the mesh. Her lovely, tapered fingers that, I think, I would have enjoyed feeling in my hair and touching my face. I would have enjoyed her stuttered, soft moans. And, possibly, quite enjoyed the taste of her lips, even with the beer residue.

If I kissed my goddesses. Which I don't.

But it's not happening anyway, so I better push it out of my mind.

She walks out into the circle of dim light under the hanging fixture in the vestibule and looks over her shoulder, waiting. She's a bit taller than most women—the top of her head comes up to the bridge of my nose. Her lovely blonde ponytail glimmers with metallic undertones as if she's woven gold and bronze and copper threads into her hair. Her curves flow beautifully, proportioned to her frame and firm under my fingers, but I suspect she's a little heavier than she thinks she should be, mostly because every woman thinks she is heavier than she should be.

Her body makes her fuckable, but it's her mind that makes her attractive.

And the word *goddess* continues to dominate my thoughts.

At this point, I don't think I want to know her name. Might ruin the magic.

I close the cage and spin the lock. She waits, watching. I carry my jacket in one fist and my pack in the other, partly to occupy my hands. But we still climb the stairs next to each other, and they creak in unison, under our synchronized steps. Her black tights hug her long legs, but she pulls her arms close to her body. It's cold, even in here.

The lights in the hallway to the apartment glow brighter than in the vestibule and I step back enough to watch her walk. Her hips swing nicely, her back straight and her step assured.

Traits I noticed before, but didn't think about.

She pulls her key from her purse but doesn't unlock the door. "Thank you for walking me home safely, Mr. Robert Quidell."

I chuckle knowing full well I'd either run my hand over my head or stuff my hands in my pockets if I wasn't carrying my PhD program in my bag. "You are welcome, Daffy."

She chuckles too, and opens the door. "My name's Isa." She pauses and glances around the door, into our dark apartment. "It's short for Isolde. My parents were going to name Mack Tristan but I'm glad they had a fight about it and my dad won. Tristan would have been creepy."

Chuckling again, I follow her in and drop my bag on the floor. The apartment is set up like most apartments: you enter into the living room, the kitchen is off to the left and the hallway to the bedrooms and the bathroom is off to the right. I flip on the living room light as she glances down the dark corridor toward the bedrooms, her shoulders angled, obviously listening for signs of her brother.

Nodding once, she glances back at me. "I think he's asleep."

I toss my jacket on the couch before taking off my bumblebee hat. It feels warm in my hands, and the sudden exposure of my head feels cold. But Isa smiles.

"Your eyes are green," she says.

My right eyebrow does the chagrined arch-dance of confusion and she laughs.

"I couldn't see before." She waves her hands at my face.

"They're not quite green." I lean toward her. My brothers and I all inherited a mix of our mom's baby blues and our dad's crystal greens.

From a distance, I always thought we looked like we had storm clouds in our eyes.

"Ah." Isa steps closer, her nose and chin out, as if she's concentrating on the details of my irises. "Ocean."

"Statues in Paris." I point at her eyes. Where I have blue flecks, she has copper and fog and the depth of ages.

Isa blinks and I think a moment of connection passes between us. It feels as weird as her piercing gaze or her uncanny ability to read my soul.

Am I frightened by it? There are so many different ways I could be frightened. My stomach does a little dance of pushes and pulls and either I'm embarrassed by the whole evening, or petulant. Or perhaps I truly am scared. But whatever makes my body act like I'm a mad eight-year-old takes control.

And I open my stupid mouth. "No sneaking into my room tonight when you figure out what you missed. I need my beauty sleep." It comes out dripping with all that eight-year-old sarcasm.

I let my internal immature dickweed tell her how mean she is.

The moment of connection snaps like a twig. Snaps and snaps again because I just smashed my foot into it, heel first, before jumping up and down for good measure.

Isa closes her eyes. When she opens them again, her face takes on the hardness I associate with someone who sees their role in my life as a narrow and precise set of interactions. She's a teacher teaching a specific subject, or she's the police officer giving me a ticket. She might be that cute girl at the coffee shop who smiles at me the same way she smiles at all the professors and the undergrads. Or Isa might be one of the many women who, after a conquest, doesn't want anything more to do with me.

I had to open my mouth, didn't I?

"Good night, Robert." Isa nods once, succinctly, and walks away toward our apartment's tiny third bedroom, the place where Mack and I used to retreat to grade or study. She's about to drop her head onto her pillow. Alone.

Because there really isn't an alternative for either of us.

CHAPTER 9

Robert

Sun streams in through the window opposite the galley that passes as our kitchen. Mack left the curtains wide open last night. I blink, squinting, and hold my hand up to shade my eyes.

The glass in the window rattles. The wind picked up this morning and has been shrieking between the sashes and the frames of every one of our apartment's leaky portals to the exterior world. I woke up to a blast of cold whistling in from the window in my bedroom.

Which means the clouds will roll in soon. And snow.

And once again, I wonder why I didn't pick a school in a more pleasant climate.

I dump the coffee into the maker as I scratch at my belly and my sweatshirt rubs across my skin. It may be Saturday, but it's still a work day. I have papers to grade and six midterm exam questions to prep. As does Mack.

So a full pot of black hazelnut-tainted caffeine will do us good.

Isa, for her part, will be on her own today.

Coffee aroma wafts through the kitchen, caught on the cold-ass draft blasting through the window. Goosebumps rise on my forearms. Maybe I should turn up the heat.

A door opens down the hall. I hear shuffling, and a knock. Then the other door. Mack and Isa mumble at each other.

My back stiffens. What is she telling him? Not that I care. Or should care. We'd be acting cordial and nonchalant even if I had fucked her.

Which I didn't.

I slam the lid on the coffeemaker.

I hear shuffling toward me, down the hall, and another door slam, farther away. One of them walks toward the kitchen, the other into the bathroom.

The pipes grumble. The shower starts. And I'm alone with one of the twins.

"What'd you do to my sister last night?" I hear a chair pull back from the table and Mack's ass hit the seat.

I turn around. He looks like shit. Pale, eyes sunken, he hasn't shaved in three days and his hair's sticking out from his scalp like a halo of dirty fungus. "You need to go back to bed," I say.

Mack chuckles and rubs his face. His fingers pull on his cheeks and the skin around his eyes yanks down. "Papers to grade."

My roommate looks like he's about to puke. "Seriously, man. Go back to bed. You can't grade like that." I point at his chest.

He slumps down in the chair before leaning his head on the table. "It's the fucking weather." A hand snakes out from under his forehead and waves in the general vicinity of the window. "Low pressure system. Normally it's not a problem but this semester's been a bitch."

Mack's TA-ing two courses this term, plus juggling a full load of classes and starting to prep for his comps. Even without the weather and his sister showing up, he's under enough stress to trigger migraines for even the most normal among us.

"I'll grade some of your section." It pops out of my mouth before I realize what I'm saying. I have a ton of studying and a paper to write. I don't have time to grade his section.

But he really does look like shit.

I pour myself a mug of low-grade hazelnut-laced caffeine and drop into the chair next to him. "Listen," I say, "half the assignment is multiple choice. I'll breeze through it first. Leave the hard shit for you."

Mack chuckles but doesn't lift his head off his arms. "Don't expect me to help you cheat on your stats test."

It's not the statistics I hate about the course, it's the program we're using to run the data. The department uses an interface-less, shareware piece of shit because of, I suspect, the licensing fees. So I suffer. If I wanted to learn to program, I would have gone into computer science. Better chance of a job once I graduate if I had. But no, I had to go with my "passion" like all the other dumbshits in my generation.

"Oh, yes you are, my friend." I sit back and sip my cheap-but-serviceable coffee. It's bitter. I better clean the maker. "I grade your papers and tolerate your houseguest, and you program my stats assignments. That's the deal."

Mack chuckles again and sits up, but he keeps his eyes closed. "I'd appreciate it if you took care of some of the grading."

What else am I supposed to do? He's hurting. "Go back to bed."

After a moment, Mack slowly stands up. "The headaches usually go away by now. I'll be better by this evening."

Maybe. "Go back to bed." I wave him away.

Mack pinches the bridge of his nose. "Student assignments are in the front pocket of my bag." He points over his shoulder at the couch, where his backpack sits.

I wave him away again. "Dude. Go. Back. To. Bed."

My roommate shuffles across the carpet of the dining area toward the hallway, but stops in the center of the living room between the couch and the coffee table piled with books and empty beer bottles. "Did Lisa say something to Isa at the party?" He rubs his head again. "She's mopey this morning."

I sip my coffee and try not to look suspicious. "How the hell would I know?" But my retort sounds as bitchy as Lisa's *I'm telling Mack* evil glare last night.

The pain cinching tight around Mack's forehead must be bad because he doesn't notice. "Be nice." He waves at me again. "She's leaving Tuesday. I don't want her to think she needs to move back into Mom's house, okay? That's not a good situation."

But he shuffles off before I can ask.

I set down my mug. I don't know a lot about what's happening in California. Only that their parents have been divorced since they were ten and their mom and dad continue to fight. Mom had a parade of boyfriends through their house while they were growing up. Dad jetsets. I get the impression Mack thinks their father is a selfish son of a bitch.

Mack always makes a face when he talks about their parents. And he seems quite protective of his twin sister.

I almost fucked her last night. Almost did my player bullshit and lived a little too much in the moment.

If my oldest brother, Dan, knew what I'd done, he'd smack me upside the head. He's the family man. The one who took up the slack when our mom died. The one who says "the hedonistic crap you pull is going to get you either dead or alone." Then he calls me an immature, weak-willed, self-centered shit.

I'm fully aware of the distancing outcomes of my behavior. What Dan doesn't seem to understand is that I like it that way.

Unlike him, I get all the sweet tail I want. And I get it without all the extra fun leftovers like emotional fallout and children.

I sip my coffee again, listening to the shower turn off.

But maybe I'd still like a new reputation. One that doesn't end with upturned noses and rolled eyes from the ladies.

Then again, maybe those rolled eyes save me from a whole mountain of bullshit I don't need. Or want. Or can handle right now. With the grading. And the classes.

I set down my mug. If I admit it to myself, the coffee tastes more like woodchips than hazelnut. But caffeine is caffeine and sometimes you need to take the burned pulpiness with the positives hitting the bloodstream. Because sometimes your body needs what it needs, no matter how bad it tastes.

Down the hall, the bathroom door creaks open. I hear the fan running, drawing out of our apartment the air sodden by ten minutes of a running hot shower. The whirring, electrically stimulated blades vomit the moisture out through the tubes and the vents into the low pressure system outside. The same weather that's giving my roommate a migraine. The same uncaring wider world that doesn't give a shit if I fuck a new woman every week.

So why the hell should I care? Why the hell should I make an effort to change my ways?

I don't care how beautiful she is, with all her copper flecks and her sweet curves. How bright and intelligent her eyes are. How, I suspect, she might be able to hold up her end of a conversation for more than five minutes.

How, most likely, she'd tell me something fascinating and wonderful and worthy of thinking about. Because she's Mack's sister and if she's not as smart as him, I'll eat my own socks.

It doesn't matter.

Because I have shit to do.

I tap the side of my mug as I reach for one of the many red pens we have sitting in the middle of our rickety table. It's time to get to work.

CHAPTER 10

Isolde

I t's hard not to fantasize about him. I have a silly school-girl dominance daydream swirling around in my head. One about a pretty boy who needs a lesson on how to treat a woman. How if he wants the best, he needs to step out of his ego and look at what's in front of him.

It's oh-so-difficult not to go back into my room, lie down on my air mattress, and rub one out while thinking about teaching Mr. Robert Quidell the lesson he very much deserves.

Warm water runs over my shoulders and steam expands through my throat and sinuses. I should be washing my hair. But in my mind's eye I see his slightly skewed smirk as he explains to me his view of the world: *I'm a god, baby. A hard-bodied, gorgeous god and I control the vertical just as much as I control all the... horizontals.*

I smirk right back at him. *Keep telling yourself that, big boy. One is the loneliest number, you know.*

He grins and chuckles and runs those strong fingers through his luscious dark hair before he leans closer. *Are you going to be the one to break through my hard exterior?*

I open my eyes. I'm wasting water. In two days I'm going to be in a part of the world where the clean, clear water running over my nipples would keep a family of four alive for a goddamned week. And yet here I am letting it swirl away because I'm fantasizing about my brother's immature but lust-worthy roommate.

Even if he does have a sweet, soft interior under his crunchy outer shell. One he doesn't want anyone to see. He made that abundantly clear last night with his little snide comment. The choice is his, not mine.

His game, his rules.

If there's one thing I've learned from growing up in the same house as my mother and her constant stream of boyfriends in need of fixing, it's that, if their idiotic behaviors keep their dicks happy, they don't give a shit about how dysfunctional they are. Or how much pollution they spread into the world around them.

So the charming, intelligent, obviously deeply-scarred-by-some-thing-or-other Mr. Quidell can suck his thumb and hold tight to his teddy bear of ouchiness for all I care. With guys like him—the entitled boys with everything going for them—the pain usually comes from something pathetic. Like they're still mad about their second grade crush rejecting them. Or they couldn't have a new car at sixteen. Because in their worlds, that pain is by far the worst thing they have ever experienced.

I soap up my hair as I curse the horrors of first world problems.

Though he really didn't seem like an entitled dickbag. A brat, yes. A dickbag, no. Frowning, I rinse off and step out of the shower. After toweling off, I slather on my nice moisturizer, knowing full well that today and tomorrow morning's showers will be the last I get for a while. And the last time I'll get to keep the skin of my shins buttery soft.

I could shave. Doesn't seem worth the effort, though. And being hairy might make that semi-dirtbag Aaron, the other assistant accompanying on this trip, not leer at me.

He's married. Never tried to touch when we worked together in Paris eight months ago. But the fucker stares.

I'm half tempted to write "Isa's boyfriend" on Rob's chest and take a picture. Set it as my phone's wallpaper so every time I get a leer I can hold it up. Make the son of a bitch who wants to make *me* feel small, feel totally, utterly inadequate.

But that, too, is another school girl fantasy. A shallow, insecure fantasy.

I pull on my t-shirt and sweats. No make-up, no blow-dried hair, no bra. Glasses perched on my nose. I may be semi-living with boys, but one's my brother and the other needs to get over himself.

When I swing open the bathroom door, the scent of hazelnut coffee slaps me full on the face. I breathe in deep. This, too, is another of life's little pleasures I'm about to say good-bye to for two and a half weeks.

Part of me likes the slimming down of my life to just my duffle and my equipment. To the mandatory malaria shots and the massive, bush-worthy hiking boots. Aaron can look at my ass all he wants when we are out on the back of our Range Rover, but he's nothing. I'm in the world and I'm seeing what needs to be seen.

It's cold in the hallway. I rub my arms. My nipples tighten, doing their usual response to the cold, and goosebumps rise on my flesh.

I need to find a sweater.

Mack's door is closed when I go by. I almost knock, but I know what it means. The storm moving in is probably giving him shit. This, too, is a familiar pattern. He needs about another eight or so hours of quiet dark to recover.

Rob sits hunched over the table when I walk into the living room, and all I see is the wide expanse of his broad back. He's wearing a ratty sweatshirt but I swear I see the cut and definition of his shoulders through the fabric. Which I can't. Because it's a sweatshirt. And no man's that perfect.

I push away thoughts of pulling up his sweatshirt and kissing between his strong, muscular shoulder blades.

He looks up when he hears me shuffle in. Blinking, he squints for a second, and I swear those wondrous, ocean-filled eyes do the same twinkle they did at the party.

Or maybe I just need coffee.

"Good mornin'," Rob mumbles. His hand wiggles toward the

kitchen. "Mugs are in the cabinet to the left of the sink. Coffee's sort of fresh." He drops his face back to whatever it is he's doing.

"Did Mack go back to bed?" I walk into the kitchen and pour myself some liquid gold. I take it black, more because the extras are just that—extras. And I'm not going to turn down caffeine because I have delicate tastebuds.

Rob nods. "Ah-huh." He doesn't look up from the assignment he's grading.

"It's the storm." I point at the whistling window. At least I'm about to go someplace warm. Hot, actually. Still better than blistering wind so cold your skin feels like it's about to freeze solid.

Rob nods again. "That's what he said."

I almost hold out my hand for a high-five, an involuntary reaction to hearing the words *That's what he said*. I snort instead.

Chuckling, Rob drops his red pen. "Sorry. Not enough coffee in me to make good jokes."

When he looks up, his face is open and happy again, the way it was for that moment last night, right after we entered the apartment. When I finally saw the color of his eyes.

But it vanishes in very much the same way it vanished last night.

I sip my coffee. The lukewarm liquid glides over my tongue and I await the inevitable snarky princess bitching that always drops off the lips of a spurned boy.

Rob sits back in his chair, his face stern yet complex, and crosses his arms over his chest. One eyebrow arches. The other draws in. And one corner of his mouth rises higher than the other. "You look angry," he says.

Do I? "Why would I be angry?" I set my mug on the counter. His gaze follows my hand as it drops away from my mouth but his eye movements stop when his focus reaches my chest. His eyes don't follow the arch of my arm. He notices my braless breasts and I swear he looks like he just saw Jesus. Not that immature Aaron leering at boobies, but a full-on look of happy wonder as if he'd just gotten a glimpse of a priceless work of art.

But he looks back at his papers before I know for sure I under- stand correctly what I was seeing. "I don't know," he says. "Maybe because you were expecting the bee hat?" He shrugs and pats his head. "It *is* cold in here."

He glances at my chest again.

"Look." I take a deep breath and grab Mack's sweatshirt off the back of the other chair. Quickly, I pull it on and drop my ass across from him. "I'm going to be living here on and off, okay? I don't have a lot of stuff and I won't be in the way when I'm here. I promise. So can we act like adults? Not get on each other's nerves?"

It's bad enough I can't stop thinking about him without also thinking about him bending me over a chair, or setting me on the counter in the kitchen and pounding me so hard the coffeemaker falls off the edge.

Across from me, wheels turn and I think Rob's trying very hard to *not* say something about my breasts. He only glances at me. "Sure." A quick pout moves across his mouth.

A very sexy, very small pout where his wonderful, gorgeous lower lip poked out just a tiny bit for a just-as-tiny moment.

God*damn* the man is photogenic. And an ass. My thighs tingle looking at him.

"You want to go back to my room right now, Rob?" I sit back in my chair, too. "Get it out of the way? Scratch that itch so you don't have an unfilled notch on your belt?"

I think I suggest it more for me than him. Because I think part of me regrets saying no last night. The part that fantasizes. But on the other hand, Responsible Brain did the right thing.

He rolls his eyes and without answering, goes back to grading his papers.

I lean closer. I don't know why I'm mad, but I am. "You think you're the first hot guy to get his hand under my skirt?" I'm exaggerating about the hotness of the guys who try with me, but Rob doesn't need to know that. "I work with models, many of whom are way, way hotter than you. Men who are *paid* to be hot."

Surprise flickers over Rob's face as if he doesn't think there are guys hotter than him out there in the wider world. Or maybe it's surprise because I think he's hot.

I'd rather think his ego wasn't so ginormous he thinks of himself as Prince Hottie, so I'll go with my second choice and hope I'm right.

A sniff twitches my nose. I don't mean it to happen, but it does. "I know the kind of fun you offer. I fully understand the rules of the game. But I also know what I saw in your eyes last night. I *know* you know when you're acting like a player. And for a moment, I thought maybe you were smart enough to get beyond it."

Rob pinches the bridge of his nose. "If you know the rules, then why the hell would you care if I got beyond my childhood traumas?"

So he knows the root causes of his behavior. Yet he won't do the work to change it. "Maybe I thought getting to know you might be worth the effort."

He blinks and his mouth opens, but he doesn't respond.

I push back my chair. "My connector flight to JFK goes out Tuesday morning. Mack's taking me to the airport before teaching his section. I need to make sure my equipment's secure."

Still silent, Rob waves me away.

In the living room, I look over my shoulder. He hunches over the papers, his attention fully on his students' needs.

Mack said his new roommate impressed him. That Rob had a mind quicker and sharper than anyone he'd ever met. My brother had seen Rob in action at a department function at the beginning of last semester. Rob, the new kid, spent three hours arguing with the department head about ethnocentrism and the emerging cyber-based subcultures formed around social media.

So the gorgeous guy sitting at the table making a point of ignoring me has a fire in his belly. And a hidden trauma.

I turn away. Someday, he might feel safe enough to get beyond his issues and find a way of living that's whole. One that meets all his needs, not just the ones easily sated.

A twinge makes me blink and I wonder, deep inside, if I'm sad that when it happens, I won't be part of his world.

Or, perhaps, I wonder if I'm worthy.

CHAPTER 11

Robert

The snow starts in the late afternoon. I frown out the leaky window at the big flakes bouncing off the glass, wondering if we're going to get snowed in. The flipping flakes tinkle against the window, each one its own little chime. The storm's brought the faery land to life at the same time it might be trapping me in a drafty apartment with the migraine twins.

One twin with a headache that's all his, and the other making a new pain in the neck for me.

I hear shuffling in the hallway and turn around in my chair half expecting to see my roommate, but Isa glides into the living room, still fresh faced and braless, her hair in a messy ponytail, a tablet in one hand and her empty coffee mug in the other.

She extends a finger, lifting it off the handle of the mug, and slides it across her tablet. The reflected light playing over her lovely face shifts, as does the mirage dancing over her glasses.

She moves into the room, looking more at what's on her screen than where she's going.

And Isa almost trips over the coffee table.

"Shit." She stands up straight a little too fast. Her old coffee sloshes out of the mug and onto a stack of student assignments on the table.

I jump off my chair, a napkin in my hand, before the "—it" part of her swearing is out of her mouth. I dab at the top assignment, swearing softly myself, somewhat grateful that this stack has been graded and they're my students, not Mack's. My section has a pretty good sense of humor, so they won't care.

"I'm sorry." Isa sets down the mug. She blinks her huge eyes and bites her lip. "I didn't ruin them, did I?" The tablet, she tucks under her arm. "I wasn't looking."

I wad up the napkin. She looks genuinely embarrassed. And she's hiding the tablet under her arm.

I point. "You looking at porn on that thing?"

Isa's brows crunch up and she frowns just like my mom used to when I was a kid and I said something bratty to my brother Tom. Stuff like, "Nice tulip you're painting. 'Cause real artists draw pretty flowers."

I was a brat who hadn't yet developed a good instinct for insults.

Isa pulls the tablet out from under her arm. "I'm applying for a position with a studio in L.A. It's steady work. Less travel." She waves the little screen in the air between us, but too fast for me to get a sense of what's on it.

But I don't see color, just gray. She must be looking at black and whites.

I don't respond. I walk away instead, to throw out the coffee-soaked napkin.

"Are you like this with Mack?" she asks. "So obnoxious?"

I stop, one hand on the cabinet where we keep the stinky garbage can. The fingers of my other tightened around the edge of the countertop.

Why do women think they have the right to psychoanalyze me? I'm just their good time evening. Why do they care? "I don't need you poking your fingers at me," I say. "Because my life's not your business."

"Your life?" Isa points at the stack of coffee-stained assignments. "I thought it was about your students' now-difficult-to-read papers."

I feel my eyes narrow. Part of me wants to yell "You started it!" but then I *would* be acting like a child. So I stay quiet.

Isa sighs, pulling in a deep lung-full of air. She holds it for a long moment, then releases it slowly. But her shoulders stay tight. And her nose scrunches up. She picks up her now-empty coffee mug. "Excuse me. I'd like to make lunch. I heard Mack moving around and my sick brother is probably hungry."

She brushes by me. Her hip bumps into my thigh and I step to the side, a little off balance, but I catch myself on the back of the chair I'd just jumped out of to save my students' assignments.

I smell her shampoo when she rubs against my side. Wisps of a sweet essential oil curl around my head—something warmly honeyed with just enough floral blended into it to make me want to inhale all the way to the bottom of my diaphragm.

Isa blinks as she glances over her shoulder, but she doesn't say more. The tablet balances closer to the edge of the counter than makes me comfortable and I stare at it, waiting for it to go tumbling the way her coffee did earlier.

But it doesn't. And I have an excellent view of the black and white she was studying when she bumped the table.

It's a young couple. They look younger than us, probably high school, and the boy is wrapped around the girl, his head on her shoulder and his arms around her waist. She leans her head toward his, her nose in his hair, and she looks as if she's breathing in his love.

There's no mistaking the story the photo tells. For the girl, the boy outlines the world. His edges are the edges of her space. And for the boy, the girl fills a space that if empty, would rip him to shreds. He'd be eaten by emptiness.

Isa doesn't comment or offer a glance in my direction or even ask where we keep the bread. She walks around our narrow kitchen, opening and closing cabinets, pulling out dishes, finding utensils. And makes a peanut butter sandwich on whole wheat toast for her suffering brother.

She walks by again, the sandwich's plate held in one hand and a glass of water in the other, and her tablet now under her arm. Isa, who knew in her bones exactly when to take that photo, how to stand to capture the image. The woman who instructed her camera and her models in how to make a moment worth capturing. A good sister who now takes into another room her ability to read humanity's deep secrets.

Away from me. Toward a man she feels is worth caring about.

I watch her go to offer a kind gesture of food to her in-pain brother.

And I feel suddenly, completely, alone.

CHAPTER 12

Robert

Mack took Isa to the airport seventeen days, six hours and twenty minutes ago. Not that I'm counting. I just remember the moment peace returned to our apartment.

Quiet that's been filled with glorious, gorgeous photos of African life sent to her brother whenever she's somewhere with service. Her eye for people continues to astound me, but also her eye for landscapes and animals. Every snap is a story in and of itself, many of which are taken with her phone camera.

Mack says she's experimenting with a "low-fidelity aesthetic." I just think she's talented. And that I really do need to learn how to use the camera on my phone.

The last picture, an orange and gold sunset over the African plain, I stared at for a full ten minutes. It's now my phone's background.

I'll take it off before she gets back. Don't need the hell of her seeing one of her photos on my phone.

Mack tidied her room, sticking the clothes she left behind into a cheap dresser he bought and stacking her boxes of software and drives and SD cards against the wall. He deflated the air bed, rolled it up, and set it on top of the boxes next to the sheets, which he washed and folded.

I think my roommate misses his sister.

I study and I don't think about her talent or her smile or her spectacular breasts.

But now it's my turn to run off. I'm flying home for the weekend, to celebrate my nephew's fifth birthday. Tom's first gallery show is Tuesday, but I can't stay. My first test of the term is Monday. So I fly home, party with the brothers, and fly back, all while reading journal articles on my phone.

Ugly, difficult to parse articles without the glorious yellows and wondrous reds of a sunset over the savanna.

I'm leaving, but Isa is coming home. I almost ask Mack if he could ask her to share more of her photos while I'm gone, but I doubt she'd appreciate my interest. So I keep my mouth shut.

Mack pats my shoulder as we walk into the ubiquitous airport bustle. "Getting sick of dropping off and picking up." He hitches the straps on his backpack and frowns at a loud family walking by. "I'm going to make her buy her own car and leave it in long term parking when she goes on these trips."

He didn't seem all that happy about taking me to the airport, either. "Why the hell don't you have on your coat?" Mack pushed up his glasses before flicking his hand at me.

"Because Minnesota is warmer than here, that's why." And my brothers have everything I need. No use packing shit I might leave behind.

Mack snorts. "Sure, buddy. Whatever you say."

Isa's coming in about an hour after my plane takes off, so Mack's spending the rest of the afternoon in an airport coffee shop grading papers, reading journal articles, and sipping syrupy coffee.

"You're a good brother," I say. At least someone is. I'll be home by the evening and in the presence of my two better-than-me brothers, meeting their new women-of-quality. And, most likely, rolling around on the floor playing superhero with the world's greatest nephew.

Mack laughs when I smile. "You're the one who dropped almost three hundred dollars on a camera for your kindergarten-aged nephew." He points at my duffle. "Why didn't you ask Isa to help you pick out something? She's opinionated, you know."

Yes, Isa has a full set of opinions. "She wasn't here."

Mack stops walking. "Give me your phone."

I stop as well. "Why?" He doesn't need to fuck around with my phone.

My roommate wiggles his fingers.

"Don't download porn." I pull the phone from my pocket and unlock the screen before slowly setting it on his palm.

"Figure out how to use the camera yet?" Mack swipes and tilts and taps in something or other.

"What are you doing?" I grab for my phone put he pulls it away.

"Not so fast, lover boy." He holds it up above his head. "How many women's numbers do you have in here?" He swipes again.

"Plenty." More than I need, that's for sure. More than will ever talk to me again. More than I want.

"You could share, you know." Mack hands back my phone.

I swipe through it but I can't tell what he did. "What did you do?"

"I added Isa's number. Take a picture of your nephew using his birthday present and send it to her. It'll make her month."

Her number's not obvious in my contacts. "Where'd you put it?" If it's in the notes, I'll need to transfer it.

Mack chuckles. "It's there with all the other ladies, Casanova." He walks ahead, shepherding me toward the self-serve check-in. "You don't have a girlfriend because you're a pig. They can smell it on you a mile away." He makes grunting noises.

I give him the finger, but quickly hide my hand when an old lady pulling a huge wheeled bag throws me a stern disapproving grandma look. Her bag *thump thumps* away and Mack laughs and laughs.

"You're twelve courses of dumbass," he says.

I tuck my phone in my pocket and jog to catch up. "You'll pick me up Monday afternoon?" I ask, determined to change the subject.

Mack grins like a cocky son of a bitch and flicks his finger across the tip of his nose. "Sending Isa. So you two love birds can have some quality time together."

I stop walking again. "Your sister does not like me, Mack."

His look transforms into a slightly annoyed frown. "I thought that whole social media issue you had when you got here might have made you reconsider how you interact with women. Not that it's my business." He shakes his head. "Which it's not. Until you started treating my sister like she's unwelcomed."

I feel my back bristle. "You're bringing this up now? I have a plane to catch." But I don't point over my shoulder or turn away. Some part of me wants a fight. To, I think, yell and punch because she keeps getting under my skin.

And I refuse to think about her. "She wants indifference. So I'm indifferent."

Mack snorts. "You are far, far from indifferent." He gives me the finger as he turns away. "How the hell are you going to do participant observations if you can't see the obvious right in front of you?"

I see the world just fine. Mack's body language is clear and precise —he's more indignant than angry. And, like so many other times I've seen him interact with people, he's backing off of a potential conflict by walking away from me.

Which is his choice. But my gut tells me he's going to stew about it while I'm home.

"Mack!"

He hitches his pack up his back and points toward the check-in before walking back to me. "Looks like the line's long. Better queue up."

He stands straight and slaps my shoulder. "One day a woman may actually *like* you. Could happen, you know."

"Fuck off, Mack." Plenty of women like me.

He laughs, but his face instantly turns stone cold serious. "You mess with my sister and I'm kicking your ass to the curb."

"You put her number on my phone, not me." Now I'm more confused than anything else. I think my mouth opens. He might be joking, but I don't think he's *joking*. This is the first time I've seen my roommate look... menacing.

"I told you why I put her number on your phone. Send her a photo of your nephew. It will make her millennium." His eyes go spacey for a second and part of me wonders if he's having another migraine. But he seems to be remembering something.

"She used to do a lot of volunteer work teaching kids how to take photos." Mack waves his hand at me. "She'll like it." But his face turns stony again. "I meant what I said about you fucking with her."

I want to snarl. To get my back up and get into a fight, but that won't help anyone. "I don't fuck *with* women, dude." Anything short of clarity of intention is rude at the best and seriously shitty at the worst. And I don't do that.

Mack sniffs. He slaps my shoulder again as he nods toward his awaiting café seat. "And that, my friend, is the true source of your problems."

He shakes his head one last time and walks away.

Shit, I think. *What the hell did that mean?* Now what?

Maybe I should move out, anyway.

No, I won't think about it. I won't think about Isa, either. I'm going home to visit my family and women are not my concern right now.

I make it through the wonders of automated ticket check-in without difficulty, then thread my way through security. At the gate, I pull out my phone and practice taking photos of the planes, telling myself they're for Bart, my nephew. But mostly I suspect I just want to take photos.

Because I'm not going to look for her number. I'm not going to admit she's under my skin. Or that I don't understand Mack's comment about not fucking with women being my problem.

I snap photos and wait for my boarding group to be called.

On the plane, I listen to music instead of studying. The kid sitting behind me kicks my seat with a rhythm worthy of an A-list rock drummer and the obese woman across the aisle keeps ordering tiny bottles of vodka. The plane roars as planes do, and the air smells not-quite-clean, as plane air always does.

When we land, I turn on my phone to text my oldest brother, Dan, who should be at the airport by now to pick me up. My phone boots, making the jingle noise of my carrier, and a text pops up.

It's a selfie of Mack and Isa in the coffee shop at the airport, but it's not from his phone. It's from a number labeled as 'Iseult.' *If your nephew has questions about his new camera, text me.*

Why did Mack label her number 'Iseult'? It must be some variation of her name.

Confusion hops from one of my shoulders to the other, digging in its claws and biting at my ears. *I thought you didn't like me*, I text back.

It's off into the ether before I realize just how juvenile it sounds. But it's on her phone now and there's nothing I can do about it.

I like your nephew. He gave you the bee hat.

Which I left in the apartment. Didn't want to lose it.

A new photo pops up. It's Mack wearing my hat and smiling a big, happy smile. *Show Bart.*

I will, I text back. I want to ask why she's doing this. Why she's not indifferent.

But I don't think that's Isa. I don't think she'd be able to take the photos she does if she were indifferent. If she didn't see what needs to be seen.

I touch the screen as if, somehow, touching the photo she sent was touching the woman.

And I don't know what to do.

CHAPTER 13

Robert

It didn't matter how many times I checked my phone, Isa didn't send more texts. I dropped my ass into the passenger seat of my brother's truck and she didn't send more. I helped read bedtime stories to my nephew, and still no new texts. I set up the whole "video chat the gallery opening" situation with Tom's smart-but-impulsive fiancé, Sammie, but still no texts.

Until I send a picture of Bart taking pictures with his birthday gift: *It's okay if Bart wants to share his photos with me.* Then all of a sudden my little nephew is talking more with the professional photographer than I am.

Dan tapped Isa's email into his tablet and Bart "submitted his first piece to a professional." The smile on my nephew's face made the whole family smile, too. But I think I got a little jealous.

Then the noise of my brothers' relationships drowned out the rest of the world, including all the bits of jealousy. I wondered how my laid-back brother Tom fell so completely for the high-energy Sammie. And how the hell my adult-in-the-room brother Dan can be such an idiot with his new girlfriend, Camille.

I rub the top of my head as I walk through the Minneapolis International Airport on my way back to school. I dodge old men and tourists and school groups off to God knows where. The airport smells the same every time I'm here—fakely fresh but cleaner than the huge ports on the East Coast. And full of happy people returning home from their journeys.

I rub my head again and stop in front of the coffee shop down from my gate. The airport bustles around me, loud with indistinct chatter and the grind of wheeled luggage on the tiled floors and the background roar of planes. It mirrors my life.

I shake my head and look up at the menu, wondering if I want some sugar with my caffeine.

Until a stupid and stray thought bumps through my head: *You get fat and Isa won't want to take pictures of you.* A pang of indignation comes with it, and for a flash, I wonder if I'm more like my five-year-old nephew than my mature-enough-to-maintain-relationships brothers.

I chuckle at what my little-boy brain spit up. Or maybe it came out a snort because the girl behind the coffee shop counter is giving me a look. I smile and order, doing my best to charm, and by the time our interaction is done, she's smiling back at me.

But part of me wonders why I would have such a shallow thought in the first place.

On the plane, I read articles. I study for my test. And I stare at the selfie of Isa and her brother that's still on my phone.

Why can't I make my way through the haze of my reputation and build something better? Why can't I use the same rigor I need to finish my degree and apply it to the rest of my life?

Why do I act like a child around Isa?

Good thing my test tomorrow's easy or I'd be in trouble.

When the plane lands, I take my phone out of airplane mode and wait for the *I'm here* or *I'm in traffic* text, hoping it's from Mack. But it's not. It's from Isa.

I brought your coat, it says.

So Mack stuck to his word and I'm about to spend forty-five minutes in a car with a woman who thinks I'm an asshole. Who will be giving me the lust-filled stink-eye the entire drive. Because she still wants me but decided I'm not worth her time. Even if my nephew is.

Because I'm a brat and Bart isn't.

I so enjoy getting the stink-eye. I love how it raises my blood pressure while at the same time making me want to punch the nearest wall. Or the car's dash.

Women are a pain in the ass.

I really don't want to spend forty-five minutes of frowning from a woman who smells like I could cuddle up to her on a nice spring afternoon, swinging in a hammock and listening to the birds dart and chirp.

Screen says luggage pick-up six, the next text says.

I only have my duffle, I text back. *Don't need to go to luggage.*

After a moment, a new text pops up: *Glad you landed safe. I'm at door three.*

I stare at my phone as everyone in the aisle seats elbow each other so they can get their bags out of the overhead bins first. There's small talk and there's impatience and I know I'll need to walk the concourse to door three any second now.

And my gut feels like shit. I'm pretty sure she's still mad and I feel like shit.

I need to figure out what the fuck is wrong with me. No woman should make me feel like this.

I stop for an overly sweet coffee at the stand next to the escalators, saying to myself it's because I have more studying to do and not because I'm avoiding. Because that would be bratty.

The annoying airport voice rolls through the concourse telling everyone to attend to their luggage. People meeting loved ones scream with arm-flailing joy while others scurry on by, more exhausted than happy.

I hear at least four different languages; see at least six expressions of non-continental US cultures. I smell sterile airport air and taste sterile, bland pseudo-coffee. I watch a tired woman shepherd her children toward a man the kids don't seem interested in greeting. And I walk toward the door, continuing to do my damnedest to not think about my roommate's sister.

Three days in my apartment eighteen days ago and the woman

managed to burrow her way down to my bones like a damned parasite and now I can't get rid of her. I need to figure out how to live with her because as long as I'm Mack's roommate, she's going to be a chronic condition.

So yeah, I had better "treat her right" or I'll be out on my ass.

I ride down the long escalator from the gates with a knot of business types and other exhausted travelers. I hear plenty of New York-accented complaints, as well as several local people happy to be home. But mostly I see Isa waiting by the door.

Her hair is up in a ponytail but it halos her lovely face like a wonderful bit of the sun she's carried back with her from her trip to Africa. Her skin glows too, bronzed and bright. She looks exhausted, but it's not weight-of-the-world exhaustion. She looks as if she just finished climbing a mountain. Or whitewater rafting. Or uncovering a long-buried secret.

She smiles when she sees me. An actual, real, bright smile and I think I must be blinking. I expected the lust-filled stink-eye. The coldest, nastiest lust-filled stink-eye Mack's sister could muster.

Instead, I get a smile.

"Rob," she says. "Coat." She hands over my winter jacket. "It's cold."

Isa shakes her head and points over her shoulder at the tunnel to visitor parking. "Ready?"

I smile back, and make small talk as I slip on my jacket. "Mack showed me the images you sent from your trip before I left." I nod toward the bag strapped over her shoulder. "Very nice."

She grins and shakes her head. "I got a couple good ones this time."

I'm sure she did. In fact, I suspect she got a couple hundred good ones.

She's staring at my arms as I pull on my jacket. One of her eyebrows arches and I'm suddenly reminded of my surprise at the lack of unhappy looks. Part of me figures it'll show, probably sooner than later, and I almost flex, just to be embarrassing. Somehow I find the strength not to be too much of a dumbass.

Behind us, a siren screeches the start of a luggage carousel. A blue light flashes. I smile and nod toward the tunnel. "Shall we?"

We walk side by side through the flickering fluorescent lights of the tunnel, me carrying my duffle and my coffee, not really talking. She comments on Bart's photos. I smile and nod. I ask her about Africa. She smiles and nods.

It's going to be a long ride back.

I dutifully situate my duffle in the trunk before plopping my ass in the passenger seat and drop my coffee into the cup holder. As she pulls out of the ramp, she doesn't say a lot.

"Want me to turn on the radio?" Anything to break up the awkward silence and the knocking of her brother's car's engine.

She pulls us onto the freeway. "How have you been, Rob?"

I scowl. I don't mean to. So the stink-eye's going to start with her acting like she's my therapist. "Why?"

Isa shrugs. "Because I think it would be best for everyone if you and I got along."

"Mack agrees."

"Do you?" Isa, the photographing therapist.

I want to say something snarky like *I'm not a child who needs guidance.* Or tell her she's condescending.

But that's childish.

When I don't answer right away, her mouth scrunches up like my sister and my mom used to scrunch up their faces after I did something dumb, like saying mean things and making the neighbor kid cry, or getting exactly the median scores on three homeworks in a row, or describing in detail for my brother Tom what was wrong with his middle school attempts at art.

Isa looks as if she clearly sees the effort I put into wiggling myself below the lowest expectations anyone cares to put out for me.

And she changes the subject. "Your nephew has a great deal of talent. Is your brother fostering it?"

I nod and take a sip of my airport coffee.

Isa grins. "You look like that stuff hurts your teeth."

I blink. "I didn't know I was making a weird face."

She takes the ramp onto the freeway. My coffee sloshes against the side of the cup and I juggle to keep it from spilling.

Isa settles us into traffic before she glances over. "Sometimes I wonder if you're aware of your body language." She shakes her head the way someone who just had a eureka moment. "You have tells."

"What?" I don't have tells. I return the too-sweet coffee to the cup holder.

Isa laughs and swirls her finger in the air between us. "You're like a kindergartner who can't decide if he wants to play nice or steal all the toys."

"Excuse me? I'm not stealing your toys." I thought maybe we could get along, but she has to go and be insulting. "I do *not* like you anymore." It pops out of my mouth before I realize I sound like the kid she just accused me of being. And that I'm pouting. I thin my lips and clamp my mouth shut.

How the hell can Mack's sister be so... mean? Because that's what she is. Plain old mean. I didn't do anything to deserve her being *mean*.

Isa stops laughing. She stares for a long moment, both her eyes and her mouth round. "I'm going to be in your apartment for two weeks before I'm off to L.A. for a month."

She's changing the subject again. I glance at her, wondering if I should be frowning or giving her the finger.

Isa tips her head, watching me again the way she did that night at the party. "I'm sorry I pay attention. I'm a photographer. It's what we do." Her finger swirls in the air again. "That hat Bart gave you brings out something in your eyes. Something I don't think you let other people know is there." She shakes like a bug crawled up her back and flops against the seat. "I want to photograph it."

"Hell *no*." This time, I don't glower. I won't give her the satisfaction of showing a "tell."

Isa shrugs. And frowns. But she doesn't ask again.

Traffic picks up again and she takes the exit toward campus and the apartment. Where we will both be living. Mack, me, and his mean sister.

She's watching me in her weird therapist way again. Like she's looking for the correct angle to snap my photo so she can steal my soul.

That's Isa, Mack's witchy woman sister.

I can't deny that the desire to fuck her still lingers. Arguments always get the blood pumping and pumping blood makes me horny. The desires of my body color how I perceive the movements of her fingers and the flutters of her lips. They draw my attention to the rise and fall of her breasts as she breathes and to the tension in the muscles around her eyes. They make me want to bury my face in her hair and sniff along the nape of her neck. And to rub my entire body against hers.

But she's not a woman whose company I enjoy. In fact, I think, right now, I truly, honestly, all the way to my bones feel something very unlike *like* for Isa Wellington. Something that's going to monopolize several areas of my brain while I figure out what it is, even though I need to study for my upcoming test. And figure out these "tells" she accused me of having. Because I can't walk through life with tells. Tells don't help you get what you want.

She parks the car in the lot behind the apartment building and unbuckles her seatbelt. The car dings for a moment until she pulls out the key. Then she hops out and stretches next to the car, her arms up and her breasts thrust out.

No, I do not like this woman. I particularly don't like how she sees into parts of my psyche she shouldn't be able to see. I don't need a woman shining her strobe into my head. Don't need the complications.

But something tells me keeping Isa out of my soul is going to take considerable effort.

CHAPTER 14

Isolde

For the next two days, Rob and I dance around each other. We're cordial. He makes coffee; I drink the coffee. I make popcorn; he sits on the other side of Mack and nods approvingly at my photos. We eat breakfast; he goes to class and takes his tests. I spend my time networking and hoping I get an interview for the L.A. position when I'm in town. And wondering why he still fuels my fantasies.

Because he does. My trip to Namibia was days filled with landscapes and nights filled with dreams of Rob licking me to blinding orgasm after orgasm under the bright African moon.

Every goddamned night. I don't think I've ever masturbated so much while on another continent.

I truly am a freak. And I think I need a hook-up. Some random guy who's in it just for the fuck.

Or I could sneak into Rob's room. Be the one who's only in it for the fuck. Which, if I'm honest, is the main bit of my cognitive dissonance that keeps my fantasies at the front of my mind. How is it that I harangue Mr. Robert Quidell about being a shallow dickbag when my body wants to hold him down and ride his cock until I come and come again? He and I are too much alike. So I keep thinking about him.

I just wish he'd make up his mind. One second, he's open and friendly and... I don't know. Supportive? Wanting to connect? Then the next, he's behind his wall of childish asshole-ery. If I'm going to set up a relationship—committed, not-committed, hook-ups, whatever—I need to know. I won't be like my mother. I'm not out to fix every dumbass who needs fixing. I like my men to be *men* and not indecisive asshats, like my father.

Probably the safest thing to do is to ignore Mr. Quidell and his perfectly proportioned abs. Right now, he's off somewhere in the warming outdoors, presumably exercising. Mack left at the same time, his bag on his back and his own hat pulled down over his ears. Said something about an appointment with a student.

So I settle back into my laptop and my networking. I have the shoot in L.A. set for the end of the week, and inroads with the studio. If this shoot goes well, they may call me back and I may end up with a consistent position. It'd mean returning to California, but with a full-time job, I could get my own apartment. Maybe upgrade my equipment, too.

I have several other options to consider as well, including a possible three-month shoot in South America at the end of the year. Lots of portfolio work to do today even if I'd rather be outside taking end-of-winter photos of Rob standing shirtless in front of the melting snow.

I stifle a sigh and force my brain back to the work at hand: finding jobs.

I could "settle down" here. Take a position with the local studio and work out of this city. I'd be living in the same apartment as my brother. And his tasty roommate. And making a lot less—and garnering less prestige—than I would with the studio in California.

I throw my head against the back of the couch, groaning. My grandma's hand-knitted, Irish fisherman afghan—the one Mack took when he moved out because I don't stay in one place long enough to have heirlooms around—the one grandma made for grandpa, curls around my arms and my torso. Grandpa, the love of my grandma's life. God, even as kids, their relationship was obvious to Mack and me.

Maybe Grams and Gramps were why Mom's post-divorce parade of idiots always made me recoil like someone had thrown a bug into my hair.

I rub the yarn. It's thick and warm, the color of the cream I never add to my coffee, and made of intricate stitchwork and more love than any human should be able to muster.

The kind of connective love I saw flash over Rob's face that night at the party. That moment when he first spoke of his nephew.

The kid really does have a massive amount of raw talent which I'm more than happy to support. If Rob lets me. I remember Mack saying something about Rob's brother's gallery opening tonight. And that Tom Quidell is quite the artist. Little Bart will be "live blogging" for uncle Robby tonight.

Rob also set up something to share the event with his father in Sedona.

I think part of me is jealous. And another part is annoyed that I wasn't invited to participate, like Mack.

Rob really can be an asshole.

He doesn't see me when he bursts panting through the apartment door, his wonderful bee hat pushed back on his gorgeous head and his running clothes shimmering over his square, perfect ass. The door almost slams against the wall but he catches it, his hand curled tight around its edge as he bends over, his other hand on his knee.

A blast of still-cold springtime air follows him in, along with the scent of sweaty man, but iced-over. My brain makes images of a fur-wearing, ax-wielding Norse god under all that black spandex and high-tech running armor.

He stands up, still breathing hard, and closes the door. The hat flies toward me, smacking me in the face, but he's not looking at the couch. He's pulling off his jacket.

And his skin-tight, dark gray, long-sleeved undershirt. It peels off his torso, then up, over his head. The fabric rolls down his arms and his biceps pop.

I think I must have wiggled. Or moaned. Or dropped his hat. Because Rob Quidell is looking at me wide-eyed and shocked.

"What are you doing out here?" he says between two breaths.

"What the hell are you doing not cooling down?" I toss his hat back at him as I try not to look at his chest.

His sculpted, muscled, exceptionally lickable chest.

Rob pouts as he fumbles the hat. "It's cold. I came in. I was going to do my pushups in here to cool down but now I have an audience."

"Don't let me stop you."

Rob walks in a circle, his running shirt in his hand and I swear steam rising off his shoulders. He watches me with his ocean-in-moonlight eyes, his dark hair messy and spiky from his workout, and a sheen of sweat shimmering on his skin.

I pick up my phone. Concentrating on making an image will give me back some perspective on Rob Quidell. No thoughts of touching. No thinking about how good he smells, even sweaty, or how salty his skin likely tastes. How wonderful his breathing sounds. Or how comforting, even if it shouldn't be.

I snap a photo. "Hmm..." I say. It looks flat. I need fill light. And a better background than the apartment's ugly door. Because I need to capture the wonder he brings to all five senses.

I close my eyes and breathe my own air. I don't like this. I don't like *him*. He's a distracting ass who probably isn't really an ass, just playing one in real life because it's easier than *not* being an ass.

Rob stops walking. He stares at me, his hands on his hips and his chest calming to normal breathing.

Didn't take him long to cool down. Which means he's got stamina. A lot of stamina.

"Why did you take a picture of me?" He pouts and points at my phone. "It's invasive."

Invasive? "Yeah, that's me. I'm the kudzu in your life, Rob. Get used to it." Maybe I won't move out just so I can continue to be irritating.

Rob smirks. The muscles around his eyes change. And I swear he puffs out his chest. "You want me naked? You know, since I need to get used to you invading my life. Best to make the most of the photos you're going to take anyway." He wiggles down the waistband of his running tights.

Fuck, I think. I see the defined invitation V of his lower abs drawing my attention down his well-trimmed happy trail. Down toward the top of the now-visible shadow of trimmed pubic hair.

The tingle starts in my breasts and moves very quickly through my chest. It fires into my throat and down between my legs. And I want to yank down those running tights. I want to free what I know has been confined and held secure this past hour while he ran around the neighborhood, his legs pumping and his body working.

The memory of his hard cock rubbing against my thighs plays over my skin and I focus on not wiggling. Because every part of me wants to be wet and to wiggle along every inch of his brilliant body. Wet, wiggling, licking, and sucking.

But I can't think of him that way. I can't give in. He's a goddamned immature brat and fucking him will cause many more problems than it will solve.

Even if I have to go into my room and take care of it myself.

"Why do you do that?" I'm off the couch and walking toward him before I realize what I'm doing. "Why the bluster?" My hands gesture without me willing them to fly around in the air. But there's something about Rob Quidell that gets me worked up.

"Bluster?" Still half naked, he crosses his arms over his chest. "I'm not the one poking my nose in other people's business."

My lip wiggles. On its own. Wiggles like I want to cry or hit him or run away. Why do I care what this man thinks?

Rob snorts like a little boy who just won his game of bullying.

"I'd rather you were indifferent to me." My words roll out of my mouth soft and low, almost a whisper. I'm not thinking about them. I'm not even sure why I'm saying what I'm saying. But it all comes out anyway.

Because I think he's *not* indifferent. Every sideways glance signals the exact opposite of indifference. Every moment he watches me for longer than an indifferent man would. Every hurt-puppy, snarky remark.

But I don't think he's mad about not getting sex after the party. His posture is the wrong kind of belligerent—sad instead of mad. Frowning instead of chest out, puffed up intimidation. Rob Quidell isn't oppressive. He's, I think, lonely.

And I think his body language screaming how much he wants connection is exactly the lack of indifference that's been fueling my attention and my fantasies and my poking at him. Because he's always poking at me. In the car back from the airport, he acted as if every word I said was a bone-cutting insult. But every time he glances in my direction or unconsciously orients his body toward me, he's showing interest.

I don't know if I'm reading him correctly. I don't know if trying to get through will lead to seeing the caring I see when he talks about his family. Or, maybe, it will lead to another one of his barbs. Does he want connection or does my presence fill him with disdain? Or maybe the disdain is for himself.

"If you were truly indifferent, I'd fuck you," I say. "Scratch that itch and get it behind us. We could at least be roommates then, even if we were never friends. But being around you is like being in a traffic accident. It bangs me up and leaves bruises and I know I need to go to the emergency room because you might be doing some deep, hidden damage and I won't know until I'm bleeding internally and end up in intensive care."

Rob blinks, his face blank, and he steps back a little bit.

He pulls his shirt over his head.

I continue. "It's not in what you say. Hell, you barely talk to me. It's in how you move. How you look at me. In how you ignore me."

"You spurned me, not the other way around." He's pouting again.

"I did not *spurn* you. If anything, I did the opposite of spurning you." I wish he understood. "The worst part of all this is I don't think you realize what you're doing. I don't think you have any sense at all of the information your body shows the rest of the world. I think you've got your 'ignore emotional resonance' set so high you refuse to see it in yourself."

Rob's brow crinkles up. "Photographer or therapist? Which are you?"

I close my eyes. "I don't think you understand what either photographers or therapists do. And here you are in school to learn how humans interact with each other."

When my feet turn me toward my laptop, I pick up my life and I carry it toward my room. I think it's time to move back to California, with or without the job. I can't live with Robert Quidell.

"I don't think you understand what anthropologists do!" Rob calls down the hall as I close my door.

At this point, I don't know if I care.

CHAPTER 15

Robert

I follow her down the hall as I pull my sweaty running shirt back over my sweaty running tights. I know I shouldn't follow her. It's stupid. I should go take a damned shower because my clothes feel sticky and clammy. She stomps away and I follow her like a confused puppy because she's confusing.

Very, very confusing.

"You'd fuck me if I was *indifferent*? What the fuck are you talking about?" I yell. God, now I'm *yelling*. The entire building has to be hearing this.

Isa stops in the shadows filling our hallway. The light bouncing out from her room sets off the copper glints in her hair. All that bullshit about me not detecting emotions doesn't mean a thing because her body posture clearly screams *angry*.

"I'd fuck you if you were indifferent. I'd *sleep with you* if you stopped acting like a wounded kitten." She stomps off into her room and slams her door.

"Now I'm a wounded kitten?" I pace back and forth in front of her door, doing my damnedest not to pound on the frame with my fists. "You don't want to fuck me. You want to fuck with my head!"

Why am I putting all this effort into arguing with her? She's just going to call me another name. I pace again.

Isa opens her door. It slowly swings into her room, the hinges squeaking like wounded little creatures—*kittens*—and she stands in the threshold, her lovely hair messy and her pretty eyes wide behind her glasses. Her lips quiver as if she's about to cry.

Isa is about to *cry* like I'm the mean one here.

"I hope your brothers are better role models for your nephew than you are, Robert." She slams the door again.

"Better role models? I'm the one who stuck with his education." Why can't I stop pacing?

The door swings open again. "You *know* that's not what I'm talking about!" She pokes a finger at my chest. If I'd been close enough, she probably would have left a bruise.

"Then why don't you tell me, Isolde? Because I'm such a wounded kitten I can't see beyond my own widdle biddy paws." I fight the urge to rub my wrist behind my ear and keep my hands on my hips. I won't give her the satisfaction of seeing me act like an animal.

She stands in her door, her head tipped to the side, watching me. Her eyelids descend slowly, and her mouth opens just a little bit. And she finally speaks. "Do you push away all your male friends the way you push away women?"

"I don't push anyone away." It rolls out of my mouth automatically the same way it has so many times before. All the many times growing up that my many therapists asked the same question. Or when my brothers walk away because they don't have the patience anymore to deal with me complaining about my girlfriends.

Not like it's Isa's business, anyway.

"When you walked up to me at the party and I asked you about your hat, you made this wonderful face when you said 'my nephew gave it to me.' A beautiful, brilliant face. That's the face I want to photograph. Not Mr. Snarky McSpurny." She moves to close the door again.

But I put out my hand to stop it. I don't touch her. I just stop the door. "Isa," I whisper.

I don't know what I'm doing. I don't understand at all why I'm reacting this way, but I do think I know why she's gotten under my skin. "Please." It's all I can say. I don't know if I mean "don't close the door," or "don't stop talking," or maybe "don't walk away."

"That's why, when we were in the alcove and I was acting weak and full of lust I said stop, Rob. Not because I changed my mind. I just wanted to see that face again."

I think my mouth opens and closes. I think maybe I mumble something, but I'm not sure. Because Isa still looks like she wants to cry and I realize, I think for the first time, that I'm the reason.

"I'm sorry I've been mean to you. I didn't understand well enough how to articulate it until now." She steps into her room again. "When your reputation took over I thought I'd never see that beautiful, brilliant face again if we stayed on the course we were on."

I don't know what to say. I just know I'm the reason she's going to cry.

She turns her body away from me but she doesn't really. Her shoulders still sweep like she's attempting to pull herself into the hallway. "Will you stop poking at me, Rob? Can we be civil? Mack doesn't need us fighting."

Why the hell have I been fighting with her? She's about to *cry* and I feel nauseous and I think it's because I'm a dick. "Then we don't fight anymore."

I never thought about her reason for stopping. I didn't consider that maybe she sees me as a person and not just some random player she didn't want anything to do with. I didn't think that maybe she had higher expectations.

"Don't you have a family thing tonight?" She still looks like she's going to cry. "Mack said something about your brother's gallery opening."

She's changing the subject. Again. She did the same thing in the car. Frustration crawls out of the discomfort in my gut and that childish part of my brain wants to scream *Pay attention to me!* But that won't help. And I think it's part of the problem. I listen a little too much to my whiny inner child.

"I'm video chatting with Dan and Bart." I feel a smile wash across my face even though I didn't mean to. I shouldn't be smiling right now. Isa's on the verge of crying.

Isa eyes round and I hear her suck in her breath. But then she sighs and looks down at her feet. "I don't want to move back in with my mom." She looks up but I can't see her eyes in the shadows. "I'll move out as soon as I can afford it."

With that, with her final words that sound as if she's given up on me, she closes her door.

CHAPTER 16

Robert

On the other side of the video connection lighting up my laptop screen, my brother Tom gives me the finger. "If you weren't my brother, I'd smack you upside the head."

I wiggle in my room's desk chair and I fiddle with my screen so Tom can see me well. "Dan tells me the same thing every single day." My brothers feign a great deal of lack-of-patience with me. Neither wants to hear about my roommate problems.

Thing is, they're the only people I can talk to about this. Mack's partial, and I'm sure he's not interested in knowing I made his sister cry. Though part of me thinks he's guessed. But I doubt he wants to hear about it. If she were my sister, I wouldn't want to hear about it.

So I asked Tom what he'd do. He pursed his lips and looked over his shoulder at his lovely fiancé as she scurried around behind him adjusting his paintings.

"Take her on a date. You obviously want to."

I can't blame either Tom or Dan for not wanting to hear about my "wounded kitten" issues. This is Tom's big night. And Dan still hasn't fixed his Camille problem. "You need to slap Dan, not me," I say.

Tom frowns. "Look, I need to finish here." Tom straightens his tie. Sammie darts around behind him, an indigo burst of energy in a very sexy dress. My brother is one lucky man. "We open in fifteen minutes."

Sammie's friend, a dark-haired guy named Andrew, waves over Tom's shoulder. "Hi, Rob!" he calls. We haven't officially met, but he seems like a good guy. And he's been a major player in my brother's blooming career as a much-sought-after artist.

"Hi, Andy," I say.

"Dan's here!" Sammie vanishes from the connection.

"I'll have Dan reconnect, okay?" Tom aims his phone at my older brother. Then a swing back so I can see his face, and he cuts the call.

I sit back. They're both offline.

I hear shuffling in the hall and as I turn around, Mack knocks on my door. "You coming out? We want to see the show."

I've been talking up Tom's opening for two months but I didn't think Mack actually *cared*. But he has a bowl of popcorn under his arm and a couple of beers in his hand.

I almost ask about Isa. If she's coming out of her room. If I did make her cry. I should have knocked again. Made sure. But I'm a dumbass.

I nod to Mack and gather up my laptop. Time to move to the kitchen table and be social.

Isa sits on the couch with her own laptop in front of her on the coffee table. She glances up but doesn't say anything. Or ask to be included. I walk by. Because I'm a dumbass.

By the time I set up again, my brother Dan's online. He sniffs and holds out the phone. "This working?" he says.

"Hey, Dan." Mack drops the beers on the table and pulls up a chair. He leans toward me and whispers so my brother doesn't hear. "He looks uncomfortable."

I shake my head and adjust the screen. My brother's been uncomfortable in a suit since the hearings he went through to get full custody of his son. I think he associates a tie with lawyer-based hell.

Dan peers at his screen. "That Mack?"

Both Mack and I chuckle.

"I'm sorry you got saddled with my little shit of a brother." Dan turns the phone around and does a panorama of the room. "Show looks good. Andy says they expect a big crowd."

Colors and forms and glorious patterns swirl across my screen as Dan adjusts his phone and I can't help but be proud of Tom. Part of me hopes that somewhere inside, I have a sliver of the talent he possesses.

"Hold on." I take a pull on my beer more for the hydration than the flavor or the alcohol, and call up our father's number.

Dan knows what I'm doing. Tom, not so much. There's not a lot of good history there. After Mom and Jeanie died, it got complicated.

I hear a little kid voice. "Uncle Robby!" From below, the top of a young head bounces into the frame. "Uncle Robby!" My nephew jumps up and down in front of his daddy's phone and his hair appears again.

Mack laughs and looks over his shoulder. "Isa! Look at this." He waves her over. "You want to meet Bart? He's here."

My back stiffens, but my dad is coming online and I can't deal with Isa and him at the same time. Too much stress from too many faces.

In the bottom corner of my screen, the silver hair and long face of the other Quidell artist appears, our dad, Jeremiah. The man my brothers are still getting used to having in their lives again.

My poor father. The fallout of depression is difficult for an entire family to deal with. But he's been making attempts these past few years. I do what I can.

My dad fiddles with his screen and leans forward. "Did I hear Bart?"

"Grandpa!" I hear squealing.

From behind me, the sweet laughter of a happy woman. "Bart's the cutest little boy I have ever seen in my entire life." Isa smacks me on the back. "Why can't you be like that? You'd be easier to live with."

Mack snorts.

Bart takes Dan's phone and for the next twenty minutes we're neck deep in Bart-isms. My nephew's nonstop commentary gives me an excuse to ignore Isa even though she pulls up a chair right next to me. So close our arms touch and I smell the organic floral notes of her shampoo. And see clearly the joy in her eyes as she quizzes Bart about the paintings and what he likes most about drawing and taking pictures.

Mack and I pretty much sit back and drink our beers.

Few words exchange between Dad and Dan, but at least there's some. When Sammie walks Bart to his "Young Artist Corner" Dan takes us through the nudes section of the show. Dad asks a few things, mostly art and composition questions. Dan doesn't know what to say so he shrugs a lot. He's obviously distracted, probably by *his* woman problems.

Dad falls silent. As does Dan. Things get awkward.

"Will you have a show soon, Mr. Quidell?" Isa leans into me and toward the screen. I think my family has charmed her to the point she's forgotten she doesn't like me. And that I made her cry.

I don't know why but I don't lean away. The outside of her leg presses against mine and it feels different than any other contact I've ever had with a woman, except maybe my sister and my mom. It feels affectionate and genuine and friendly.

And I really do think she's forgotten how much she dislikes me.

My dad laughs but it's sad and my attention flits back to the screen. Dan's looking away. His wide-eyed gaze turns up and across the room as if an angel descended into the gallery directly from Heaven above.

I lean toward Isa. I don't mean to, but I know what the look on Dan's face means. I saw it again and again while I visited over the weekend.

"Ten bucks his girlfriend just walked in," I whisper.

Isa frowns like I'm the biggest lout in the world, but keeps her eyes on the screen. "You need a lesson in manners."

"Camille's here," Dan says.

Isa bites her lip. When she sits back, I swear she looks as if she's going to cry again.

On my screen, Camille appears and waves hello. Dan is still looking at her like a goddamned puppy. "Gotta go," he says, and cuts the call.

My dad blinks a couple of times and visibly moves back from his screen. He says good-bye and cuts too. He knows about the trouble Dan and Camille are having right now. I don't think he likes seeing his boys having lady issues.

"You all look like your dad," Isa says. She's still watching my now dark screen.

We do, Dan more so than Tom and me. We get our big and broad frames from him. But the pretty is all from our mom.

Dad still misses her and Jeanie. We all miss them. It's been over a decade but my dad's heart hasn't healed yet.

Mack pats Isa on the shoulder as he stands up. "Make him buy you ice cream with that ten bucks. He deserves to get fat." Stretching first, my roommate picks up the empty beers and popcorn bowl off the table. "I'm going to bed."

I doubt Isa would go for ice cream with me. I snort and close my laptop.

Isa frowns but she doesn't move. "I like caramel chocolate."

She doesn't look angry. Just sad, like Mack. But I think maybe this might be my chance. "The coffee shop next to the florist on the corner sells ice cream." Maybe we can be friends.

Isa watches her brother saunter down the hall. He looks more sad than I've seen him in a while, like her.

"Do you think he's got another headache coming on?" I ask. We both teach tomorrow. A migraine will just cause him a new and different set of headaches.

"No." Isa turns toward me when we hear Mack's door close. "Let's get that ice cream."

CHAPTER 17

Isolde

Rob stuffs his hands into his pockets. It's warmed up enough his hat looks uncomfortably hot, but it stays where it is, a bumblebee stinger-butt perched on the top of his head. His breath curls in front of us as we walk, the same as mine. The street-lights make it glow from above and it fogs the air, a brief cloud of our warmth lingering for only a moment.

Then it's gone.

He's been quiet. Watching me, mostly, with keen eyes and his body angled toward me. I'm beginning to wonder if maybe, possibly, he understood what I said before his brother's gallery opening.

I don't want to fight with him. I don't want to have to move out before I can afford to either, or run off to my mom's place because I can't get along with my brother's roommate. But at this point, I'm wondering if I can tolerate my mom's drunk-ass douchey boyfriends asking me if I want to "make it a threesome" better than Rob's belligerence.

"I deserved you yelling at me earlier." He does a little sidestep dance to accent his comment.

It's odd and out of place. It's as if he's happy I called him on his behavior.

He does another little two-step dance and twirls around. "You're right and I'm sorry."

I tap my foot. I can't help it; watching him makes me want to dance, too. "That's it? You're sorry?" He could just be saying it. "The last thing I want is to come out of the shower to find you standing there all pouty and huffy because I'm mean and you think I used your soap or something."

Rob laughs, but his face is serious. "You were crying."

He noticed. "You were dense."

The cold tickles my nose and I turn away, not feeling like dancing anymore. Maybe ice cream wasn't a good idea.

"Still am. Doesn't mean I can't learn." He bops in front of me, his hands still in his pockets. "I resolve to be a good roommate. You don't need to move out."

He's smiling but his eyes are serious. And he's tapping his foot like he wants to fidget.

I think he honestly wants to try.

"Thank you," I say.

Rob takes a small bow. "Were you really going to cry?"

A micro-expression of terror flashes across his face the way I'd expect to see it on someone before that moment when they realize the thing on the path in front of them is a stick and not a snake. Or that pre-understanding moment when they hear a loud pop and somewhere in their amygdala they think it's gunfire and not a car or a firecracker.

That fear moment that for most people vanishes once their rational brain takes over, but for a few unlucky souls, develops into something nasty and ongoing.

Rob twitches. Not a lot. Just a little. And I wonder.

"You did a good thing tonight." He needs to know. It might help. "I think your dad smiled more in the forty minutes you facilitated the chat than I ever saw mine in the entire time he lived in the same house as us."

Now Rob frowns. "Really? That's sad."

I laugh. I can't help it any more than I could help the dancing.

"Dad's got impulse control issues." I shrug. "Which I sometimes think I inherited."

Rob pulls a hand out of his pocket and adjusts his hat. "Quick thinking gets you the good photos."

"Yeah, but we be the sad twins, aye?" I do a sidestep the way he did earlier, my footwork opposite his. "You and I."

"I do say we be." He nods approvingly at my feet. "You that good with your camera, miz photographer person?" He does a different, more complicated step, one shuffling him backward first, then to the side. His foot thrusts out.

I tap my chin, wondering just how much I can get this man to dance. Because I like this new and improved, non-ass, open version of Rob. "Of course." I imitate his steps and flick out my foot to tap my heel on the cold concrete.

"Oh no you don't." Rob does a full arm swing and a hip circle before taking my hands and spinning me around in the cold night air. He's smiling and I feel light like the sun's shining. Warm like it's summer and not the tips of spring's ears.

"You're laughing." Rob stops twirling us around.

The surprise on his face makes me feel silly. Or sad that I let our issues get to where they did. Because I think my first impression was right: He's a good person.

"I'm sorry I was a dick." He's blinking sort of like he expects me to slap him right across the face.

"Can we be friends now?" Stroking describes much better the action my fingers want to take. Stroke his chin, touch his cheek, caress his hair. Pull him down on top of me and kiss him until he moans into my mouth. Until he can't take it anymore and pumps into me with his incredible granite-hard cock.

But if we're to be friends, I can't have these fantasies about him anymore. Because they're not going to happen.

"Friends." Rob stands erect, his chin up and his bee hat perched on the back of his head, and pulls off his thin and ratty glove. He extends his hand to shake.

He looks ridiculous, but I like it. And I smile. "You need new gloves." I pull mine off too, and glide my fingers over his palm.

Even in the cold, his skin feels like a dream. He's warm. Gentle. Soft but firm and masculine. I stare at his fingers as he curls his hand around mine and I don't want him to let go. But we're friends, not lovers. So I allow my hand to slide away from his.

He slams his hands into his pockets again. "Coffee shop's down the street."

Rob's gorgeous eyes gleam in the light reflecting off the sidewalk and his black hair pokes out from under his hat. He's a handsome god of a bee-filled underworld and part of me can't help but wonder if he's serious about changing. If he really does want to be friends.

We walk for a few minutes, Rob next to me. He's quiet, watching the street, until I start asking questions about his brothers.

Rob lights up. "I swear Tom's painted twenty portraits since he met Sammie." He kicks a small stone out of the way and leans closer. "She moved in with him a week after they met. Can you believe that? One week and now they're engaged."

A smirk moves across his face and once again I don't think he realizes what his body language says. The square shoulders and the raised chin show confidence. The slight skip to his walk signals he's proud of his behavior. The glances toward me show that he wants to share.

And that he likes the idea of knowing immediately when someone's the right one.

"Sometimes that's what happens," I say. "Other times, it takes years. Every couple's journey is different." His brother Tom seems to have a good head on his shoulders. None of the distancing Rob does, or the workaholic behaviors Rob says his other brother shows.

When we walk under another streetlight, he glances around, his eyes bright and watching. "Hey," he says, his voice louder than usual, and authoritative, and he wraps his arm around my waist. "I changed my mind. Let's go to the other coffee shop. The one closer to campus."

He won't let go, either. His hand pulls me close and the next thing I know, we're jaywalking across the street, walking quickly toward the major road next to the dorms.

"Don't take out your phone and don't let go of my hand." He grips my fingers so tight it hurts.

"What's wrong?" What did he see? Then I notice the figure in the shadows about a hundred feet in front of us, or what would have been in front of us, if we'd stayed on that side of the street.

A skinny person dressed head to toe in dark colors with his or her head completely hidden in a hood. No distinguishing features. No indication that there's even a face in there at all.

"Shit," I mutter. "I didn't see him."

"Doesn't mean he's up to anything, but I'd rather trust my gut." Rob's fingers tense and for a second, I think he might want to weave them through mine. "I'm not going to let anything happen to you. Mack will kick me out. Then what will I do?"

His grin is more disarming than any I've seen from him.

"Thank you," I whisper.

He grins again. "See? I'm not a complete dickbag." We walk along faster than my usual pace until we're out of sight of the shadowy figure. "Do you still want ice cream?"

I think, more than anything, I want to spend time with this new Rob. The one not hiding anything anymore. The man with the bright eyes and the happy smile. "I think I want to take pictures."

Rob stops walking but doesn't let go of my hand. "Now?" He looks around. "I'm not taking off my shirt out here," he says, but he's grinning and I know if I asked, he probably would.

I grin, too. I *have* to take pictures. I can't let this openness get away. "Where should we go? I don't want to go back to get my equipment so it'll have to be the phone." I nod toward the shadowy figure.

"The fountain in front of the Alumni Center has floodlights. Will that work?" God, his eyes sparkle in the moonlight, the same way they did the night we met.

"Yes," I say, and pull Rob Quidell toward the center of campus.

CHAPTER 18

Robert

I sa screws up her face and closes one eye as she looks me over. Her phone rises through the air, riding on the sensual curve of her lively fingers, and I hear the electronic shutter sound. She screws up her face again and shakes her head "no."

I'm beginning to think I'm not as photogenic as all my dates tell me I am.

The Alumni Center fountain covers a massive open concrete field that spits water out onto a flat surface, but in the winter they shut it off. This year, a melting exhibition of student ice sculptures dots the open concrete. The floodlights make all the ice glow and Isa has me on the edge of the fountain space, my toes inches from a wet, slick area of very cold water.

I frown at my feet. "I don't want to stand in slush." Frozen toes don't sound like fun.

Isa laughs and twists my shoulders toward one of the floodlights. "You pout a lot."

"Says the crybaby." I grin and shift to the side, the way she wants.

The floods make everything unearthly and too bright. Her hair glows almost white. Our breath curls like cotton candy. And the gold and copper flecks in her eyes fluoresce.

And I can't help but hear *goddess* echoing in my mind again. Diana rode a moonbeam to the Earth and now she's posing me in front of ice sculptures.

"This crybaby wants a good picture, so hold still. And don't stiffen up like that. You look like a damned robot." She wiggles my arms like a massage therapist loosening up a football player.

It feels good. It's not sexual but it's intimate in a way I'm not used to. Her fingers—her touch—focuses on me and I don't give a damn if it's because she wants a certain look for her picture. I just want her to wrap her long, graceful fingers around my arm again.

When I glance up, she's not looking at my arm. She's looking at my face. And she's smiling. "Yeah, I'm pretty sure you're clueless about your body language."

She dances a few steps back and snaps another photo before I can respond. This time, her smile only grows.

"I take it my nostrils aren't too big this time?" I stick a knuckle into each side of my nose and stick out my tongue.

Isa chuckles. The phone's fake shutter sound rings through the chilly air. Somewhere behind us, an undergrad laughs at her date's silly joke. I look over my shoulder in time to see the young woman lean against the kid.

My dates always narrowed their eyes, assessing mutual lust, and straddled my lap. Sometimes they take a selfie with me pressed against their back, to make all their shallow friends jealous. No one ever leans against my shoulder.

When I look back, Isa snaps another photo. Shaking my head, I pull the bee hat over my eyes and grin like a fool, hoping to give her some fun photos, too. I don't want to think about shallow right now. Now that for once in my life, I think I'm friends with a woman.

A wonderful, talented woman who the immature part of my brain thought was mean. But I see the truth now. Only immature assholes make women cry.

Isa grins and steps right up to me, her back against my shoulder. She holds out her phone to allow me to see the screen but I lose any interest in the photos. I breathe in her sweet and warm scent. I feel the weight of her hips against mine as she moves closer. All I want is to pull her against my body and kiss her deeply.

But I was a dick. I should thank the stars I've been allowed to be her friend.

She swipes through the photos. "I like this one."

It's the moment before I pulled the hat over my eyes. The undergrads behind me are out of focus, one blurry smudge of two people happy together. I'm glancing away, looking down, my hand rising to yank the hat down, my shoulders slumping, like the moment's too much. My face looks like regret rooted into my soul long ago and seeing the undergrads has made it blossom into something massive and entangling but strangely lovely.

"Wow," I say. How did she capture all that with a camera phone?

"We need to work on your stiffness, mistah cyborg maaann." Isa elbows my stomach.

"Most of the time, when women take photos of me, it's to make me look bad on social media." I shrug.

She tucks her phone into her pocket. We walk side by side toward the apartment, silent for a long moment.

At the corner, we wait for the light to change. Cars buzz by. Exhaust fills the air. But Isa still fills my senses.

"I have no interest in posting photos like that, Rob." Her head angles up and away, her eyes focused on a sign across the street. "You deserve better." I barely hear what she says.

Part of me doesn't believe it, anyway. The part that yells and screams and says women like to be cruel because I do deserve it.

The streetlight glints in Isa's beautiful eyes when she turns to me, and I know she's not lying. I know she speaks the truth. And the schema I built for myself—that fuck-buddy bad boy reputation that's kept me confined to the women who want bad boy fuck-buddies— crumbles. I feel it crack and I see it fall away from how I see the world and I have Isa to thank for it.

But it's new. And it's terrifying. I don't know if I can breathe through this. Or if I can let go of what's become the only way I know how to live, no matter how much I want to be free of it.

"Thank you," I whisper.

Isa's hand curls around mine. And we walk across the street, hand in hand, as friends.

CHAPTER 19

Robert

Three days later, Isa left for an eight-day gig in California. She mumbled something about the studio being a major operation and that working with the lead photographer was going to do wonders for her career. When she gets home, she'll be here for two weeks, then off again, away to somewhere else.

I gave her a hug and squeezed her fingers and tried not to look like a kitten. She smiled and squeezed back and disappeared into her room, to pack.

The evening of the first day without her, the creaks and the rattles of the building drowned out everything else. Mack and I ate our pizza and graded our students' assignments. Isa messaged me photos of her room at her mother's house outside L.A. Wide doors open onto a panoramic view of the hills separated from the house by a vast wrought iron fence. Off-white curtains billow in a breeze. A long shadow falls over a large bed made up with a flat white coverlet and a gigantic, generic painting that to me, looks like a drop of blood.

Her room looks more like a mausoleum than any place a human with so much brilliant creativity should live.

When I asked why her photos weren't displayed on every surface, I got only the texted version of a shrug.

If it were my house, I'd freakin' project her photos onto every single goddamned wall. I already ordered a big print of one of her Africa photos and bought a frame. It's going to be hanging over the couch when she gets home.

The second evening, she wanted to video chat so she could show me the sunset. We talked for six hours about her mom and her life growing up and how everyone in her family but Mack rushes headlong into situations. The worst of it caused her parents' divorce.

That night, I didn't go to bed until two a.m. and ended up sleep-walking through teaching the next day.

The third evening, she had a dinner she needed to attend. Mack and I spent our meal in stitches because of her two-hour-long, under-the-table messaged commentary on the grandiose douchebaggery of the shoot's client.

On the fourth night, I called. We talked for three hours about my classes and her production boredom and the differences in the flavors of California and Florida oranges.

On the fifth, I joked I was mad she took her shampoo but that her pillow, the one sitting on top of her rolled-up air mattress next to the cheap dresser full of her clothes, still smells like her. I know this because I needed printer paper from the closet in what used to be our den. Which is the only reason I went into her room. I don't want to be creepy.

She laughed and laughed and laughed.

The next evening, we texted all through dinner and the four hours it took me to grade my student's latest assignments. She sent me a new photo of the Los Angeles sunset each time I made it through ten essays. The last one is the new wallpaper on my laptop.

Mack's eyed me the whole week. We teach and we grade, and we both keep our noses to the grad school grindstone, but I think he wonders about my intentions toward his sister.

The truth is, I miss her, too.

Last night, she told us she had news she'd share when she got back. Mack scratched at his beard and said she probably got another big shoot someplace where she might get cholera or kidnapped or a bullet in her head.

I spent the night staring at the ceiling with his words echoing in my head, trying very hard not to let my mind wander from one horrible scenario to another.

This morning, Mack got mad when I grabbed the keys from his hand. He frowned, but I think a new migraine had started knocking on the inside of his skull. So I sent him to bed with a promise that I'd fetch Isa from the airport.

I sped all the way. I'm lucky I didn't get a ticket. But today's the first day driving with the window down that wouldn't ice over my corneas.

The weather's beautiful—warm and sunny. The birds sing their loud springtime songs and the trees try to rustle in the breeze as if they all wish their leaves had unfurled weeks ago. Puddles cover every street and sidewalk. Isa comes home today.

I stare at my phone as I stand next to the benches between the two luggage carousels of her carrier, numbers six and seven. The airport's the same as always—loud and cleaned-by-bleach smelling. The coffee is unsurprisingly bitter. Exhausted people mill about. The fluorescent lights blink.

And Isa's coming home.

A text pops up: *Landed*.

I smile and text back *Waiting by luggage pick-up*.

A little thumbs-up symbol and a smiley face appear followed by *I got some shots I'm really proud of*.

Pride rushes through my veins even though I have no right to feel the way I do. But supporting her talent feels right. *I can't wait to see them*, I tap out.

Just you here?

In the back of my head, I hear that little voice again. The one that used to call her mean. This time it's scared. *Sorry to disappoint*, I type. *Mack had a proto-headache so I sent him to bed*. What if she doesn't want me here?

I'm not disappointed.

My breath releases and I close my eyes. What's wrong with me? I'm acting like a high schooler. We're friends and I don't think we can be anything else. Not after the way I treated her for the first month she lived in the apartment.

I fucked up and I need to live with it.

Every time I visit my family, Dan points out my flaws. Between him, Tom, and my many therapists, I have a pretty good understanding of my behavior with women. It used to work for me. It worked for the women, too. I may have disappointed, but in my undergrad days, I never made anyone cry.

Another text pops up: *Off the plane. There in a minute.*

For the last ten days, we've been friends. Good friends. And maybe, I think, Isa might be becoming my best friend. So she can't cry again because of me.

Heads bob along in the sea of people. I watch the crowd, looking for Isa's beautiful goldspun hair. Her confident gait.

A knot parts. Fifteen feet down the concourse, Isa walks between a big guy wearing a cowboy hat and a slow moving little old lady, her main gear bag on her back and her second case in her hand. She bends forward a little under the weight and I think the bags throw her balance off. She shifts to the side and the guy in the cowboy hat almost bumps into her.

The look he throws borders on vicious. He's less than five feet from my best friend and every muscle in my body tightens. "Isa!" I shout.

She looks up but I'm not looking at her. I'm glaring at the asshole in the hat as I stride toward her, making sure he sees me. She glances at him then back at me, and her expression changes. Something I don't recognize moves across her cheeks and settles in her eyes. And when I'm close enough, she reaches for my hand.

Every other sound in the airport blanks out. Every sight and every scent. Isa looks up through her glasses with her big eyes and I don't think. I take her bag and pull her close and wrap my arms around her waist. The sweet notes of her scent fill my nose when I bury my face in her hair and the wonder of her skin covers my lips when I kiss her forehead.

Her hands grip my back. "I missed you, too," she whispers.

My hold tightens and again I don't think about what I'm doing.

About where we are or who's around us. About her luggage or how tired she is. She's against me and she missed me too. I kiss her on the lips like the silly stupid high school kid I'm trying not to be. Right here, in the middle of the fucking airport, I kiss a woman who's my friend because she means more to me than I realized.

"Rob!" Isa pulls back. Her mouth rounds and she glances around. But she smiles and slaps my shoulder.

"Sorry," I say. She's beautiful beyond reason with her hair in the chaotic ponytail and her clothes wrinkled and disheveled. All I want is to kiss her again, but she's right. Not here.

Her eyes narrow. "Robert Quidell, you are a *terrible* kisser." She slaps my shoulder again.

"I am not." The immature part of me wants out again. It's miffed. But I'm just being stupid. Because I'm pretty sure another kiss, one somewhere more private, would go over better.

But it's hard for me not to kiss her again, just to prove my point. I may not kiss my dates, but I know my skills. Skills I want to use to bring Isa to the exact opposite of crying.

I didn't realize how deeply I missed her until I felt her touch again. Until I breathed in her honeyed and slightly rosewater scent. How much I wanted our relationship to be more than friend and roommate.

She grins and takes my hand, but doesn't say much more. I hold her bag and we get her luggage and Isa watches me with concerned eyes. She clutches my hand, but she's far enough away our arms bow out like a rope between us. When I move to close the distance, she moves away, first to get her luggage, then to lead me toward the car.

And now I'm wondering if she wants another kiss as much as I do.

Isa pulls her seat belt across her lap and I press the key into the ignition but I don't start the car. I rub the top of my head instead. "Do you want to get dinner tonight? Not at home. At a restaurant. You and me?" I rub my head again. It'd be nice to spend an evening away from the apartment. Someplace where Mack can't stare accusingly at the back of my head. "I thought maybe we could spend some time together." I pluck at my t-shirt. "I'll put on a decent shirt. Promise."

"Rob..." Isa folds her hands over her lap. Her face does the same drawn, pale look it did when we argued in the hallway. When I made her cry.

"What's wrong?" My mind goes to all those catastrophic places with cholera and bullets even though she's sitting here right now so close that if I leaned over the shift I could kiss her cheek.

Why is my mind flipping over to thoughts of her sick or hurt? Why do I feel helpless? She may be exhausted but she's home and I can spend the next two weeks making up for the terrible behavior of our first month.

Isa opens her mouth, but it closes again and she looks down at her hands.

"Did I do something?" She's everything. I didn't realize until she walked up the concourse and that a-hole in the hat looked like he might hurt her, but it's true. Absolutely true. I think it's been true since the party.

I won't hurt her again. I won't.

Isa presses her lips together. "I'm moving out, Rob. I'm going back to California."

CHAPTER 20

Isolde

We spent the past eight days talking and texting and becoming better friends. We talked about sunsets and shampoo and I didn't tell him I'd been offered a position with the studio in L.A. That taking it would boost my career to the next level and might, if I'm lucky, lead to major magazine deals. Maybe gallery shows like his brother, Tom.

I don't know why I didn't tell him. Why I didn't ask his opinion.

Rob sits on the other side of the apartment's dining room table, an uneaten slice of pizza on a paper plate in front of him and two empty bottles of beer next to his twitching fingers. He's barely looked at me since we got home, and has said even less.

I think, maybe, I didn't say anything because I knew I'd break his heart.

Mack, on the other hand, took it well. My brother shrugged and ate his pepperoni pizza, though he did suck down an extra beer, just like Rob.

But Mack's sideways glances at Rob all through dinner bothered me. The slightly narrowed eyes. The tightening of his neck and his shoulders. My brother looked like he wanted to punch his roommate.

The man I'm pretty sure feels more than friendship for me.

Gorgeous Rob, a guy who, two weeks ago, acted more like a child than a man. Who pouted and poked and would have thrown sand if we were preschoolers on a playground because he likes me and he didn't understand any other way to respond. Beautiful, handsome, family-oriented Rob who, I think, uses his looks and his bluster to distance people.

But I wanted to see the real Rob. I wanted to take his picture. And I wanted to lean against his shoulder, safe and happy and, I think, sharing in his moments of strength. In his sense of family.

I wanted to be part of his life even though I kept telling myself it wasn't possible. How could I be part of his life? I'm just another conquest. Even when men change, they don't change. *Friends* was the best I could hope for.

So in the airport, when he kissed me, I thought he was teasing. How could Rob Quidell see me as someone other than the woman who forced him to see her as a friend?

Yet he sits in his chair two feet from me, his eyes averted. Every time our feet touch, or we rub knees, electricity fires through my limbs. But Rob won't look at me and pulls back as if I just cut him with a knife.

All I want to do is crawl onto his lap and kiss away his hurt. I want to see his beautiful eyes gleam and I want to spend hours feeling his hands roam over my body.

But I'm moving back to California.

Rob will be three time zones away.

Mack drops his napkin on the table. He looks at Rob, then me, then Rob again, frowning the entire time. "Opportunities like Isa's don't come around often." His words come out as narrow as his eyes. He means it for Rob, not me.

"If this works out, I could be well on my way to my own studio in a couple of years. Shooting for myself. I'll have more control of when and where I travel." Maybe settle down, at least a little. But I don't say it.

Rob looks up and I swear I see *Really?* play through his eyes. I can almost see the calculations bounce around in his head. Semesters he has left. Time to write a dissertation. Job hunting.

The possibility of moving to California.

It's all there, on his face and in his body posture. And I don't know what to do.

Years in reality are very different than years in fantasy, and I can't do that to him. To me. I can't expect Rob to change and sacrifice. I can't be worrying about a boyfriend on another coast.

"Work." Mack slaps his knee. "Must do." He jabs a finger at Rob's nose. "Don't be a dick and fall behind in grading."

He's up and dumping his paper plate into the garbage. After a moment or so, he walks away toward his room.

Rob watches him go. "I have all weekend to grade." He sounds tired. His words rolled out of his mouth slow and sad, and I wonder just how much beer's going to be consumed over the next two days.

Over the next two weeks, to be honest. Two weeks before I permanently move out and temporarily move into my mom's house again.

I refuse to stay with her longer than I need to. My new gig will get me steady work and income and I'm going to get my own place. How my mother has managed to keep her house both sterile and terrifyingly clean at the same time it's full of alcohol-filled chaos and yelling and weird boyfriends, I don't know.

Rob doesn't move from his place at the table. He stares at the hall-way, frowning.

"I'm getting my own place. In L.A." I rotate on my chair so I'm facing him. "Come visit, okay?" Though having Rob sleeping on my couch is going to be a hell all its own. Friend or not, relationship or not, I have my own set of fantasies and many of them star my favorite ocean-eyed bad boy.

I think every time I close my eyes and imagine his tongue working across my nipples, or down my belly, or buried in my pussy, it makes him a little less real and a little more distant. He becomes inaccessible in real life, and it makes moving out easier.

Fantasy Rob and real, my-friend Rob, are two different men.

"I'll fly out every weekend, if you want me, Isa." Rob takes a pull on his beer.

If I want him. I blink wondering if what I feel is as obvious on my body as his emotions are on his.

"My dad used to travel a lot," I say. "Business." Slowly, I stand and pick up my plate to clean up some of the mess. "Our parents say they had an open relationship." I shrug and point down the hall, toward my brother's bedroom. "Mack and I know they didn't. They both cheated. Dad was—is still, really—a player. So's Mom. New lovers every few weeks for both of them. So we're sensitive."

Rob stands and helps finish clearing the table. "My parents never strayed. I don't think my father ever looked at other women." He smiles and chuckles. "I still remember the moms at my soccer games eyeing him. I don't think he noticed." His plate lands in the garbage. "My mom got harassed all the time." He waves his hand at his face as if he's a magician. "My excellent bone structure comes from my mom's side of the family."

I chuckle, too. "You *are* a pretty one."

Rob smiles big and throws a pose worthy of a perfume ad. "Maybe after I'm done with school, I'll model. God knows I'll need a job."

"You'll need to take a shower, first." I give him a little push before pinching my nose and crossing my eyes even though Rob smells warm and deep, like his voice. Masculine and fresh, and a little like clean ocean spray. It's his natural scent. No body sprays or perfumes. With Rob, what you see and smell and hear—and touch—is what you get.

I was so surprised by his kiss at the airport, I didn't think about how he tasted. Now I wonder.

Rob drops onto the couch, his beer in his hand. He sets it on the coffee table and pats the cushion next to his side.

I flop close, but not too close, my own beer in my hand. Friend close. Because we need to establish our boundaries. Or at least I'll keep telling myself that. I think, though, that I'm being weird about things. "I should have been more open about my moving out." I'm as confused as Rob looks.

His nose wiggles and he looks away. "Before I flew home for Bart's birthday, Mack told me that if I fucked with you he'd kick my ass to the curb." Another sniff works across his face. "I don't think he trusts me to act like a gentleman."

CHAPTER 21

Isolde

Rob picks up his beer but doesn't drink. "He's probably right."

His shoulders slump and he blinks slowly, his lids dropping over his beautiful eyes before snapping open. A shiver runs through his entire body. Rob sits up straight, a masking grin on his face, and puts on his best player face.

Seeing him fake not caring makes my stomach drop.

Rob leans back against the couch. "Tom has one of those magic relationships. The kind that happens fast and perfect and the next thing you know you're living with the love of your life." Rob's nose and eyebrow twitch.

He does the little shoulder roll men do when they don't believe someone's telling the truth.

"I take it you don't think so?" I wiggle on the couch, trying to get comfortable. My brother's shitty sofa has lumps.

Rob shrugs and takes a long pull on his beer. How the man stays as fit as he does while drinking so much is beyond me. Must be his handsome Quidell genes.

"I think Tom's artist mind wants his life with Sammie to be as exquisite a picture as the ones he paints."

"Oh?" I think he needs to get this out. To change the subject but not change it at the same time. Rob needs to talk about the social world he's part of, not just the social worlds he studies.

He scratches his cheek. "I think they have a lot more work to do than they realize. And I think they should wait longer before getting married."

"You don't believe in fairy tale romances?"

The day I took pictures of him by the fountain, he seemed to think his brother has a good thing going. But that may have been more about *liking* a woman than loving one.

I've seen fairy tale romances work as often as I've seen them fall apart. My mother is a serial fairy tale romancer, but I don't tell Rob that. My family's issues aren't his.

"It happened with our mom and dad. They eloped ten days after they met. Dan was born nine months later. Their marriage lasted through four kids and a lot of ups and downs." He stares at the coffee table instead of looking at me.

His lips thin, too. And his neck tenses. There's more to this than he's telling me.

"Dan's the family man, ya know?" Rob continues to stare at the table top. "The protector. He's clueless. Always has been and always will be." He chuckles and taps his beer against his thigh. "His new girl-friend is the first woman in his life since that psychotic twit Lori divorced him."

I take a sip of my beer. "They doing okay?" I haven't asked.

Rob shrugs again, but this time, he glances up. The look in his eyes takes me by surprise. Rob Quidell, the man okay with being on his own, looks as if every ounce of the world's loneliness has burrowed under his skin. As if somewhere in there, he misses his family more than he lets anyone see. More than he lets himself see. And that he wants, more than anything, for his brothers to be happy.

And his father, too. And his sweet little nephew, Bart.

"They are." He tips back his bottle but it's empty. He makes a face and it clinks when he sets it on the table. "But the moment she gets pregnant, he's going to become Mr. Super Protector Family Man again and become a bore."

Rob snorts and sits back against the throw on the back of the couch. His gaze stays on the one spot on the table, like he's drilling through the glass top with his heat vision.

"That's what happened after our mom and sister died. Dan stepped up. Became the dad Tom and I needed."

"I'm sorry."

He looks so distraught I want to pull him to my chest. Hug him until he smiles again. I squeeze his forearm.

When I don't let go, he covers my hand with his own. His palm slides over the back of my wrist, warm and strong and alive, but there's a tension I don't expect. His hand feels as distraught as his eyes look.

"My sister was three years younger than Dan and three years older than Tom. Her birthday falls almost exactly between my two brothers." Rob smiles. "She used to read me bedtime stories."

I swear he hiccups. Not a big one, not one that would be visible to another guy, but it's there. Right there, in front of me. And I didn't think my heart could ache any more than it does right now.

I move closer, to offer comfort. Rob leans toward me. He doesn't take his hand off mine. He doesn't ask for anything more.

"I heard the crash. I was in the front yard, bouncing my soccer ball against the garage door. I ran down the street. Dan got there after me. We were the first two people there, my brother and I." He blinked. "Dan and I saw it first."

"Rob—" I pull on him trying to draw him closer. I don't know if it's for me or for him, but it happens.

But Rob stiffens. He doesn't push me away. He just sucks in his breath.

"I did the therapy. I'm fine."

But I don't think so. Not really. How can he possibly be okay?

"Tom doesn't know. Dan and I never told him we were there first. It never came up. It..." His face scrunches up. "He was at a friend's house. Didn't seem to be necessary to tell him."

I lived through my mother's parade of shitty boyfriends. The ones who were better fathers than my real dad and who broke my heart when they left. The one who tried to grope me in middle school. The ones who didn't care either way.

But nothing like this.

"Rob—"

He sniffs and turns toward me, and the distraught look is gone. Vanished away into whatever space Rob puts it when he doesn't want to think about it.

I know all about those spaces. The pocket universes where we put the distress.

I'm relieved he has one. And that it looks strong enough to hold this for him. Some people would get mad at me for supporting what they see as a corrosive coping mechanism, but they can go to their little hug festival corner and whine to each other. We do what we need to do to get through the day.

"So," he says. He's changing the subject. Just like that, because he doesn't want to talk about the bad stuff anymore. Which is fine. "You want to do some night shoots?" He plucks at his shirt. "We better do them now before you're gone forever."

CHAPTER 22

Isolde

Rob stands next to the door gripping two open bottles of beer between the fingers of one hand while he fidgets with the collar of his jacket with the fingers of his other. "Need help with your gear?" he points down the hall.

I shake my head *no*. "Just my camera, my monopod, and one pocket strobe. It's all in the bag. Don't want anything that might draw too much attention."

"Ah." Rob smiles. "I'll wait for you at the top of the steps." He opens the front door. "There's usually a nice puddle of moonlight."

The door swings open. He watches me more than he watches where he's going as he backs out. "Don't take long."

The door clicks shut and Rob Quidell vanishes into the hallway, leaving only a slight hint of microbrewed beer behind.

I think he wants a moment alone before we're off into the wilds of the night to shoot in the dark. To center himself. It's time to be jolly and friendly.

I grab my smaller, cheaper DSLR case from my room, along with one Speedlight and my rope-and-monopod homemade tripod set-up. It's a lightweight and will get me good, real-looking photos.

With my real-life friend. I duck out the door, careful to close and lock it behind me, my jacket in my hand and my bag over my shoulder.

Rob sits on the top of the stairs with his back to the hallway. When the tumbler lock clicks, he looks over his shoulder. I can't see his face. He's backlit by the moon streaming in through the big window over the building's foyer.

I walk down the hall and set my bag next to the railing. I drop my jacket on top of my equipment and dust the top step before seating my backside next to Rob's.

Outside the apartment, I smell the lives of all the other inhabitants. Cooking grease and fried meats waft up from the second floor. Cat from down the hall. Cold air and exhaust fumes from outside. And pizza and beer from our apartment.

Sounds filter out, too. Faint hints of someone's television echo up the stairs. A voice rises against the background noise of the street outside, then vanishes again.

Next to me, Rob breathes. Moonlight reflects off his skin and shines in his eyes. He grins and scoots toward the rail to make room for me.

I take one of the beers. "Probably should leave these here." The bottle glints as I hold it up first to Rob, then to the moon.

"Aye." Rob winks and takes a pull before setting his next to his thigh. "I'm going to miss you."

I look away. The moon's not full, but it's close, and silver light spreads up the stairs and across the landing where we sit, filling the moment with a surreal sheen. Edges sharpen. Colors blend and turn blue. It's beautiful.

"You know," I say, "I had this fantasy that I'd write 'Isa's boyfriend' on your chest and take a picture so I could make another assistant—a jerk who ogles me—feel bad about himself." I don't know why I tell him this. Maybe so he knows *he's* not a jerk.

Rob grins and looks up, and after a shake of his head he takes a long pull on his beer.

The moonlight plays over his face and the bottle, and an ethereal glint flits through the space between us. It sparks and vanishes, a moment of subdued brightness that sums up perfectly my relationship with Rob. There's power there. A burst of brilliance that only appears when we're close to each other, the way we are right now. But then the world interferes, first by tainting his reflective surface. And now, by warping mine.

Rob winks. "Ah, yes. That old fantasy."

I chuckle and he sets down his bottle. And it seems, once again, that possible connection, that brilliant flare, vanishes.

Why do I let it go? Why don't I snap a photo and hold it up for him to see? Show him the caring in his eyes and the desire for connection radiating off his chest and his shoulders and his face? Because I'm good enough to capture those moments. I'm good enough at my job to gather evidence of his body language and play it back for him.

Which, really, is the problem. I'm good. And California is where I need to be to become excellent. California, Australia, Africa. Europe for months on end.

Rob will be here, becoming his own version of excellent. Not alone because he has his family. And he has my brother. And, I suspect, he'll have a girlfriend in no time after I'm gone, another woman capable of seeing all the brilliance I see sitting next to me. Someone who can see beyond his handsome face and his strong, gorgeous body. Someone who will love him as much as I do.

Maybe I sigh. Maybe I, too, have body language I don't realize I have. Because Rob reaches around my side for my bag. "You got a pen in there?"

His arm against my skin feels miraculous. My fantasies whirl through my head, fueled by his proximity and the light of the moon: Semi-public sex. Tying him to the railing and jerking him off until he comes all over my hands. Rob pressing me against the wall and growling like an animal as he takes me from behind.

But that's not Rob. That's my fantasy man I use to bottle up my sexual attraction to this person who is my friend.

"You can't be serious," I say. He can't actually be playing out one of my fantasies, even the silliest of the set.

But he's got my bag and he's rooting around in the front pocket. "Hah!" Out comes the felt-tipped marker I use to mark memory cards.

And off goes his shirt.

He twists in the moonlight of the landing, his fingers gripping the edges of his ratty t-shirt, and the fabric wisps as it scrapes over the skin of his face. He shakes his head a little as if the action will resettle his hair, and blinks. The shirt slides down his arms, over his well-shaped biceps, and down his beautiful and strong forearms. For a second, he glances at his hands bound up in the fabric. They sit on his lap, two masculine fists clenched around the cotton of his shirt, making his entire upper body tighten.

I have a flash of carnal need so strong I almost grab his hands and tie that shirt into a knot. An immature little voice in my head wants to punish him for all the times he acted like an ass. To hold him down and ride his cock and taste his lips and the warm wonderful skin of his neck and shoulders. To feel the heat of his stubble against my nipples as he takes one into his mouth then the other. To whisper that he'd better not come until I have at least three times.

But they're just more fantasies I need to release. That time's past.

Rob drops his t-shirt next to his beer. He looks down at his chest and his mouth screws up as he tries to figure out how to write in a way that would be readable in a photo. "Like this?" He pantomimes writing his name with his finger.

"You're insane."

His gaze feels like it's boring a hole through my skin. "If he's a douche who gets off on making you feel uncomfortable, then I say we fuck with his head."

I can't help but smile. It's a juvenile fantasy. Rob's my friend and he wants to support me doing something silly and... naughty. Because he's my best friend.

I reach for my bag. Quickly, I work my camera out of its straps, determined to distract myself by setting up for the low light. And taking a good photo.

The moonlight sparkles across the apartment building's long hallway. I twist a little and motion for Rob to twist too, to get his chest into the light. He nods and moves, and watches me for cues.

"Good." I could set up my mini monopod and wrap the rope around my legs, but I'd miss this moment. I brace my back against the wall and one elbow against the railing instead, the other against my knee. I crank the shutter speed down and the aperture open. "You'll need to hold as still as possible."

Rob takes off the pen's cap and a small snap echoes through the hallway. He watches me, his eyes bright, and I snap the first photo. There's motion blur, but it adds a shimmer to the moment. I snap another photo.

Rob leans back and the line between the moon's light and the wall's shadow falls over his face. His features vanish. He raises a knee, bracing himself to hold still, and slowly starts writing.

My name appears first, three letters followed by an apostrophe and an 's' of possessiveness. He's mine, this man. Robert Quidell writes my name on his chest and it feels real even in this surreal moment. It feels as if he's giving me something he's never given anyone else. And he's doing it in a way that's both public and for us, very, very private.

In front of me, Rob moves in and out of the light, a body writing "Isa's boyfriend" across his flesh. This gesture goes beyond any of the social media haze around his past. I may never show these photos. It's about him giving of himself, not just of his skill with his body, and I feel showing the images would diminish his gift.

And it feels as if he's more naked, right now, than he was when we were in the cage down three floors, below our feet. More naked than when he pulled off his shirt to tease me after his workout. This feels as if he's peeling off his armor.

He looks up and I snap one more photo. Rob holds the pen between his fingers, just off his skin. "How's that?" he asks.

I turn off my camera and cap the lens. Carefully, I return it to the bag. I zip its pocket, listening to the sound fill the cool air of the hallway. And I take the pen, snapping on the cap, and return it, too, to its pocket.

Rob doesn't speak. He doesn't touch, either, though I see his hand move as if he wants to stroke my cheek.

His face is more raw than I've ever seen it. More emotion plays through his eyes than I thought possible, and I can't take it anymore. I can't take what I'm doing to this man.

I run my finger over my name, tracing the letters one at a time. As my fingertip twists around the bottom curve of the possessive 's', Rob closes his eyes. His chest tightens and I wonder just how ticklish the skin of this gorgeous man is. But when my finger glides over the 'b' at the beginning of 'boyfriend,' he opens his eyes.

His hand curls around mine, his fingers weaving between each of my own, first his pointer, then his index and ring, his skin warm and gentle and as brilliantly wonderful as the color of his eyes. When his pinky hooks around mine, he smiles.

And Rob Quidell nods his head *yes*.

CHAPTER 23

Robert

Isa glides her finger over my chest. I feel her touch, smell her warm scent. I hear only her breathing. I see the woman who I want to be more than a good friend.

"I'm leaving in two weeks," she whispers. "I won't be back. Not for a long time. This can't be."

"Yes, it can." I'll do whatever she needs. We can build what we need it to be. "I'll do the work—"

Isa's arms curl around my head. Her fingers weave into my hair. She pulls me to her, all of her, and her lips, her chest, her body presses against mine.

She's not gentle. One hand moves to my shoulders and her nails bite into my skin the way a woman's nails dig deep when she's about to come and she can't stop herself. Isa's body responds right now as if I've been fucking her for hours.

My cock is instantly, completely hard and the rush that comes from the change in blood flow makes me almost lose control. I can't think but I can touch her breasts and smell the faint musk of her arousal. "Isa," I growl.

I yank her onto my lap.

"You deserve... a real girlfriend." Her hand works into the waist-band of my jeans. "Not someone who..." She sucks in her breath before my lips steal more of her air. "... leaves for months."

I pull back enough to see her eyes. She's serious. She doesn't think we can do this long distance.

Maybe she's right. Maybe she's not. But tonight, I'm proving to her how much she means to me.

I pull her hand out of my hair. Carefully, I stretch her fingers, flat-tening them along my own. Her palm presses against mine and I want to clasp my hand tight around hers but that's not going to get my point across.

I lay her palm over the words on my chest. And over my heart. "We have two weeks. It's going to be real, Isa." *As real as I can make it for you.*

Because every single moment I've spent with her has been real. More real than any other time with any other woman. I've been fucking ladies since I was fifteen and not once was it more than solving the puzzle of the moment. How do I make her feel comfortable enough with me that she'll fuck me? How do I get myself off while making a woman feel good? How do I live with myself in the morning?

Never how do I connect. How do I build a relationship.

Isa's lips glide along my neck. Her tongue touches my stubble. Her arms curl around my chest. She's closer than any woman has ever been, holding tighter than any other woman.

I can't let this end.

"Two weeks with you?" she asks.

She holds onto my front and the closeness, the connection, vibrates through my muscles. I almost whisper the truth. Tell her the strength of the emotions flowing through me. But I can't find the words. No sound I make could possibly express the need I feel right now.

So instead, I kiss her with my lips, my shoulders, my entire body. She needs to know.

"Two weeks." Two months. Two years. Spending two *centuries* with her would make me the happiest man in the world, but I don't say it. She'll run if I do, saying she can't hurt me by breaking up when she leaves.

But we have this moment.

I scoop my hands under her bottom and turn us so her back presses against the wall. The moon plays over her lovely features and across the lenses of her glasses. For a second, her eyes vanish. But I know I hold all her attention.

I press her against the wall, shifting her hips enough to press my now-painful erection against her crotch.

"I'm weak, Rob." Isa moans and arches her back. "I was weak when we met at the party. I'm weak now. My responsible brain is telling me to be responsible but I want to be with you."

I snake my hand under her shirt. She's wearing one of those thick-cupped bras, the formed ones which I hate. Can't feel nipples. I yank on the damned cup hard enough I think I hear it rip.

I bite through her t-shirt. "Fuck responsible," rumbles out of my throat. "You're staying with me tonight."

"All night?" Under her glasses, her beautiful eyes are open and wide.

When I stroke my thumb across her cheek, she kisses my fingers.

Every night, I think. "Tomorrow morning, I'm going to wake you with kisses and cuddles and a pot of *good* coffee."

A moan makes it through Isa's smile and her mouth opens just a bit. "I fantasize about you all the time," she breathes. "*All the time*. No one sparks my imagination the way you do, on so many levels. It's why I want to take pictures of you."

My entire body vibrates. "You get off on torturing me, don't you?" She better fuck me tonight. I'm not going to be able to handle wanking myself off. I need her body, her touches. I need Isa. "Being mean."

She chuckles. "One of my fantasies is tying you to the bed and teaching you a lesson."

In my head, words stop forming and my brain toggles over to making only images. The rush is fast and intense and exhilarating. I see her straddling my hips, her luscious breasts bouncing so close I feel a little breeze every time they go up and down. Her ass in the air as I pound her from behind. Her with my cock deep in her throat.

"I have other fantasies," she whispers. "Some involve your revenge the next day."

More images: Shuddering as I pinch on nipple clamps. Her begging and begging for me to fuck her again and again.

I tighten my core and stand up. Isa's back slides up the wall, her legs around my waist, but I don't let go. I don't let her fall. "Condoms in bedroom." Goddamn, I sound like an animal.

"Get my gear." She's growling, too.

I'll have to let her go.

Isa grins. Her lips land on the hollow above my collarbone and she suckles on my skin. Gently at first, then with a little teeth. I shiver.

"I like that I can read you so well." Her lips move up to my neck. "I know what you want before you do. You want me naked like this, against the wall, pounding me so hard everyone in the building thinks we're in an earthquake."

I'm beyond exclamations. I need to fuck her now. I cover her mouth with mine before she responds and I sweep my tongue over her teeth and inhale, to form a vacuum in her throat.

"Oh...." Isa moves with me when I try to pull away.

Which is exactly what I wanted. But I pop the seal. "You feel that? I'm going to do that with my cock."

Another, breathier "Oh..." flows from my beautiful girlfriend.

"I told you two orgasms while fucked, one licked." I rub against her pussy. "I expect the same from you, woman."

Isa drops her feet to the floor. She yanks away fast, and swipes for her equipment bag and coat. Her hand snags my jacket and t-shirt too, but she abandons the beers. Before I know it, she's down the hall and in front of our door.

"Damn it, my hands are full." She looks up at me, a smirk on her lips. "Key's in my front pocket."

I flatten her against the door and press my erection into her back. I could come on her now, out here in the hallway in the silver moonlight. Yank down those jeans and rub against the cleft of her ass and come all over her. Maybe I will.

I jam my fingers into the front pockets of her jeans, diving in deep, pressing on her hip bones and her pelvis. Her ass thrusts against my cock. Her legs spread. I grind my fingertips into her flesh as close to her pussy as I can.

"*Fuck*..." she breathes.

I swear she's going to come now and it makes me want her all the more. I yank the key out of her pocket and slam it into the lock, but I can't wait. Quickly, I glance side to side, listening for doors or voices or anything else that might mean a neighbor. Only Isa's moans fill the hallway.

I unzip her jeans. If I had a condom, I'd fuck her now. But I can finger her until she screams.

My hand works between her jeans and the soft skin of her belly, roaming down, looking for the fabric of her panties. God, they're tiny. Just enough to cover the trimmed hairs on her mound.

I press harder against her back and fight the need to bite the nape of her neck.

But then I remember what she said about fantasies.

She's slick. I slide my index finger into her folds, but don't rub. I just press on her clit. My mouth descends toward her hair. I use my teeth to flick away her ponytail before I latch onto sweet skin just below her hairline. And I nip at the same time I flick my fingertip across her clit.

Isa's entire body quakes as an orgasm rips through her. A moan rolls out, loud and sexy as hell. I yank my hand out of her panties and push open the apartment door.

Isa falls through.

And right into her brother.

CHAPTER 24

Isolde

I have never been so embarrassed in my entire life. My fly is open and I have my half-naked, hard-as-granite boyfriend with his arms around my waist.

Why the fuck is Mack in the living room?

He's ruining the moment. And giving me the same exact I-do-*not*-approve stare Dad gave me every time I brought home a date. As if his continued love was predicated on whether or not my boyfriends lived up to his standards.

Or maybe Mack is disappointed in Rob, and not me.

My brother's face alternates so fast between totally shocked and totally *not* shocked I think he's going to pull a facial muscle. "Oh for God's sake, what the hell are you two doing?" he yells.

"None of your business." Menace colors Rob's voice. His arms tighten around my waist and he pulls me against his front. His shoulders curve forward and one of his hands moves to cover my open jeans as I set my equipment on the floor just inside the door.

My breath hitches. When I look up at his face, I see why he's responding the way he is: No one yells at his girlfriend. Not some random person. Not my brother. In Rob's mind, my safety—both physical and mental—comes first, even if it means he might piss off his roommate enough to get kicked out.

I don't think he realizes what he's doing. Or how barely he's controlling the protectiveness in his stance.

I turn in his arms and hug his chest. He blinks, surprised, and returns the hug.

"We won't bother you anymore." Rob's attention flits away from Mack and returns completely to me. A kiss lands on the bridge of my nose, and another on my cheek.

I take his hands, folding my fingers into his, and squeeze.

"How is this a good idea?" Behind me, Mack sounds like he's about to throw a pillow at us.

Rob tenses again and his gaze flicks to my brother. I see a snarl start on the corner of his lips.

"Rob," I say. He's wound up like a spinning top and he's going to burst. But it can't be onto Mack. I want it on me.

The snarl turns to a smirk when he sees my face. And the next thing I know, he's pulling me down the hallway to his room.

"Don't be stupid! Either of you!"

Mack yells, but I don't care. I slam Rob's door the moment he pulls me through.

He doesn't flick on the light. The moon's light floods through the open curtains and it's perfect. He's perfect. Tonight will be perfect, no matter how much my brother yells.

Rob understands. He knows I won't ask more of him than I think he can give me. The future might pull us to different coasts but we have right now. We don't have to hold back.

His room is cramped, filled wall to wall with a large bed, his dresser, and his desk. The closet door's mirror reflects his gorgeous, naked back. A desk chair sits in the middle of what little walking space he has. And a small, three-drawered nightstand stacked with books and a lamp sits next to the head of the bed.

The condoms must be in there. The condoms I don't want to use, but I'm not on any form of birth control, so we don't have any other options.

It's never been an issue. I travel too much to form intimate relationships. But tonight, I feel a little annoyed by my lack of planning.

I want all of Rob Quidell.

He yanks up my t-shirt and his face descends into my cleavage.

"Thank you," I groan.

His hands yank down my jeans but he can't get them off with his face in my chest.

I've never had a man respond to me like this. Not even my first boyfriend that night at the charter house when we both lost our virginity. Not my only long-term boyfriend in college who told me he loved me, even though I don't think he knew how to love anything other than his BMW. Not the couple of random guys I've had sex with because we were both so horny we needed release.

No one wanted to be this close.

Rob pulls his face from between my breasts and I feel as if I'm truly exposed. He's my protection from the world, not my clothes or my equipment, and when he moves away, I don't like it.

Having his strong arms around me holding so tightly I can barely breathe feels right. I feel as if I've found a place of peace. Rob Quidell wants to be the steady rock in my life.

Rob, the player, who's never been anyone's rock. This man who has always pushed away everyone wants to be my center for as long as he can.

For the next two weeks.

"Thank me for what?" he asks.

For loving me, I think. I almost say it, but I don't want to terrify him. I'm selfish. I don't want him to realize the connection we're forming and to pull back from it. But I also don't want him to associate anything bad with allowing out this part of himself. He needs to learn to love as much as I need to be loved by him.

He touches my cheek, his fingers gliding over my skin. His ocean eyes shimmer in the moonlight, wonderful and full of life. My beautiful Rob looks happy.

"You are beautiful," he whispers.

The intensity in his voice flows into his next kiss. We aren't naked. He doesn't have his hand on my ass or cupping my breast. He holds me as close as to his chest as he can, his wonderful lips gliding over every micro-inch of mine. He tastes warm and a little like the beer, but genuine and healthy and fresh.

I step back. I need to see his face. His body. I need to watch him move and to feel the strength of his wonderful arms. I need Rob to be the living man he is.

His fingers caress my arms, gently gliding over my biceps to my elbows. He sweeps his palm along the outside of my forearm and an intense, bone-vibrating shiver runs up my arm and into my chest. A moan escapes.

Rob smiles. "I'm good at sex, Isa." He dances his fingers over my wrists, pressing and tickling the cleft that forms at the base of my palm when I wiggle my thumb. "I'm going to make this the best two weeks of your life."

Even if we stop now, even if I say no we can't do this because it can't last, even if we are just friends, I think these next two weeks will be brilliant. Special. And I don't think I'm going to want to leave.

"Hey." Rob kisses me again. "What's wrong?"

What do I say? Do I tell him the truth? *I shouldn't love you but I'm head over heels.*

So I give him one more opportunity to escape. One more moment before we tangle together. "Are you sure you want to do this?"

Rob's forehead contracts. He closes his eyes for a long second, then opens them again. "I want to be with you. If it's two weeks, it's two weeks." The look of consternation turns to one of concern. "Do *you* want to do this?"

I press myself against his chest, my face against his neck. The temple of my glasses rubs but we adjust. "Two weeks," I whisper.

I'm with him now and I'm not letting go.

Rob pulls back. His hands cup my shoulders, then my cheeks. Carefully, he takes off my glasses. When he steps away to set them on the nightstand, I feel cold. I need his touch and his warm skin.

All of the room's edges fuzzy out. Life without my glasses is soft and sort of shimmery. It's out of focus but not so bad I can't function. But it fogs distant places.

And, maybe, distant times. Two weeks from now, we will deal with breaking up. But right now, right here, Rob is hard and close enough to see clearly. And my focus returns to where it needs to be.

CHAPTER 25

Isolde

Electricity fires between my fingers and to the skin of Rob's chest. He closes his eyes and tips his head upward. I see the edges of his teeth and they glow just a little in the moonlight. When a low groan filters out over his tongue, his entire torso elongates. His wonderful chest. The waves of his exceptional abdomen. The words he wrote on his skin.

"Isa's boyfriend" ripples and I feel a surge of possessiveness course through my belly. It's stupid and childish but it feels so damned good. The gods offered me two weeks with Rob. The man I love brings out a level of pure, primal lust I didn't know I had.

Or maybe I did. My imagination's vivid enough.

I rub my palm over his constrained cock. My prize is about to burst out of his jeans and it makes me want to vacuum him until he comes in my throat.

His belt clinks and rubs under my fingers as I move him backward, toward the bed. I make quick work of the buckle and his fly, and push his jeans down his hips. They're off before I suck in another breath.

"You too." Rob's voice sounds dark, smoky. His eyes mirror his voice, as if he's looking at me from a new place.

I think he's a little afraid. His fingers vibrate as they undo the clasp of my bra. His palms too, when he cups my breasts. Nothing predatory moves from his skin to mine, but there's energy. Strong, wonderful, new energy.

His thumbs alternate flicking one of my nipples, then the other. The oscillation adds another layer to my lust and I can't take it anymore. I can't worry or whimper.

So I give in to my not-so-responsible self. And I let out the fantasies.

I wiggle off my jeans. They rub down my legs, constricting and lashing them together, and another rush of thrill strikes like lightning right into my pussy. Which do I want more? To be the animal first? To teach Rob his lesson? Or lie back and let him release his lust onto me?

I need both. I will have both. And more.

"Every one of those pretty-boy models you work with wants to fuck you." Rob's smoky voice takes on a dreamy edge. "No straight man would pass up *you*."

Why his words affect me so, I don't know. I float along their surface, buoyed by the lust I hear woven into the love in his voice. His certainty catches me off guard. Rob sounds as if he's hooked into the male hive mind and he knows, without a doubt, that he speaks the truth for every man on Earth.

And he's the one who won the prize.

I chuckle and run my palm over the soft cotton covering his diamond-hard cock. The vein running along the underside of his erection pulses against my fingers. The ridge of his cock's head quakes as I tickle it.

Rob groans and looks up at the ceiling again, his mouth slack and his shoulders tensing. "Jesus above," he breathes.

He wears super-soft boxer-briefs. The ones with the fabric covered elastic and the smooth, flat stitching. I hook the pinkies and ring fingers of both hands into his waistband and pull the fabric up and out, and stroke my thumbs and index fingers across the ridge of his crown.

A "*Fuck*," rides his breath as he grabs my shoulder and neck.

His kiss bends me backward and pushes against all my effort. My mouth opens on its own, my tongue dances with his all by itself. He tastes exactly right; exactly like Rob—savory and a little like sea salt touched by deep earth minerals forced up by a volcano. Rob, my man with more strata than he shows the world.

His lips work down my chin to my neck. His hands squeeze and massage my breasts. The head of his cock rubs against my belly and I almost come right now, standing inches from his mattress in my little black panties.

Can we make this last all night? Or is the need too strong? When it erupts, will we both let loose everything? I don't think I'll be able to control myself.

I push him toward the mattress. He slides his feet backward but keeps his grip on my breasts. His thumbs work my nipples again, sliding left to right, up to down. I know my mouth opens. I know I'm shuddering.

He flops onto his back, bringing me with him, but I break his hold on my nipples. And yank his boxer-briefs off his hips.

Heat rises off his long, thick cock and over his trimmed hair as I kneel between his legs. A thin line trails up to his navel and I dance my fingers through its soft hairs. Rob chuckles and the ridged muscles of his abs tighten under my touch. I massage along the groove between his abs and his hips and he wiggles again.

"You're ticklish," I say. Watching him squirm makes me want him more.

"Am not." Yet he squirms again and pushes up on his elbows.

"I want to taste you." I want him all the way in my throat and hitting against my gag reflex. I want to ride that edge. God, he's thick and I want to run my tongue over his crown.

Rob's face takes on all the dark smokiness from his voice. His eyelids droop. And I know that once I take him between my lips, he won't be able to hold himself up any longer.

The first lick pulls a loud groan from Rob. With the second, he drops onto his back again. Gently, I massage his inner thigh, working toward his balls, doing my best not to tickle too much. I want this to be the best blowjob of his life, not the time he spasmed because I wasn't paying attention.

A hint of his sea salt spreads over my tongue when I close my lips over the tip of his cock. I relax my throat and slowly slide him in, my lips cupping over his crown, then his shaft. When he hits the back of my throat, I suck hard to keep him in, even as I move up again. I take him deep again and again, one hand helping my mouth and the other caressing his balls.

His hips tighten. He likes my mouth so much I can tell he wants to pump.

I *want* him to thrust. I want to feel him on the verge of losing control. So I pop my mouth off his cock and strip his boxer-briefs completely off his legs. He sits up, his beautiful cock right there, right in front of me, and I pull him off the bed.

Rob kneels next to me. He grabs for my breasts, for my hair, and catches me in a deep, soul-burning kiss. "My turn," he groans. His fingers work into my panties. "I'm going to lick you until you scream."

The desire in his voice sends a real, bone-rattling quiver through my body. The man gives me nipple-hardening, orgasm-making chills. But I'm not done with him yet.

I crawl up onto the bed, ass away from him, my lips right where I want them. Leaning over the edge, I massage his hips, running my thumbs over the muscles of his lower abs. "I'm not done torturing you."

Rob chuckles. "You're *mean*."

He tries not to thrust when I pull his hips toward my mouth. I feel his glutes harden and his abs tighten. But he's off balance and he buckles forward, his chest coming over my head.

I take him deep again. His lips rest in the middle of my upper back and when he groans, it vibrates through my ribcage.

It feels good. So damned good. I suck hard on his cock, twirling my tongue against his shaft, and feel his pleasure roll through my shoulder blades.

The next thrust goes deeper than I expect but I hold the gag. Rob works his hands up the side of my body, his fingers digging into my flesh, until he reaches my ass.

And the next thing I know, I get another pump into my throat and a good hard smack on my right butt cheek.

I almost come. It almost happens. Rob must have realized because he shifts enough to curl an arm under my chest.

He clamps my nipple between his finger and thumb at the same time another slap hits my ass. And another thrust into my mouth.

The orgasm reverberates from the sting on my backside to the sting in my nipple. I moan around his cock but he pulls out of my mouth and flips me over.

He looks pleased. "That's two."

What is he going to do? "Fuck me now," I plead. "Please. I don't need—"

Rob presses the entire length of his body against mine, and his cock against my hip bone so hard it hurts. His kiss silences my pleas. I forget everything but him, sense nothing but his lips, and curl myself into his embrace.

My focus shifts from his taste to his touch. The vibration I noticed earlier dances again across his skin to mine. His lips find mine and his kiss is more intense, more alive, than any I've experienced in my life.

"Rob," I whisper. He's wonderful. Right now, he's everything.

"I want this to be the best sex of your life." He sounds as if he doesn't believe he can finish what he started. Rob Quidell seems to think he's not up to the task.

"It is. It already has been." I stroke his cheek and kiss the tip of his nose.

His kisses, how he embraces me, the touch of his fingers, are better than any other time. Better than any fantasy. "I'm with you."

Rob strokes my hip. When his fingers find my mound, I buck against his hand. "I want to make you come and come again and I want to be in you when it happens. I want to see your face and hear you sigh."

I think beautiful Rob who just spanked me to an orgasm wants sweet, missionary sex. He wants to see my eyes and feel my breath and see me respond to every thrust and every kiss.

I stroke his cheek, wondering if he's ever experienced the connection he craves. If sex has always been acrobatic and more about one-upping each other with skills than about feeling one another.

But that's not what he wants with me. Not our first time.

"Yes." I want to share this with him. To be, in some ways, his first.

He digs in the nightstand. I pull off my panties and scoot up the bed next to him, and curl my arms around his waist. We're both naked, both bathed in light from the moon outside. He tears open a condom, and the wrapper crinkles when he drops it on the floor. He makes fast work of rolling it on before snapping open the cap of the lube.

I kiss his shoulder. "Just a little." I'm wet enough.

He explores, his fingers rubbing over my clit and my opening, and I shudder. A new kiss finds my mouth as Rob moves between my legs.

Slowly, gently, he presses into me. His first inch sends an intense wave of pleasure through my belly. The second makes me whisper his name. With the fourth, I'm ready to scream. When his sixth and seventh move into me, I grasp the muscles of his backside. I need all of him. Every inch, every thrust.

He watches my face, his eyes wide open. Oceans swirl above me, glinting with emotions I never thought I'd see on a man's face while making love. But they're there and they're real.

I kiss his neck and grasp his back. He rocks against my clit, his hips as intense as his expression. He moves gently, slowly, making it last.

Making it real.

"Rob," I whisper. I want to cry. I want to speak the emotions welling higher in my belly and chest each time he slides into me. I want him to know.

He leans on one elbow to keep his leverage and strokes my face with his other hand. "I…" No other words move out of his throat. No other sounds but his breathing and his moans. He thrusts, a few shallow, a few deep, and kisses me again.

Greens and blues dance in his eyes. His dark hair blends into the shadows. Silvers spark and moonlight highlights. His hard body presses into mine, against mine, rocking, thrusting, and I read his desires. Rob wants this moment. He wants to move beyond arousal and simple touching.

His lips lock onto my neck, his shoulders hunching over, and he moves higher along my body to hit my clit with more force. The loud groan rolling from my throat surprises me, but not Rob. He knows how to do this right.

Hot-cold rakes every nerve in my body. My skin feels too big at the same time it feels too small—I feel each of his finger wisps and the gentle brushes of his breath. But I also feel the weight of his solid body. How much he stretches me. Every swirl of his cock caused by the rolling of his hips.

Rob ignites the upper limits of my body. He's found the edge beyond which my nerves will simply disintegrate. We glide along it, kissing and fucking. And, I think, loving.

My fingers dig into his shoulders. A new moan erupts. I spasm under Rob's thrusts and the world blanks out.

"*Oh...*" Rob pumps one last time.

My orgasm matches his, pulse for pulse, stuttered moan to stuttered moan. New kisses land on my neck, my cheek, my oversensitive lips. His fingers weave into mine. Each kiss is gentle, sweet. I kiss the tip of his nose and he grins, his eyes happy and, I think, amazed. But also a little sad.

All I want is to make sure I see only his happiness. I don't want to let him go.

"I need to take care of the condom," he says.

I nod. Rob lifts off me but I sit up too and lean against his shoulder. His arms curl around me for a long, strong, entwining hug. Rob holds me as tightly as I hold him, and his lips dance over my ear.

"I'm sorry for every stupid thing I did. For the stupid things I said to you," he whispers. "I'm so sorry."

I press my lips against his jaw and his cheek, and I give him my own apology. "If I had chosen you over my lust, it never would have happened." And we would have been together much, much sooner.

I know we would have been together. But loving longer would make leaving him much, much more difficult.

Rob kisses my temple and my forehead. He pulls away only long enough to roll off the condom, but he's paying more attention to me than his work. He ties the condom and drops it in the wastebasket and he's immediately back in my arms, curled around me, exactly how we were when we both orgasmed.

A new kiss lands on the bridge of my nose. "We'll figure it out," he whispers.

I nod and press myself against his chest. We will. I just hope I have the strength to do what's right.

CHAPTER 26

Robert

Isa fell asleep in my arms. Beautiful, fun, adventurous Isa cuddled against my side and fell asleep with her head on my shoulder.

For the first time in my life, a woman wanted to *sleep* with me.

I didn't say anything more than "We'll figure it out." I knew what would fall from my lips if the words continued to roll out: *Don't leave. I need you here. We can do this.*

I love you.

Part of me still wondered if she would be gone in the morning. If she'd sneak out the moment I fell asleep and that we'd be doing the cordial nods and embarrassed smirks over coffee. But she's here, sleeping next to me, her lovely hair fanned out over my pillow, snoring softly and smelling of sweat and sex and love.

Isolde Wellington, my roommate's "mean" twin sister. Isa, the woman I love more than I thought I was capable of loving. She's here. She stayed. Slept with me because she's my friend and my lover and I'm happier than I should be.

Maybe seeing my brothers with their new loves rubbed off on me.

Maybe I just needed examples of relationships worth fighting for that haven't ended in ripping metal and...

I blink and rub my face. I won't think about the accident.

But Isa travels a lot.

I kick that irrational thought in the gut. I'll hold it down and beat the snot out of it if I have to. The ten years of therapy can't be for nothing, no matter how hard I worked at making sure it didn't take.

But it did. My girlfriend is with me this morning.

My stomach growls and my cock does its normal morning stand at attention even though it got plenty of satisfaction last night. My girlfriend's adventurous. Which, I suppose, shouldn't surprise me one bit. She flies around the world to take photos of moments ranging from skinny models standing on beaches to poachers murdering elephants.

And for some reason, my globetrotting lover chose boring, shallow me.

For two weeks, she chooses to be with me.

I'm not giving her up. If I go six months without her in the same room with me, then I go six months. But when she flies home, it's going to be to me and not to some tiny, pathetic, lonesome place in California.

No, we're not breaking up when she goes. I'm not giving up without trying. I'll work myself to the bone for her.

I think she feels the same. I hope she feels the same. But I need to be careful. Can't come on too strong or she will run. Then we *will* have the awkward smirks and sideways glances over breakfast. And I'll never see her again.

Sun filters in through my window and I swear Isa glows. She snorts. Her nose wiggles. A hand bats at a few stray hairs wrapped around her face and she pretty much slaps herself across her cheek.

I can't help but chuckle. She's amazing and wonderful and real.

Her eyes open. "Oh!" And she sits up so fast I'm afraid she's going to smack against the headboard. "Rob!"

Worry whacks me with the same force I thought she might inflict on herself. What if she regrets last night? What if she would have snuck out, if she'd woken up first? "You okay?" I ask.

Isa rubs her eyes. "I was dreaming."

She reaches for me. I pull her into my arms and her luscious breasts flatten against my chest. My skin tingles where she touches.

I can't help but kiss her hair and her forehead. "Not bad, I hope."

"It seemed important." Isa cuddles in close. "I'm glad I woke up with you."

I think perhaps I suck in my breath. It's not manly. But I can't let her go.

Her kiss feels better than anything in my life. Better than a birthday party. Better than the time Tom dared me to climb over the roof and down the other side of the house and I did it in less than ten minutes. Better than my no-debt-accumulated scholarships.

I squirm when she traces her finger over the words on my chest. "I'm getting it tattooed on." I wink. "I'm thinking blacklight ink."

Isa chuckles. "My boyfriend-for-two-weeks is insane."

Not two weeks. It won't be two weeks. But I don't say the words. "You like me insane and you know it." I kiss her with enough energy my morning wood notices.

"Hmm..." Isa runs her hand over my hip. "Two weeks of waking up to this is going to be heaven." A new kiss lands on my shoulder. She glides a finger up my firm cock, base to tip, and smirks.

I try not to groan but her touch is brilliant.

"You are a thing of beauty, Robert Quidell." Her hand wraps around my erection and she strokes up once, then slowly down again.

My worries flop into the pond of subconscious buzz in the back of my head. I'll deal with them later. Right now, I have my woman.

I glance at the clock. I also need to be on campus in an hour and a half.

Groaning, I pull away. "I need to go to class." I'd rather spend the day fucking my girlfriend into pure bliss.

Isa makes a wide-eyed, exaggerated pout. "But it'd be a shame to waste a good, hard cock." She strokes me up and down again.

Playful and adventurous. I hit the jackpot with this one. "It's a renewable resource." God knows it won't go away and I'll be spending my day uncomfortable and distracted.

"I'll drive you to campus if I have to." Isa rolls over and reaches for a condom.

The perfect twin mounds of her gorgeous ass are right there, waiting for my attention.

I grab hold and press my thumbs into her flesh, spreading her cheeks to get a good look at her pussy in the bright morning sun.

Goddamn, I think I'm going to skip class this morning. I'll email my TA later. Say I'm sick. Or maybe I'll just tell him the truth— spending the morning boning my sex kitten girlfriend trumps stats lectures any day.

Isa wiggles her ass higher at the same time she widens her legs. "You're not going to get kicked out of grad school because of me, are you?" She wiggles her ass again. "If we're quick, you'll get to class on time."

I get a quickie before my boring day of classes and office hours? I think I like waking up with someone I love.

The condom flicks over her shoulder and lands on the curve of her ass. "Do me, baby," Isa drawls.

She glances over her shoulder, her expression cocky and naughty and full of a different emotion I don't quite understand. Acceptance, maybe. Desire, for sure. The desire to share this moment of bad behavior with me. We're intimate in our juvenile disregard for authority's hourly schedule.

"You're a bad influence." I smack her left ass cheek before kneading the muscle.

Goddamn, she's gorgeous.

"Oh!" But her expression just gets naughtier and she wiggles her ass again.

I'm directly behind her, using my knees to spread her legs farther apart. The condom sitting just at the top of her ass's cleft slides a little toward me. I grip her backside and wiggle it, to move the wrapper back to its original position.

"I need to take a shower." I smack her other cheek.

She responds by wiggling again and pressing her ass toward my belly.

I run my palm over her slick pussy. Her trimmed bush is slightly darker but the same basic blonde as her hair. Her inner lips blush and quiver when I rub my fingers over their warm, slick surface.

Yes, I'm missing stats class. "Can't miss my office hours this after-noon. Have a student coming in."

Isa bites her lip as she glances over her shoulder. "So you're not as bad a boy as you claim to be?"

And she calls me the brat. I smack her ass again, then knead her flesh, squeezing hard.

"I never liked spanking before." Her head drops down. "But when you do it, it's amazing."

Chuckling, I pull up on her ass cheeks. Her back bows and she drops her front down onto the bed, her chest flat and her arm out along the pillows.

I could tie her up. But I'd have to leave the glorious pussy in front of me. I ask anyway. "Blindfold?"

Isa looks surprised when she pushes up again and looks over shoul-der. But her face quickly changes back to the naughty expression I saw earlier. "You like it?"

Sometimes. "I want to see you writhe because you can't stop coming."

"Oh..." Isa plants her face in the pillow and stretches out her arms. "Please."

"Don't move." I move to the head of the bed and dig around in my nightstand. The silk scarves wait in the back of the drawer, one for her eyes and one each for her arms.

The purple one, I brush along the back of her neck. She shivers and wiggles her ass and I want to fuck her right now. No toys, no playing, just a hard, fast fuck.

Maybe tomorrow morning.

I make quick work of tying the scarf around her head. Isa lifts her front off the bed. Just a little, but it's enough I see her open mouth. Her tongue darts out and I know immediately what my fiend of a girl-friend wants.

Slowly, so she knows what I'm doing, I lean over the side of her face and rub the underside of my cock against her cheek. Electricity flickers up my shaft and into my lower belly. Is she going to turn her head enough to take me in her mouth? Is she going to give me another mind-blowing blowjob, like she did last night? This morning, I'm not sure I could stop myself from coming on her face.

"Tie my hands," she whispers.

I immediately tie one end of a red scarf around the wrist of her hand opposite me. The effort rubs my cock against her face again. It's distracting. I can't think. But I manage to pull the long end of the scarf toward the headboard.

When I shift, she rolls slightly. Her lips wrap around the head of my cock and her tongue traces the tip.

I try not to groan. I try not to thrust. *Feel it*, I think, but shit, it's like I'm fifteen again and this is my first, formative moment of a woman sucking me.

When I move into her mouth, she pulls her head back, not taking me deep the way she did last night. She wants only the head of my cock.

Fuck, I think. *She's killing me.*

Her lips pop off and she wiggles her wrapped wrist. "Work first."

I immediately tie the scarf to the headboard, allowing some give, but not a lot, and do the same for the arm close to me. Isa lies on my bed on her chest, her ass in the air, the condom still perched on her lower back, her arms spread and her eyes blindfolded, ready for me to delight her senses.

Or just fuck her as I please.

I run my hands over her shoulders, teasing and tickling. She whimpers and pulls against her restraints, and her muscles tense under my touch. I move one hand around to the front of her neck and gently stroke her jaw. I run a finger over her lips.

"Hmm...." I hum into her ear. My other hand roams down her spine and over the curve of her back. I press the condom packet into her flesh. Then I move my hand around her hip.

Isa pants against my fingers. Slowly, I press a finger into her pussy, then another, and mirror the movements with my other hand, pressing one, then two fingers into her mouth.

"I will tell you when to come," I breathe into her ear. She can come and come again, but this is our first time playing this game. Better play by the conventional rules.

"What are you going to do?" She sounds wistful. Faraway. Which means she's enjoying the game.

"Fuck you." Quickly, I take hold of her head, positioning my hands to make sure she's not torqueing her neck or holding her head in a way that will hurt, and lift her shoulders off he bed. And just as quickly, I thrust deep into her mouth once, twice. Three times.

A sigh tickles my cock at the same time her tongue presses against the underside of my shaft. God, she knows what to do and it's divine. "Before you leave for California, I'm coming in your mouth," I growl.

Another sigh tickles along my shaft. I pull out of her mouth and rub my cock over the side of her face and up to the sensitive skin around her ear. Isa drops her face to the pillow again and I press my cock against her shoulder, her side. Each point of contact elicits a moan.

Her responses make me want to plunge into her. To just lose control and slam her hard.

I move between her legs. Slowly, I grind my palm against her glistening, upturned pussy. The condom slides to the side and I glare at it. That sheath of latex is going to keep me from feeling all the wonders of Isa's tight, hot pussy. For the first time in my life, the desire to be completely in contact with a woman almost overcomes my safety protocols.

I let out my frustration and nip her left ass cheek.

A breathy "Best boyfriend ever..." rolls out of Isa on the back of a moan.

No woman has ever trusted me this much. Even my "lifestyle" girlfriend was more into power games than trust and connection, no matter what she told me. But Isa likes what I do and wants everything I have to offer.

This can't be only two weeks. It can't. So I'm going to make her addiction to me as strong as her feelings.

I widen her legs again and flip onto my back. Digging my fingers into her ass, I pull it down until her pussy is right above my lips.

And I blow on her clit.

"Rob..." Her belly shakes and I swear she just came a little.

"No orgasms until I say." I accent my growl with a new slap to her ass.

"*Ah*..."

I lay a quick, gentle lick across her clit. Her pussy tastes like the rest of her skin—sweet with a hint of rose—but stronger. I lick again.

A new moan rises from my trussed up girlfriend. She wiggles, pulling against her restraints, and it makes me want her more. I suck on her clit and roll my tongue around her opening, lapping at her like a starved puppy.

She presses her pussy into my face, grinding and whimpering, but I keep licking. I keep sucking. And I slap her ass one more time.

Her orgasm spasms through her body and I feel her contractions against my lips. Pulses I want around my cock. I slap her ass again.

"I didn't say." I roll out from under her. The condom fell off while I ate her and now sits on the sheet next to her hip. I run its edge along her skin and rip it open next to her ear. "Time for your punishment."

I swear she quakes again. That another small orgasm rolls through her body.

Yes, I think. *I'll get what I want.* I want to feel her come while I'm buried in her, the way I came last night.

I roll the condom on. My balls burn. My cock feels ten times too big for my skin. And once again, I hate the damn latex.

I'm not careful. I thrust in, feeling the friction before her slickness takes over. Isa bucks against my hips and I pump deeper. She stretches more with each thrust but I bottom out and hit her cervix. She groans and shakes, and I think it might be the wrong kind of pain.

So I yank on her hips and reposition her ass to hit a different spot, at a different angle. The next shudder around my cock feels right—hot, intense, perfect. I slam into her again.

Fast, deep, I pump my hips against her ass. We slap together. The bed rocks and creaks, and I'm sure the neighbors below are getting an earful, but I don't care. Her sweet scent mixes with my lust and I'll fuck her this way all day if I can.

I can't hold my orgasm. I need release. She's gorgeous and tight and we fit together exactly right. Finding her spots is as easy as walking. And she's already found all of mine.

She arches back toward me, taking every thrust. "I'm going to come..." Another loud moan pushes from her throat.

"*Shit*," I groan, and pound into her again and again, faster and faster.

My orgasm hits me like a slam into a wall. It's sudden and surprising and reverberates from the point of impact through my entire body. My brain bounces against my skull. My knees buckle. And my entire weight drops onto Isa's back.

Isa twists her wrists and her hands pull out of the scarves. The blindfold comes off. She rolls under me and pulls me up to her shoulder, her entire body curling around mine the way she did last night.

I don't usually like being touched after an intense orgasm. I want the woman to let me be, at least for a moment or two, but not with Isa. I want her as close as I can get her. Tasting the set of her lips and her joy in her breath.

Like now. She grins and chuckles and presses the entire length of her body against mine and I'm in heaven. Real, wonderful heaven.

I move only far enough away that I can pull off the condom. She's breathing hard and so am I. We're both warm and bordering on sweaty. The sheet rubs over my skin as she pulls it up but cuddling together is what I need. Quickly, I return to her arms. And my bliss.

But the clock says if I shower now and run to the bus stop, I'll only miss the first part of my stats class. "I gotta go."

Isa sits up. She pulls the sheet over her chest and cocks her head to the side, watching me. "Go be otherwisely brilliant, gorgeous." She pats the mattress. "I think I will spend the morning lounging naked in your bed."

No pout. No frown. My girlfriend smiles and sends me out into the world to work my job and it's the best post-sex moment of my life.

I kiss her cheek knowing full well I'm not letting her go.

Not at the end of the two weeks. Not in two years, either. Or twenty. She's who I need. "Shower with me."

Isa wags her finger and flops onto the mattress. "Tomorrow."

Leaving her in my bed takes considerable will power. Showering without her, even more. I don't scrub the words on my chest. If they fade, I'll trace them. They're staying all fourteen of our days.

I brush my teeth, but don't shave. I'll get food on campus. Back in my room, Isa props herself up on an elbow and nods approvingly the entire time she watches me dress. Her gaze feels different from the dismissive lust I'm used to. She seems to enjoy watching me move even when we aren't having sex. It's nice.

"I gotta go," I say again.

Isa rolls off the bed and pulls my t-shirt from last night over her head. It falls over her exceptional breasts and down to her exceptional hips. Quickly she pulls on her panties.

"What time does Mack leave?" Isa cracks the door and looks into the hallway. "We alone?"

"He was out of here at dawn. Early class." I wrap my arm around her waist and pull her out to the living room with me. Once again, letting go takes more effort than it should. She fits against my side. Her warmth gives me calm.

But I have class. And office hours. "I'll be back around four." I toss my bag onto my back. "So will Mack."

Isa nods. When I swing open the outside door, she kisses my cheek. "Be careful."

I don't want to go. For the first time in my life I've found someone good for me and I want to spend every waking moment with her. But duty calls.

I nod. "Miss you already."

A blush rises along her cheeks. She looks down and away but squeezes my fingers. "You're wonderful."

"Let's talk tonight, okay? Figure things out." Then sit down with Mack. He can't be mad. I'm staying with Isa, no matter what happens.

She nods yes. "We need to sort out permanent addresses."

She wants to stay with me. I see it in her eyes and in the set of her cheeks and I almost blurt out how I feel. I almost say it. But I have class, so I kiss her instead. "Four."

Isa nods again. "Don't be late."

I back through the door. "I won't."

"Bye." She watches me step into the hall.

"Bye." I walk backwards toward the stairs.

"Go on." She shoos me away, but her face says *come back*.

I nod and turn away. The door clicks closed and I hear the lock tumble behind me. I should run for the bus, but I can't. Not yet.

I knock.

When she answers, confusion twists her face. I step in and hoist her up in my arms. My kiss steals her breath. I want to take away her worries and replace them with comfort and joy. "I'm going to think about you all day."

More blush creeps up her neck. "Go *on*. You're already late."

This time, I wait until I hear the lock click again before I dash away, toward the bus, my head full of possibilities and plans. My future wants to be with me. And we're going to make it happen.

CHAPTER 27

Robert

I don't remember my stats lecture. Don't remember sitting in my cubicle for office hours, either. But I do remember sexting with Isa all afternoon.

We sent back and forth more than naughty innuendos. Turns out, she managed to convince Mack to let her borrow his car tonight. Looks like I'm going on a real date with a gorgeous woman. She spent the day planning the whole thing.

I glance out the bus window and watch the dorms go by. It's nice today, warm and bright, and the air smells fresh. A night out will be fun, though so would another night full of fantasies.

I shift in my seat. Two excellent rounds of excellent sex within the last twenty-four excellent hours but my balls ache anyway. And I've been semi-hard since she texted me the first *I just took a shower* this morning.

Which she followed with *You like my black panties, don't you? I have a red pair I'm pulling over my thighs right now.*

Smart, talented, and a bad girl. I'm marrying that woman.

The bus lurches and I blink, suddenly aware of my own thoughts. I need to convince her we can handle a long-distance relationship first.

Hell, I need to make sure we can handle the next two weeks. It's not like I have a good track record. Neither does she, to be honest. Traveling has always taken priority to intimacy.

My sudden awareness of my thoughts shifts from future plans to the very real present. To expectations. Finishing school. And to likely sacrifices.

I shift again in my seat and tuck those thoughts away. It's not like I'm proposing. My beautiful girlfriend is taking me out for a night on the town and we're going to talk. Make plans.

The bus groans and rolls up to my stop. I jump off the step into the spring sunshine and the bus exhaust, my pack on my back and enough dance in my stride to make me smile.

Because this is going to work. For once in my life, I'm going to make sure I play for two people and not just myself.

I dodge a puddle. Birds sing and cars honk. A beer awaits, as do the cuddles of my glorious girlfriend. Though I do have a stats assignment due in a couple of days. At this point, I doubt Mack will help me with the programming. I don't think Isa can, though some of the image software she uses looks more like moon rocket controls than cropping tools. She'd probably figure out my stats program in under an hour.

Grinning to myself, I pull out my phone and tap my brother Tom. Time to get some relationship advice from an expert.

Though "expert" is more "lucky dumbass" in his case. Still, Sammie moved in a week after they met, so he's got insight on the whole "living together while you establish your relationship" problem.

You around? I tap out.

After a moment, *Why aren't you in class?* pops up.

Walking home. I glance around more to make sure I'm not going to run into someone as I stride along the sidewalk. *Got a woman question.*

To spank or not to spank? You need to ask Dan that, not me.

I shake my head. *TMI,* I tap out.

What's your problem, little brother?

I don't know how to phrase what I want to ask. When did you know Sammie was the one? When did you decide you wanted to marry her? Or maybe it's not so much deciding you want to make it permanent, but deciding to put in the effort to work toward making it permanent.

I think I'm in love, I tap out.

The pause before his answer is excruciating. What if my responsible brother chastises me? Tells me I'm too immature to even consider a real relationship and that I have way too much work to do on myself before I should open up *that* line of communication with Isa?

His answer isn't what I expect. *Don't hide something that important from her.*

I should speak up. Lay it all out. *What if I—*

I didn't see the guy squatting in the bushes next to the sidewalk. I didn't expect the punch.

Or the knife.

CHAPTER 28

Robert

I'm bleeding. I'm... *bleeding.*

I'm—

A person. Someone I don't recognize. "Hey, dude, hold on. We called 911. They're coming."

I can't see his face. The sun's too bright. "What?" He's pressing on my side.

A warm, metallic tang sits on my tongue. It fills my nose. I think I hurt but I don't know.

"Hold on. I hear the ambulance. You're going to be okay. Hold still."

Sirens. I'm *bleeding.*

Two new faces appear, one an older cop and another a woman in blue with a medic patch on her shoulder. She's wearing bright blue latex gloves.

"Son," the cop says. "What's your name?" He fishes around my pockets. I think he's looking for my wallet.

"Rob..." Breathing's harder than it should be. "Robert Quidell." I try to point at the apartment building. I was almost home. Why didn't I make it home? "I live there."

The cop looks over his shoulder. "What unit?"

"3E. My girlfriend..." Why can't I talk?

The cop yells something over his shoulder. The woman wearing the blue gloves puts a mask over my face.

I hear the screaming.

Isa's *screaming*.

CHAPTER 29

Isolde

The waiting room of the University hospital smells like puke and bleach and dirty diapers. The television blasts some stupid daytime show. Canned laughter blares from the speakers and hits my eardrums as a concussive wave of emotionally manipulative noise.

I want to punch something. Someone. Putting my fist through the wallboard might relieve some of my anxiety but it won't help Rob.

Mack paces. He's on the phone with Rob's brother Dan and I'm pretty sure they're making plans for Dan and Tom to fly in tonight.

Rob's been in surgery for two hours. The doctors won't give us information even though I rode in the ambulance, but they will talk to Rob's brothers, so Dan is telling us everything. Rob lost a lot of blood. The slash runs across his entire stomach but the puncture looks to have missed his organs. The doctors say no major damage. But they need to check. And sew him up.

I almost lost him, keeps spinning through my head. At the end of our two weeks, I would have at least known he's alive.

But he's going to be okay. He *has* to be okay.

I'm up, off the ugly orange burlap of the waiting room couch and pacing right alongside my brother. How did this happen? Rob was out in broad daylight on a busy street. The perp snatched his phone. Why did he need to slash too?

Mack touches my arm. "Dan will be here around midnight. One of us will need to pick him up."

I nod. I'm not really paying attention.

"He can sleep in Rob's room."

I nod again. A doctor in scrubs appears in the waiting room and I don't really care about the sleeping plans of another Quidell man.

The doctor who walks into the waiting room is a short, skinny guy. Muscular too, like a cyclist. He saunters over and stands in front of us with his feet apart and his fists in his waist like he's a superhero. Or a cowboy. Or a superhero cowboy.

Or a narcissistic workaholic cowboy surgeon. At least he's got enough of an ego to always be correct. Which means he more than likely stitched up my boyfriend correctly.

"You are Mr. Quidell's girlfriend and his roommate? The nurses tell me his brother faxed the consent to allow me to talk with you about his recovery." The doctor extends his hand. "Dr. Patel."

I shake his hand. He looks genuinely relieved to be talking to us. I don't think he likes dealing with family out of state.

Mack waves his phone. "I'm talking to Dan right now."

Dr. Patel nods. "Mr. Quidell is stable. He is in Recovery and we'll move him to the post-op ICU shortly." He turns away from Mack and addresses me directly. "If you wish to stay tonight, you will need to make arrangements."

Mack throws me a disapproving look, but doesn't argue.

"Thank you," I say.

Dr. Patel drops onto one of the waiting room chairs and motions for us to sit, as well. Mack sits on the couch across from the doctor and I plop down next to my brother, my ass on the edge of the cushion, and try very hard not to tap my foot. What if Rob's not okay? What if the doctor is only telling me this to keep me calm?

But that's not how surgeons work. Protecting people's feelings isn't important. Sewing up body parts is.

Dr. Patel drops his elbows to his thighs and leans forward, toward Mack and me. "He required several units of blood. No major damage. Thirty-seven sutures." He sniffs and waves at Mack's phone. "We've started antibiotics and anti-inflammatories. He's lucky he's as strong as he is. He responded quickly and with the correct rotation away from the assailant to protect his organs."

The unsaid words weigh heavy in the air between the doctor and Mack and I: *Any deeper and his guts would have been all over the pavement.*

Any deeper and your boyfriend would be dead.

I can't stop the hiccup. Nor can I stop the suck in of my breath. Or the tears.

Mack wraps his arm around my shoulder but talks to Dan on the phone. "I'll pick you up." A pause. "Isa's staying."

He gives me a little squeeze.

Dr. Patel nods once. "I estimate a week before he will be cleared for release. We will watch the wound and make sure it is healing well. Once he's home, he can't be up and around. No extra walking. No power lifting or skiing, either." He grins at his joke. "And I suggest six to eight weeks before he returns to classes."

Mack nods. "Thanks, Doctor."

We watch the skinny Dr. Patel swagger back into the halls of the hospital. Rob's going to need care for at least two months.

Not two weeks.

Six weeks beyond the point in time where I was going to accept the most important opportunity of my career.

We were going to talk. I was going to suggest, perhaps, we try long distance until the end of summer. Then regroup before school starts in the fall. Decide if we can honestly do this. Or if my sexy gorgeous boyfriend needs more touch than I am able to offer.

More contact, more caring, more support than globetrotting me can provide.

Rob's degree is as important as my photography career. I figure I'd commute. And when he's done with his coursework, maybe, just maybe, he might consider moving to California.

But I'd need to be making enough money to support both of us.

Which means I need this job. But he's going to be recovering for six to eight weeks.

Mack pats my leg. "Dan will be here tonight. I'll bring him around tomorrow morning."

I nod.

"Listen, he'll want to take Rob home to Minnesota until he fully recovers." Mack frowns and stares down the hallway Dr. Patel vanished into.

Where Rob would spend his recovery hadn't crossed my mind, but Mack's right. Rob needs to be with his family, not here in a student apartment.

Mack pats my shoulder. "I need to go to the department. We need to find someone to teach his section. And I need to get the paperwork started to set up incompletes for him for this semester."

My brother stands up and rubs the top of his head. After a moment, he frowns and adjusts his glasses. "Tell Rob I have the department under control."

I nod again.

"Are you going to be okay here by yourself?" Mack digs around in his pocket for his car keys.

"I won't go outside by myself if that's what you're worried about." The hospital is on the opposite side of campus from the apartment. It's a half hour walk. But Mack's question wasn't about leaving me here without transportation.

Mack shakes his head. "That's not what I meant."

No, it's not. "Are you worried I'm going to pull a Dad?" Because I think deep inside I'm worried I'm going to channel our father and retreat from the entire situation. Retreat from Rob.

Mack's expression says very clearly that I'm right. And, I think, that his worry was the underpinning of his anger when I fell through the door into the apartment last night.

"Why would you think that, brother?" I shouldn't snarl. Now is not the time for me to be fighting with Mack.

He frowns and looks at the floor. "I'll be back in the morning with at least Dan. Not sure if Tom is coming tonight or not."

So Mack's avoiding. I watch him for a long second, not at all surprised.

"Call me if there's issues." Mack twirls his keys around his finger. "Let me know when he wakes up, okay?"

I nod again. "We're both stronger than our parents, Mack." Neither of us needs to fall into the narcissistic bullshit that's kept our parents in serial relationships their entire lives.

"I used to think that when Lisa and I dated." Mack scratches at his stubble. "You know how that turned out."

Yes, I do. Sacrifices weren't going to be made even though they ended up at the same school. And, at least according to Lisa, they tried. Communicated. But professional life is professional life.

And here I thought I could make it work with Rob across two time zones.

"I'll text as soon as I pick up Dan."

Mack squeezes my shoulder again and walks away, down the hall toward the hospital entrance.

CHAPTER 30

Robert

I don't open my eyes but I hear beeps and buzzes and indistinct chatter. Feel air blowing up my nose. My tongue sits like a weight in my mouth more than functions to taste. When someone shuffles and a curtain rattle-shrieks open, I still won't look around.

"Mr. Quidell?" A maternal hand touches my forehead before moving to my shoulder and I know part of my brain thinks it belongs to Mom. But it doesn't. And I'm lying in a hospital bed watching my body from behind closed eyes as it processes smells and touches and thinking that it's a little boy again. Because that would mean Mom and Jeanie are still here. And I almost didn't die, too.

"Can you hear me? You're in Recovery. We'll be moving you soon." The nurse touches my face again. "Your girlfriend is here."

Isa? The muscles around my eyes don't want to cooperate. They don't want to raise my lids and they don't want to focus my eyes. But I make them, because Isa's here.

"Hey, handsome." Isa runs her finger over my cheek. "Doc says no skiing for at least eight weeks."

All sensation of Mom vanishes. I'm floating on antiseptic hospital noises and I think someone stabbed me but my girlfriend's here. I blink because my eyes refuse to adjust but my girlfriend's with me.

"I love you." I have no idea if I say it or just think it, but I'm pretty sure Isa hears me.

"Oh, Rob." Isa kisses my cheek.

Her expression might be surprised, or it might be angry. Or she might be happy. I can't tell.

Behind her, the woman who touched me like Mom and must be the nurse, smiles. She's a round woman wearing round green scrubs and a round blue puff of plastic hair constraint on her head. She leans close and winks. "All the nurses think you're a keeper, young man." Her hand waves at my chest.

"What?" My chest?

Isa snickers. "She's referring to your mark of boyfriend-hood."

"Oh." I remember writing something on my skin. "I love you." She needs to know how I feel. I almost died.

Isa bites her lip. "I love you, too."

She loves me. "Will you marry me?" I almost died. I can't live life regretting losing her.

The nurse chuckles as she fiddles with the tubing running in and out of my body. Isa, though, blinks rapidly.

"When I'm done with school I'll get a good job and you won't have to travel anymore." She won't be out there waiting to get in a car crash. Or knifed. "We'll buy you studio space. You can take photos wherever we land."

The rapid blinking turns into a full rounding of eyes and mouth. Is she shocked? She shouldn't be shocked. I almost died.

"Hey there, young man." The nurse is throwing me a stern maternal look. "You're not thinking clearly because of the meds in your system, so be careful, huh? Don't pull the pretty stitches Dr. Patel wove into your belly." She runs a thermometer over my forehead.

Isa's sitting back in her chair, still wide-eyed. Still as round as the nurse and her plastic puff of hair containment. "I think we need to talk about this when you're... coherent."

"I want to marry you." I don't feel my arm reach for Isa but the nurse stops me from twisting. I glance at my wrapped-up, IV-encrusted wrist. "I love you and I almost died."

The nurse pats my shoulder. "No, you did *not* almost die. You'll have a showroom-worthy scar but the EMTs got you here in plenty of time."

The nurse leans toward Isa. "We see this all the time. In two hours, either he won't remember what he's saying or he'll be so embarrassed he'll try to crawl under his bed, so don't be too freaked out."

Isa nods but doesn't stop making the round expression at me.

I don't care what the nurse says. I *know* I almost died. "I'll remember. I love you. Will you marry me?"

"Rob, please don't. We'll talk about it later, okay? You need to rest." Isa pats my arm.

She doesn't move closer. She doesn't blink. She looks as stiff as the splint on my IV arm.

The nurse glares at me and makes a small *Quit it* shake of her head.

"But..." I'm suddenly very tired. Tired like I ran a marathon. Or got knifed in the belly. I close my eyes.

When I look again, Isa and the nurse are talking outside my curtained-off recovery area. I can't hear them, but I see the nurse squeeze Isa's arm. Isa hiccups and wraps her arms around her chest.

She glances up at me but she won't look at my face.

And I don't understand why.

CHAPTER 31

Isolde

The ICU waiting room smells like turpentine. The chairs squeak and the lights flicker. But I need to be someplace by myself for a couple of minutes.

I can't leave. I promised Mack. And what would that say to Rob if I just up and vanished? What kind of girlfriend would I be?

The kind who's terrified by the demands of her white-picket-fence-wanting boyfriend.

The nurse said Rob babbled because of the anesthetics and the pain killers. That he'll be back to normal by morning and probably begging for my forgiveness. But I don't know. If he wasn't thinking it, he wouldn't have said it. And some of his words made my stomach lurch.

My gut gyrated and jumped as if I got knifed, not Rob.

Did he understand what he said? *Settle down, Isa. Become a good little wife.*

"Oh my God," I breathe.

I'm overreacting. I *know* I'm overreacting, but I can't help but see my mom's flat expression anytime she speaks about her career. About her camera or her brief year and a half photographing wildlife in northern Canada. About the polar bears and the moose.

Rob asked once why Mom's house didn't showcase my photos. It doesn't showcase her photos, either.

It showcases Dad's surgical career.

I pinch the bridge of my nose and try very hard not to rock back and forth. "Oh my God," I breathe again. How do I handle this?

A nurse swings around the corner into the little alcove where I'm hiding out. She's young, probably my age, with pretty blue eyes and a bouncy brown ponytail. "Ms. Wellington?"

I look up. "Yes?"

"I made up the cot in Mr. Quidell's room." She points over her shoulder.

I'm sleeping here tonight. Someone needs to be here. To keep an eye on Rob. He needs care, now. "Thanks," I say.

Machines beep and pumps whiz but he's sleeping soundly when I come in. The nurse said that if he wakes up they can increase his pain meds, but she figures he'll sleep until morning.

Quietly, I wash my face in the room's sterile bathroom and brush my teeth with the tiny, flimsy hospital-provided toothbrush.

The cot's lumps press into my back and neck but it'll do. I just need to remember what the nurse said: He'll be embarrassed in the morning. And we'll laugh it off.

But I don't know.

I don't know if I can.

⬧

ROB'S BROTHER DAN IS THE LARGEST MAN I HAVE EVER MET. HE'S A good four inches taller—and wider—than Rob. He's also just as square-jawed and handsome, but a lot less scruffy. His head of chocolate brown hair sits tidy and well-trimmed next to his scalp. He stands with me in the wide, too-bright hallway outside Rob's room and watches the world with the same blue-green ocean eyes.

Rob said Dan used to be a firefighter. I swear the first thing Dan did when he and Mack walked onto the ICU floor was to make sure he knew the locations of all the exits.

I can tell he's trying not to be imposing.

He glances into Rob's room. We're in sight of the nurse's station out here in the hall. Two of the nurses are trying very hard not to watch over the countertop. Dan obviously gets his share of the stares, as well.

"Ms. Wellington," he says. His giant hand engulfs mine when he reaches out to shake. He's got the same smooth, warm baritone as Rob, as well.

"Sorry we had to meet this way," I say.

Behind us, in the room, Rob stirs. Dan squeezes my hand and walks by, his attention diverted. I watch him pull a chair around and drop next to his brother.

Mack touches my elbow. "Tom will fly in when Dan goes back to Minnesota. They want to make arrangements to get his stuff. Dan wants to take him home as soon as the doctors okay a plane trip."

"What are you going to do with the apartment?" My brother's rent effectively just doubled.

Mack shrugs. "I might list for a new roommate. Or not. Depends on what Rob wants to do."

I can tell he's anxious about it.

In the room, Dan laughs and squeezes Rob's shoulder.

"I need to go back to California, Mack." I blurt it out all high-pitched and as anxious as Mack seems to be about the apartment.

My brother inhales slowly, and exhales even slower. His mouth twists and untwists as if he doesn't know what to say. "I think Rob's the one you need to talk to about that."

He's right. I do. I also told Rob that I love him.

Which I do. But, I think, I need space.

"Just be careful about causing him extra stress." Mack points over his shoulder. "I'm going down to the cafeteria. You want me to get you something?"

I give my brother my order and follow him into the room to ask Dan. And I watch as the men make food-eating plans.

Rob lies on his crumpled hospital bed, turned on his side, and watches me more than his brother. When Dan asks to go with Mack, Rob waves him away.

And reaches for my hand.

CHAPTER 32

Robert

My brother Dan pulls a chair toward my bed and sits his big ass down across from my head. "Nurses say you only get one day on the costs-more-per-hour-than-a-Porsche floor." He waves at my room. "Then it's off to a regular person's room."

If anyone knows about hospitals and costs and all that bullshit, it's Dan. He spent two months in the burn ward after his accident.

"Why didn't you tell me the pain meds were this good?" I'd sit up on the bed but the nurses won't let me and my belly doesn't want to bend.

"They alter parts of your brain you don't think they're altering." Dan laughs and clasps my shoulder. "The doc won't let you take the meds home when you leave, so don't get *too* used to them."

I want to make some snarky comment but my brain's not up to it, so I shrug. "I'll miss the pretty robes, though."

Dan laughs again, but this time he leans close, his face serious. "The pain meds stop being nice when you don't need them anymore. Remember that."

I sniff. "Geez, you look like you think I'll do something stupid."

Dan sits back. "Why would I think that?"

I close my eyes. They took the oxygen tube thing out from under my nose when they moved me onto this floor, but I'm still surrounded by buzzing, wheezing machines. At least my beeps are strong and rhythmic.

And so is my tendency toward bratty behavior. Dan's warning comes only because I have a track record. Not with drugs or things mostly illegal, but it's there. And he's been dealing with it all his life.

"I'm trying to grow up, Dan." I'd roll over but the nurses don't want me to do that, either.

Dan twists his lips and glances into the hallway. "I like Isa. She's nice. And concerned about you."

"I said something in Recovery. The nurse said I probably wouldn't remember." *Shit.* I do. "Motherfucker." I slam my hand into the mattress.

"What'd you do this time, Robert?" Oh, the number of times I've heard that tone of voice from my dear brother. Every time I pulled a penalty playing soccer while we were kids. That one time I made the neighbor girl cry. But she deserved it. She was spreading rumors about Tom. I made sure her mouth bit her in the ass.

And now I'm wondering if what I said in Recovery is about to bite me in the ass, big time. "I told her I love her."

Dan grins and shakes his head. "Well, that might or might not go over well."

"It probably would have been fine, if I hadn't asked her to marry me." I'm an idiot.

Dan laughs. "It's going to be fun watching you clean up this mess."

"It's not funny." It's not. She withdrew. Goddamn it, she clearly, completely withdrew from me when I said I wanted to marry her.

What the hell did I do?

Dan watches Isa and Mack outside the room more than he watches me. "I take it Ms. Wellington thought your proposal was med-fueled and inappropriate?"

"I don't know." I don't know shit anymore. "She's going back to California. She has a wonderful opportunity to advance her career. It's big. She can't miss it. We were going to talk about trying a long distance relationship."

Dan looks like he wants to sigh. His face draws down and his corners of his mouth make a father-frown. But he nods. "I'll talk to the doctors. Mack, too. We'll figure out the best way to deal with your recovery. I'd like you to come home. But if that doesn't work, we'll see what we can do. Maybe Dad will come up from Sedona. Who knows?" He sits back and sniffs, still watching Isa more than me. "But you can't go to California, Robert. Not until you're healthy and done with your schooling."

"Yes, Dad." At this point, I'm not sure Isa would want me in California, anyway.

Mack knocks on the door. "Hey, Dan, I'm getting food. Want to come along?"

Dan pats my shoulder. "Your only option is to talk to her about it." He pushes back his chair.

"When did you come to the conclusion that communication is the best course?" When I left after Bart's birthday party, Dan was in full not-talking-about-it mode with his girlfriend, Camille.

Dan pulls his wallet out of his pocket and checks his cash, I'm assuming to see what he can afford in the cafeteria.

"Therapist." He sniffs but seems satisfied with his fund supply. "Doing the needed work." He stuffs his wallet back into his pocket. "I'll be back in an hour or so."

My brother and my roommate wave, and disappear into the hallway.

Isa, though, stands in the door, watching me.

CHAPTER 33

Robert

She sits in the chair Dan pushed back from the bed. She doesn't move it closer. She stays too far away to touch.

The machines around my head beep and buzz. I don't hurt too much at the moment, but the dressings around my belly feel tight. The stitches and staples in my flesh constrain.

Pretty soon, the slash is going to start stinging. And, I suspect, that little energy boost that came with the fresh and happily donated blood pumping in my body will wear off. I'll be lying here wrapped like a mummy with only my own sad body to keep me company.

"Doc said it could have been a lot worse," I say.

A small grin appears on Isa's perfect lips.

"Nothing important got pierced." Lucky me only got slashed.

"If you need anything, or if Bart needs anything after I go back to California, or if you want to talk, text me. Or call. Okay?"

Is she breaking up with me? *Fuck*, I think. She already decided. I see it on her face. "What happened to our two weeks?"

Isa blinks and frowns and her shoulders slump. "I haven't left yet. You'll be out before I go. I just…"

She trails off and looks away, out the window.

"What, Isa?" What's going on here? I can't parse her responses. I'm suddenly too tired from talking to Dan. And too spaced on my meds.

"We're friends," she says. "I want us to stay friends. But I need to go to California. This job is a make or break for me. I can't stay here."

"I know. I don't want you to pass up an opportunity that's going to catapult you where you need to be, Isa. I'll do anything you need to help get you there."

Isa looks at her hands. "Anything, Rob?"

Anything? My brain freezes up. The fatigue suddenly rolls over me like a wave of hot, humid air and I can't think. I'm not processing. "Isa, I'm not thinking well, here. Can we talk about this later?"

After a long moment, she nods. "I'm sorry I brought it up now."

"It's the meds." I think I must have closed my eyes for a moment. When I open them again, she's leaning over me.

"Go to sleep," she says.

"Okay." But part of me cringes. Part of me thinks she's never coming back. "Miss you already," I whisper.

Isa's breath hitches. But she kisses my cheek anyway. "You *are* a keeper, Rob. For someone, even if that someone isn't me."

"What?" She said something I didn't catch.

But I don't think it was good.

I hear her shoes on the tile floor and I hope she's giving me another good-bye kiss. One that says *I'll be back later.* But that's not what I hear.

When I open my eyes again, I'm alone in my whining, beeping hospital room.

OVER THE NEXT WEEK, ISA BRINGS ME ARTICLES I ATTEMPT, BUT fail, to read with my med-crossed eyes. We do puzzles and word searches together. I do my best to quiz her about her travels and spend most of my waking time staring at her pretty photos.

We don't talk about what she meant by *Anything, Rob?* It's... too much right now. But she's here. She didn't completely withdraw.

Dan leaves, citing work. Tom arrives and trades off sitting at my bedside with Isa and Mack. A few friends stop by to check on me, all as equally wide-eyed as they are freaked out. Classmates deliver assignments and balloon bouquets from the department. I'm set to take the rest of the semester at the pace I need. All my professors agree and are helping out.

Cops ask questions. Attorneys offer no answers. I mostly sleep and feel tired. The slash alternates stinging like a son of a bitch and aching as if Satan himself crawled into my gut. The nurses give me more pain meds to make it stop, but *everything* stops, and I wonder if I can even handle incompletes.

So I ask Isa to show me more photos, because at least then I'm thinking about beautiful things.

The doc says I'm healing remarkably fast. The shit they swab onto the slash smells like bug killer but it gets the job done. I'm suffering very little inflammation. No infections, either. So they're going to send me home in a day or two.

I'll need to use a wheelchair for a week or so. No walking up the steps until I'm cleared by the docs either, so I get to ride our building's rattling, mildew-smelling elevator. Tom rolls his eyes and calls me a whiner when I tell him I don't like being in a windowless box hanging from some random cable. But he nods because I know he doesn't like elevators any more than I do.

They send me home with a strong prescription and orders to continue with my newly formed sleep habits. Mack drives. Tom and Isa sit in the backseat, courteously chatting about Bart and Tom's art career. I listen, chiming in only every so often, as I try not to look too sick because the bumps and sways of the drive pull on my stomach like I'm on a fair ride.

Tom pushes my rented wheelchair through the building's back door and up the first floor hallway. It's dark down here, darker than our floor, and kid noises bounce through the super's apartment door.

"Mack says he told the super you were coming home today." Tom sniffs and keeps pushing me forward. Like Dan, Tom needs to stoop to push the wheelchair. They're both taller than me, and wider. I'm the runt.

Isa did the same blinking *oh my God you're so big* expression with Tom that she did with Dan. And like a lot of people, she seemed fascinated by how well he paints, considering the size of his hands.

I got a bit jealous. I couldn't help myself. Tom, though, took it in stride. Spent a lot of time chatting up Sammie to Isa. Said his fiancé wants to start an official artist's representation and promotion company, and that she'd love to talk to Isa.

Tom pushes the elevator button. He leans against the wall with his hands in the pockets of his jeans, my giant eighteen-months-older-than-me big brother. "So, Isa's not your girlfriend anymore?"

Shit, I think. "What she say?" Because she hasn't said shit to me.

"I don't think she wants to stress you."

"So you're doing it for her?" My brother's got an eye for body language. Much better than mine. Especially right now, with the drugs in my system.

And the fact I don't want to think about it.

We have three days left before she leaves. Three days I hoped we'd talk. *Shit*, I think again.

Tom stands straight. "We talk about Bart, not you." He shrugs. "She does a lot of avoiding. Which made me wonder, that's all."

The door pings and glides open. Tom wheels me into the dark confines of our building's vertically climbing coffin and we both frown. I fucking hate elevators.

"Dan told me about the issue you two had in Recovery." Tom taps his finger on the handle of my chair. The vibration snaps through the back and into my spine. "Just realize you may need to talk about it several times before the problem is settled."

I hear a semi-groan. I don't think this is completely about Isa.

"And then you'll need to revisit." Another semi-groan fills the elevator. "Maintenance."

I crank my neck around and look up at my frowning my brother. "You sound more married than Dan."

Tom shakes his head as the elevator door slides open, but doesn't say any more. Isa's standing at by the door, waiting.

She grins too, and points at my face. "You got him to smile."

Tom wheels me out. "That's because we were talking about you."

I don't know if he winked at Isa, or smiled, but his tone sounds genuine. And I swear she blushes.

CHAPTER 34

Isolde

Dinner the first night Rob's home consists of an ordered pizza topped with every form or savory ground-up animal available from the pizzeria, as well as chunks of what I suspect are mushrooms and onions. It's tasty and filling, and I spend the rest of the evening on the couch next to Rob wishing I'd eaten two fewer slices than I did.

Before bed, Tom moves his suitcase into my room. And I move into Rob's.

I'm weak. I should sleep on the couch but our two weeks aren't up. And someone needs to keep an eye on him.

And...

I'm going back to California. Responsible Brain nags me to act like a grown-up but Rob doesn't need the extra stress.

Even for the few days we have left. I need Rob. I need to be near him because professional life is about to step between us and call an end to our special time. I can't be the good little wifey. But I can, at least for the rest of our two weeks, be a good girlfriend.

Rob doesn't want to go back to Minnesota. His doctor is here and he has access to the University physical therapy department. Tom doesn't seem all that happy about it, but he shrugs and makes Rob promise to come home for the summer.

The sunset spreads golden-red light through Rob's room. I help him sit on the edge of his bed. He closes his eyes as obvious pain plays over his handsome face. The red hue of the light streaming through the window doesn't help and for a second I swear he looks like he's about to curl into a ball.

Or maybe it'll be me clutching my knees weeping.

What am I doing? How is it that I think this is a good idea? But...

I miss him already. It's going to end and I won't be coming back to the man who loves me and I know I'm going to spend the next three months crying myself to sleep every night.

Rob pats the bed. "Sit down."

I drop next to him. He watches me carefully, his beautiful eyes showing as much concern for me as they do for the ache in his flesh.

Slowly, he weaves his fingers into mine. "I'm going to miss you," he whispers. "A lot."

"Oh, Rob." I tuck myself in between his side and his arm and wrap my arms around his chest. "We'll talk, okay? Lisa and Mack are still friends. We can be, too."

Rob's lips glide over my forehead but his body vibrates. From anger? From pain? I don't know.

"So that's it, Isa? We're breaking up?"

I nod against his shoulder. "I'm going back to California in a few days." How do I say this? "I need..."

I think he wants to yell at me. I think he wants to pound on the wall and throw his nightstand light across the room. Because I think he knows what I'm about to say.

"You said 'I want to marry you.'" I back away. "Marrying me isn't a good idea." He deserves someone more in tune with his needs. "I'm not good at settling down."

He closes his eyes. "Don't blame me for wanting to share my joy about not dying. Blame the meds."

I hiccup. He *is* angry.

But he should be. *I* would be. Maybe I am.

When I don't answer, he opens his eyes.

His expression changes instantly from the hard tremor of anger to a wide-eyed concern. "Isa, don't cry. How is it that I make the woman I love want to burst into tears? Don't—"

My words burst out in a single breath. "You wouldn't have said what you did if somewhere deep inside you weren't thinking that way."

Rob leans back. His face moves out of the reds and oranges and golds of the sunset and into shadow. "Why is loving you a bad thing, Isa?"

Loving isn't the issue. "Don't ask me to sacrifice my career for yours." I wipe away a tear.

When did I start crying? Why can't I hold it together around Rob? My body feels as if I got the slash, not him.

"When did *Marry me* become a death sentence? Why would I ask you to sacrifice any part of your career? You're beyond talented."

The emotions swirling through my brain and my body make me nauseous. They're calling up memories from my parents' split and I see my therapist's office in California. I see the warm orange-red of the walls and smell the soothing sandalwood aromatherapy she always doused the room in. I feel the sun's heat on the breeze from her open windows. I see her face. I hear her voice: *Are you seeing what's in front of you, Isa? Are you looking?*

I'm a photographer. I'm a scientist. And I very clearly see what's coming.

So I stuff those nauseating emotions back into the pocket universe from which they escaped.

"You said 'When I get a job, we'll get you studio space.'" I sit up tall, because I need to be strong. "I know what that means. You intend to become a professor, like Mack. You're going to do the post-grad one year appointment move-around from one university to the next for what, five, six years until you get an associate professor position? Where?"

"I won't know until I graduate where positions are available. That's how it works."

"This is why Mack and Lisa broke up. They'd have to separate when they graduated, so they ended it before they combined their lives to the point it would tear them apart when they split." But it did anyway. I don't think my brother's recovered yet.

I don't know if I will either, when I leave in a few days. Why did I agree to two weeks? Why can't I control my impulses?

For the first time since meeting him, I don't think I can read Rob. It doesn't help that he won't look at me.

"Let's say we do get married." I'm whispering now. And trying not to sob. "I can't spend my life in isolation. I can't just take snapshots of the pretty flowers and do high school graduation pictures for the locals."

"That's not what I meant."

But I think it is. Rob looks more defeated, more exhausted, then incredulous.

Then something else rolls up to my surface. A terrible, tiny voice. One I didn't realize had been whispering to me all this time. "How long are you going to be willing to live with me traveling all the time? What happens when the department secretary flirts with you? Are you going to have a threesome with some buxom cowgirl and the local librarian because you're lonely? When I get home, are you going to ask for an open relationship because you're living that way anyway?"

I wipe away another tear. "Because that's not going to happen."

Rob turns away. His shoulders. His chest. His eyes. Every molecule of Rob backs away from me. "I like your other fantasies better."

What did I just do? I jump off the bed. I can't be this close to him. I can't see him suffering this way.

"I can't argue with you anymore." Rob waves me away. "I need to sleep."

I look at the floor. The only movements either of us make is to breathe in, then out.

In, then out.

"I'm not as immature as you think I am, Isa."

Rob rolls away and all I see are the last of the sunset's reds playing over his back.

CHAPTER 35

Isolde

Mack flicks the signal and changes lanes. I rebooked my flight to an earlier day. Seemed to be the kindest thing to do.

Rob will find a nice new girlfriend in no time. One who doesn't mind tagging along to Middle America University and who is willing to accommodate his career.

I don't have that option.

"What you did was cold, Isa." This from the man who gave me shit for giving into my desires in the first place.

"I said good-bye." If I'd been stronger, if I hadn't let my fantasies get the best of me, if I'd talked to Rob about my career before I slept with him, none of this would have happened.

But we also would not have had our brilliant few days together.

"I suppose you did."

"He knew I'd be leaving anyway."

Mack scratches at his cheek stubble.

"It's better this way, Mack." It is. "What if we'd gone the two weeks and made plans and accommodations and in a year he drops the whole

'Let's live in this university town!' bomb? I'm not doing that. I'm not going to become Mom."

Mack pulls into the parking ramp. I'm leaving for good so he wants to walk in with me. "So you've decided to become Dad instead?"

"No." I glare at him. "I'm ending it before there's any chance of cheating. Or children."

"Or responsibility." Mack pulls the key from the ignition.

I throw open my door but grab it before it slams into the sedan in the next space over. "I'll text you when I land."

"Will you at least explain to Rob why you're doing this?" He slams his door, too.

I lean against the car. Exhaust fumes fill the ramp and I'd like to go inside. Not that the inside of the airport smells any better. "Does it matter anymore?"

"To me? No. But I can tell you right now that it damn well matters to Rob." Mack opens the trunk and pulls out my bag. "At first I thought you getting involved with him was the worst idea you've ever had. He can be... immature. But damn it, Isa, I think when the meds wear off and he realizes you aren't coming back it's going to fillet his heart. Not just break it, but shred it into bleeding strips."

I pull out my suitcase. A loud *shink* echoes off the concrete pillar in front of the car when I yank up the handle. I think it's echoing off my heart, too.

Because I think I just *shinked* Rob and me. And maybe Mack, too. "What do you want, Mack? For me to tell you we can overcome our nurture with our nature?" Because I've seen what our nurture leads to. "Smart and talented doesn't always overcome the shit life throws at us."

"No, Isolde, I want you to use your smarts to figure out how to overcome those shitty little moments of nurture planted in the backs of our brains." Mack slams the car's trunk and the entire frame shakes.

A big pick-up truck rolls by, looking for a space. The airport's constantly-droning, canned overhead announcements bounce off the ramp's concrete. And I'm about to walk away from the man I love.

Because he loves me too much.

"You and I had it shitty, Isolde. Be we did not have it Quidell shitty.

So maybe you should cut him some slack." My brother walks toward the skyway to the airport proper, my equipment pack on his back. "Maybe talk to him instead of accusing him of behaviors you don't know if he will commit."

But maybe I'm saving him from *my* future behaviors. *I can't stay here, Rob. I can't be tied down.*

Again, the nauseous emotions swirl up in my gut. And again, I stuff them away into their little pocket. I don't need them right now.

"I still have to leave!" I yell. "I have work!"

Mack glances over his shoulder. He doesn't respond, but I very clearly see on his face what he's thinking: *Just like Dad.*

Somewhere, out there, an airplane takes off carrying people to someplace or another. People leaving. People returning home. People with a calm place of roots and anchors. People a lot different from me.

Mack's right. But the sad thing about all this is that I know I'm right, too. And our rights don't overlap into the true correct path out of this situation.

So I'm taking the path I know will lead to the type of fulfillment I want the most. I'm going to photograph the world.

Alone.

CHAPTER 36

Robert

S he's not coming back.

Mack looked away when I asked him why and he mumbled something about family history. Then, out of nowhere, he hugged me and said he's sorry.

I wish she'd talk to me about why she's so scared.

Tom stayed for a couple of days, then flew home. My dad will be here tomorrow. But Isa's gone forever.

I think I cried myself to sleep last night. When Mack asked about it I said I need more painkillers.

I try to focus on my classes. Mack's helping me catch up in stats and a couple other students in the department come by every day with notes and assignments. One of my professors even worked with the department to set up a video conference link during class so I can participate.

Dan was right; the meds do make basic thinking difficult. But I need to try. I need to keep myself busy.

They caught the guy a month after he slashed my belly. He confessed to get a reduced sentence on another aggravated robbery charge. I haven't heard if he's going to be back on the street menacing people. I figured there's nothing I can do about it either way. My job from this point forward is to pay attention to the world around me. And, I think, to buckle down. Work harder. Make sure I make the most of what I've got.

My doctor pulled the staples out of my scar a couple days ago. They numbed it but feeling the metal yanked out of my skin was weird and nasty. Felt like someone had put down a very small vacuum cleaner nozzle to suck up my skin along the scar, then did it again. And again.

Doc said I can fly next week, if I want to. So I think I will go home for the summer. When I tell Dad, he nods and pats my shoulder and mumbles something about doing what's best for the family.

I don't have the energy to fix our father issues right now, so I don't try. I just wave when Mack takes him to the airport, too.

So I immerse myself in articles. And writing my next paper. And producing the slides to share with my afternoon class. I'm almost caught up, meds or no meds in my system. I figure a couple more hours tonight won't hurt.

Mack's finished his comps and is now officially All But Dissertation. It's teaching and data gathering for him from this point forward.

Keys rattle in the door lock and I look up from my studies and my spot on the couch. Mack walks in and immediately wags his finger in my general direction. "Why are you awake?"

"Hmm?" Carefully, I stretch out my legs. My physical therapist—a sweet middle-aged guy with a bald spot—has me rubbing some sort of scar-care stuff on the slash. It smells like horseshit, but it's helping with the pulling and tightening. Still, I need to be careful.

"Shouldn't you be sleeping like the invalid you are?" Mack tosses his keys on the coffee table and seats his ass next to mine.

Mack's been amazing. It's not like we were good friends before all the shit went down. I was just his kid roommate who started a fling with his sister. But he stepped up and took care of all the department paperwork and questions for me. Without his help, I probably would have had to drop out for the semester.

I'm fortunate, that's for sure.

"Studying. Almost caught up. I'm thinking I'll be able to go into campus and to take my finals on time." My therapist and my doctors want me to start "low impact exercise" again, which means walking. No rock climbing or soccer yet, but it's a start. As long as the scar doesn't hurt too much, I'm good.

Mack nods. "Finalized summer plans?"

I think he's worried I won't be around to pay rent over the summer, but hasn't wanted to ask because of the whole "stressing Rob" business. Which, I suspect, has more to do with his sister than my lovely scar at this point.

"I think I'll go home for a while. Can't TA until Fall Semester anyway." I shrug.

"Are you moving out?" Mack stares forward and doesn't look at me.

"Are you kicking me out?" Because this is the first he's insinuated that I may not be welcome. I close my textbook and set it on the table. It thumps louder than I intend it to, but Mack doesn't seem to notice.

"No. Would you be upset if Isa visits on Friday?"

Dumbfounded, I stare at Mack. Isa visiting is totally out of the blue. I know he's been talking with her but he's been kind and not doing it in the apartment where I can hear him.

"This week?" I ask. She must be coming to celebrate his ABD status. "She's willing to be in the same building with me?"

Mack's nose crinkles. "No. I lied and told her you were visiting your family for the weekend."

I snort. Which quickly turns to a chuckle. Which turns into a full-on laughter roar. "Oh my God that hurts." I wrap my hand over the scar.

Mack shakes his head, laughing too. "She totally deserves me fucking with her." His laugh turns into a loud, honking snort out of his nose. "It's payback for that time she told my first girlfriend I was secretly fucking the lonely housewife down the street."

"She did that?" Now I'm laughing uncontrollably. "And she says I'm the brat."

Mack pokes me in the arm. "Oh, you two are way too alike for your own good. That's why I yelled at you. If you haven't figured it out yet, you were sleeping with the female version of yourself." He snorts. "Except for the sex with every woman on the planet bullshit. Or the not pulling your nose out of your books. Or the lovely cheekbones and the pouty lips."

Mack makes a kissy face. "Or the fact that you're talentless and my sister has the gift." He rolls his eyes.

"That's not fair. I draw a mean happy face, so I'm not a complete hack." I can't stop laughing. I don't know if it's because it feels good to laugh, or because if I stop, I'll start crying.

Crying and yelling and ripping apart the couch cushions.

"She was afraid, Rob. We grew up with a mother who sacrificed her dreams to tend to our father's career. Then it fell apart and we dealt with a lot of drinking and random men." He shrugs.

"I'm not like that. I would never do that." Why didn't she talk to me about it?

Mack inhales sharply and cuts off his chuckles. "That's not what she heard in the hospital. At the time, I don't think you two talking would have done any good, anyway."

He pats my knee. "I'm picking her up tomorrow." Then frowns. "Mom says she cries herself to sleep every night."

"She does?" My words come out a whisper, reverent and real. I feel it in my chest. Around my heart. And until this moment, when the possibility that I'd see her again became tangible, I didn't realize how much I miss her.

Isa, another vanished woman I don't think about because I can't.

But she's coming back.

Mack nods. His words come out reverent and real, as well. "If I were you, I don't know if I could forgive her." His eyes look vacant and distant.

He's serious.

Isa isn't the only Wellington with trust issues.

"It's not about forgiving," I say. Forgiving is the easy part. "It's about growing out of the hurt." And learning not to let the hurt fester to the point where it coats the entire world with its slime. Or so I supposedly learned from my therapist, all those years ago.

"It's a lot harder to do than it is to say." I pat the couch cushion. "Maybe that's why I'm so easy, you know. With the forgiveness."

Mack snorts. "You're just *easy*."

Maybe I am. Maybe my family has an easy way about us. Tom's certainly easygoing. And Bart's quite the charmer....

A plan bubbles up. I grin and shake my head.

"What?" Mack looks rightfully suspicious.

"So, you okay with a little revenge?" Maybe the meds aren't cutting into all my brain spaces after all.

My roommate laughs. "Always, my friend. Always."

CHAPTER 37

Isolde

I'm pretty sure my brother's fucking with me. The whole "Oh, Rob's gone so let's celebrate me passing my comps," and "Oh, Rob flew to Minnesota so you can sleep in his bed," is total bullshit. The way he's trying not to smirk as he pulls into the lot behind the apartment building clinches it.

My brother thought he could pass off his ABD status as a reason to party so I'm about to come face to face with the man I jilted.

"I hate you, Mack." I slap the roof of the car. "This is *not* a good idea."

"It's a fine idea." Mack scowls. "You know what was a bad idea? You fucking my roommate in the first place. But we already discussed that, haven't we?" He pulls my bags out of the car. "So why don't you go upstairs and make nice with the guy you're going to end up seeing again sooner or later anyway. Because he's my friend and he lives here too and I am *not* flying out to Mom's place every time you need a freakin' hug."

Mack slams the car door and walks toward the building.

I look around, making sure no one's in the lot with us, and follow him to the back door. "Take me to a hotel!" This isn't fair. To me, to—

The door swings open.

"What's not fair, Isolde?"

Rob grips the door as if it's going to run away from him and launch itself into space. He wears baggy sweats and a huge t-shirt I suspect is his brother Dan's. He looks thinner, like he's lost some of his muscle tone. The smudges under his eyes cast a shadow of exhaustion, as does his scruffy, unshaven face.

He needs a haircut, too. But he's up and he's alive and he's made it through his ordeal intact.

Or mostly intact.

"A lot of life's not fair, Robert," I say.

He snorts and grins. Shaking his head, he moves to the side to let us pass.

I'm surprised, to be honest, that he didn't just lay into me the moment he opened the door. *I* would have laid into me the moment I saw me. I know I broke his heart.

But better I broke it before we'd combined our lives. Cleaner, this way. Less pain in the long run.

At least I'll keep telling myself that.

I move by and start up the stairs, but stop and look over my shoulder. "You okay walking up three flights?"

"Yes." Rob shakes his head again and slowly, steadily, starts up the steps.

I smack my brother's arm. "You let him climb steps like this?"

Mack's expression says he would have given me the finger if his hands weren't full. "Doctor cleared him for exercise."

"Sex, too." Rob doesn't glance over his shoulder at us, though I know he's smirking. I see it in his shoulders.

Mack snickers.

I think the boys are picking on me.

At the top of the stairs, Rob steps by the spot where he wrote "Isa's boyfriend" on his chest and continues his slow and steady pace toward the apartment door.

When he swings it open, I hear a little boy.

441

"Bart's here?" I ask. What are they doing, running an intervention on me?

I balk, refusing to step in. "What the hell is going on?"

Mack rolls his eyes and pushes me through the door.

Rob's laptop is open and sitting on the coffee table next to a pile of books.

On his computer screen, I see a room brimming with little artist toys: An easel. Multiple boxes of action figures and crayons and paints. And another open laptop, this one connected to the camera Rob gave Bart for his birthday.

I must be looking at the living room of Dan's house.

A little head bounces into the bottom of the frame. "Uncle Robby! Are you back?" The little head bounces in again. "Is Ms. Isa with you? I want to show her my pictures!"

"Dan set the webcam on top of the television." Rob walks into the living room. "Bart's figured out how to toggle, haven't you?" he calls.

"I have!" The screen switches to the web cam on the computer hooked to Bart's camera. "See?"

Five-year-old crystal blue eyes smile at me through the web cam and little Bart waves. "Hi, Ms. Isa! I took pictures." The camera and its cable wiggle.

A stream of photos blips by. Most are his classes at the Community Center. Several are a dark-eyed woman with black hair I think is Dan's girlfriend, Camille. A few are a five-year-old's angle up at Bart's very tall father.

They all show remarkable intuitive framing. He's learning how to use his camera's depth of field, too.

I drop my bag on the floor and kneel in front of the computer. "How are you, Bart?"

The display switches back to my little friend. "I graduated from the Community Center!" He jumps up and down but stops and looks over his shoulder. Quietly, he leans toward the computer. "Ms. Frazier moved in *for real* on Saturday," he whispers. "She's going to be my mommy."

I touch my mouth. He looks so happy I want to cry.

Or maybe I want to cry because I'm not moving in. For real.

"Uncle Robby is coming home this summer and we're going to the lake!" Bart bounces around again. "Uncle Tommy and Auntie Sammie are bringing Mr. Pickles!"

I glance up at Rob. "Mr. Pickles?" Does Tom have a horse I don't know about?

He nods toward the computer. "Cat."

"Ah."

"Will you come, Ms. Isa?" Bart bats his baby blues at me. "Please?"

There it is. I'm being expertly manipulated by the world's cutest five-year-old.

"Depends." I don't know why I say it. I should just say *No* and be done with it, but Bart's showing real talent.

And he's a great kid.

"Please?" He holds out his kid's camera. "Will you teach me how to take *good* pictures?"

Oh my God, I think. "Did your Uncle Robby put you up to asking me to come to the lake?"

Bart bats his eyelashes again and makes the unmistakable Quidell pout. "He said I'm supposed to say no if you ask."

Behind me, loud chortles burst from both Rob and Mack. I look over my shoulder. Rob smirks and shrugs.

Mack mouths *Don't be a douche. Tell Bart yes.*

From the laptop speaker, I hear a woman call from the kitchen behind Bart. "Is your uncle back?"

Bart points over his shoulder and smiles a huge smile. "My mommy."

Every little bit of anger and frustration that had been stewing in my gut melts away. How can I say no to Bart? No one with a soul could say no to that boy. "I have a shoot in California but then I can visit."

Or stay at home, alone in my crappy little loft. I frown.

"So you'll come to the lake?" Bart jumps up and down again. "Daddy! Ms. Isa's coming to the lake!"

I throw a *What the fuck did you just get me into?* look at Rob.

"Go get your daddy, Bart. So we can finalize plans." He looks right at me, one eyebrow cocked and his bad boy smirk all over his face.

You're terrible, I mouth.

Yes, I am, Rob mouths back.

"Okay!" Bart runs off.

"Only as a friend," I say. "I'm going to spend time with Bart."

Rob nods. "I know." Slowly, he drops onto the couch and waves good-bye to Mack, who walks off toward the kitchen.

I think Rob wants to groan as he settles into the couch. He's been through hell and how did I help? I ran off and left my brother to tend to the misery. "I'm sorry about what I did."

A sadness the exact opposite of Bart's joy descends over his face. "Good."

I feel my eyes narrow and my mouth thin to a flat line. "I know you're not okay with what happened."

"With what you *did*."

I deserve this. I do. "I'm sorry. I am. Do you want to talk about it?" He's not okay. I can tell. It's going to take him some time. It's going to take *me* some time. But maybe being friends will help.

"Yes." Rob shrugs and leans against the back of the couch. My grandparents' throw is still there, still soft and intricate, and I swear it's mocking me.

Why did you hurt him? it's asking. *Why didn't you try?*

"I'm here for a couple—"

"We do it on *my* timeline, not yours." He waves his hand in my general direction.

"What?" What does that mean? But Dan appears on the laptop before I have an opportunity to ask.

"Hey, Isa. How are you?" Dan asks. His smile looks as sad as Rob's. "I hear you're coming to the lake to teach the little master the fine art of photography."

"She is!" Bart bounces into the frame again.

Rob leans forward and the three of us make plans. I'm totally locked into this trip. There's no getting out of it, now. I'm off to a Minnesota lake to teach a brilliant five-year-old how to hold his camera.

Dan signs off and I wave good-bye to Bart.

It's going to be the best week of my life, I think.

I shake, wondering where that thought came from. Or why I would think it, especially with Rob's obvious anger.

Slowly, he closes his laptop. "I still miss you." His speaks hushed, as if Bart, or the world, might overhear. "I miss the time that was stolen from us, even if it would have been brief." Rob looks away. "I told myself seeing you would be good for me. That it'd be a nice dose of exposure therapy. I'd get used to Mack's mean sister again."

"We would have broken up anyway." I might as well be honest.

Rob chuckles and shakes his head. "Yes. As you decided already. For both of us."

I look away. My body feels as if it's crunching in on itself. Because he's right.

"I need to study." Rob looks like his scar hurts. "In my room. By myself. Though some days focusing through the meds makes it difficult."

"I'm sorry." I want to squeeze his hand but I don't dare touch. "I'm sorry you've gone through all this."

Rob absently scratches at his belly, right over his scar. "Maybe by the time you visit the lake, we can talk."

This time, I don't stop myself. I take his hand. "I'll see you again at the lake."

Rob stares at our hands. His fingers twitch as if he wants to wrap his digits through mine, and I think the dark circles under his eyes turn a deeper shade of purple. "If I text, will you talk to me?"

Responsible Brain screams *Clean break!* But Not-So-Responsible brain yells *You miss him as much as he misses you!*

And I'm weak. Head-to-toe, heart-driven weak.

"Yes," I say. "Every day, if you want to talk."

Every single day.

Rob nods. "Good night, Isa."

CHAPTER 38

Isolde

Every day, I wake up to a new text from Rob. Some are random quotes. Others, forwarded pictures from his little nephew. I think he's engaging in more of his "exposure therapy."

I throw on my clothes and I drive to the studio and some days, I shoot photos. Some days, I production assist. Some days, I edit. But every day I check my phone at lunch time, hoping to see what new wonder Rob's sent my way.

The second week after Mack's ABD celebration, Rob began texting questions about the many places I've visited. Asking things about the people and the cultures and if any of them interested me enough that I'd want to go back for an extended time to do in-depth work.

We video chatted. Turns out he's doing preliminary planning for his dissertation. His advisor wants to see a concrete idea of Rob's future by the time he returns in the fall.

He left for Minnesota the third week. I got a lot of lake photos. He's right; it is beautiful. I pack accordingly.

The fourth week, I borrow Mom's crossover hatchback with the storage space and the good gas mileage. The studio owner takes his vacation this month, so I'm taking mine, too. I'm driving through the Rockies, all under the guise of teaching the little master, and photographing the wilds on the way back to California.

It takes me four days to drive from Los Angeles to the wonder of green freshness that is Minneapolis and St. Paul. Dodging road construction and evening traffic, I settle in for the final four hour drive north to the Quidells' lake house.

I roll down my car's window as I slowly make my way along the dirt drive toward the house. The air here smells just as fresh, but heavier, than it did in the mountains. Insects and frogs buzz. Water laps a shore not too far off. Animals rustle in the trees. Something dog-shaped scurries out of the way of my headlights. Gravel crunches under the tires.

I feel as if I'm being drawn in by a giant magnet. Teaching Bart will be fun, but I know the real pull. The Quidell family has me in their orbit. *Rob* has me in his orbit. Maybe I need to admit it. Maybe I should settle in and enjoy the ride.

Enjoy this time of exposure therapy. Because ultimately, Mack's right. I'm going to see Rob again and again. He's my brother's roommate and friend. He's part of my life.

The car sways as I inch it down the drive, and I sway right along with it. I think I need to admit how much I want to be here. How much I've been looking forward to spending time with a functional family, even if it's the family of my ex-boyfriend.

The drive curves and opens into a wide, cleared area in front of a big, two story cabin that looks, architecturally, as if it was built quite a few decades ago, and added onto in the fifties or sixties. Natural cedar siding sucks in my car's headlights and make the cabin's shape slightly blurry, but I see a wide porch that I suspect circles the entire building.

Off to the side, down an open walkway toward the beach, the Quidells all sit around a big, roaring fire pit. Bart's off his dad's lap and running toward my car before I finish parking next to the other vehicles in the clearing.

"Ms. Isa's here!" Bart, dressed in what looks like superhero jammies, a hoodie, and hiking boots, bounds up the walkway, his arms wide, with Dan and Rob right behind him.

When I open my car door, I'm greeted with the nicest, strongest five-year-old hug I've ever experienced. He smells like bonfire and burned candy. I drop down to my knee and hug him back, though he's pretty tall for a kindergartner. "Hello, Bart."

"Daddy said I could stay up until you got here." Bart yawns. "You drove all the way from California?" He looks over my shoulder. "Did you bring your camera? I brought mine!"

My back complains about standing straight, but at least I don't have to drive anymore. "All my gear is in the back of the car."

Rob stops at the end of the car, watching me. Dan, though, steps up. He's wearing a long-sleeved t-shirt and cargo shorts, and big hiking boots, much like Rob. Grinning, Dan offers a quick hug. When he steps back, he places a hand on Bart's shoulder. "Bart, what did I say earlier?"

"Oh!" Bart stands tall. "Thank you for visiting our lake house, Ms. Isa. Thank you for being my teacher, too!" He offers his hand to shake, even though he just squeezed the life out of me with a hug.

I shake his hand. "You are welcome, Bart."

"Do you want a roasted marshmallow?" Bart points at the fire. "Mommy's making s'mores but I'm supposed to go to bed now." He frowns.

Rob pats Bart's shoulder, but he's still looking at me. "Let's get Ms. Isa's suitcases inside first, okay?"

"Okay!" Bart jumps up and down next to my car.

Tom, also dressed in a t-shirt and cargo shorts, saunters up and pats Rob on the shoulder. "Take Isa down to the fire and introduce her around." He nods toward the car. "Dan and I will take her things in."

Rob nods. "What do you say, Bart?" But he's still watching me more than anyone else. "Should we go get those s'mores?"

"Okay!" Bart takes my hand as if he's the only person allowed to touch me.

Grinning at Rob, I let Bart pull me by.

Dan opens the back of my car. "Your room is upstairs, first door on the left. You want everything in?"

"Please," I call. Bart's got me half way around the cabin by the time Tom and Dan start unloading.

Rob walks behind us with his hands in his pockets. "The drive tire you out?"

He's back to his normal level of scruffy, with his five-day beard and his messy, almost luminescent hair. He looks refreshed, too, less exhausted. The lake's done well by him.

Bart pulls me down the path. "A little," I say. "How are you doing?"

Rob points. "Watch your step."

"Oh!" I dance down a short set of stairs toward the long, wide dock. The big Quidell cabin comes with a small boathouse, a wide, flagstoned patio area bordering the pebbled beach, and a long dock. The fire pit sits at the edge of the patio, next to the sand.

Two women get up from camping chairs and wave. The taller of the two, the one with the auburn ponytail, must be Sammie. I recognize her from Tom's opening. The other dark-haired woman I recognize from Bart's photos.

She extends one hand toward me and another to Bart. "Camille," she says as we shake. "Bart, careful so Isa doesn't trip."

Next to me, Rob chuckles.

The other woman also offers a hand. "Sammie," she says.

"Hello," I answer. They're both quite beautiful, and very different from each other. I think I'll be getting some interesting photos.

Camille looks at Sammie, who looks at her. "We were just going in," she says. "Time for Bart to go to bed."

Camille makes a show of yawning. "We came up late last night and the little man here got us up early this morning, didn't you?" She ruffs Bart's hair.

"I heard Mr. Pickles meowing." Bart frowns.

Sammie smiles. "Rob said you're not allergic, correct?" She points at the house.

"Kitties are fine." I ruffle Bart's hair, too. "You get a good night's sleep, okay? I brought lots of stuff to do. We'll start tomorrow."

"Can I have another s'more?" Bart pouts.

Camille and Sammie look at each other, then both look directly at Rob.

"Tell you what," he leans toward Bart. "We'll do another fire tomorrow and make a lot of s'mores for everyone, okay? I think Ms. Isa is tired."

Bart yawns again, but doesn't argue. "Okay, Uncle Robby."

I think he really is tired.

Camille smiles and takes Bart's hand. "Good night." She takes Bart and Sammie with her toward the cabin's back screen door.

I watch them go. "I brought a stack of travel magazines and atlases, and a scrapbook, so Bart can help plan the return drive."

Rob's standing close enough I feel his warmth. The breeze flowing off the lake adds a misty chill to the air, and the water gently laps at the pebbles. The fire crackles and sparks twirl upward from its licking flames. In the circle, Dan and Tom chat about the cabin and, I think, about adding on studio space. But it's Rob who holds my attention.

"Bart will like that." He doesn't move.

I could wrap my arms around him if I wanted to. Right now. Out here, with his brothers in front of the cabin working diligently to bring the trappings of my life into theirs, and their soon-to-be wives tending to Bart in the kitchen, on the other side of the door.

"Do you want to go inside, with your family?" Instead of staying out here, with mean me.

Rob watches Camille through the window as she wipes Bart's face. "In a minute."

Inside, Tom walks into the kitchen. He curls an arm around Sammie and kisses her cheek. When she smiles, he waves to us through the window.

They vanish into the hallway.

"Your stuff must be in." Rob looks out over the lake. The fire crackles and he moves away, toward the camp chairs. "Want a marshmallow? Some water?" He holds up a bottle.

"Thank you for inviting me." My voice all but vanishes into the pops and snaps of the fire.

Rob looks out over the lake. "We're friends."

I sniff. He's looking away, thank God, and I don't think he notices. Because if he did, I'd fall apart right here.

I'm not over him. I wasn't when I left after the attack, and I wasn't when I visited for Mack's celebration. And I definitely wasn't on the four day drive through the mountains.

My brain made new fantasies. Begging ones, with Rob on his knees with his arms around my waist. Fuck-buddy ones where we ignore everyone and spend the next few days in the woods fucking under the bright sun. The fight ones, where we wrestle and get sweaty and I always win. Always ride him until a mind numbing orgasm shudders through his gorgeous body.

Or the one where we spend two days talking and kissing and making love.

Why was I so cruel? Why did I think two weeks was enough? Or that maybe, just maybe, long distance might work?

The screen door opens. Dan sticks out his head. "Gear's in your room. We locked your car." He points over his shoulder. "We'll see you at breakfast."

"There's only one shower in the house." Rob watches his brother shut the door. "There's another in the boathouse."

The firelight plays over his cheeks and when he sighs, I think it sets his pale eyes blazing. For a moment, Rob burns as bright as the bonfire.

The pull I felt driving up to the house wasn't from the lake. Or the Quidells in general. It came solely from Rob. From the magnetic connection I've felt for him since the moment we first met in the dead center of winter, in the cold, under his bee hat.

The symbol of family he doesn't need now, because he's embedded in it. Here, he's safe. He has Dan and Tom and Bart. No one's going to knife him here. Not physically.

Not emotionally, either.

Rob picks up a bucket and dumps it on the fire. "Let's get some sleep." When the fire vanishes, he offers his hand.

"Okay," I say, knowing full well that he's sleeping alone tonight.

But not alone. He has his family around him.

Me, he's keeping in a separate room, where I belong.

CHAPTER 39

Robert

Isa spends the next few days teaching Bart how to take photos. They sit on the dock with her magazines and her scrapbook and my nephew plans out my ex-girlfriend's overly circular route back to California.

Dan and Camille hold hands a lot. Tom and Sammie touch, but they seem edgy. And exhausted. They're both working two full-time jobs, with their corporate work and Tom's blossoming art career.

I take a lot of naps. And a lot of walks with Bart and Isa. We don't talk about why we broke up.

I'm being mean. I know it. Dan and Tom know it. Isa obviously wants to talk but I'm letting her stew.

A lot of things get hard, though, when she puts on her blue bikini and goes swimming with Sammie and Camille.

Tom and I sit on the dock in our camp chairs with our beers, watching the show. Out on the float off the end of the dock, the women laugh. Tom gets his *I'm going to paint this* look on his face. Sometimes I envy him his visual memory.

He takes a sip of his beer. "Bart's been asking Dan why you're moping. He doesn't understand, since Ms. Isa is here. He thinks you should be as happy as him."

Out on the float, Isa laughs at something Sammie says.

God, they're beautiful, our three muses, with their auburn, black, and blonde ponytails and their skin glowing in the sun. Yeah, I understand why Tom wants to paint this scene.

I shrug and take a sip of my beer.

"It's childish not talking to her the way you are." Tom chuckles. "Though I'd do exactly the same thing."

Now I chuckle. "It was Mack's idea."

"Seriously?" Tom laughs. "To keep her uncomfortably uncertain for an entire week? Damn, he's more of a player than you."

I don't know how much more I can take, though. How many more longing glances I can handle. How many more walks in the woods holding Bart's hand and not hers.

Sammie waves from the float.

Tom sets down his beer and stands up. "Ladies be returning." My brother obviously has adult activities on his mind. He and Sammie might be having a difficulty here and there—not that he's said—but it can't be too bad.

I chuckle again.

The women walk up the beach. Tom's right there, handing out towels, like a cabana boy. Camille wraps hers around her middle and pats Isa knowingly on the shoulder. Moments later, Sammie and Tom follow her up the steps to the porch.

Isa towels off her hair as she watches them go. "I like your family," she says.

I motion to the dock and we walk up to the railing. Gnats buzz in the shade thrown by the boathouse, but it's cooler, and not so bright. Somewhere off in the reeds, a fish *plops* in the water. A turtle scuttles around on the beach. The lake smells fresher today than usual, with its warm, not-quite heavy scent of plants and animals. Birds chirp and the high notes of Sammie's laugh peal from inside the cabin.

"I like them too," I say.

Isa wraps her towel around her chest. "Mack and I grew up in a very different environment."

I lean against the rail. The boathouse blocks some of our view of the cabin and out here, only the golden glow of the lake throws shadows. They creep over Isa, across her face, into her hair, and hide the sadness in her eyes.

I can't take it anymore. The uncertainty. I need to get the emotions out of my system. "How could you *not* see that the guy who wrote 'Isa's boyfriend' on his chest was head over heels in love with you?" I want to slap the railing but I grip it instead. "In permanent marker!"

Her mouth opens and closes. "Rob—"

She reaches to take my hand but I step away. The anger's surfacing. I've kept it down. Kept it tucked away, mostly for Bart. It's good for no one. But I don't think it's willing to stay buried any longer.

"How the hell could me saying 'I love you' and 'I want to marry you' have been such a shock?"

"But that's just it! It *was* a shock, Rob!" She throws her hands in the air. "When I realized—really, truly understood—I got scared."

The lake's calm, like I need to be, so I look out over the water hoping to internalize at least some of the stillness. "And you tell me I'm the one unaware of my emotions."

"That's not fair."

"Not fair, Isa? You know what's *not fair*? You unilaterally deciding that we're through. You, all by yourself. Why'd you do it? Because I'm a bad boy?"

I understand intellectually the reasons. Mack explained their childhood. But emotionally, it doesn't make sense. I'm not her father.

I see her chest tighten. She's holding in a sob. "I don't see you that way!" she yells. "I've never seen you that way!"

The volume of my voice drops. I'm almost whispering. "I don't do that anymore." My words float over the lake. Somehow, I need to declare my confession. This goes deeper than my social media persona. Or my undergraduate years. I'm not immature anymore.

"Rob..." Gently, Isa touches my wrist.

She doesn't stroke or glide her fingers, she settles her hand onto my skin. I think she's hoping to offer a small moment of comfort because I'm angry. Even though her face says she wants to yell *You're mean!*

"I'm sorry." Isa can't hold her sob any longer. "I'm so, so sorry. I shouldn't have..." A hiccup interrupts her words. "I acted like..." Another hiccup cuts off her voice entirely.

"Isa..." I pull her to my chest. Part of me is yelling that she deserves me being mean. Another part wants only to drop to the dock and cradle her on my lap.

She sobs against my shoulder and it feels as if she's holding onto me for dear life.

"No one's ever loved me like this," she whispers. "No one's fought for me. Or supported me the way you do. Unconditionally."

She blinks and stiffens in my arms. "Not even Mack's been so... open about supporting my goals. My parents, never. Mom lets me live with her, but doesn't show my photos. Mack lets me live with him too, but I saw him walk away from the love of his life because he wasn't able to compromise."

I don't say anything. What can I say? She needs to get this out.

"Yet I pushed you away and you still wanted me to teach your nephew, even though me being here obviously causes you pain."

I bury my face in her hair. She smells like the lake, but hints of her sweet, organic shampoo cling to her scalp. My beautiful Isa. "Your photos are still the backgrounds on all my devices. New phone. Laptop. Everything."

"Really?" She pulls away enough to see my face.

"You look like you just licked an electric fence." I suspect my expression isn't much different.

The anger still bubbles inside my chest. It's like a fountain in the middle of a pond brimming with every emotion my body can produce. I want to swing at the wall of the boathouse at the same time I want to curl up into a ball. I want to hunt the asshole who slashed me at the same time I want to cry like a baby.

I want to love Isa just as much as I want her to understand how much she hurt me.

Gently, she lays her fingers over my scar. My t-shirt rubs over the ridge, flicking slightly as she touches. "This is going to sound really stupid," she says.

I almost snort. My well of contradictory emotions sloshes inside my gut and the scar tingles. Isa pressing against my chest feels both comforting and uncomfortable. She touches, but is she really touching? She wants forgiveness, but can I give it?

I've bottled it up. I've stuffed it down. Exposure therapy should have made this easier but really, I asked her here because one way or another, I need closure. My emotional fount needs to pick which color filter it's going to use on its lights.

Bitter, angry, scab-colored red or the warm, sweet gold tones of Isa's hair?

"How stupid?" I ask.

She looks like she wants to bite her lip. "I've been watching you and your brothers."

I let go and cross my arms. My desire to punch the wall of the boathouse makes my muscles twitch.

"Watching and marveling at how good you all are with Bart. How no matter what he does, he's always loved."

My brows pull together. Of course we're good with him. "He's a good kid."

"Yeah, but you'd all love him even if he wasn't. You did a lot of naughty things as a kid, didn't you? Acted out? Your brothers still love you." The towel loosens and she readjusts it so it doesn't slide off her sweet hips.

Horniness rears its head in my overflowing fountain. It swims around like a snapping turtle, lapping through all my bratty meanness, and my bubbling anger, and right through the need to rock back and forth crying.

How is she doing this to me? Why the hell did I let a woman get this far under my skin?

Why the hell won't she just say what she means? "Why wouldn't they love me? We're family."

Isa sniffs and looks out over the lake. "Mack and I acted out, too. Dad won't talk to us. Says we need to 'learn from our mistakes.'"

Jesus, I think. "That's stupid."

She glances at my face before wrapping her arms around her chest. "See, I told you it would sound stupid."

My inner brat screams *Stupid!* and I want to walk away. Or pick her up. I don't know which. "Are you blaming your shitty father for your shitty behavior, Isa? Because that's shitty."

She wipes her eye with the back of her hand.

I realize I'm pushing her toward real tears. But this time, I think it needs to happen.

"I'm explaining why I acted the way I did." Her face and her body harden. "Because I thought what we had was a fantasy. I didn't believe it could happen in real life. No one's that good to me."

"You're right. That's stupid." I uncross my arms and slap my palm on the railing. Is she always going to be like this?

She clamps her mouth shut, then opens it with a pop. "I don't have the right to ask you for a second chance," she says. "You're past your limit. I went over the edge and there's no turning back and I should just be grateful you're willing to be friends."

Isa blinks and steps closer. "I'm so sorry. Will you...?"

I stand up straight. She's going to say it. "Will I what?"

Isa nods as if she understands. "Even if there's no turning back, will you forgive me? I'm being selfish asking. I shouldn't. I'm sorry. But I—"

I can't talk. The words don't form, so I let my kisses carry my need and my anger. My frustration.

And my love.

CHAPTER 40

Isolde

A fish surfaces just off the dock before flicking its tail and vanishing again. The air buzzes with the sound of crickets and cicadas and gnats. Someone in the house slams a door.

Rob's breath heats the skin of my neck. He yanks me toward him, his fingers digging into the flesh of my upper arms. His slight scent of ocean mixes with the humidity in the air and I swear I hear waves crashing on the shore. Waves of his anger. His frustration. Every ounce of his love.

He's crashing into me.

"I will *never* hurt you again," I breathe.

He nips at my skin just under my ear and I shiver. "Say it again," he growls.

"No more hurting you. I won't do it again." My towel drops to the slats of the dock. The only things between me and his erection are his cargo shorts and my bikini bottom.

I rub against his front.

"Are you going to talk to me?" His grip tightens for a moment, but

458

he seems to realize how strong he is and he backs off. "If we're together, then we make decisions together."

I curl a leg around his. God, I want to climb on him now, out in the open. Or drop to my knees and suck him off right here. "Together."

One hand releases from my arm. He glances up and at the cabin before turning me slightly to block any view of what he's doing to my front.

Rob works his fingers under the cup of my top. "If you get any more of those *he's just like Dad* notions you forget them immediately, you understand?"

"Yes," I breathe as I nibble on his chin.

"Because I'm not."

"You're not." He's Rob, my boyfriend. And the man I love. Oh, God, *love*. Head over heels. "I'm sorry."

"That's right, you're sorry. You're very sorry, aren't you? You've never been sorrier in your whole life, have you?" He flicks my nipple.

My breath stutters. I can't speak.

"Tell me how sorry you are." The authority in his voice makes my legs quake.

I can barely hold myself up. "I'm very sorry." Why did I push him away?

"Do you still believe I'm going to consign you to some shithole backwater and make you spend the rest of your life taking pictures of raccoons?" His anger growls out through his constricted throat. His skin reddens across his neck, too.

"No, I don't."

"You better not. Because that's not going to happen."

"It won't." Even if I didn't believe him, the commanding tone of his voice makes me. "I need to do a better job of separating fantasy from reality."

"Yes, you do." Rob twists me again so my back is completely to the cabin. His other hand works into the front of my bikini bottom.

But he only strokes across my pubic bone.

I want to scream. "I will. I swear I will."

"Do you have any idea how in love with you I am?" Both his hands pull out from inside my suit and his arms curl around me. I'm suddenly, completely enveloped by Rob's embrace. By his strong forearms and biceps. His wonderful chest. He's all here. All with me.

"Rob..." I kiss his ear, his neck. "I'm sorry. I'm so, so sorry. I love you." The next kiss finds his lips. "I absolutely love you."

"Don't push me away again. Please." His hold is so tight, I can barely breathe.

"I won't. I swear."

Another thump echoes down from the house, followed by a laugh. Rob backs away enough to take my hands. "Boathouse?"

I blink and look over my shoulder. Can't have Bart bursting out of the screen door.

I snatch my towel off the ground and pull Rob toward the little house's entrance. The door slams against the wall and Rob chuckles as he pushes me inside.

He still sounds angry. And his grip is still firm and demanding. The boathouse is a rickety place big enough to nestle in their fiberglass motorboat, along with a shower opposite the door, two canoes hanging from the ceiling, and several shelves full of tools. A lawn mower sits unused in the corner.

The water sloshes against the boat's hull. The lake side door of the boathouse is closed and locked, but there's still a good three foot gap between the structure and the waterline. Sun sprinkles in, reflecting from outside.

My bikini top is off before Rob presses my back against the cabin-side door. My bottoms follow. I'm naked between the dirty window and a couple more camp chairs hanging on the wall just inside the door.

Rob strokes my mound and his index finger works between my folds. "How much do you want me to fuck you?" His other hand twists and kneads my breasts.

"I think about you every time I'm in the shower," I groan. "By myself. Taking care of my urges."

His kiss floods my senses. I'm under its surface, bobbing in its wonder and praying for air. He's the world I see. The world I hear. He's all I taste.

"I don't want an open relationship, Isa. I want you. I don't want you fucking other guys when we're apart, you understand? I love you."

"I won't. I'll call you. Ask you to talk me through it."

Rob responds with a crooked grin, but his face quickly turns serious. "I will never cheat. Even if we're apart for years, I will never cheat."

He's offering a level of commitment I didn't think I would ever get... or deserve. "I can't put you through that," I whisper. "I won't—"

His kiss silences my worries. "Trust *me*, Isa. Not the version of me you've built up in your head."

"Oh." He's right. That fantasy can't rear its head anymore. It can't.

"I'm real."

And he loves me.

I work at the buckle of his belt. "Take off your shirt."

His t-shirt flips up and over his head.

I stop with my fingers on the button of his shorts. The scar curves across his belly and around his side. Rob got slashed coming home to me. I run my finger over its raised edges. He almost died.

"I know what you're thinking." He looks down at my face. "I didn't die. I'm fine now. I'm going to finish school and we'll figure out how best to make this work. If it means me finding a non-academic job in California, then that's what I do."

More commitment. More love. "Are you sure?"

The anger's gone. Rob strokes my cheek and gently kisses the tip of my nose. "I've never been more sure of anything in my life."

"Oh, Rob, I love you." More than anything. "We'll figure it out."

"We will." He unzips his shorts.

Slowly, carefully, he picks up my naked backside and sets me on the edge of a bench next to the lawnmower. I push down his shorts, then his soft boxer-briefs. He's rock hard in my hand, and when I stroke him, he shivers.

"I want to feel you," he whispers. "But I'll go in for condoms if you need me to."

We shouldn't do this. We should be careful. "I need to feel you as much as you need to feel me."

"Are you sure?" He presses his cock against my belly. "Because I'll go inside. We can both go in."

"I'm sure." I don't know why, but I am. Sure the way I knew after the party that I couldn't be just a conquest for this wonderful man. But also sure the way, I think, his mother was the night she eloped with his father.

Carefully, Rob presses into me. He feels so good, so real. I've never been with anyone without a condom. Never trusted someone this much.

My Rob with his wonderful, ocean-colored eyes. His scruffy stubble and his brilliant, quick mind. His incredible body.

He feels amazing as he slowly pushes into me. Slowly gives me an inch. Then another. And another. I'm the luckiest woman on Earth.

"I love you," I moan. More than anything.

He shivers again and his face falls to my shoulder. His strong arms tighten around me once more, cinching in a hold that could keep me stable for years. Rob thrusts deliberately, with a wonderful, slow rhythm. "Isa..." A new kiss takes all my breath. "Marry me." Another thrust. "Even if it's ten years from now. Marry me."

I hold his shoulders as he pumps into me, and press my face into his neck. "Yes..." I whisper. "Oh, God..." With each thrust my voice grows. "Yes, Rob." And my pleasure. "Rob! This is... *ah!*" An orgasm rolls through my abdomen and out to all my fingers and toes. Whimpering, I fall backward, against the line trimmer sitting at the back of the bench.

He kisses me again, but his face is serious. Intense. He feels so damn good when he shifts his hips and slams me hard. "Jesus, Isa..."

Rob pulls out but keeps pumping against my mound, rubbing against my naked skin. He groans and his lips latch onto my shoulder. He bites. Lightly, but it's going to leave a mark.

Oh my God he's *marking* me.

Rob's back tightens. And hot cum spurts onto the underside of my breasts.

It's unbelievably sexy. I don't know why, but seeing Rob so excited by my body makes me immediately horny again.

Incredibly nipple-hardening, panting because I need him again now, *horny*. But a lot of guys don't like being touched right after coming.

But I need him and—

He must sense my horniness because he flips me around. His mouth latches onto the back of my neck and I almost howl. Almost let it all out.

"God *damn* you are hot," Rob rumbles into my ear. "I am the only man who touches you, do you understand?" The anger's back. I feel it pulse from his hard, newly re-tensing body. "You fantasize about them. Think about them. But those pretty boy models don't touch. Only me."

Rob presses his still-hard, still-perfect cock against my ass.

No one compares to Rob. No one occupies so much of my thinking, or my feeling. "Why would I fantasize about anyone but you?" He's all I need. My gorgeous Rob.

Possessive hands roam over my back. Possessive hands smack my ass. "I'm still angry, Isa." He sounds almost apologetic.

Almost.

"It keeps welling up, even though I think it's gone. Part of me wants to fuck you until you scream, just to prove my point." He rubs against my ass but doesn't thrust against my skin. "I want you every way I can get you."

He fingers my anus.

Holy shit, I think. "You are so much better than *any* fantasy."

A low *heh* rolls from Rob's lips into my ear. "We have our entire lives."

He's not going to—

Rob flips me around again. "Into the boat," he orders. "On your back. Now." He pushes me toward the small, rocking craft.

I crawl in, looking for a place to lie down. It's cramped. Two benches cross the middle, both with storage underneath. I won't fit between. There's really nothing I can do.

Rob's shorts and boxer-briefs drop onto my bikini bottoms and he jumps in, not paying attention to the boat's position. It rocks to the side, almost dipping all the way into the lake, and a big wave spreads out across the water.

Rob braces the boat with his feet and it suddenly, completely stops rocking. His incredible cock is right at eye level, glorious and springing against his lower abs. He came on me once already, and he's already good to go again.

I am most definitely the luckiest woman in the world.

I move forward to take him in my mouth but he grabs my ponytail. "Up on the back of the boat." He nods toward the curved fiberglass sweeping over the squared end of the boat. A low, rounded wall houses the interior parts of the motor and makes the back end of the little boat a smooth arch.

I immediately lie on the arch next to the motor housing. My back curves away from Rob, my breasts up and out, my pussy presented and waiting for him to do with as he pleases.

A new growl rolls from his throat and he grabs my waist, hoisting me higher until my head almost hangs over the boat's end. And my pussy is easily accessible to his roving fingers.

And tongue.

I drop my head back. I'm looking out at the open, upside-down lake, at the sparkles and the surfacing fish and the sun's sheen. Rob cups a breast, massaging with a tight grip. With his other hand, he spreads my legs.

Two fingers glide along the edges of my slick parts, one on either side. He runs them up, then down, then up again. On the final up stroke, he flicks my clit.

I shudder, but I won't come again. This needs to last.

"This time, you do as I say." He stares at my pussy, his face and body humming with his desire and need.

Before I can respond, he slaps my clit.

"Oh!" No one's ever slapped me there. It's... intense. I don't think I'd like it if another man did it, but with Rob, it's amazing.

I grin.

"No orgasms until I give you permission." He slaps me again. His other hand trails over my abdomen, touching gently, the exact opposite of the slaps.

"*Fuck...*" My head drops back over the edge of the boat. The dissonance is going to set me on fire.

Rob works his tongue across my bellybutton and I moan, wanting his lips working my clit instead. He knows exactly what to do and how long to do it. The right pressure, the correct tease. God, he's incredible.

His tongue flits across my opening before drawing ever tightening circles around my clit. Just before I think he's going to kiss or suck or lap, he pulls back.

I see the lake, the water where the sky should be, and I feel nothing from where Rob should be, between my wiggling thighs and licking me to splendor. I pull up my head and look, trying to frown at my gorgeous boyfriend.

His hands latch onto my hips. Slowly, he works them up over my waist, to the underside of my breasts.

The look on his face is one of fierce, animalistic joy. "You have the most spectacular breasts." His thumbs work over my nipples. "When I'm at school and you're off shooting in South America, I want topless selfies."

I blink, my mouth rounding. "You are so *demanding*."

"Still mad." He slaps my pussy again. "Do you want me to lick you to an orgasm?"

Oh my God. "Yes!" I hiss like I'm deflating. When he runs the pad of his thumb around the outside of my opening, my hips buck.

"I want to watch you shower." A finger probes. "I want you to call me. I want to know how horny you are. How much you miss my kisses and my cock."

Rob blows on my clit. I shiver. Even if we're half a world apart, he wants to see me every day. I don't think Rob will ever give in to separation.

It works both ways. I don't want to be apart from him anymore than he wants to be apart from me. "Only if I get to watch you jerk off," I growl.

One of Rob's eyebrows arches. A grin appears. "I serve only my goddess."

His mouth descends onto my pussy.

It's heaven. He flicks his tongue. He probes and massages my thighs and my ass. One second, suction makes me squirm; the next, kisses make me moan. The ecstasy spreads like a tingling, warm presence over my entire body, across my breasts, into my shoulders. Up my neck and into the roof of my mouth. Down to my toes and my fingertips. Robs licks and my world flips upside down, like my view of the lake.

"I'm going to..." I can't stop the orgasm. I can't.

"Come," Rob commands.

The orgasm thunders into my belly, riding on the tingly, hot brilliance already woven into my body. Rob rides it too, first changing his pressure, then his speed, to draw it out as long as possible.

I snort, maybe squeal, and slap the hull.

The next thing I know, I'm being pulled down the slick fiberglass into the boat. I can't fight, I can't do anything but continue to gasp and quake. My knees buckle. I fly forward, legs spread wide open, onto my kneeling man.

Rob's cock thrusts deep into my pussy. "Yes..." he groans. "You're still coming..." Another deep thrust and a new spasm rocks my core.

An arm threads under my ass and Rob presses me against the part of the boat I just slid down. He pounds me hard and steady, thrusting with all the strength of his thighs and buttocks.

His gaze locks to mine. "This is what I want." Another deep, powerful thrust. "You looking at me this way." A warm kiss dances over my lips. I taste myself, but mostly I taste Rob's slight saltiness. "In love with me."

The warm tingling of my orgasm changes into an electrical tingling around my heart. It dances through my chest, up my neck, and onto my face. My cheeks round. My eyes widen. And I kiss Rob with everything I feel as he thrusts again and again.

Rob will care for my heart as carefully, and as well, as he cares for my body. He won't withhold because he's upset. He's proving how unconditional his love is right now, with each plunge into me. With each touch to my cheeks and kiss to my lips.

And all he asks is the same in return.

"Will you..." My words barely form. "... marry me?" Part of me can't believe I just asked him. Another part dances with joy.

A new orgasm rips through me, one held steady by Rob's embrace and strong body. A soft *Ah...* floats to my ear. He bucks against me one last time, his cock jerking sharply inside me.

The boat rocks as the final kinetic energy of our lovemaking dissipates. He holds me against his front, still buried deep inside me, still warm and wonderful.

His next kiss gives me his answer. Joy fills his eyes and his smile. "My goddess," he whispers. "I'm yours. Now and always."

He's what I want. He's what I need. Now and always.

For the rest of my life.

CHAPTER 41

Robert

I peer at the video feed on my phone. Bart's messing with something out of the camera's view. "What you doing there, buddy?"

His head pops back into the frame, along with one of the atlases Isa gave him before we drove away from the lake house together three weeks ago. Road-tripping through the Rockies with the love of my life sounded like just what I needed to finish my recovery.

Mountain air does wonders. As do the touches of a loving woman. I'm now as right as rain, even if Reno is too hot and a bit dry for my tastes. Colorado, though, is beautiful. We spent three days in Grand Mesa National Forest alone.

Bart waves his atlas. "Where are you, Uncle Robby?" He pages through the maps. "Are you still in Colorado?" He folds back the book to show me the big yellow circle he made around Denver.

"We're in Reno, Nevada. Do you know which way we drove to get to Nevada?" My nephew's been closely following our travels. He drew a picture of Mr. Pickles for us before we left and Isa's been photographing it on every boulder and bush we come across. In Denver, she did an entire series of random people—a cop, some kid on a bike, one of our waitresses—holding it up, just for Bart.

He jumped up and down and clapped for three minutes straight when he saw.

Bart's head disappears below the frame again. "I'll find Reno!"

The webcam pans back to my brother. Dan chuckles and adjusts his laptop. "I've never seen him this interested in anything outside his paints and crayons."

"It's because Isa sends him new pictures every three hours." Or at least every time we stop and she's got good wifi.

Dan chuckles again. He leans toward the webcam like he's going to tell me a secret. "Tom and Sammie postponed the wedding, by the way."

I shake my head. I'm surprised but I'm not that surprised. "Why?"

Dan shrugs. "First it was her family. Then it was all 'let's have a double wedding!' Now, I don't know." He shrugs again.

Bart pops up. "Found it!" He holds up the map. "Will Ms. Isa send me new pictures?"

"Of course, little man." He really is excited. His atlas looks well thumbed. "Later, okay?"

Bart frowns but nods. "Where are you going next?" He holds up the atlas again.

"Tell you what. Why don't you look at the map and find me the closest big city, okay?" That'll keep him busy for about thirty seconds.

"Okay!" Bart vanishes again.

Another chuckle rolls out of my brother. "So, what are you two up to in Reno?" He peers at his screen. "Are you in some cheap-ass theme hotel?" After a moment and an exaggerated eye roll, he sits back. "You are."

I grin and pan my phone around the room, to show off our evening's accommodations. All of Isa's equipment is stacked in the corner under a huge, hanging, bright red lava lamp. Shiny silver wallpaper decorated with little red hearts glints on the walls. The entire place smells like stale champagne, but we couldn't turn up the opportunity to spend a couple of days making love on the massive, heart-shaped rotating bed in the middle of the room.

"Are you in the honeymoon suite?" Dan sounds incredulous.

I can't stop laughing. "Yep." The most obnoxious honeymoon suite this side of old school Vegas.

"Why the hell are you in the—" Dan stops talking when I hold up my hand and my wedding-banded ring finger.

"You didn't." Dan peers at the screen for a long moment. "You did." He shakes his head and turns around. "Camille! You have to see this!" Then back to me. "You're an idiot."

"Sure. I'm the idiot. When *you* going to make it legal, brother?"

Camille stops about five feet behind Dan and lets out a scream loud enough it overtakes my phone's speaker and turns into a buzz worthy of a hive of bees. "Oh my God!" She jumps up and down behind my brother.

Before Dan can say anything, Bart pops back into the frame. "What?" He looks around, all five-years-old and confused.

"Uncle Robby and Ms. Isa got married!" Camille gives her soon-to-be stepson a hug.

"You're making me look bad, little brother." Dan frowns. I can't tell if he's happy for me, or in total shock.

I shrug. I am, to be honest, the last one of us anyone expected to get married. But I'm no longer falling down to expectations. Mine or anyone else's.

Neither is Isa.

Camille drops onto Dan's lap and adjusts the screen and the cam again. "Where's the bride?"

"Getting ice." She hasn't been feeling well the last few days, but I don't tell them that. They'd get worried.

"Oh." Camille gives Dan a hug. "So I take it you're staying in L.A. until school starts?"

"I'll be bicoastal as of September." It's only a year and a half before I'm ABD. "I'm thinking I might write my dissertation about how social media affects the boundaries between the various subcultures in Colorado." Both Isa and I like the state, and there's a lot to study. "Isa's thinking of doing a photo essay at the same time."

Maybe doing a gallery show, too.

Camille smiles. "I knew you two would figure it out." She hugs Dan again.

"San Fran... Fransisto!" Bart holds up the atlas. "Highway 80 goes into California." He points. "Is that right?"

"That's right, buddy." Dan lifts him onto his lap when Camille stands up. To me: "But you'll be home for Christmas, right?"

Camille waves and walks back toward the kitchen. "You better!" she calls.

I nod. "Probably. I don't think Isa's family is big on holiday celebrations."

"Well, hell." Dan sniffs like a dad who smells weed in his son's bedroom. "Bring Mack, then."

My brother-in-law might like spending time with my loud family. Or he might be overwhelmed. Either way, it'll be a new experience for him.

Dan traces a road on Bart's map. "See here? That's the Monterey Bay Aquarium. We'll look it up when we're done talking to Uncle Robby, okay?"

Bart's eyes get big. "Do they have sharks?"

I chuckle.

Dan rubs his son's head. "We'll have to look."

"Okay." Bart folds up his book. "Can I have a cookie?"

Dan pats Bart's shoulder and nods toward the kitchen. "Go ask your mom."

A big smile lights up my nephew's face. "Bye, Uncle Robby!" he yells, and runs off toward Camille and his snack.

"Listen, I gotta go," I say. Isa's been in the bathroom a long time and I want to check on her. Besides, my battery is running low.

Dan shakes his head. "You got married first."

I wave. Dan waves. We sign off and I glance around our honeymoon suite as I plug in my phone. The chair next to the window is upholstered with the ugliest crushed red velvet I suspect was available in the early eighties, when the hotel opened for business.

The place is truly the tackiest room I've ever been in. Which, I think, just makes it more special. It makes Isa happy. Which makes me happy.

We have a few more weeks, then I need to fly back to school. I'm going to be walking through LAX, lonely and frowning and missing her terribly. I miss her now, and she's just in the other room.

"Honey?" The bathroom door's open and I hear her moving around inside. "You okay? Still feeling queasy?"

I push open the door.

My beautiful wife looks up, her face a perfect circle topped by her lovely blonde ponytail. She's in her pajama tank top still, and her tight little sleep shorts. Just looking at her feminine curves makes the deepest parts of my brain and body very happy.

But behind her glasses, her eyes are as round as her cheeks. As is her mouth.

In her hand, held in front of her chest like it's a hot poker, is a long white plastic stick that looks like a thermometer. But it's not.

It's not at all a thermometer.

Oh boy, flits through my mind. *Oh boy* followed by a very quick, intense tactile and emotional re-experiencing of our make-up sex in the boathouse. Our "marry me fuck," as Isa called it, when we were lying in our sleeping bag under the Colorado stars and she was looking for a good pounding.

She holds out the white plastic stick. A word shows in the little window next to her fingers. One word. One precious word that smacks the world upside the head: Pregnant.

I stare at the little window. And the word. "We're going to have a baby?" *Looks like we get a souvenir from our sexy fun time*, I think. But I don't say it. It's flippant and smartass and it popped up from the immature part of my brain. The one that no longer gets any say.

"Yes." She's still shocked. And her face is still round.

I'm shocked. My face is probably just as round as hers. "Is that why you've been feeling sick?" My wife has morning sickness.

"I think so." Isa blinks. "Rob? What are going to do?"

I pull her into my arms. She shivers and I feel as if she's holding on to my chest because I'm the only thing keeping her from drowning.

"We're going to have a baby." I hold onto her the same way. "This changes the logistics of the next few years." I kiss her forehead. "We're pregnant." I may need to work out taking a semester off and...

The reality of the moment hits me like I just stumbled into a wall. I fell in love, eloped, and now I'm going to be a daddy nine months later. Just like my father.

"Bart's going to have a cousin." I'm grinning like the idiot Dan likes to tell me I am.

"You're not mad?" Isa shivers again. "I didn't know yesterday when we went to the chapel. I didn't." I feel her crunch in on herself as she returns to clinging to my front.

She's genuinely upset.

"What?" Why would I be mad? My part in allowing this happy accident was as big as hers. "Of course you didn't know. You just took the test." I kiss her again.

"Oh, Rob." Isa hiccups against my chest.

I nuzzle her jaw, doing my best to make her feel better. "Guess you don't have to worry about going on the pill when we get home, huh?" I kiss her neck, playing up the naughty. "Hmm, pregnant woman sex."

Isa chuckles and hugs me close with her cheek over my heart. "I thought you might be mad."

"Why would I be mad?" I lean down and make her look at me.

"I don't ever want you to think you're trapped." She hiccups again.

I'm not trapped. I think, strangely, I've been set free. Or at least released into a whole, new, wild part of my life. It's out there, just waiting to be mapped and explored. "I'm the happiest man in the world."

Isa wipes away a tear. "I love you, Robert Quidell."

I hold her close in the surreal and tacky bathroom of an equally surreal and tacky theme hotel room in Reno, Nevada. A place I never thought I'd be, at least anytime soon.

Yet here I am with the most talented and wonderful person I know, ready to step into a whole new part of both our lives. "I love you too, Isa Wellington-Quidell."

Now and forever.

The Story continues
in book four, **Thomas's Need**

Careers and wedding plans swirl around Tom and Sammie until a parent falls ill and a job vanishes....

THOMAS'S NEED PREVIEW

CHAPTER ONE

Thomas

"Put this on, Uncle Tommy." Bart holds out a child-sized, bark-brown vest complete with child-sized arm holes and a child-sized bug "abdomen" hanging off its back. "You can't go in unless you're an ant like me."

My nephew tugs on his own vest before looking up at me with his big, blue, five-year-old eyes.

Kids are exhausting. We've been in the Children's Museum for just over an hour and I already want to run for the hills, or for a beer. Either would work. But I promised my brother's boy an afternoon of "fun in the city" so here we are, a happy-if-precise kindergartener and his big oaf of an uncle, at the mouth of an indoor "anthill" play tunnel.

This particular exhibit has been a staple of the Children's Museum since I was a child. Hell, I think it was here when Bart's grandfather was a child. It was probably here before Minneapolis became a city. The first human to step onto this spot fifteen thousand years ago slammed a spear into the ground and declared, "Let's build the kids an anthill right here!"

Some things never change, including the murals rolling over the costume area where Bart now stands, and the air around us. An odd mixture of aged dust, cleaning chemicals, and that specific, sweet-yet-sour scent of child hangs in the air as thick as the shadows deep in the tunnels.

I run a finger over the pockmarked paint. Refreshing the blues in the mural would go a long way to adding a little brightness.

Funny how I never noticed the blandness of the colors when I was the kid playing. I just wanted to run fast and lose my younger brother inside the tunnels. It never worked; Rob always lost *me*. I suspect Bart would do the same.

I point at the vest. "I don't think that'll fit, buddy."

Bart frowns. He's already taller than all the other five-year-olds and I suspect he's destined for the full Quidell height and broad build, like his father and his uncles. Small we are not, which is fine, except when you're supposed to crawl through an insect mound.

"Oh." Bart's hand—and the vest—drop to his side. He looks at the floor for a moment, then out into the open area in front of the exhibit, his face open and hopeful. "Auntie Sammie can come in with me!"

My fiancé looks up from her task of stuffing Bart's action figures into his backpack. "What?" She smooths the front of her t-shirt as she stands up.

Sammie is slightly older than me—four years to be exact. She graduated from the University the same year I started. We'd crossed paths as students, but only in a disconnected, lost-opportunity kind of way. Thankfully, we met again last year when I started in the Art Department where we both work.

We've been making up for lost time ever since.

Her t-shirt hugs her curves, as do her jeans. Sammie's perfect female shape and luminescent auburn hair set her apart from the tired parents herding little ones through the exhibits. In my eyes, she's a vision.

But she doesn't seem as overwhelmed by the noise as I am. Sammie, unlike me, understands how to replenish her reservoir of energy.

"Bart would like you to be an ant with him." I point at my nephew. He smiles.

Sammie's face takes on an *Oh my God you are so adorable* look. The one every human with a soul makes when in the presence of kids or kittens. That wide-eyed pout, the one that only flits across features because everyone knows adults don't make that face.

But it's hard not to, when a kindergartener wants you to play.

And I think I fall even more in love with Sammie than I was after our quality cuddle time this morning, if that's even possible.

A little girl with golden skin and equally golden eyes runs around Sammie's side. Her big, curly ponytail bounces as she darts by me and right up to Bart.

"Hello," says the little girl. She's his height, which means she's probably slightly older than him, and she obviously knows her way around.

Bart doesn't say anything. He just stares all dumbfounded at the pretty girl.

Sammie's gaze shifts from Bart to me. She shakes her head as she walks over.

The little girl takes the ant-vest from my nephew's hand. "I'll be an ant with you."

Bart smiles a new, big, happy smile. "Okay."

The little girl slips the vest over her shoulders. "This way gets to the slide faster." She points behind me, then looks up at my face. "Are you his daddy?"

"That's my uncle," Bart says. He steps between his new friend and me as if I'm competition. "He's an artist."

I can't help but chuckle.

Bart throws me a look, but when the girl takes his hand, he's utterly, completely lost.

"Let's go!" she says, and my nephew disappears into the anthill with his new friend.

Sammie sets the backpack at our feet and leans her head against my shoulder. "Ah, young love."

I take her hand as I watch an older woman guide my young nephew through the tunnels. At least Bart didn't miss *his* chances.

I kiss Sammie's cheek. "I guess he's better at seeing his opportunities than his uncle."

Sammie looks up at my face. Her brows twist up for a second, and her warm, hazel eyes take on a shadow. But she shakes her head again and pats my elbow. "What's that saying? You make your own opportunities?"

"Yeah," I say, and kiss her cheek again. She's my muse, my Sammie. What would I do without her?

⁂

"Her name is Serena!" Bart kicks the back of Sammie's seat.

There's not a lot of room in the back of my truck's cab. Sammie waves her hand over the headrest. "Watch the toes, please," she says.

Bart ignores her. He's too wrapped up in his cougar moment. "Like the tennis player." Bart swings his arm. "How do you play tennis, Uncle Tommy?" He swings his arm again. "Serena says she plays tennis and volleyball. She knows how to ski down hills!"

He makes a loud *whooshing* noise. Sammie throws me a bemused look.

Bart leans forward. "Can I learn to ski? I want to ski." His next noise sounds more like a monster truck than the swishing of snow.

I turn into my brother's neighborhood. It's nice—suburban and full of mature trees and well-maintained, middle-class split-levels. Dan says the schools are good and the streets safe. The area reminds me a lot of our neighborhood growing up, which, I suspect, is why he chose to buy a house here.

That's my brother, the painfully perfect family man.

"I think we've created a monster." Sammie nods over her shoulder.

Bart continues his monologue about the wide range of sporting activities available to today's youth.

The truck's engine grumbles one last time as I park in Dan's driveway. Dan's girlfriend, Camille, steps out onto the front step. She's freshly showered. Her damp black hair hangs over her shoulders and her muscles look loose as if she just finished a good workout.

"I think you and Camille need to pose for me." A full suite of classic painterly poses run through my head. "I could do a full series. Call it 'The Muses.'"

Sammie smiles as she opens the door and steps out. She helps Bart undo his seatbelt and he's running for Camille before I pull the key from the ignition.

Sammie taps the side panel of the truck as she watches him go. "I think he had fun."

I walk around the front of the truck and wrap my arms around her waist. "How could he not?" I gently kiss her upper lip. "He's a Quidell. We have a weakness for cougars."

Sammie slaps my shoulder. "Me-*ow*," she says, and saunters up the driveway, toward my brother's house.

I chuckle as I follow.

"Concert's at nine," she says over her shoulder.

We had an afternoon with the nephew. Now it's time to party like adults. I will never understand where Sammie gets the energy for it all.

Other than she sleeps better than I do. But I made a promise, so I smile. "We'd better get home so we can get ready."

Sammie's eyes brighten. Her hips swing as she follows Bart. She holds her back erect and her shoulders high, but her head tips just a little to the side as she takes in how Camille hugs Bart.

And again, I think I'm more in love now than I was this morning, even if I am tired.

My Sammie. My muse. I follow her into my brother's house for a quick good-bye with Bart.

I watch my nephew run off for a cookie and a juice box.

Sammie grasps my hand. "Ready?" she asks.

I guess it's time for a whole other anthill. I kiss her again. Any night with Sammie is special, concert or no concert. "Let's go."

The Story continues in book four, **Thomas's Need**...

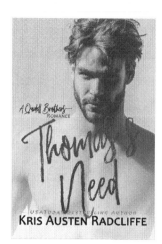

THE WORLDS OF
KRIS AUSTEN RADCLIFFE

Hot Contemporary Romance:

The Quidell Brothers
Thomas's Muse
Daniel's Fire
Robert's Soul
Thomas's Need
Andrew's Kiss *(coming soon)*

*Genre-bending Science Fiction about
love, family, and dragons:*

WORLD ON FIRE
Series one
Fate Fire Shifter Dragon
Games of Fate
Flux of Skin
Fifth of Blood

Bonds Broken & Silent
All But Human
Men and Beasts
The Burning World

Series Two
Witch of the Midnight Blade
Call of the Dragonslayer (*coming soon*)

༄

Smart Urban Fantasy:

Northern Creatures
Monster Born
Vampire Cursed
Elf Raised
Wolf Hunted (*coming soon*)

ABOUT THE AUTHOR

As a child, Kris took down a pack of hungry wolves with only a hardcover copy of *The Dragonriders of Pern* and a sharpened toothbrush. That fateful day set her on a path traversing many storytelling worlds —dabbles in film and comic books, time as a talent agent and a textbook photo coordinator, and a foray into nonfiction. After coauthoring *Mind Shapes: Understanding the Differences in Thinking and Communication*, Kris returned to academia. But she craved narrative and a richly-textured world of Fates, Shifters, and Dragons—and unexpected, true love.

Kris lives in Minnesota with her husband, two daughters, Handsome Cat, and an entire menagerie of suburban wildlife bent on destroying her house. That battered-but-true copy of *Dragonriders*? She found it yesterday. It's time to pay a visit to the woodpeckers.

Fore more information
www.krisaustenradcliffe.com
krisradcliffe@sixtalonsign.com